THE PERFECT NEIGHBORHOOD

A NOVEL

LIZ ALTERMAN

CROOKED
LANE

NEW YORK

Copyright © 2022 by Liz Alterman

All rights reserved.

Published in the United States by Crooked Lane Books, an imprint of The Quick Brown Fox & Company LLC.

Crooked Lane Books and its logo are trademarks of The Quick Brown Fox & Company LLC.

Library of Congress Catalog-in-Publication data available upon request.

ISBN (hardcover): 978-1-63910-021-7
ISBN (ebook): 978-1-63910-022-4

Cover design by Melanie Sun

Printed in the United States.

www.crookedlanebooks.com

Crooked Lane Books
34 West 27th St., 10th Floor
New York, NY 10001

First Edition: July 2022

10 9 8 7 6 5 4 3 2 1

For Rich, who took care of everything
while I went to Oak Hill.
Thank you for the time and space and,
most of all, your faith in me.

Even the devil's eyes can't be as sharp as the neighbors'.
—Heinrich Boll

1

Thursday, June 13
Rachel

FOR THE PAST two months, we spoke of little other than the Langleys.

"Did you hear? She's gone!"

"No! It can't be true."

"If they can't make it work, none of us stands a chance!"

"Allison and Christopher Langley? Oh, it's over. Totally. Someone saw him jogging with the dog. Just the two of them. That's a first."

"How long do you figure he'll be alone?"

"Less than a minute. Look at him! I bet he won't even have to set up an online dating profile."

"How fast do you think he'll decide to move back to the city? That house has to have, what, four bedrooms at least? And so close to the elementary school! Let me know the second he decides to sell! I know a couple who'd kill for that location."

On and on it went for weeks as May slipped into June. Nearly everyone within a three-block radius of the Langleys' well-maintained Colonial whispered about them over hedges, in the parks and playgrounds, while walking their dogs and toddlers around the pond in the heart of our otherwise sleepy town.

Some refused to believe it.

"The Langleys? No way!"

"I'm sure she's just off filming another commercial. Probably somewhere fabulous. I wonder what she's pushing this time? Toothpaste? Rental cars? What a life!"

That might have seemed plausible if Mary Alice Foster's son, Phil, hadn't seen Allison hurry into an Uber at four in the morning without a suitcase.

"Can we trust Phil? No disrespect, I'm just saying, he hasn't seemed quite right since he got back."

"Yeah, no offense, but Phil's not exactly credible. And why is he watching their house? That's creepy."

Others insisted they'd seen it coming.

"I saw Allison looking teary at the drugstore a few weeks back, but I chalked it up to allergies. Trees budding and all. Show me a person whose eyes aren't watering, right? Anyway, I said hello, and she sort of waved back. It wasn't like we had a conversation. We didn't really know each other. Did anyone really know the Langleys?"

"I bet she met someone else, maybe a hedge fund guy with a fat bank account."

"Chris's got money, doesn't he? Royalties from that song? Wasn't it in the background of those beer commercials? Plus, she's probably made a bundle from those acting gigs."

"I'm talking about private jet, fuck-you money. She's what? Thirty-two? Thirty-four? Her window to bag a billionaire's closing, and she knows it. Probably got tired of life in the 'burbs. Can you blame her?"

Finally, we were able to purge every ill-formed, mean-spirited thought we'd ever harbored about them. Neighborhood-scale vomiting. Sickening. And delicious. I was part of it too. The gossip. It was wrong yet impossible to resist. Some of us were almost rooting against them from the start. You couldn't help it. So much to envy. Even their names—Allison and Christopher Langley—sounded clean, rich, regal.

With her thick dark hair, perfect smile, and bone structure that implied she'd still be gorgeous at eighty, everyone in the neighborhood treated her like royalty. Our very own Kate Middleton.

And him? His rock-star status, though faded, had even the most aloof mothers in Oak Hill swooning as they dropped off their budding musicians for the piano, guitar, and voice lessons he gave in the afternoons. Nannies, too, left minivans idling at the curb to walk their charges to the door for a chance to see him up close, maybe even talk to him, drink in a few sips of his voice, which carried the faintest hint of a Southern drawl, a souvenir from the years he lived in New Orleans.

Last summer, when Frank Chadwick convinced Chris to join the town softball team, women who'd never watched their husbands play suddenly appeared on the sidelines. They pretended to cheer while admiring Christopher's butt, round as two firm cantaloupes, beneath the thin polyester of those uniform pants.

"Is he wearing a cup, or is that, er, natural?" one woman whispered to another.

All the running they did left the Langleys enviably fit. How many mornings had I looked out the bathroom window and nearly been blinded by their radiance as they jogged past the house? Good health oozed from their pores, the opposite of the image reflected back at me in the mirror. Graying hair sprouted at my roots and temples. My face, most days, appeared pale and puffy as an angel food cake. My tongue felt sandpapery as a cat's and tasted faintly of the wine I'd downed quickly the night before to take the edge off the day and force my evenings to blur into something more bearable.

In early spring, through the window screen, I could hear their laughter, the way they held a conversation and bantered easily, never out of breath, and I despised them. Golden and good-natured, even Murphy, their dog, was beautiful. If he stopped to chew grass, one of them would command, "Keep it moving, Murph!" and the dog obeyed.

How could you not loathe this couple? We were merciless in our constant need to dissect them. Like hawks circling, we waited to spot their weaknesses.

They had no children. Some chalked it up to that "selfish millennial" stereotype. Others felt sorry for them. "Such a shame! Their kids would be stunning!" But a group of us, the ones who'd fallen into codependent friendships, ones forged for survival at Mommy and Me classes or preschool drop-offs and pick-ups, envied the Langleys. United in our easy-to-maintain haircuts, comfortable shoes, and yoga pants, we resented them as we imagined the perfect pair doing all the things we no longer could: staying awake past ten on a Friday night, sleeping in on Saturdays, savoring Sunday brunches.

Deflated balls and mold-speckled riding toys weren't ruining their lawn. Their driveway wasn't littered with crushed-up pieces of forgotten sidewalk chalk or pulverized Goldfish crackers covered in ants. Phantom whiffs of vomit didn't waft up from their couch cushions.

Sometimes, after too many glasses of wine, we'd speculate, "They probably still have sex in the shower. Remember that? Remember shower sex?"

"Ever see them stretching in the park? They're so fucking limber!"

On and on we'd go until, even to our drunken ears, we heard how jealous and ridiculous we sounded.

At the annual block party or the neighborhood holiday cocktail gathering, the Langleys had their own gravitational pull. Necks swiveled. Heads spun in their direction. And the way they looked at each other? We were the spellbound audience catching the joyous final scene of a Hallmark movie.

"Don't forget, she's an actress," the more bitter among us reminded the group.

But most of us believed it wasn't an act. They seemed so insular, as if all they needed was each other. It had to be real.

So, naturally, the shock of Allison's abrupt exit left us reeling, clamoring for answers. What went wrong? Had she met someone else? Maybe he wanted to get the band back together and tour again? Did they disagree about starting a family?

No one knows what goes on in someone else's home. I know this better than anyone. And, of course, it was none of our business. But after living so long in our quiet town, people craved news beyond soaring property values and preferred preschool teachers.

How could Allison's decision to suddenly run off in the early hours of a late-April morning not become breaking news that worked its way into nearly every conversation? What else did we have to talk about? The Petersons' new shed? Who might get a Labradoodle?

The Langleys would've continued to be our primary topic until Allison returned, Christopher moved away, or another couple's shocking divorce came to light, forcing our jaundiced eyes to shift in a new direction.

The thing that brought the gossip to a shameful halt wasn't a reconciliation, a departure, or another couple's demise. It was the disappearance of Billy Barnes.

Billy, who would turn six in July, vanished as he was walking home from kindergarten on a perfectly ordinary afternoon. Not a trace of him was left behind. Not the house key that dangled from his Yankees keychain. Not a sneaker. Not the dinosaur backpack that had his initials monogrammed just above a Tyrannosaurus rex's roaring mouth. W. E. B. William Edward Barnes. He'd wanted "Billy" in navy blue block letters, but every parent knows putting a child's name out there constitutes an open invitation for a pedophile to attempt to lure them into their van.

And yet, even without his name stitched there for all the world to see, he disappeared.

Had a predator been watching, waiting for the right time to make a move? There's no evidence to suggest that's what happened. But what other explanation could there be?

Could Billy have wandered off? Possibly. Like most five-year-olds, he was insatiably curious. He asked a thousand questions a day, even ones he already knew the answers to, a habit that irritated his father. Billy fancied himself an explorer—the pockets of his cargo shorts bursting with a plastic magnifying glass, compass, and miniature flashlight. But would he have ventured far from the sidewalk that led him home every afternoon? No. Never. He'd been told that if he wanted the privilege of walking to and from school by himself, he had to be back on his porch by 3:15 PM every school day. No detours.

Of course, there were times when he wasn't completely alone. His neighbor and classmate Oliver Jordan frequently walked with him. Behind him, really. Because of Oliver's short stature and tendency to stop to crush ants or leap in the air to shake raindrops off low-hanging leaves, he typically trailed Billy by at least ten paces.

"Hurry up! We're going to be late!" Billy would call over his shoulder, though they usually had plenty of time.

"Um, it's kindergarten. Who gives a shit?" Oliver, raised with older brothers who lived on a steady diet of offensive YouTube videos and memes, would respond.

Billy had a half brother, Evan, from his father's first marriage. But even when he was in college, before he'd officially moved out, Evan had barely taken the time to say hello to Billy, let alone offer him swearing lessons the way Oliver's siblings had.

The classmates often walked home together. But on the afternoon Billy went missing, he was by himself. Oliver had been picked up by his mother, who was whisking him to an emergency dental appointment. One of Oliver's brothers had tripped him that morning, and he'd fallen face-first into a metal radiator. He'd arrived to walk Billy to school with a bag of frozen peas covering his mouth. It was a baby tooth. Still, his mother wanted assurance there wasn't root or nerve damage that would cause the next tooth to come in gray.

So Lindsay Jordan had scooped up Oliver in her black SUV. She told police she'd offered Billy a ride home, but Billy had simply called back, "No, thanks!"

Another mother thought she'd seen Billy take a lollipop from Veronica Baker, the crossing guard, before disappearing into the crowd of kids busily counting down the days until summer break. They skipped alongside mothers or nannies who were far less excited about the weeks of endless togetherness.

One au pair thought she remembered seeing Billy turn the corner onto Cherry Lane. From there, it was just three short blocks home. Even if he dawdled to study a ladybug or look through a sewer grate, he should have arrived no more than ten minutes later.

That was seven hours ago.

And no one had a clue where he was.

Parents marshaled to help search, hanging posters from every telephone pole in town as well as on bulletin boards in the post office, library, and even the supermarket, I'm told—not that I've been there.

Billy's photo appears below the word "Missing." His smile beams above information about his height and weight. The picture was taken a week ago on the kindergarten field trip to the zoo. Even in the black-and-white copies, his bright brown eyes shine. If you look closely, you can see that his cheeks are dotted with freckles from getting too much sun at a T-ball game. An untamable cowlick pokes up from the back of his head.

The gossip, which had been so focused on the Langleys, shifted, settling swiftly and decisively on the Barnes family.

"Did you hear about Billy Barnes?"

"Oh my God, I did! It's unimaginable!

"Do you really think he was taken? Abducted? In this neighborhood?"

"A nightmare. An absolute nightmare."

"He was a sweet kid, right? Always friendly. Betsy told me his mom is in shock, walking up and down streets screaming his name."

"Wouldn't you?"

"Kindergarten is too young to walk home alone, right?"

"I said the same thing to Pete as soon as I got the alert that Billy was gone."

I heard their hushed, urgent voices as together we frantically searched the neighborhood this afternoon, believing maybe Billy had followed a chipmunk and wandered into a garage, hoping perhaps he'd accepted a last-minute invitation to a classmate's home, praying he'd simply gotten lost trying to corral a stray dog.

Their fervent whispers floated over hedges, through picket fences, around corners. Their words traveled across lawns and hung in the branches of oak trees like poisonous fruit. But all conversation stopped as soon as I came into view.

This time I'm not part of the chatter. I'm on the outside. Not included. No one wants to talk to me now.

Because I'm Rachel Barnes.

I'm Billy's mother.

2

Saturday, June 15
Allison

Rachel Barnes. Billy. Their names float through my mind. I'm barely awake, but I picture them—her neatly bobbed brown hair, his sweet freckled face—behind my closed eyes. Was I dreaming about them?

I roll over on Vivian's couch. The hammering inside my head speeds up as the blender shrieks to life. Viv's pulverizing pomegranates, oranges, kale, flaxseed, and whatever else she can find to create the sludge she swears is both a hangover cure and the secret to her flawless skin. Thanks to Viv's early-morning smoothie-making, the June sunlight streaming through her curtains, and the rumble of the city as it comes to life, I'm getting less sleep than I did at home. Still, I'm relieved to be here.

I peel my tongue off the roof of my mouth. It's thick and scratchy as a Brillo pad.

"Billy Barnes is missing?" I whisper, testing the words to see if they make sense or if I just imagined it. Viv can't hear me over the whirring of the blender. I roll over again, convinced I've had a nightmare. It wouldn't be the first time I woke up with an aching head, haunted by thoughts of lost children.

When the blender stops, Viv walks over, places a glass tumbler on the coffee table, and says, "Bottoms up, girl!"

The colors of all that produce bleed into a gray-green-purple slime. Not wanting to seem ungrateful, I sit up and rub my eyes.

"Thanks," I croak and take a sip. It's every bit as bad as the one she made yesterday, and I can't help but wince. "Seriously, Viv, how can you drink this?"

"Are you kidding? I'd swallow scalding hot monkey semen if it slowed the aging process." She laughs, takes a long swig, and licks her top lip. "Yum!"

When I pretend to gag, which doesn't take much, she says, "What? Some of us still need to make a living."

Viv and I have known each other since we were thirteen. We met when we were cast as soccer teammates in a sports drink commercial. Over the past two decades, we've found and lost each other a dozen times. When she reached out to me on Facebook a few months ago, I'd never been happier to reconnect. I'd almost ignored her friend request because she used the name Noradeen Ballmanze, but then it clicked. Noradeen was a character she'd portrayed in a teen horror movie franchise.

Great to hear from you, Noradeen. But why the alias? I messaged her.

Just keeping the assholes, exes, and perverts at bay, girl. You know how it is! she wrote right back.

Our lives always had an odd symmetry, a strange way of diverging and realigning. We could go long stretches without communicating only to find ourselves up for the same part, vacationing in the same city, or in this case, simultaneously looking to make a fresh start.

When she told me she was moving to Manhattan, the idea of leaving Chris and my life in Oak Hill had been slowly forming, hovering out there at the edge of my mind. My biggest dilemma—where could I go if I wanted to disappear?—was solved when Viv resurfaced.

This isn't my *Gone Girl* moment or anything like that. I'm not hiding exactly. But I don't want to be found either. In the letter I left for Chris under Murphy's leash, I explained that I was sorry, but I couldn't do it anymore. I couldn't pretend that everything was fine, that we hadn't become reminders of each other's disappointment.

Technically, I could pretend. I'm an actress, after all. But the reality was I needed to be someone new. And it had been so refreshing, exhilarating even, to make a clean break. I cast myself as "Young-ish Woman Starting Over in the Big City."

Initially, the idea of embracing a life where I wasn't constantly reminded of the past or forced to think about the future, where I could just exist in the present, oblivious to the ticking of an imaginary internal clock, made me giddy.

But I'd forgotten that you can't ditch your history like an expired Metrocard. You can pretend that you don't think about it, but that only lasts so long. Memories clobber you when you least expect them. Something as simple as the opening notes to a song or the scent of roses in full bloom can call up an image, and suddenly you've gone from "Carefree Gal Living in the Moment" to "Weirdo Weeping in the Subway." And it hits you: Your past has been with you every moment, no matter how much you try to will it away.

I imagined Chris reading the letter, Murph tap dancing beside him, ready and waiting to go for that morning run. Chris would be surprised but not shocked. Everything I'd written in the letter I'd already told him—more than once. But even when I'd said the words to his face, "We can't keep doing this," he hadn't believed me.

On the windowsill, beside the hand cream and an alphabet's worth of vitamins, I left my cell phone. Taking it would've made it too tempting to answer the texts he was bound to send: *Come home, Al. We'll work this out. It'll be different this time. I promise.*

In my note, I asked him to give me space, not to try to find me again, to let me be. Then, I slipped out of the house at four in the morning. Chris could sleep soundly anywhere: on a train, in a movie theater, at home on the couch—even after suffering another crushing disappointment. I hated and envied him for it.

For years, I'd lain awake watching the hours slide into one another on the clock on Chris's nightstand. Sometimes I'd get up, read a book, or wander from room to room dusting picture frames and rearranging throw pillows, until the sun came up. Murph, so accustomed to my roaming, didn't bother to follow me.

Noticing the purplish-gray rings beneath my eyes, my doctor had given me a prescription for sleeping pills. Chris convinced me not to take them.

"Don't start with that shit, Al. It's not healthy," he'd said.

"Easy for you to say. You're the one who could sleep through an explosion." I waited, expecting him to relent, to show the slightest hint of sympathy. He had none. "I'm exhausted all the time. My eyes burn. I look like a zombie," I continued.

"Those things have side effects, and they're addictive as hell. What if this is the month, Al?" His bright blue eyes pleaded with me.

As if that wasn't the question that kept me up in the first place.

*   *   *

Viv's bedroom door opens. The guy who was waiting for her on the stoop last night saunters out, shoes in hand. Maybe I've met him once before. These men all blur together.

"Want some?" Viv holds out her glass to him. She's sitting in an overstuffed chair, her long, elegant legs crossed at the knee.

"Nah, thanks." He shakes his head. "Gotta run."

I'm twisted in the sheet I spread over the couch each night and fold up every morning. Before I untangle myself, I check to make sure I'm wearing more than just my underwear. Last night, like so many nights now, is fuzzy. Glancing down, I see the camisole and boxer shorts Viv lent me. I stand, ball up the pale pink sheet, and gesture for Viv's latest guest to have a seat.

"Al, you remember William?"

"Of course," I lie. My temples throb like someone's slapping bongos inside my skull. "Nice to see you again, William."

"It's Bill, actually," he says, fiddling with a knot in his shoelaces. My eyes flick to Viv's, and she winks at me.

"Sorry, sorry!" She nudges his knee with her foot. "I guess I'd pay more attention if we ever did any talking, Billy."

Billy. Billy Barnes. Rachel. Their names and faces drift like clouds through the foggy sky of my mind. Why am I thinking about them again? I suddenly remember turning on the news last night after we got in.

Most nights, I fall asleep with the television for company, soothed by its warm glow. Enthusiastic infomercial voices drown out the questions swirling through my head: *What have I done? What am I doing?* And worse, *what should I do next?*

I'd just settled on the couch when I saw the Barneses' house flash up on the screen. I recognized it immediately. Chris, Murph, and I had run past it nearly every morning for the past six years. But seeing it there unexpectedly made me sit up so fast I dropped the glass of water I'd hoped would prevent this hangover. A familiar ache filled my stomach, transporting me right back to Oak Hill. The place I'd been trying to forget for the past two months.

In the news segment, Rachel sobbed on the front lawn, pleading with the public to help her find her son. Her forehead looked like an Etch A Sketch, all fine lines, and her face was washed out, ashen. They cut to a shot of Billy smiling in front of a giraffe exhibit at the zoo. That's as much as I remember.

It's already eighty-five degrees in Viv's third-floor walk-up, yet chills wash over me, creeping up my spine until the hairs on the back of my neck bristle.

I put my smoothie glass down and reach for Viv's laptop on the coffee table where I left it yesterday afternoon. I'd been searching for an apartment before Viv insisted we go for drinks, which turned into dinner, which turned into more drinks.

I type Viv's password, MarryMeLiamHemsworth, and enter "Billy Barnes Oak Hill" in the search bar. Within seconds, the page floods with headlines.

Oak Hill Boy Disappears on Walk Home From Kindergarten
Town Fears the Worst When 5-Year-Old Vanishes
No Clues in Case of Missing Oak Hill Boy as Search Continues
Have You Seen Oak Hill Kindergartner Billy Barnes?

Some articles include photos of Billy. Others show Oak Hill's favorite landmarks—the clock, gazebo, and pond. I click on an article with a video and check the date: Saturday, June 15. Today. Staying at Viv's without a job has caused me to lose all track of time.

A reporter stands at the entrance to the park. The sound is off, but as she gestures toward the playground behind her, the ache returns to the bottom of my belly. Loss and sorrow grow and expand like orbs inside a lava lamp, swimming, toxic and free, inside me.

I start the video from the beginning and unmute it.

"When five-year-old Billy Barnes didn't arrive home from school Thursday afternoon, his concerned babysitter called the boy's mother . . ."

I'm so focused on her words, I don't notice Bill's gone until Viv settles in beside me on the couch.

"I thought you were apartment hunting," she says, peering at the screen and pointing to the words "Oak Hill" beneath the reporter's name. "Isn't that your old town?"

"It is." I click one story after another, my eyes scanning for new details.

"You're not thinking of going back to Dullsville, are you?"

The day I moved in with Viv, I tried to explain life in Oak Hill, how the biggest thing that ever happened was when a new vendor joined our farmers market and brought alpacas to town. She'd laughed so hard she spit out her mojito.

"The last time we hung out, we danced on a bar in Ibiza. Now you're sampling apple cider and hanging with farm animals?" she'd said.

It seemed funny at the time, but now I wonder if that wasn't part of the problem. Because Oak Hill was straight out of a storybook, it perpetuated the myth that no harm or hardship could ever befall anyone lucky enough to live there. Our neighbors believed they were untouchable. Chris and I had bought into it too. How wrong we'd been.

"I'm reading about this boy who's been missing since Thursday. He lives in my neighborhood." I pause. "My old neighborhood."

I point to a photo of the Barnes family at SeaWorld, posing with a costumed shark. Rachel has a hand on each of Billy's shoulders. Protective. Her smile looks strained; his giant grin is the real deal. There's a resemblance in their big brown eyes. Ted, Billy's dad, wears sunglasses and stands off to the side, like he's afraid of being devoured by the theme park's plush mascot. More likely, he doesn't want to be there.

I'd seen the Barnes family around town, of course. Rachel always seemed like a cold fish who only turned on the charm when there was a commission to be made. Ted, her husband, gave off a vibe like he was somewhere between tired and angry. He had a son, Evan, from his first marriage. But once he left for college, Evan rarely returned to Oak Hill. According to the rumor mill, Evan and Rachel don't get along. Go figure. Evan's mom had only been dead about a year before Ted remarried, and before long, Billy was born.

The first time I talked to Billy was at the neighborhood block party last summer. We bumped into each other, literally, and my hot dog had rolled off my plate and into the street.

"Oops, sorry," he said.

We reached down to pick it up at the same time and nearly bumped heads.

"Billy, get over here, and quit causing trouble," Ted bellowed. "Sorry!" he barked in my direction.

I hadn't minded. I wasn't going to eat anything at that petri dish potluck where macaroni and potato salad curdled in the sun, and flies drowned in spinach and bean dips. Plus, because he was five, Billy was probably one of the few people there I could talk to who wouldn't gossip about me later.

I imagined the conversations my neighbors would have behind my back after Chris and I headed home.

"She's put on a bit of weight, right? Think she's preggers?"

"Was she drinking? Did anyone notice?"

I wasn't paranoid. I heard them whispering about one another. That's life in a small town like Oak Hill, as much a part of the community as churches or sidewalks.

I watched Billy skip away toward his dad with a longing that left me breathless.

As if she can read my mind, Viv laughs. "Shit, I don't even want kids of my own. Who would take someone else's?"

"Jesus, Viv. That's not even remotely funny."

There's so much I haven't told her, mainly because there's nothing she can say or do that will make me feel better about any of it, and I'm trying to move forward.

"Sorry! Sorry, I'm joking!" Viv yawns as she stretches, placing her pedicured feet on the coffee table.

I continue skimming and stop when I come to the next photo. Viv leans in closer.

"What happened? Did they find him?"

"No." I point to the smiling girl with blond hair in the field hockey uniform. She's standing between teammates, their faces blurred. "Cassidy McLean—the babysitter who called Billy's mom when he didn't come home at the usual time."

"Damn, she's gorgeous. Look at that skin—no visible pores."

"Of course her skin is flawless, she's eighteen!"

"Remember life before thirty? Before worrying about crow's feet, Al? Wait, who does she look like?"

"Blake Lively," I say. "I thought it the first time I saw her."

"Yes!" Viv claps her hands.

This is one of her favorite games: Figure out which celebrity a person most closely resembles.

"I know her too—the babysitter, I mean." I rub my temples.

"First, you know the missing boy, now the babysitter. Maybe you should've run for mayor!" Viv elbows me.

I laugh not because it's funny but ironic. "I was totally unpopular in Oak Hill, actually. No one even invited me to join their book club or their Bunko group."

"No surprise there, Al. You know the rules. Everyone hates the prettiest girl in the room. I'd imagine having a super-hot husband doesn't help either. Not that I have any experience there."

After a while, not being included was better. That way, I didn't have to see their framed family portraits lining the walls and stairwells—all those clichéd barefoot beach shots with everyone in matching jeans and white T-shirts. I didn't simmer with jealousy when fresh-out-of-the-tub toddlers came down for a good-night kiss in their footie pjs, their fine baby hair smelling like strawberries. Being excluded meant I didn't endure the questions that would inevitably arise after these women had a few glasses of rosé:

"So, what about you and Chris? When are you guys gonna start a family?"

"How many years have you been married?"

"Are you trying? If you are, you'll want to get on a preschool waitlist ASAP."

These women looked forward to time away from kids they didn't even have yet. They had everything and took it all for granted. Maybe they knew how ungrateful I found them, and that's why they never included me.

"Cassidy's one of Chris's piano students," I say, searching for more information. "It says here she was a few minutes late getting to the Barneses' house. She must feel awful. She's a sweet girl. Smart too."

"Well, her future is over. This will haunt her for the rest of her life."

"Don't say that."

"I think you spent too long in Pleasantville, Nancy Drew. When I played Juror Number Six on *Justice Is Served*, I learned that if the cops don't have some good leads in the first three hours, it's usually not a happy ending." Viv stands and stretches again. "I'm hitting my usual Saturday morning Wake & Drake spin class. Wanna come?"

"Nah." I shrug. "Thanks."

I've lost all interest in exercise and healthy eating. As soon as Viv leaves, I'm going around the corner to the deli for the best hangover cure I know: a bacon, egg, and cheese sandwich.

Maybe I'll have it delivered. The last time I went out, I swear some guy followed me. He was standing across the street from Viv's building when I stepped outside. Tall, thin, with a strong jaw and sunken eyes, he walked behind me, even after I turned the corner. When I stopped to pick a bouquet of flowers to refill the vase on Viv's coffee table, he slowed, fished out a cigarette, and lit it. He stood so close, smoke filled my nostrils. Maybe he was a fan who recognized me and was working up the nerve to say hello. If he wanted a photo, he could've just taken it and moved on. This guy lingered.

When I came out of the store, he flicked his cigarette into the gutter and trailed me back to Viv's. I angled her spare key between my trembling fingers to use as a weapon if it came to that. If it hadn't been a sunny afternoon, the streets filled with people, I'd have completely panicked. Still, my heart hammered. The thought that Chris might hire someone to find me was always with me, making me anxious and flinchy.

But that was impossible. Years ago, I'd played the part of Marlowe Malloy, a woman who needed to escape her abusive husband, a powerful and beloved politician. I simply followed the script. Once I made up my mind to leave Oak Hill, I withdrew thousands of dollars little by little, hitting the ATM every few days, getting cash back at grocery stores, purchasing prepaid gift cards. I changed all my passwords and announced on social media that I was going on a digital diet to spend a few months "unplugging and recharging"—the kind of celebrity self-care bullshit that typically lasts a week tops. I left my cell phone behind so my location couldn't be tracked. Chris could be relentless, but there's no way he'd find me in the middle of Manhattan—especially because I rarely went out.

After I got back inside Viv's apartment and arranged the sunflowers, I looked out the window. The man was gone. I told myself I'd imagined it.

"Too much time away from acting, and you create your own drama!" Viv would say if I mentioned it. So I didn't.

I thought about that guy on and off for days. Now, I can't stop thinking about Billy and Oak Hill. I want to put the laptop down, but I can't. I click back to the article with the video shot in the park and play it again from the beginning. On many late afternoons, I'd taken Murph there to keep him from distracting Chris's students. A few kids were afraid of big dogs, but others wanted to spend their entire lesson petting him.

When we'd get to the park, I'd let Murph off the leash, and he'd sprint across the grassy field in the dog run area. I'd throw him a tennis ball over and over again, my back to the playground. I couldn't stand to watch all the nannies and parents on their cell phones, paying no attention until a toddler toppled off a slide and landed in a sobbing heap on the wood chips. More than once, I'd thought about how easy it would be for someone to come along and take one of those kids since no one was watching them closely. How much time would pass before anyone noticed? How far away would the kid be when they finally did?

It scared me that I'd even think like that. But sometimes on those darker days, when my lower back ached and I knew my period was on its way no matter how much I willed it not to come, I'd imagine taking one of those children by the hand and leading them away from the park toward home. My home.

As the video segment wraps up, the reporter frowns. She asks that anyone who passed through the neighborhood between three and four on Thursday afternoon reach out with any information that could help find Billy.

Chris took Murph for his afternoon walk around that time. In good weather, they'd make long meandering loops through town before the kids began showing up at our house around four for lessons. I never asked Chris which route he took, but I'd wondered if he and Murph passed Oak Hill Elementary. Or did he also find it too painful to see all those little faces, to hear their high-pitched squeals of delight as they threw themselves into the knees of a waiting parent?

But, of course, Rachel Barnes wouldn't have been there on the sidewalk. She'd gone back to her real estate career last fall. She couldn't stop talking about it at the block party.

"It's time! I have to do something to avoid empty-nest syndrome," she brayed as if Billy were going off to college instead of kindergarten. "So, if you're thinking of selling, or know anyone selling, or know anyone looking to buy, send them my way, okay?"

After too many glasses of sangria, she'd teetered over to us, wobbling on wedges she wasn't used to wearing.

"Ever think about downsizing?" she'd asked. "What do you need that big house for? It's just the two of you!"

Her words landed like a hatchet hurled directly at my heart. Chris felt me stiffen beside him and said, "You might want to get yourself some coffee, ma'am."

He added the "ma'am" for me. I'd been called it recently by some teenage cashier at a grocery store. It made me feel old. Dried up. I'd told Chris that it had bothered me. Vain, I know. Still, it felt like proof that the last few years had taken a noticeable toll.

But Rachel, too tipsy to be offended, only grabbed Chris's arm to steady herself and laughed. "You're probably right! I'm sorry if I'm being too forward. It's just that your home is so stunning. They all are. Look around."

She swept her arms from side to side like a game show host's assistant before stopping to gesture toward her own house. A trio of shiny black rocking chairs waited on her sprawling porch. They matched the black shutters, while the lush greens of hanging ferns appeared brighter, more vibrant in contrast to the home's white siding.

"It's magical. Who wouldn't want to live here, am I right?" Rachel continued.

Without waiting for our response, she'd wobbled off to ask another couple if they'd given any thought to moving.

I didn't need to study the well-manicured lawns to remember that I, too, once thought of this as an ideal place to put down roots, grow a happy family, and then sit back and watch all my dreams blossom into existence. But now I know that looks can be deceiving.

People think terrible things can't happen to you if you live in an upscale community, in a fancy house with enviable landscaping. You certainly wouldn't think a child would go missing in this sweet, sleepy town.

But I'm not surprised. After all, I lost myself in Oak Hill. And my children too.

CHAPTER

3

Saturday, June 15
Cassidy

I LEAN AGAINST A tree listening to crickets and whispers, aka Oak Hill's summer playlist. Everyone stands still as statues waiting for the dreaded "Over here!" or "Got something!"

I hold my breath, watching the police comb Oak Hill Pond as Kyle Kinsley claps me on the back.

"Kyle!" I jump. "Holy crap! You scared me!" I gasp for air as if I'm the one at the bottom of the muck. Police officers in boats the size of bath toys have spent the last hour dragging the still water while the crowd looks on.

"Hello, Cassidy," Kyle says with a wave, as if this were just an ordinary Saturday night. "How are you doing?"

How do you think I'm doing? I'm a person of interest in a missing child investigation. The bad babysitter every parent in Oak Hill hates. I'm completely falling apart, asshole! I want to scream. But Kyle's a good guy. Brilliant but awkward. Odd, sure, but not a dick. So I bite my lip, shake my head, and turn back to the pond where the officers move so slowly, it's like they're scared they might actually find something.

"Do you think he's in there?" he asks. "Billy, I mean. Do you think he's in there?"

I narrow my eyes and stare at him. The harsh glare of flood-lights turns Kyle the yellowy-white of a potato chip. The lawn surrounding the pond shines like that cheap plastic grass you stuff in an Easter basket. Everything looks fake in this creepy glow, and for the millionth time since Thursday, I wish none of it were real—that I'm tripping like the guys in my gym class who mess around with microdosing and mushrooms.

It's 10 PM. The police and the mayor agreed that searching the pond for Billy's body should be done at night so it won't alarm local families. That's Oak Hill for you. Never let anyone think this is anything other than a quaint little Norman Rockwell town. Like, if you search for a missing kid during the day, Oak Hill won't top those stupid "Ten Best Towns to Raise Your Family" lists. Everyone around here makes a part-time job out of pretending their lives are perfect.

Meanwhile, they can't go seven seconds without gossiping about one another. I would know. Since Thursday, stories about Billy, his family, and me have been spreading faster than lice through a preschool.

Eighty, maybe a hundred people have come out tonight. Only a handful look worried. The rest seem straight-up interested, like they've got a front-row seat to the best show in town. I imagine them shoveling down their dinners and reminding their spouses, "Set the DVR! We've got ourselves some real live drama right here in Oak Hill tonight!"

Vultures. They talk to the reporters whose news vans ring the pond, and I lean a little closer to the tree. Mom says I shouldn't be here, that it'll only make me feel worse. Maybe she's right. I haven't really slept since Billy's been gone. I can't, and I've stopped trying because when I wake up it all rushes back. When I nap, I dream of Billy calling my name. I can't see him or get to him. We're in a maze. I follow the sound of his raspy little voice, but every time I turn a corner, he isn't there. I try shouting, "Billy! Billy! Where are you? Answer me!" but can't get the words out. That feeling of being paralyzed startles me awake, my heart galloping, skin clammy.

"Caaaaass!" Kyle whines loudly even though he's still standing right next to me. "I asked you a question. Do you think he's in there?"

The thought makes my stomach churn and my mouth go dry. I can't answer him. Instead, I watch bats swoop and dive beneath the floodlights.

Oak Hill Pond is usually the most scenic spot in town. On Saturdays in December, Santa sits inside the white gazebo nodding and ho-ho-ho!-ing as children whisper their wish lists into his frozen red ears. In spring and summer, bridesmaids smooth their gowns and check their makeup while ushers pretend to toss a groom into the chemically treated water, a photographer capturing shot after shot. In autumn, families frolic in piles of gold, copper, and amber leaves that have fallen from the soaring oaks that give the town its name. They pose for the photos that will become their Christmas cards.

Oak Hill Pond is a bit like the community itself. Picture perfect at first glance, but you probably don't want to know what's going on beneath the surface.

If these officers dig around enough, maybe they'll dredge up some beer bottles and condoms. They may pull out a bicycle or a set of car keys tossed in as a prank. Oak Hill Pond may be the keeper of certain dark secrets, but it can't have Billy. He'd never come here alone. His mom forbids it. "Steer clear of the pond!" is number five on the list of a dozen rules that hangs on the fridge. Each mandate ends in an exclamation point. Billy knew if he wanted to continue walking to and from school with his buddy Oliver, or on his own, he needed to follow every single one.

Even if Billy took a detour and walked here hoping to see a goose or catch a tadpole, even if something caught his eye and he waded out into the muck, he knew how to swim. I taught him when I first started babysitting for him two years ago. His mom—she told me to call her Mrs. B.—hired me because I lifeguard at Oak Hill Country Club and help with swim lessons.

The Barneses have an in-ground pool, the shape of a kidney bean, in their backyard, and even though Billy was just a toddler, he'd throw himself right in. Fearless. It didn't matter if the water was so cold it made your fingers and toes tingle. He'd duck under in the shallow part and bob up giggling and spluttering in eight feet, flapping his arms like he was part penguin. Mrs. B. thought I was a great instructor, but it was all Billy. He's braver than most kids.

"Having a job that shows you're responsible impresses college admissions officers!" my guidance counselor loved to remind me. Good thing I've already been accepted because I've screwed up spectacularly now.

Since Thursday, I've told myself that Billy's going to come back safe, that he'll use his beloved flashlight, compass, and all that courage to make it home. I have to believe that. Anything else destroys me.

Billy and I got really close over the last couple of months. Mrs. B. went back to work full-time last fall. When she fired her au pair in April, Mrs. B. asked if I could watch Billy a few afternoons a week until she found a replacement.

The timing couldn't have been better. I need to make as much money as possible before I leave for school, and Mrs. B. is one of the more generous moms in town. She's the kind who'll hand you a bunch of tens and twenties and say, "Keep the change," a dream compared to the others who prefer to use Venmo or PayPal and then round backward to the previous half hour. Like even if I'm still there at four fifteen, they'll only pay me until four. *Cheap Range Rover–driving assholes spend more on their dog walkers than their babysitters.*

"Cassidy!" Kyle windmills his long arms in a failing attempt to fight off mosquitos. "Answer me!"

People turn and stare. Exactly what I don't want. I'm wearing jeans and a basic gray hoodie, hoping not to attract any attention. Since Thursday night, reporters have been calling the house and trying to connect with me on Instagram, like I'm ever going to answer their questions:

"Where were you, Cassidy—why weren't you at the Barneses' house at 3:15 PM?"

"Do you think those extra minutes would've made a difference? Would Billy be safe at home if you'd arrived on time, Cassidy?"

"Was this the first time you were late? Let's set up an interview! Don't you want to share your side of the story, Cassidy? Clear your name?"

"Jesus Christ! Shut up!" Words fly out, directed at Kyle and the voices in my head. "No. I do not think he's in there!"

I focus on the pond, but out of the corner of my eye, I see Kyle flinch. I take a deep breath like Mom reminds me to do when she sees that I'm on the verge of freaking out.

Kyle's shoulders slump. He won't look at me. We've been in honors and AP classes together since freshman year, so I know that once he asks a question, he won't rest until it's answered. That's who he is. It's also probably why he doesn't have many friends, which makes me feel like a major asshole whenever I lose my patience with him.

"Shit, Kyle," I say, "look, I'm sorry. I'm just really worried about Billy." I force my voice to sound calmer, but my insides jangle. All I can do now is wait.

Up until Thursday, my biggest worries were what to wear to graduation and if my future college roommate was really as cool as she seemed when we FaceTimed. And there was one other thing—person, really—who'd been on my mind nonstop.

"Don't curse, Cassidy!" Kyle says, again louder than necessary. "You're smarter than that. Remember at the prom when your heel broke, and you said 'motherfucker' and I told you there are other ways to express yourself?"

Yes, I went to the prom with Kyle Kinsley, quirkiest kid in our grade. Why? Because he asked. Because he's harmless. Because I can't stand guys my own age. These idiots with their memes and their dick pics? Not happening.

Of course, if I'd been hanging out with them, maybe I wouldn't be here now, watching men with hooks pretend that they're fishing for trout instead of the lifeless body of a boy who could list the batting averages of all his favorite ballplayers.

If I hadn't been where I was, if I'd been at the Barneses' home at the regular time, maybe none of us would be here.

But nothing was regular about Thursday. The annual senior class pizza party started at noon on the football field. We were all supposed to sit around and reminisce while signing each other's yearbooks. But I had better plans.

When I told Lexi, my best friend, that I was bailing, that I had no desire to melt in the sun writing "HAGS!"—as in "Have a Great Summer!"—over and over again, she made a *tsk tsk tsk* sound.

"When good girls go bad," she joked, shaking her head.

"Stop!" I laughed. We stood outside the school's entrance. I lowered my voice when a couple of lacrosse players walked by. "You know you'd do the same if you were me."

"I didn't say I wouldn't." Because of her mirrored sunglasses, I couldn't see her eyes, only my distorted reflection. "I just think this has gone from a crazy, one-time thing to a . . ."

Lexi fiddled with the spaghetti strap of her floral romper. It violated the school's dress code, but with a week left until graduation, no one cared.

"This thing's gone to a what?" I asked, tilting my head to the side, waiting for her to finish her sentence.

"A mistake." She held her hands up in a *how-do-you-not-get-this?* gesture. "It's gone from an 'oops' to a 'what the fuck?' pretty damn fast, and I think it's going to seriously screw you up if you don't end it. Just stop now before you get in deeper or someone finds out."

She placed one of her outstretched hands, still cold from the school's air conditioning, on my arm. It felt condescending. I shook it off.

Lexi and I had made a pact in fourth grade to never tell each other anything but the truth. This came after her mom had lied to her for two weeks insisting her dad was away on a business trip when actually he'd moved across the country and was too much of a shithead to say goodbye in person.

I stared her down. "Why don't you admit that you're jealous that he picked me and not you," I said, a dare.

Lexi snorted and looked around to see if anyone could overhear before she said, "Yeah, right, only because you threw yourself at him! For someone so smart, you're acting really stupid lately."

"Well, thanks for your concern." I pretended her words didn't hurt. They stung, of course, but even with her warning and her insults, I couldn't stop smiling. My heart and mind were already blocks away. "If anyone asks where I am, tell them I'm in the bathroom dealing with an eyelash extension crisis."

"Whatever." She hitched her backpack higher on her shoulder and walked away.

I reminded myself to chill and not to sprint to my car in the senior lot like the needy, lovesick girl that I'd become.

When I got to the ancient beige Camry that belonged to my grandmother, I opened the door and stashed my cell phone under the front seat just in case Mom checked my location. That wasn't her style, but still, better safe than sorry. Then I locked the door and bolted toward my better plans.

*   *   *

That was before noon. I had more than three hours to get to the Barneses' house, and I still messed it up. Had it been worth it? I'd thought so at the time, but now I'd give anything to go back to Thursday and do it all differently. Would it have mattered? Maybe Billy would still be missing. But if I'd been in the right place at the right time, at least I wouldn't feel responsible.

I've seen the stories, read the comments. If you believe them, I'm a "checked-out," "thoughtless," "selfish teen," already condemned by social media. Every time my phone pings, I die a little. If Billy isn't found safe, everything I've worked for—college, my small but very necessary scholarships, my shot to get out of Oak Hill—all disappears.

Low whispers rise to a steady hum that spreads across the pond.

"Look!" Kyle juts his chin in the direction of Mrs. Gallagher.

While most people wear shorts and tees, she's sporting one of those look-at-me Lilly Pulitzer sundresses and matching fuchsia espadrilles. She moves from one group to the next, offering her clipboard and pen as if she's passing hors d'oeuvres at a party.

"What does she have there?" Kyle asks.

I know what she's got. Part of me is horrified, another part is grateful.

"She's asking people to sign a petition that wouldn't allow kids to walk to or from school without an adult until they get to Oak Hill High." I cringe because her latest crusade makes it seem like Billy's parents were negligent. But it also takes the spotlight off me—the bad babysitter—and for that, I'm embarrassingly relieved.

"Wouldn't it be more efficient and environmentally friendly if she used Change.org?" Kyle frowns.

"Yes, but then she wouldn't get the attention," I say, and think back to Thursday night at Oak Hill Elementary. Volunteers gathered there before splitting into search parties.

When I walked into the gym, Lexi bit her lip like she had to stop herself from saying something, then pulled me into a hug.

"We'll find him," she whispered.

"I wasn't there, Lex," I blurted, barely able to keep it together. "I was supposed to be there for him. I was late. I fell asleep, and then I had to race back to get my car. I never should've—"

"Well, Mrs. Gallagher is basically blaming Mr. and Mrs. Barnes for not hiring a bodyguard to escort Billy home. She's talking about starting a movement to stop kids from, like, being outside unattended or something just as ridiculous."

Tears burned my eyes. I couldn't speak.

"Stop, Cass." Lexi squeezed my arm. "We'll find him. C'mon."

She grabbed a stack of flyers. Beneath the word "Missing," Billy's face smiled up at me and I thought I might collapse under the crushing weight of failing the person who least deserved it.

I had never been late before. I could remember what it was like to be a kid walking into an empty house by yourself. The weird echo that only existed when you were alone watching otherworldly dust particles float through a patch of sunlight. The skin-crawling anxiety that came from imagining someone, something, was there waiting, lurking in a closet, under a bed.

I'd never wanted Billy to feel that way, so I usually got to the Barneses' house by three at the latest.

I'd let myself in with the key Mrs. B. made for me and prep Billy's apple slices or rinse the fresh berries that waited in the fridge, complying with rule number eight: "Healthy snacks only!" Then I'd go sit on the porch steps and scroll through my phone while I waited for him. He'd usually come running down the block by 3:15, filled with tales about show-and-tell or who got sent to the nurse's office.

As soon as I realized I wasn't going to make it there on time Thursday, I texted him. "Running late, sorry!" with a frowning emoji. "See you in a few!"

I had a momentary freak-out when I remembered that Mrs. B. checked Billy's phone at the end of every day. But, still, she didn't know where I was when I sent that message. I could tell her I'd been just up the street but didn't want Billy to worry if he didn't see my car right away.

I expected him to send a yellow thumbs-up emoji, but he didn't text back.

I ran up the Barneses' porch steps, crossing my fingers that Billy would be sitting in a rocking chair with his magnifying glass studying the spiderwebs spun between hanging ferns. He wasn't there. I grabbed the mail and tried the doorknob. Locked. My racing heart slowed. Maybe I'd arrived ahead of him. It seemed like a miracle.

It was hot for mid-June, and the humidity made the front door swell and stick. I leaned into it with my shoulder as I turned the key. A blast of cool air hit me, a shock and a relief.

"Billy!" I yelled just in case he'd beat me there. The foyer looked as if someone had gotten drunk and binge-ordered every item on the Pottery Barn website. A dark wood bench sat beside the staircase. It had cubbies for Billy's school supplies and baseball gear. I looked at the one where he usually stuffed his backpack. Empty. The tray where he was supposed to leave his sneakers because of rule number ten ("No shoes in the house!") held only a pair of flip flops. I stepped out of my sandals and shivered. I'd been wearing a light cardigan over my sundress, but, in my rush, I'd left it behind, a swirl of cotton on a bedroom floor that wasn't mine.

"Billy?" I called again, ignoring all the clues that told me he wasn't there. I walked through the kitchen and placed the mail on the giant marble island, hoping to spot a note from Mrs. B. Finding one was unlikely. She'd have texted me if their plans changed. She was good like that. Lately, though, she'd been distracted, busy with some contractor and their house-flipping project.

No note. Just a bunch of herbs in clay pots. On their sides, Billy had used chalk to scribble "rosemary," and "basil." I smiled at how he'd misspelled "thyme" though I was surprised Mrs. B. hadn't corrected him. She'd hired a tutor to help with reading and writing.

I looked in the family room, past the throw pillows and the wall art preaching all that inspirational bullshit everyone spouts but no one actually practices: "Good Vibes Only" and "Follow Your Dreams." My favorite was the "Collect Moments Not Things" plaque Mrs. B. placed on the fireplace mantel right under a massive flatscreen TV.

Beneath my bare feet, the hardwood floor felt warm from all the sunlight spilling in through the windows and French doors. Still, I shivered. I looked outside, hoping to find Billy in a lounge chair by the pool. He wasn't there. I turned to the right and caught a flash of movement out of the corner of my eye, just behind the couch.

"Come out, come out wherever you are!" I called.

Some afternoons we played hide-and-seek. Maybe he'd started this round without me. As I took giants steps in that direction, Jeter—Billy's cat—leaped up from behind the couch, landing perfectly on the back of the sofa.

"Holy shit!" I shouted, my heartbeat thumping in my ears.

When I caught my breath, I started getting annoyed. It wasn't like Billy to not come home on time. Or to hide from me. But school was almost out and everyone had that itchy, restless feeling that makes even the smartest people do dumb things. Dangerous things. If anyone knew about that, I did.

At the front door, I thought of Mom's advice about the power of positive visualization. She always told me to picture myself already doing the thing I wanted to achieve. She probably meant for me to use it to ace a test or score a goal in field hockey. But instead, I had seen myself kissing the man of my dreams. And then I did it.

Because it had worked, my proof as real as the smell of him still on my skin, I closed my eyes, and envisioned Billy skipping up the walkway, magnifying glass pressed to his eye, breathless and babbling about the Yankees. I stepped onto the porch and opened my eyes. It didn't work.

I went back inside, calling, "Hey, Bill! Billy boy! Billy Barnes!" Nothing. "William Edward Barnes! Answer me! Please!"

Upstairs, the bathroom doors stood open, toilet seats down, lids closed, as if Mrs. B. was preparing to show her own home. I went from bedroom to bedroom, wondering why they needed this big, old house when it was just the three of them. Well, four, if you counted Evan, which I didn't. I'd babysat a handful of times when Evan had shown up. Billy'd been so excited to see him, he jumped up and down like he was inside one of those inflatable bouncy castles.

On a good day, Evan might throw him a "What's up, dude?" Other times he acted like Billy wasn't even there. He'd look me up and down and then give me side-eye as if Billy and I were a homeless couple he'd found hiding out in his kitchen.

Standing in the guest room, I got this weird, disoriented sensation. I was still floating on a post-sex-and-sleep cloud, but a sense of dread was waking me up. I listened for Billy's key in the lock and forced myself to look at the time. 3:33 PM. Billy was almost twenty minutes late. That never happened. I raced down the steps and out the front door. On the sidewalk, I looked left, then right.

I'd put off texting him again because I pictured Mrs. B. reading his messages later that night and firing me.

People talk about helicopter parents, but Mrs. B. was more like a low-flying drone. Even when she wasn't there, her presence loomed over you. A lot of Oak Hill moms are that way. They try to act like they're all zen in their yoga pants and Namaste tank tops, with their "Wag more, bark less!" bumper stickers, but they're stress bots. "Jackson! Jackson! Let me help you with that sweater!" or "C'mere, Willow, let me blow your nose for you! Let me breathe for you!"

I'd imitate them at dinner for Mom, and we'd laugh until she begged me to stop.

"You have no idea how hard it is to be a parent," she'd say.

"But, Mom, they fill water bottles with wine to get through trick-or-treating or kids' birthday parties, and they're still vein-popping-in-their-foreheads tense," I'd argue. "You raised me alone, and you never acted like that."

"Finally!" She'd smiled. "How come just when you're about to leave for college you start to appreciate me?"

I couldn't wait any longer. I had to text Billy again. I pulled out my phone, typed, "Hey, Billy! I'm at your house. Where r u?" and willed dots to dance inside that gray bubble, letting me know he was there, writing back.

Nothing. 3:38 PM. My screen hadn't changed. "Billy?" I texted again and waited a second before typing the words I'd been saving as a last resort, the ones I was sure would get a quick response. "I'm going to have to text your mom if you don't write back to me. Now!" I added a purple devil emoji, trying to strike a balance between threatening and fun, so he'd know I wasn't really mad.

I waited, sure that the fear of his mother, whose smile could come and go like the Joker's, would be enough to get Billy's little fingers flying across the tiny keyboard.

My phone pinged. I jumped, sure it was Billy or Mrs. B. It wasn't. It was a text of two ties: one green, one blue.

What the heck is this? I wondered as the phone rang. Kyle.

"Hey, what is it? I'm kind of in the middle of a crisis here."

"Well, Cassidy, I was calling to get your opinion on which tie I should wear to graduation. I just sent you a text so you'd be able to make an informed decision. But I suppose my sartorial dilemma can wait. What's your crisis?"

"I'm supposed to be babysitting this afternoon but the boy—Billy Barnes—he hasn't come home from school yet."

"That's not good, Cassidy. Oak Hill Elementary School has been out for," he paused, "thirty-nine minutes and thirty-three seconds. Does he take a bus? Maybe it broke down?"

"No. Shit, Kyle, he walks home. I was late, so I don't know. Maybe he was here, and he left? I don't know what to do."

"Why were you late?"

I should've known Kyle would ask. No way could I tell him the truth, that I was rolling across periwinkle sheets with the hottest guy in Oak Hill on top of me, under me, everywhere, making me feel like we were the only people on the planet.

"Cassidy?" He repeated. "Where were you? I didn't see you at the pizza party."

A thought popped into my head—a picture, really. From Instagram. A detour near the train station and downtown. A guy in my grade posted it with the caption, "Another day, another bomb scare!" #ThanksPhil #FUPhilFoster

"I got stuck in that detour," I lied.

"Oh."

I exhaled, relieved he didn't ask any follow-up questions, until he said, "Have you called his mother?"

Billy usually called his mom at 3:45 PM to tell her about his day. When she didn't hear from him, would she reach out to me or Billy first? If she found out he wasn't home and I hadn't called her, would that make me look worse? Even more negligent? I needed this job. She paid fourteen dollars an hour, and Billy was by far my favorite kid to watch.

"Not yet," I confessed. "I've been hoping he'd—"

"If a child is missing, you shouldn't wait to tell someone!" Kyle's usual flat tone flipped to exasperated. "The first couple of hours are crucial. Call my brother, Dan. He's a police officer. I wore a red tie to his graduation from the academy. Do you think I should wear the red tie to our graduation?"

"Kyle!"

"You sound stressed. I'll text Dan. Maybe he can help you. My dad calls him Sherlock Holmes, but I think he's joking. You know I struggle with sarcasm."

"Whatever, Kyle, thanks." I hung up.

I knew I had to call Mrs. B., but I didn't want her to have a full-on shit fit. How do you start that conversation? "Um, hi, it's me, your babysitter. I think your kid is missing?"

You're overreacting, I told myself as I typed. *Hi, Mrs. B! Billy isn't home yet. Did he have other plans today?* I waited, held my breath. *Can you call me when you get a chance?* I sent it and looked up, hoping Billy would magically appear. He didn't. I bit my thumbnail, a bad habit I'd probably never break. I told myself Mrs. B. would call. She'd sound calm but bossy—her usual—and tell me she knew exactly where Billy was. It would all make sense.

I stared at the phone, praying it would ring. Three minutes later, it finally did.

* * *

"They found something!" an older woman shouts, snapping me back to the present, to the scene unfolding beside the pond. Her voice, shrill as a fire alarm, shatters the eerie stillness. Murmurs mutate into gasps as we wait. Even though the night air has turned cooler, I'm suddenly burning up, my pulse pounding throughout my entire body.

Kyle's brother, Dan, lifts his pole slowly, gently, out of the water. A dripping jacket dangles from the end of it. A collective exhale ripples through the crowd.

"Is it his? Is it Billy's?" the older woman shouts as she limps toward the water. When the light catches her silver hair, I recognize her. Billy's grandmother. Mr. Barnes's mom. She stopped by randomly when I watched Billy, sneaking him sweets his mother would never have allowed.

She waits at the edge to inspect the jacket even though it's obviously five times bigger than any child's coat. I can't bear to watch. My stomach flips. I'm glad I haven't been able to eat anything since Thursday because I'd probably throw up.

Turning away, I spot Phil Foster walking laps around the pond like he does most nights. I almost wave to him but don't. Phil's been different since he got back.

He was still at Oak Hill Elementary when his dad died. To help pay for college, Phil accepted an ROTC scholarship. He never expected to be deployed to Afghanistan.

When Mrs. Foster was a teenager, she babysat Mom, so our families have always been pretty tight. Phil and his mother would come over to our house or we'd go to theirs when I was younger. Phil taught me cool things like yo-yo tricks and how to whistle. Sometimes he'd bring walkie-talkies or binoculars, and we'd spy on the neighbors.

"Mary Alice hasn't had an easy life," Mom says anytime the Fosters come up in conversation.

When Phil got back last fall, Mom and I visited. I brought my yo-yo, thinking it might remind him of old times. His hands trembled so badly, he couldn't "walk the dog" or "rock the cradle," and I felt like an idiot. He didn't say much either, just rubbed his eyes and grunted in response to our dumb questions.

"He's got his days and nights mixed up," Mrs. Foster whispered, "like a newborn."

"He's seen some terrible things," Mom said on our walk home.

I didn't ask what exactly. I didn't want to know.

* * *

I watch Phil circling the pond, muttering to himself. My head aches thinking about how he used to carry spiders and ladybugs out of my basement and set them free in the backyard. I hate the way people act like he's a freak now, even if he does regularly screw up traffic by reporting "suspicious" packages.

The Fosters live across from the Langleys. Sometimes I spot Phil in the window or pacing across the porch on my way to my piano lesson. I used to wave or yell, "Hey, what's up, Phil?"

before I went inside. But for the past month, I've snuck around the back to the side door just in case he's watching.

"Why would Billy wear a jacket in June?" Kyle asks.

I turn away from watching Phil and back to Kyle.

"It's not his," I say. Even though it's a relief, my skin crawls like a million ants are marching through my veins.

As if he can read my mind, Kyle says, "It's not your fault, Cass. You probably think that if you'd been there on time this wouldn't have happened. But you don't know that, and there's no way to prove it would've made a difference. Well, except that you'd probably feel better. Not better, but less responsible. Is that helpful?"

"Not really, but thanks for trying."

I take out my phone, the screen's full of Instagram notifications—probably more people telling me I'm a shitty person. I swipe them away with shaky hands and focus on the time. 11:11 PM. I make a wish. That Billy is found. Alive. Soon. Then I power it down completely.

I turn and walk away from the pond, pulling out the burner phone I bought with cash Friday morning at the 7-Eleven a couple towns away. I send a quick text, "U up?" and walk faster.

"Wait, Cass, where are you going?" Kyle calls but doesn't follow.

"Home," I lie.

I could go to Lexi's, and we could drink in her basement until we pass out. It's Saturday night, so her mom's probably on another awful date. But I want to go somewhere better, somewhere that makes me forget about everything and everyone else, no bad cocktails required.

I'm going back to the place that made me late on Thursday.

4

Saturday, June 15
Lindsay

I TIPTOE INTO THE house close to midnight, praying the kids are all in bed, asleep.

Sergeant Pepper, our Labradoodle, stretches across the sofa. He yawns as I kick off my wedges. A black dog, three wild boys, and a white couch—what the hell was I thinking?

"Pepper, get—" is all I need to say. He hops down, tags jingling, and follows me into the kitchen, where I grab a San Pellegrino and toss him a treat.

The house is deliciously—or suspiciously—quiet. I don't know which until I climb the staircase and peek into each of the boys' rooms, making sure there's no late-night Xbox tournaments happening, no devices smuggled under covers.

A faint light spills into the hallway from beneath my bedroom door. Behind it, Scott's propped up on pillows, scrolling away on his phone—as addicted as our kids.

"Hey!" His voice takes on this sexy, throaty quality each rugby and baseball season. All that yelling from the sidelines.

"Hey," I whisper back and cross the room, ignoring his balled-up work socks and dress shirt, which have been nesting in a heap on the floor since Friday afternoon.

"So, how was it?" he asks.

"Creepy. Terrifying." I slip off my shorts and tug my shirt over my head as the scene from the pond flashes through my mind—the super-harsh floodlights making everyone look like waxy replicas of themselves, their low, echoey voices interrupted by the squawk of police radios.

I shake off a shiver, unhook my bra, and let it drop to the floor—at least this gets my husband to look up for a second. His face glows a soft blue, lit by the screen, before he puts the phone down, and frowns.

"Did they—"

"Find him? Nope. You know I didn't think they would."

I pull a long cotton tank top from beneath my pillow, slip it on, and lean in to kiss him.

He sniffs. "You smell like . . ."

"Robin made us try this eucalyptus essential oil she sells. It's supposed to repel mosquitos." I scratch my shoulders. "Clearly, it doesn't work."

"I was going to say wine." He arches his eyebrows. "You smell like wine."

"Sarah invited a bunch of us back to her house."

"You went drinking after you watched cops drag a pond for the body of—"

I wait for him to say "our son's friend," or even "Ollie's class-mate," but he can't finish the sentence. Scott played tight end in college, but, on the inside, he's soft as a litter of kittens. "That seems kind of inappropriate—even for your crew."

I roll my eyes, my back to him, as I remove my earrings and bracelets.

"Some reporter interviewed Betsy about her petition. She thought she might be on the eleven o'clock news. Sarah's house was closest. But if she was on TV, we missed it. I wonder if that's why she was all dressed up? She said she'd just come from a graduation party, but now I wonder."

I walk into the bathroom. Strange as it sounds, this is my favorite room in the house. We remodeled it in March, hiring the contractor Rachel Barnes recommended. I had a hard time convincing Scott at first. Nothing was wrong with the old bath-room. It just looked outdated—too much reclaimed wood. I felt like I was bathing in a barn.

"I'm surrounded by males! Don't I deserve something pretty? Feminine?" I'd lobbied until Scott finally relented.

I'd used photos from this Napa Valley spa we visited for our anniversary as inspiration. Derek, the contractor, nailed it. Every time I step onto the white marble floor and see that decadent soaking tub, the elegant crystal chandelier suspended high above it, it brings me joy. Whoever said money can't buy happiness should see this bathroom.

I stand at the sink, removing my makeup, admiring the vase full of peonies I picked up yesterday. Scott leans against the doorframe, an expectant look on his face. He's waiting for me to explain how I could sit in a neighbor's backyard sipping cocktails when a little boy our son walks to school with is missing.

"It wasn't like we were celebrating," I insist. "They're all pretty freaked out."

"And you're not?"

"I told you what I think happened." I look at him in the mirror as I dab dots of rose-scented cream beneath my eyes.

"You're not serious about that?" Scott crosses his arms, stretching his white T-shirt tight across his biceps.

He's tan from coaching the boys' teams and somehow looks better than when we met nearly twenty years ago. Or maybe it's the wine and seeing Betsy's husband, Doug, at the pond tonight, his belly protruding like he's expecting twins. I was walking Sergeant Pepper a few months ago when their Peloton was delivered. I don't think Doug's using it.

"Rachel had to leave. She thought she was going to be sick. Frank Chadwick drove her home. Ted wasn't there." I turn around to face Scott. "Betsy noticed too. When we were sitting on Sarah's patio—did I tell you she's thinking of having a pizza oven built for Brian? As a Father's Day gift. It won't be ready until fall. We should look into that. The boys would go bananas for one." I reach for my tube of elbow butter, squeeze out a dime-sized drop, and rub in small circles. "Anyway, Betsy said, 'Does anyone else think it's odd that Ted wasn't at the pond tonight?' Sarah jumped right in to defend him, saying, 'But imagine if they found Billy?' I guess she has a point. Still, something's off. I'm telling you."

"Just because Ted wasn't there, that doesn't make him a suspect, Linds, c'mon." Scott takes the tube from my hand, squirts out a puddle, and massages it into my shoulders. It feels so good, I don't tell him this shit costs more per ounce than caviar.

"I was right about the Langleys, wasn't I? Remember? I told Kelli at book club back in February, 'Allison didn't wish Chris a happy birthday on Facebook. Nothing on Instagram either.' Next thing you know, Allison Langley's gone. Poof! I'm telling you, babe, I can sense these things."

I attempt to squeeze toothpaste onto my toothbrush but a white gob falls into the sink. I scoop it up with my finger and lick it.

Scott grins. "Geez, Linds, how many have you had?"

"Two, maybe three glasses. Not even glasses—cups! Cups! Sarah said she didn't have any clean wine glasses, so she made us drink out of red Solo cups! Can you imagine? I saw Betsy make a face, and then she whispered, 'I'd sooner drink straight from the bottle than from a plastic cup! So I said, 'Shh! Pretend you're back in college!' Then, this is the best part! Do you know what Sarah served us?"

I take my time brushing my teeth, heightening the suspense, waiting for Scott to guess. He smirks. My husband pretends to hate that I'm part of what he calls Oak Hill's "Mommy Mafia," but I know he secretly enjoys my tales of suburban drama.

"Fritos!" I dry my mouth on a fluffy, monogrammed towel. "You know the tiny bags you stick in kids' lunches? Those! We each got one! How hard is it to put together a decent cheese plate? Or even little dishes of almonds or cashews? I seriously expected Betsy to DoorDash a charcuterie board if anywhere in this lame-ass town was still open."

Scott laughs, so I keep going. "I felt bad, Sarah was obviously embarrassed. She tries so hard. Like, you can literally feel how much she wants to fit in. She apologized and said she grocery shops on Sundays. Hello, Instacart? Who still goes to the store?"

"Not everyone's the hostess you are, my dear. Isn't she the one who just had a baby?"

"That was nine months ago! We were on the patio, three feet from her house, and she was clutching the baby monitor the entire time as if her kids might be snatched at any second. The whole town is on edge. I've never seen it like this."

"So, did you tell them?" Scott says, slowly easing my tank top over my head, kissing my neck.

"Tell them what?"

"Your theory." He slips off my panties. "About Ted."

"No. Not yet. It seems—I don't know—too soon."

Between biting my earlobes, he whispers, "Did you remember to set the alarm when you came in?"

"Please tell me you're not buying into the madness. Like, there's really a predator on the loose? In boring old Oak Hill?"

I slide my hand inside his boxers as he lifts me onto the open space between the undermount sinks, the cool marble giving me goose bumps.

"I have to say, I didn't love paying for it, but remodeling this bathroom was one of the best ideas you ever had," he says, sweeping my hair off my shoulders.

"Why do you ever doubt me?" I moan as he thrusts his way inside me. "You know I'm always right."

5

Sunday, June 16
Rachel

I T'S NEARLY FIVE in the morning, and I'm alone on the porch. The floorboards groan beneath the rocking chair as I move back and forth, the steady rhythm offering no comfort.

Earlier, around midnight, Darcy, my sister, draped a blanket around my shoulders when the air turned cool and rain began to fall.

"Come inside, Ray Ray. Please," she whispered, holding my hands in hers.

"Billy loves to sit out here during a storm and wait for lightning," I told her as I stared at the swaying treetops. "When he sees a flash in the sky, he starts counting, and when he hears thunder, he says that's how many miles away the storm is. Or is it thunder first and then lightning? I don't know. I can't remember."

That was all it took. Long, choking sobs clogged my throat. I couldn't catch my breath until, in a streetlight's glow, I spotted movement, shadows. I leaped up from the rocking chair.

"Billy?"

From twenty feet away, Christopher Langley, a bag of dog poop dangling from his wrist, offered a feeble wave before he and his beautiful retriever crossed to the other side of the street and disappeared around the corner.

I dropped back into the chair, dizzy with loss.

Darcy tried again. "Please, Ray. You've been up for days. Let's go inside. You need to lie down and rest."

"I'm not going inside until Billy comes home."

She reached over and stroked my back in slow, sweeping circles.

"I think you should take something, you know, to take the edge off maybe, help you sleep. The doctor called in a prescription. Ted left it in the kitchen. I'll—"

"I can't!" I hissed. "I won't. I need to be right here. Waiting. I have to be right here!"

I wanted to pound my fists on the arms of the rocking chair, but every motion required strength I couldn't summon. Just breathing seemed as impossible as trying to sprint across the bottom of the sea.

Darcy sighed. Six years older than I, my sister has always been my fierce protector. One of my earliest memories is of Darcy and me huddled beneath the dining room table, her hands covering my ears to block the sound of our parents fighting about money.

Now Darcy has been rendered helpless, humbled by the unknown. Police still have no clues about what happened, no leads, no idea where Billy might be.

"We're asking that neighbors review their home surveillance and contact us immediately if they spot something. Let me assure you, we're leaving no stone unturned," Detective Dubin had said when he stopped by Friday evening to provide us with that worthless update.

When I think about the fact that my son's life is in the hands of a man who isn't clever enough to not speak in clichés, I want to vomit.

"You go inside. Rest for both of us," I told Darcy around 2 AM, when even the birds and crickets had gone silent. But she wouldn't budge. She finally relented, limping toward the door, when the navy of the night sky gave way to dusty pink, signaling the dawn of another day. Another day without Billy.

It's been sixty-two hours since he went missing, almost seventy since the last time I saw his face. Did I kiss him goodbye before he skipped out the door and jumped down the porch steps? What were my last words to him? What were his to me?

I'm numb, suspended between horror and disbelief. I pinch the inside of my wrist, hoping to wake myself up from this nightmare. The red marks only serve as ugly reminders that I'm wide awake. Every moment, my thoughts flit to the darkest corners—murderers, molesters, sex traffickers. I shut my eyes tight, hoping to stop the storm of gruesome images—blood, bones twisted in unnatural positions, a stranger's hands on my son's small body—that flood my mind. I picture the cub scout master—young, single, childless. The lurking custodian. Billy's overfriendly T-ball coach, Scott Jordan, patting every boy on the back, offering his usual, "Nice work, bud!" No one is above suspicion.

When I think back to Thursday, it seems like a lifetime ago. Who was that Rachel? How had she remained so calm? How could a grown woman be so stupid as to think tragedy couldn't strike her family?

Crimes, abductions—those didn't happen in places like Oak Hill. Children went missing in big cities, in dangerous neighborhoods. They didn't disappear from affluent communities, from places where parents and caregivers were vigilant, attuned to their every need. And yet.

Billy is gone. I could've been there on the sidewalk Thursday afternoon with all the other mothers. If I had been, everything would be different. But I wasn't. I chose not to be. I'd left someone else—a teenager—in charge of my precious child while I sat stifling yawn after yawn in an attorney's office, taking the simplicity of the uneventful day for granted.

That's where I was, debating if I should make dinner or order takeout again, when the messages started coming, letters typed one after another, forming words that would rip my life apart.

I was watching my clients sign their names over and over when I felt it—my purse on the floor vibrating against my shoe. At first, I ignored it. It started again. I looked at my watch. 3:45. It would be Billy calling to tell me about his day. I imagined our conversation, him breathlessly recounting his "Flat Stanley" presentation, me repeating, "Great job! I knew you could do it! I have to get back to this closing. Tell me more tonight!"

For the final project of the year, Billy's kindergarten class had read the tale of Stanley Lambchop, a boy who accidentally gets flattened. Students decorated their own cut-out paper doll. They then had to give these Flat Stanleys to a friend or relative who'd take it on adventures, photograph those travels, and return the doll to the student along with accompanying snapshots of Stanley at large. On their appointed day, children would stand in front of the class and share everywhere their Stanley had gone.

"Who do you think we should send him to?" I asked when he'd put the finishing touches on Stanley's orange shirt and had begun to panic about the prospect of speaking in front of his class. "How about Aunt Darcy?"

"Can Evan do it? Please?" he begged.

"Evan's busy looking for a job, pal," Ted said. "Let's not bother him."

"He's been looking for a job for a year, while you pay his rent, his outrageous-even-for-Manhattan rent. It's the least he can do," I argued.

Boy, had that backfired. Days before it was Billy's turn to present, Evan dropped by to "borrow" more money from his father.

"Here you go." He smirked as he handed me Billy's Flat Stanley folder.

Fortunately, I was alone when I opened it. If I hadn't been so irritated, I might have laughed as I flipped through photos of Flat Stanley in Times Square beside Naked Cowboy, Stanley heading into a Weed World in the shadow of Penn Station, Stanley with a shoe print on his forehead on the floor of the Staten Island Ferry.

"Fucking idiot!" I fumed.

It took me hours to add that stupid doll to digital images of Manhattan landmarks and then print and label everything. According to the kindergarten-class moms, Billy's teacher, Miss Harrington, spent an egregious amount of time surfing Pinterest boards for the perfect favors for her upcoming wedding. I counted on her being so distracted she wouldn't notice my poor man's version of Photoshop.

"Wow! Look! Evan did so great!" Billy squealed, spreading the photos I'd placed inside the folder across the kitchen island.

"Hey! Not bad!" Ted said, peering over his shoulder.

I hadn't told Ted that in Evan's version, Flat Stanley had gone to a rave and was probably well on his way to contracting an STD.

When it came to Evan, I was always wrong. Too critical. Lacking empathy. According to Ted, I'd never understand what it was like for Evan—all he'd been through losing his mother so suddenly, having to open his home to a stepmother and half brother so quickly, and at such a tender age. I'd learned over time to save my breath and focus all my attention on Billy.

A shy child, Billy dreaded getting up in front of the class—a class where, if I'm honest, he didn't have many friends. I blamed myself for that too. I wasn't home to orchestrate the types of playdates—trips to trampoline parks and laser tag—that solidified friendships in Oak Hill.

I made time to help him practice, lining up stuffed animals in rows on his bedroom floor, an attentive, albeit fake, audience. Seated in his desk chair, I nodded, offering two thumbs-up, gently correcting him each time he said, "Umpire State Building."

"Bravo! You're going to do great!" I clapped and cheered as he finished, the photos slipping out of his small hands, spilling across his bedroom floor.

I heard Ted coming up the stairs, back from a round of golf, and went into the hall to meet him.

"He's doing better, but still really nervous," I said. "Maybe you could go in and say something encouraging?"

"Have you ever considered that he can't function in these situations because you micromanage him? You coddle him so he thinks he can't do anything without your constant approval."

I reeled back, his words a slap. Before I could respond, he continued, "Are you going to go off to college with him too?"

I narrowed my eyes and lowered my voice. "He's five, Ted. He's looking for extra love and acceptance from me because you're so . . ."

"I'm so what?" he asked, mopping his sweaty forehead with a new dish towel.

"Withholding," I said. It was the perfect way to describe him. I'd begun seeing a therapist, and her ability to sum up my husband's behavior so succinctly had been well worth the co-pay.

Rather than respond, Ted shook his head, emitted his signature *pfft*, and strode toward our bathroom, wiping dirt and dead skin across the once-white towel.

*   *   *

When the phone buzzed again beside my foot, I jumped as if jolted by an electric shock. I needed to know that Billy's presentation had gone well, that Ted was wrong, that I was supporting our son, not smothering him. I picked up my purse, excused myself, and walked into the hall.

I opened my bag, and that's when I saw it. Billy's phone. I forgot I'd taken it. Blocked it out, more likely. He'd been dawdling at breakfast, playing Subway Surfers or Temple Run or some game with a song that would invariably lodge itself in my head—welcome as an ice pick— for the rest of the day.

"Let's go! Come on! Finish your banana, then brush your teeth! You're going to be late! Oliver will be here any second. Don't forget to pack Flat Stanley! Hurry up!"

"Okay, okay, I will, just let me—" His voice trailed off as his thumbs continued tapping away.

I swooped in like a hawk and snatched the device out of his small hand.

"Hey!" he started to protest before he looked up and saw my mommy mask fall away.

I'd awakened with a migraine and a sour stomach, which left me short-tempered and irritable.

As I watched my son's cheeks puff in and out, my first instinct was to rush to him, whisper an apology into his soft seashell ear, and hand back his stupid device. But then I heard Ted's voice: "You coddle him," and I stopped myself.

The doorbell rang.

"Pull yourself together! What's wrong with you?" I seethed. At Billy? At the thought of Ted? At myself?

Billy hopped down from the stool, tossed his banana peel in the trash, and said, "I'm hurrying! I'm hurrying!"

I shook my head in annoyance and hurled his phone into the open mouth of my cavernous handbag.

As I stood in the hallway outside the attorney's office reaching into my bag for my phone, I found his first. Regret wriggled under my skin as my mind replayed the image of my hands grabbing the device, housed in the bright green case he'd been so excited to pick out last August when Ted told him he could get his own phone.

"It's the same color as an alien!" Billy said when I tried to persuade him to choose something classic, like navy.

Initially, I'd insisted that he was too young to have his own phone. I didn't want him on social media or watching filthy videos on YouTube like Oliver Jordan and his brothers, and I didn't have the time or energy to block and monitor it all the way I needed to. And could a kindergartner be responsible enough to not lose such an expensive gadget?

"If he's going to walk to and from school, it's a good idea," Ted argued.

"I don't think he's ready to walk alone, Ted! He's only five!"

"Relax," my husband said dismissively. "It's a short walk, for God's sake. What's it take? Eight, maybe ten minutes." Ted had shrugged. "Evan did it. It's good for the kid. Let him get some fresh air, exercise, independence. Besides, if he's got a phone, you can track his location."

That was the sole reason I'd relented—on both the device and the walking to and from school. I devoted time to helping him learn to read and text simple phrases. Like the rest of his generation, he took to it like a pro.

As I fished around for my phone, Billy's screen glowed to life. His background photo, the selfie he'd taken with Oliver's enormous black Labradoodle, Sergeant Pepper, was obscured by a series of texts. Joy washed over me. Finally, Billy was making friends. It had taken all year, but it was happening.

Then I saw the sender: Cassidy. I skimmed her messages last to first, my initial excitement draining, anxiety replacing it. I scrolled bottom to top and read again.

"Where r u?"

"Write back to me. Now!"

Weakness flooded the crooks of my arms. My hands went slack. I nearly dropped the phone. I tried not to panic as I stared at her words, sure I'd misread them.

"I'm going to have to text your mom."

The purple devil emoji glared at me, mocking. Attempting to quiet the maternal instinct that told me something was wrong, I leaned against the wall, struggling to ignore those initial vibrations of fear that made me break out in a cold sweat.

Of course Billy couldn't respond to her texts; he didn't have his phone, I reasoned. Still, my stomach pitched, sending the sour taste of the yogurt I'd eaten for lunch inching up into my throat.

But why wasn't he home yet? And why was Cassidy running late? She was usually so punctual, so responsible. She'd been distracted lately. Even Billy had noticed. I'd heard him repeating, "Cassidy, did you hear what I said? Did you see Aaron Judge's homer last night? Did you?"

She'd been busy with prom, graduation, and preparing to leave for college in August. I'd felt lucky she'd agreed to watch Billy. It was nearly impossible to find a babysitter in Oak Hill. Parents supplied their teens with steady streams of cash so they had little incentive to work.

Everyone ran late occasionally. Cassidy and Billy would find each other any minute. He'd call from our home phone and tell me all about his presentation, and I'd exhale and laugh at myself for rushing to believe the absolute worst.

If Billy arrived home and didn't find Cassidy there, wouldn't he let himself in and wait for her? Would he go to a neighbor's house? Did he know her cell phone number or mine by heart? My brain scrambled to piece it all together. Nothing clicked.

I pressed her number, my fingers thick and slow. She answered before I even heard it connect.

"Billy!" The relief in her voice was palpable, a thing I could hold in my hand.

"It's me, Cassidy. Mrs. B." My words spooled out in slow motion as I waited for her to interrupt, to tell me Billy was there, safe and sound, giggling and popping raspberries into his mouth.

I heard only silence.

"I have Billy's phone today. I just got your texts," I said, my breath coming in short, quick bursts.

She didn't say a word, forcing me to continue. "Is Billy home yet? Is he there with you?" I tried to stay calm, commanding my heart to slow down as I clung to the thought that this was probably just a mix-up. But from the way she answered before it rang and the urgency in her voice as she said his name, I knew it wasn't. I waited, each second stretched taut, a balloon inflating toward its breaking point.

"No, I don't know where—I'm on your porch. I thought maybe . . . Did Billy have plans you didn't mention?" she stammered.

I tried to think. A wave of nausea rolled through my belly. My mind went blank. What day was it? Had I signed him up for an after-school enrichment class? Painting or cooking? No. No birthday parties. Everything except T-ball had wrapped up ahead of summer.

"No. He doesn't have anything today. I'm coming home. Stay there and wait. I'll make some calls from the car."

"I'm sure he's—"

I didn't let her finish. I couldn't listen to reassurances from the eighteen-year-old who was late, my mind already busy assigning blame.

* * *

I think back to the moments before I read Cassidy's texts, those minutes I sat in the attorney's office daydreaming about chicken and eggplant in a gingery garlic sauce, watching my clients sign their names dozens of times. I now view those final fleeting instants of oblivion as the last time my life would ever be good, the last time I'd ever be whole. And I wasted them.

That morning, I'd seethed over a text from one of the class moms asking if I could send in two dozen mini-bagels the following day for some end-of-the-year celebration.

"Since you work, we know you won't be there for setup or cleanup, so this job is perfect for you!"

Very few mothers in Oak Hill returned to their careers. Last fall, my news about getting back into real estate had been met with frowns, confusion, and the obligatory, "But Billy's still so young! Are you sure?"

The story I'd told most people was that I needed fulfillment, a challenge. "Not that chairing the annual kindergarten plant sale won't be scintillating, but you know what I mean," I'd joked.

What I didn't say was that my marriage was in trouble. It had been from the start.

"An unplanned pregnancy is a tough way to begin," my mother had said, pointing at my swollen stomach, letting out a low whistle when I'd told her Ted had proposed. "Does what's-his-face think you trapped him?" Early hints of dementia had eroded her internal filter.

"Stop, Ma, geez," Darcy said. "You wanted a grandkid, now you're getting one. Be happy!"

"Darcy's right, Mom. Maybe by your standards I'm doing things out of sequence, but it's still a blessing," I'd attempted to convince her and myself. "I'm thirty-seven. I'd pretty much given up on finding a husband or starting a family. It's all going to be fine."

It hadn't been fine, and I didn't know how to fix it. I needed a safety net, my own money, a way out when the time was right.

And now here I am, shivering on my porch, sick to my stomach, keeping a lone vigil for my son because I went back to work, believing it would allow Billy and me to leave Ted, a man who chose to sleep while his own child was missing.

Around six last night, our neighbor from two houses down, Betsy Gallagher, brought over chicken cacciatore. Her eyes grew wide as charger plates as she peered past Darcy, hoping for a glance inside our hellscape, searching for some detail she could report to the rest of the block.

"No rush returning my Le Creuset." Betsy waved her floral oven mitts as if she were hosting a tea party. "I have plenty."

"Is she fucking serious?" Darcy asked, kicking the front door closed with her foot, bare hands burning against the cast-iron cookware.

As soon as I saw Betsy approaching the house, I ducked inside, refusing to be the object of her pity, scorn, or the cautionary tale of what could happen if an Oak Hill mother tried to have a career.

When Darcy placed the meal on the island and lifted the lid, the sight and smell of poultry drowning in tomatoes, covered in pepper slices slimy as earthworms, made me gag.

Ted consumed two servings. Then, he swallowed one of the pills the doctor had prescribed. I watched him from the corner of the kitchen.

"What?" he asked, shoulders raised. "I'm going to lie down. Someone needs to be well-rested. Clearheaded."

I snorted, an ugly little laugh of disgust. Was he implying I wasn't clearheaded because I'd been weeping and walking in circles since Thursday? Was he suggesting that my hysteria was unwarranted? I blamed myself for Billy's disappearance, but he was responsible too, with his stupid "let him get some fresh air"—not that he'd ever acknowledge his role in this.

I opened my mouth to scream "What the fuck is wrong with you? Your son is missing, yet you feast like you're at a Super Bowl party, you detached piece of shit!" but before I could get any words out, he said, "If there's any news, the police will let us know."

As if Darcy and I weren't there, he walked out of the kitchen and switched off the light, plunging the room into an eerie twilight. Another night settling in, another bedtime without Billy.

I looked out the window at the butterfly bush Billy and I had planted last spring. He'd been so excited the first morning he spotted a pair of monarchs flitting from branch to branch while he ate breakfast.

"Mommy! Mommy! They're here! It worked! Come see! Come see!" He'd pointed and giggled as he stood atop the barstool beside the island, though I'd told him a thousand times to be careful and sit nicely so he wouldn't fall and crack his head open. I'd anticipated so many horrific scenarios, but I never thought I'd live out the worst one imaginable.

I turned back toward the large arched doorway where Ted had stood and hated every inch of my home. The walls I'd overseen painted an impractical alabaster closed in. The kitchen island I'd insisted I needed appeared hulking, monstrous.

If I'd kept it professional and sold this house when I had the chance, none of this would have happened. Working as a real estate agent was how I'd met Ted. He'd stopped by the office one evening when I was working late, alone. He was tall with thick, dark hair and a quiet sadness I mistook for thoughtfulness. He'd wanted to sell his home, downsize. His wife, Jane, had recently died. Saint Jane, as I'd eventually come to think of her, had been killed, hit by a car in the middle of the afternoon.

On a windy December day, just a few weeks before Christmas, she'd dropped off Ted's dress shirts at a dry cleaner in Pine Ridge, several towns away and was hit by a drunk driver coming from a holiday luncheon.

Ted said the house held too many memories, that Evan would be better off making a fresh start elsewhere. I could tell Ted was lonely. The first time I saw the house, he kept me there longer than necessary, asking questions he easily could've googled. I got the listing, and he insisted on hammering in the For Sale sign so my heels wouldn't sink into the lawn. On my next visit, he walked me to my car after I'd installed a lockbox on the front door.

I brought him and Evan homemade dinners under the guise of going over marketing strategies. I arrived early on Sundays ahead of an open house, bearing coffee and pastries along with my staging expertise.

I remembered from my father's death a decade earlier that even the smallest hint of kindness meant the world to the grieving. It didn't take long before Ted kissed me in the backyard beside a dead holly tree I suggested he replace. A few months later, I was pregnant. With a baby on the way and no offers on the house, I convinced him to stay, redecorate, put a pool in the backyard for Evan.

"It'll have a completely different feel, a new energy, you'll see!" I promised.

It was after I'd moved in and Billy was born that Ted changed. His quiet sadness shifted to simmering resentment, as if I'd hijacked his life, robbed him of his rightful role as wounded widower.

When he'd arrive home from work, I'd catch him staring at the brightly colored baby toys that littered every surface, a bewildered look in his eyes, like he'd returned to the wrong house.

"I don't remember Evan screaming like this," Ted would grumble before storming off to the guest room on the nights Billy's newborn cries interrupted his sleep.

He hesitated to introduce me to colleagues or old friends, as if embarrassed that he'd replaced Saint Jane, his college sweetheart, so quickly—and with the first woman to cross his doorstep, the first real estate agent who answered his call.

My mother's voice echoed inside my head: "Does what's-his-face think you trapped him?"

Initially, I ignored it, telling myself I'd gotten what I'd wanted, or what I thought I'd wanted. So what if it wasn't perfect? Whose life was? I'd grown accustomed to putting a positive spin on everything. It was in my job description.

"Install a dehumidifier, and this basement will be your favorite room in the house! A smaller backyard means less time spent pulling weeds on the weekend! Stall showers are so much easier to clean than a big bathtub—not to mention eco-friendly!"

*   *   *

With that same idiotic optimism and my mantra, "Pull it together, Rachel!" I found myself taking a deep breath and heading back into the conference room after I hung up on Cassidy.

I focused only on figuring out how to get through the moment right in front of me, a coping strategy I used whenever I felt a real estate deal going sideways. But this wasn't a deal, this was my son. My son, who hadn't come home. My son, who couldn't call me if he were in trouble because I'd taken his phone.

As I pushed open the glass door, small black dots floated at the edges of my vision. I placed my hand on the table for support as that distant, pre-fainting feeling swam through me. *Pull it together, Rachel!*

With my insides knotted, I forced a smile. My clients, Frances and Jack Lewis, a young married couple from the Midwest who still held hands, were nearly finished signing the documents that would make them first-time homeowners. When Frances looked up at me and returned my smile, I thought I might burst into tears. Reaching inside my handbag for my car keys, I mumbled a fast apology about needing to leave to handle a family emergency.

"I hope everything's okay." Frances frowned with genuine concern, and for a moment, I wondered how long it would take before Oak Hill changed her.

"Thanks, I'm sure it will be." Like a fool, I believed this even as the clammy sheen creeping across my skin confirmed that subconsciously I knew nothing was okay. "Best of luck in your new home. Call or text me if you need anything at all," I added, a throwaway line that mercifully few clients took seriously.

At the elevator bank, I jabbed the down arrow button impatiently, whispering, "Please! Please! C'mon, please open!" before giving up and rushing toward the stairwell. I raced down four flights, panting by the time I exited.

As I hurried through the parking garage, I dug inside my bag for my phone. Cassidy's texts and call, mixed with others I'd missed, flooded the screen. I flicked between texts and voicemail, praying for a message from Billy or a classmate's mom telling me he was there, playing in her backyard. I spotted a text from Derek, my house-flipping partner.

"Hey, when you get a sec, let's talk," he'd written.

We'd exchanged curt text messages all morning. I wished they were about insulation solutions for the drafty shack we'd foolishly thought was a solid investment. I couldn't focus on him, the house, or the other issue we needed to discuss, so I continued scrolling. A reminder about the kindergarten end-of-the-year breakfast popped up, followed by a text insisting that at least a dozen bagels be gluten-free. Nothing from Billy.

"Thirty-three minutes to home!" my phone's GPS chirped.

Less than ten miles separated the attorney's office from our house on Cherry Lane, but an ocean of traffic and a dozen stoplights stood between them.

"Fuck!" I screamed, throwing the car into reverse, stopping millimeters from a cement column.

Sweat pooled above my bra's underwires and the leather of the car's seat seared the back of my thighs as my mind ricocheted from one awful thought to another.

What if older boys at school had Billy trapped inside a bathroom stall? The principal had sent a notice about a similar incident that happened months ago. What if Billy tried a new way home and got lost? He was obsessed with testing out that stupid compass. What if a stranger in a van asked him to help find a lost puppy?

I shot out of the parking garage, horns blaring on both sides. At a crosswalk, the car in front of me lurched to a sudden stop.

"Fucking go!" I shouted and beat the dashboard with my fist before pulling into the next lane, ready to race through the intersection. A woman pushing a stroller suddenly appeared in front of my car, so close she put her hand on its hood for fear I'd hit her and the toddler. She shook her head, disgusted at my impatience.

I waved a weak apology, tears clouding my vision. It felt like just hours ago that I was pushing Billy in a stroller. Where was he? How had I thought it was okay for him to be out in the world alone?

I needed to call one of the parents who might have seen Billy as he left school, who might know which direction he took, maybe overheard him talking about going somewhere other than straight home.

But who could I call? When I'd gone back to work last fall, I'd asked to be removed from the neighborhood moms' group text chat. All the beeping and buzzing was a constant distraction. Worse was how guilty their messages made me feel because I wasn't there to take Billy to the park or to the library to see a puppet show.

When I'd asked Betsy to take my number off the list, she'd made a face as if I'd suggested formula was superior to breast milk.

"You really don't want to be kept in the loop?" she'd asked.

Because I'd deleted that group, I'd have to find each mom's number, and when I did, what would I write?

Hi! It's Rachel Barnes. Have you seen Billy?

Admitting I didn't know where my son was felt far too serious a subject for a text. It wasn't as if I'd left a pair of Prada sunglasses on someone's deck. Even if I tried to make light of it—*Hi! I seem to have misplaced my kid! Billy isn't at your house, is he?*—it would spread like a virus through the entire town. I could already see the messages they'd exchange: *Rachel Barnes just texted. She doesn't know where Billy is! Can you imagine losing track of your only child?*

Even if Billy was at a classmate's home, I'd forever be the mom who didn't know where her five-year-old was.

Pressing the phone button on the steering wheel, the dial tone throbbed through the speakers. I didn't know how to make this call. Saying the words "I'm not sure where Billy is" aloud would make it real. I wasn't ready. I hung up and tried again to focus, to convince myself everything would be fine.

"He'll be there. By the time I get home, he'll be there," I repeated. As much as I tried to block them, the same thoughts kept circling: *Why wasn't Cassidy there on time? What if Billy came home, didn't see her, and walked off? Where would he go?*

The tires squealed as I turned the corner onto Cherry Lane so fast my purse fell off the passenger seat, dumping its contents all over the floor.

I barreled into the driveway, plowing up the curb. The car rocked as I threw it into park.

Cassidy stood between two men—one in a police uniform, the other in plain clothes. Had I asked her to call them? I couldn't remember. With one look at their solemn expressions, their hands on their hips, guns in their holsters, my stomach churned.

The whole drive home I'd told myself Billy would be there, eating a plum, jumping up to greet me with a sticky-sweet kiss. He would tell me he'd stayed late to talk about baseball with a classmate. He'd say he wanted to call, but I had his phone. I'd kiss him on the head, breathe in the scent of his coconut shampoo, and try not to let him know he'd scared the hell out of me.

But he wasn't there. Just Cassidy and the policemen—one old, one young, staring—waiting.

I staggered out of the car and vomited all over the walkway.

Cassidy jumped back on to the lawn.

"Oh Jesus!" the boyish cop said. "Ma'am, have you been drinking?"

"Of course not," I spat, doubled over.

Though I'd only glanced at him, I recognized the older cop. He'd directed traffic in uniform outside the wine and cheese shop on holidays. During the Fourth of July parade, he walked the route, keeping kids on the sidewalk, out of the way of marching bands and floats. He reached into the pocket of his worn tweed blazer and handed me a wad of warm tissues.

I wiped my mouth, mortified, the sour smell of half-digested yogurt filling my nostrils.

"Go get a hose," he told the rookie before turning to me. "I'm Detective Dubin." He nodded to the other cop. "That's Officer Kinsley. You're Mrs. Barnes?"

"Yes." I nodded. "Rachel."

"Do you want to sit down, ma'am?"

"No." I stood up straighter, then slumped. "Yes."

I didn't know what I wanted other than to never let my son out of my sight again.

I collapsed on the porch steps. They'd been painted black to match the rockers and the window frames, but they were peeling in places. I'd asked Ted to touch them up. He hadn't.

"Ms. McLean said she arrived a few minutes late and Billy wasn't here. When he didn't turn up right away, she searched the house and backyard but couldn't find him. She suggested this—not coming straight home—is out of character for your son. Is that accurate?"

"Yes." I nodded, keeping the tissue pressed to my mouth, afraid I'd be sick again.

"Have you called your neighbors or the parents of his friends?"

I shook my head no, my mood lifting. It sounded so logical when he said it. Of course, Billy would be close by. All of this would turn out to be a misunderstanding that someday, maybe after he'd graduated from college, we'd laugh about.

"I'll have Officer Kinsley go door-to-door when he's finished here." He gestured toward the walkway, where white chunks of my curdled lunch skidded toward the sidewalk under the garden hose's powerful spray. "What about Billy's dad?" Detective Dubin looked at the platinum wedding band on my left hand. "Your husband?"

"What about him?" I asked, focusing on the ground. I felt light-headed, while at the same time my neck seemed unable to support the weight of my skull.

"Have you called him?"

"No, no, I haven't."

When I first got in the car, I'd thought about calling Ted. But what if Billy had stayed late in the playground for a game of tetherball? What if he'd stopped at the lemonade stand Polly Peterson and her twins set up on warm afternoons? They had a Shar-Pei. Rumples. Billy couldn't resist dogs.

If I called Ted and this turned out to be nothing more than a false alarm, it would prove his theory that I hovered. He'd say that Billy absorbed my anxiety, making it my fault our son couldn't get through a presentation about a stupid one-dimensional doll.

I'd wanted to stall for time, knowing that as soon as I told Ted I wasn't sure why our son still wasn't home, he'd make a cutting remark about outsourcing my maternal responsibilities to a teenager—something Saint Jane never would've done. I was in constant competition with a dead woman. She always won.

"I . . . was hoping there'd been some miscommunication and Billy would be here by now," I added.

"Is there a chance Billy's dad might have picked him up from school today?" the detective asked.

"I doubt it," I said, wishing Ted were that kind of father—a dad who showed up as the school bell rang with tickets to a ball game or simply to take his son out for an ice-cream cone.

"Why don't you call him now, just to be sure—before Officer Kinsley goes door-to-door," he said. "We don't want to alarm anyone unnecessarily."

"No, right, of course." The words I spoke were at odds with the ones screaming inside my head: *Just fucking find my son! I don't care if you have to break my neighbors' doors down!*

I walked back to the car, knees rubbery as I waded through disbelief. Was this really happening? I found my phone under the passenger seat along with my lipsticks and everything else that had fallen out of my purse. Beneath the time and date—4:32 PM Thursday, June 13—Billy's face beamed up at me. The picture I'd taken of him on the zoo field trip. My heartbeat rang in my ears. I gripped the dashboard, thinking I might pass out. *Pull it together, Rachel!*

I pressed Ted's number, fifth on my Favorites list, below Billy, Darcy, our mother's assisted living facility, and the home number, aware that all eyes were on me.

I dialed twice before he picked up.

"Yeah? What is it?" From his restrained tone, I knew he was with a client.

"Ted—" was all I could get out before I started crying.

"Rachel? What is it?"

"Ted—" I started again.

"Rachel! What is it? I'm in a meeting. Is it Evan?"

"It's Billy. He—"

"What now?" he interrupted. Ted wanted only the headlines, as if he were above the small details of everyday life.

"He hasn't come home from school yet," I said.

"Well, where *is* he?" he hissed, unable to disguise his impatience.

"We don't know," I said, trying to hold it together so he'd take me seriously.

"What do you mean you don't know? Who's we?"

"Two police officers and Cassidy. She was waiting for Billy but he—"

He sighed, annoyed with me, his overprotective wife, worrying needlessly again. For once, I wanted him to be right.

"What time does he normally get home?"

"Three fifteen. He knows the rules, Ted. Something's wrong."

He sighed again. "Did you try calling him? Did you check the app that tracks his location?"

"I can't. I . . . I took his phone away this morning because he was playing some stupid game when he was supposed to be brushing his teeth." I barely finished the sentence before I broke into tears again.

"Jesus Christ, Rachel! That's why we got him the thing!"

"I know. I don't know what to do. Can you come home?" I waited. "Ted?"

He'd hung up.

"He says he'll be here as soon as he can."

That was the first lie I told the police.

I slumped back onto the porch steps, trying to remember to breathe. Cassidy stood nearby biting her fingernails. She'd been crying. With her eye makeup washed away, she looked much younger than eighteen. I couldn't stop staring. What was I thinking entrusting my son to someone who'd been a child herself not that long ago? Had I learned nothing from what happened with the au pair?

"I'm so sorry, Mrs. Barnes." Cassidy sat down beside me, too young, naive, or honest to understand that in today's world apologizing meant you were guilty, culpable. "I waited—I looked everywhere . . . I love Billy. He's like a little brother to me."

"Why were you late?" I asked, unable to stop myself even though I knew her answer would change nothing.

He gestured toward the walkway, where white chunks of my light lunch skidded toward the sidewalk under the garden hose's powerful spray.

"There was a detour," she said, looking down, her long strawberry-blond hair blocking her face.

"You didn't hear about that?" Officer Kinsley interjected. "A resident spotted a suspicious package at the train station. We had to block off several streets and evacuate nearby homes. Turned out to be nothing, but still, crazy day."

Fucking Phil Foster. Police would never confirm it, but it had to be. Since he'd been back, Phil suspected every discarded soda can housed a live grenade. My heart went out to his mother. Mary Alice knew he needed help, but resources and support were limited.

"Mrs. Barnes, Officer Kinsley's about to canvass the block. It'll be helpful for him to have a complete description of Billy: height, weight, hair and eye color, what he was wearing today, any distinguishing marks or features?" Detective Dubin stared at me, pen poised above his notepad as if he were simply asking me to share ingredients for a recipe. Tears slid down my cheeks, into my mouth, warm and salty, washing away all my words.

"Have you got a recent photo? We'll issue a 'Be on the Lookout' bulletin to all nearby patrols, Mrs. Barnes. So, please, I know this is difficult, but try to focus."

My insides shook. It took all my willpower not to stand up and scream, "*You* try to focus! Find my son!"

I thought about darting away from them, these men who moved in slow motion. I wanted to run from house to house, pound on doors, beg my neighbors to help me. But I was paralyzed by fear, and I knew that if I broke down, let every emotion loose, I'd be dismissed as a hysterical woman. The police would discredit everything I said from that moment on. So I remained on the steps, muted by shock.

"He's got brown hair and brown eyes," Cassidy jumped in. "He's got a backpack with a dinosaur and his initials, W. E. B., on it. I'm sorry, I don't know what he was wearing today."

"Mrs. Barnes, did you see your son before he left for school?" The detective frowned. "Can you tell us what he was wearing?"

What was Billy wearing? Was I a terrible mother? Could the average parent remember their child's outfit on any given day? I closed my eyes and tried to picture breakfast. Breakfast, when I'd snatched his phone.

"Flat Stanley!" I shouted, my eyes flying open. "He's dressed as Flat Stanley."

"Fat Stanley, is that a relative?" Officer Kinsley asked.

"An orange polo shirt, light blue shorts, that's what he's wearing! Just like his doll!" I said, relief coursing through me.

"He carries a doll?" Detective Dubin looked up from his pad, confused.

His words became background noise as I watched Ted pull up behind the police car. I stood and walked to meet him on the sidewalk. We embraced awkwardly, like eighth graders forced together in a school production of *Romeo and Juliet*.

The rest of the afternoon dragged on in a sickening swirl of answering obvious questions like, "Did Billy ever mention running away?" and "Have there been any adults who've taken an unusual interest in him lately?"

Precious seconds ticked by, each echoed inside me, a drumbeat reminding me we weren't any closer to finding Billy.

Detective Dubin kept us outside while he searched our home.

"Kids go looking for things and get stuck—in the attic, sometimes the basement. I once pulled a little guy from a sump pump pit," he said, a failed attempt to offer us some hope.

I'd had the house childproofed before Billy could walk.

"He's not the type of kid who'd climb inside a clothes dryer," Ted said, irritated.

"You'd be surprised." Detective Dubin shook his head.

* * *

Now I sit here shivering, nauseous, replaying every part of Thursday, my mind filled with a thousand *if onlys*. *If only* I'd done this, *if only* I'd been here and not there. But Ted was at work too. He isn't consumed by regret. No, while every moment that passes leaves me feeling as if I'm slowly being poisoned, Ted sleeps, belly full, content as a house cat.

Soon the sun will rise. In a few minutes, sprinklers will snap to life, their gentle *tsk tsk tsk* shaming me further. Polly Peterson will jog past, AirPods planted in her ears, twins in their double stroller. No one is letting their children out of sight now.

Will this be the day Billy comes home? My eyes flit left to right and back again. I know I'm delusional from fear and lack of sleep, but I expect him to walk up the porch steps and tell me he followed a butterfly into the woods.

"I was so close, I almost held it in my hand!" he'll say. Then, he'll wrap his arms around my neck and whisper, "I won't leave again, Mommy. I promise."

But there are no woods left in Oak Hill. Developers razed nearly every inch of land to slap together big, boxy houses for people like me to sell. They go up overnight. Takeout cartons are sturdier, but hang some barn doors, install a farmhouse sink or a subzero fridge, and somebody will buy them. Constant demand led me to partner with Derek to renovate that run-down Cape Cod, confident we'd turn a quick profit. Everyone wants to live in this zip code with its quaint downtown and good schools, not a single registered sex offender among us. I know; I've checked.

In the terrible, predawn silence, I hear Detective Dubin's voice again, a low rumble inside my head, repeating a question he asked Thursday—one that's haunted me since: "Do you have any enemies, Mrs. Barnes? Anyone who might have a grudge against you?"

I'd only just stood up, but his words and their brutal implication toppled me. He didn't believe that this was a mix-up—that my son was at a neighbor's. "Enemies," "a grudge" suggested that this was personal—that Billy was taken. On purpose. I sank to the steps. How could I respond?

Did I tell him that my husband behaved like a hostage, brooding and scowling as if I'd tricked him into the second family he never wanted?

Did I bring up my stepson whose mean, dark-eyed stare could send shivers down my spine in the middle of an August heat wave?

Did I try to explain where things stood with Derek? My investment partner, my . . . We were hemorrhaging cash, bound to take a beating on the fixer-upper, which had been my idea. And that was only one of our issues.

Did I mention Rose, the au pair I fired in April? I could still hear her begging me to reconsider, pleading, "Please! It'll never happen again! I swear to you. I'm sorry. Please!" in the Irish brogue I'd once found endearing. I could picture her boyfriend, Trevor, the scar the length of an index finger slashing through the pitted skin of his cheek. I could feel the spray of his spit through the gap in his teeth when he got right in my face, and hissed, "You're the one who's gonna be sorry!" after I ordered Rose to pack her things and get out.

It had been a bad day—even before I'd arrived home to find Billy alone, parked in front of the TV, gnawing his way through a bowl of Swedish fish. Rose was out, picking up her seedy boyfriend from the airport—an airport that was, without traffic, thirty minutes from our house.

In no mood to be threatened, I'd leaned into Trevor's face and shouted, "Come near my family again, and I'll make sure your girlfriend is on the first flight to Carlingford."

It took a moment, but he'd backed down. Still, it had been an ugly scene—one that left me so shaken that when I saw Betsy at the boys' T-ball game that night, she'd said, "Rachel, what's wrong? You look ill."

I hadn't intended to, but I told her everything. And once you shared something with Betsy Gallagher, it was only a matter of hours before all of Oak Hill knew it too.

I could've told Detective Dubin any or all of those things as he stood above me, waiting for my response. But my suspicions seemed ridiculous—the wild, paranoid delusions of a mother at her most desperate moment.

And so, when he repeated, "Mrs. Barnes? Do you have any enemies?" I simply whispered, "No."

That was the second lie I told the police.

What I should have said was, "Where would you like me to start?"

CHAPTER

6

Tuesday, June 18
Allison

"You have to stop." Viv shakes her head. "Trust me. I fell down a yearlong JonBenét Ramsey rabbit hole, and I still don't know what happened to the girl!"

Viv's right, but I can't make myself close her laptop. It's Tuesday afternoon. There hasn't been an update about Billy since Sunday morning when The Acorn, Oak Hill's online news site, reported that police officers dragged the pond Saturday night and found nothing.

"Remember when they put missing kids' faces on milk cartons, and you stared at them while you ate your Froot Loops?" Viv shudders. "How fucked up is that? Seriously? No wonder we're all on antidepressants."

She's busy rushing around the apartment, putting glasses in the dishwasher, recycling junk mail, plumping pillows. It's all part of her pre-travel ritual.

"If I die in a plane crash and my mother sees that I've been living like a frat boy, she'll use only the worst photos of me in my memorial service slideshow," Viv had joked when I first asked her about these sudden cleaning frenzies.

Even though she's been all over the world, Viv's still an anxious flyer. This afternoon she's headed to Arizona to play the "trophy wife to a silver fox" in a commercial for a golf resort and spa.

"The pay sucks, but maybe I'll get a hot stone massage out of it," she told me last week when she said she'd be gone for three days. "I've gotta book as many jobs as I can before the only gigs I'm offered are ads for yogurt that helps you take a shit."

"Damn, this place looks pretty decent when it's not a complete mess," she says, surveying the now-tidy apartment. "Don't host a rager without me, okay?"

"I don't think you have to worry." I laugh. "You're the only friend I have in the city. No one else knows I'm here."

When Chris and I lived in Brooklyn, we had a group of friends. Most migrated to the suburbs like we did, spreading across Westchester, New Jersey, or Connecticut, lured by thoughts of toddlers crawling through lush acres of green grass in backyards big enough to host summer barbecues. And storage. Everyone wanted more storage, as if the thing standing between us and true happiness was the ability to buy in bulk.

"Oh, I'd say Jayson in apartment Three-C knows you're here." Viv winks. "You can't really get much cuter," she sighs. "That wavy hair? The way he pushes that one lock off his forehead when he laughs?" Her eyes light up. "Did I tell you he's a chef? And have you seen his hands? Those are man mitts! Imagine them all over your—"

"Stop." I hold up my palm. "We're not having this conversation again."

"I don't get it." She shakes her head and flops into the armchair, worn out from her speed cleaning. "We both just got out of relationships. How long were you married? Six years?"

"Seven—nearly eight, actually," I say, though I really can't remember my adult life without Chris.

"This should be our hot girl summer, Al. When I played sassy slut Suzy Stanford in *Psycho Sorority Sisters* I wore this T-shirt that said, 'The Best Way to Get Over Him Is to Get Under Someone Hotter.' I've taken that shit to heart." She pulls a push-up bra from behind a throw pillow, sniffs it, and then flings it in the direction of the growing laundry pile in the hallway.

"I was thinking about doing some volunteer work at this—"

"Oh my God, you just said you were married for seven years! Isn't that penance enough? You're in Manhattan, the capital of the fucking world. Shed your suburban skin, Al. Seriously, there's a pole dancing class you should try. Release your inner J.Lo. You need to have fun again."

She's not wrong. I've been in this funk for years. Sometimes I think I've forgotten what it's like to experience pure bliss. But I'm certain sex and shimmying up and down a metal rod aren't the cure.

"Tell me this: Do you think your rock-star husband—or ex-husband or whatever—isn't bangin' his way through the MILFs of Maple Hills?"

"It's Oak Hill," I correct her, "and I really don't know what he's doing."

"You're so mature," she sighs. "If I were you, I'd be cyberstalking him instead of checking for updates on Bobby Baxter."

Of course, it's impossible not to think about Chris, not to wonder what and how he's doing. Does he hate me for giving up, abandoning our life? I want to believe that after everything we went through, we'd want each other to be happy. If that couldn't happen with us together, I hoped he could find it with someone else. Viv might think of it as maturity, but it's more about survival. Enduring so much loss ate away at me. I had to guard what was left and try to leave the hollowness behind.

But because that's too much to explain, and Viv has a plane to catch, I simply say, "Billy Barnes, not Bobby Baxter."

"What are you going to do while I'm gone? Please tell me something other than set up Google alerts for a lost boy."

"I have an appointment with a real estate agent tomorrow afternoon." I watch her face, trying to gauge her reaction to see if she's looking forward to having her one-bedroom back to herself. But she's an actress. She could hide her relief if she wanted to.

"So, you're really not going back?" Viv asks.

"Nope."

I'd wondered if Viv viewed my running away from home as temporary. Did she chalk it up to bored housewife stuff? Believe that I'd miss my old life with Chris after a week or two?

"You know you can stay here as long as you like," Viv says.

"Thanks, but I need my own place, and I've probably overstayed my welcome as it is. Plus, look at this space in all its prewar charm—a fireplace, exposed brick, tall ceilings." I point toward her laptop. "You could list it on Airbnb or Vrbo when you're out of town, and then you wouldn't have to make out with grandpas at desert resorts to pay the rent."

"I could, but I'd rather not think of some hairy-assed stranger sitting on my toilet or jerking off into my shampoo bottles." She wrinkles her nose. "Besides, I love having you here. Who else would buy me flowers or water my half-dead plants while I'm in Sedona tooling around in a golf cart pretending I'm in love with an old man? Speaking of, I better hop in the shower."

"Wait, can you look out the window?" I ask. "Tell me if you see a man across the street."

Viv grins and sweeps the curtain aside. "Got a date? You're not holding out on me, are you?"

"No, I just—sometimes I look down and there's this skinny guy standing there smoking, staring up at the window." I don't tell her that I'm sure he followed me at least once—maybe other times before and I didn't notice.

"I don't see anyone," she says, "just a couple of pigeons. I think there's a psychologist in that brick building. Maybe the guy's waiting for his appointment."

"You're right," I say, wanting it to be true. "I'm probably just paranoid. Maybe I should make an appointment with that therapist." I force a laugh.

"Listen, I had a stalker back in L.A. It's scary." She moves away from the window, crosses her arms, and hesitates. "It's been almost two months, and you still haven't really said much about why you left—and you totally don't have to—but you know you can tell me anything, right?"

"Totally." I nod. "Thanks."

But really, could I tell her that my husband became fixated on the thing that was destroying me? When I said I wanted to stop, he pulled me into his arms and, in a tone that was part-whisper, part-warning, reminded me, "You and I didn't get where we are by quitting, Al, and that's not what we're going to do now either."

Could I tell her that I rarely leave the apartment because I'm afraid of being found before I'm strong enough to resist going back?

Viv walks down the short hall to prepare for her trip. Selfishly, I want her to stay. When she's around, I don't have to think. When she's gone, silence floods the apartment. But if I'm going to move out and live on my own, I have to get used to it. And if someone out there is keeping tabs on me, I need to leave here. Soon.

I check my new email account. A message from the agent I contacted waits. "Pick as many as you like. I've cleared the afternoon for you. See you at one."

She's sent more listings. As I scroll through the photos, descriptions, and layouts, I feel a flicker of excitement. For the first time in a long time, decisions about my life are mine alone.

* * *

When Chris and I found our home on Woods End, we hadn't even been thinking of moving. We'd taken a drive out to western New Jersey on a lazy Sunday because Chris heard a music shop had a rare guitar he wanted to check out. On our way back, Chris's vintage Rickenbacker snug in its silver case, we stopped for coffee. It was late August, and we knew there'd be shore traffic, so rather than take the highway, we followed back roads past fields and through small towns. We found a cafe and sat outside, an umbrella shading us from the afternoon sun. The leaves had just started curling up at their edges, turning from green to gold, and the air held that first promise of fall, a scent that always reminded me of sweaters and new shoes, sharpened pencils and fresh starts. Chris devoured a chocolate croissant while I picked at a blueberry scone. An endless parade of toddlers in fancy strollers and nearly identical Labradoodles passed us.

"How are there no parking meters?" I asked, checking my phone for the time, a reflex from so many years in the city. "What is this place?"

We wandered up and down the streets, enchanted by the indie bookstore and the old-fashioned ice-cream shop. We were headed back to the car, waiting for the light to change, when we spotted it—a flyer taped to a telephone pole. The word "Found" appeared above a photo of a calico cat.

"Where are we again?" Chris asked as we stared at green-eyed Whiskers.

"Oak Hill?" I guessed, recalling the Welcome sign we'd passed before we parked.

"Oak Hill: a town where pets are found rather than lost!" Chris said in his earnest, newscaster voice. His band, Regrets Only, had broken up six months earlier after Roddy, the drummer, had been poached by a pop star and the lead guitarist, Edward, who wrote most of the lyrics, wanted to strike out on his own. Chris was struggling, trying to decide if he should find new bandmates, continue making music, or branch out and try something else, like voiceovers. He didn't need to work. He'd inherited a fortune from his parents, and he was still making money off the band's earlier work, even though their final album, *Last Exit Before Rehab*, had tanked.

"Oak Hill! A town where pets aren't lost! They're found!" he said again, trying a more upbeat, deejay-like inflection.

I looked around and admired the library. A tiny Tudor with turrets, it resembled a miniature castle straight out of a fairy tale.

"This place is kind of magical. I still can't believe there aren't parking meters. Must be nice," I said.

As the light changed, we stepped off the curb. Chris stopped me mid-intersection, his hands on my shoulders. "Let's move here, Al. Let's live here!"

"Sure! Why not?" I laughed. "We've been here what? Twenty minutes? Let's just pack up and put down roots in a random New Jersey town where people reunite lost pets with their owners, and we never have to worry about parking tickets!"

"Exactly!" he grinned.

A driver attempting to make a turn waited patiently as we blocked the intersection. I braced for the wail of a horn, accustomed to impatient city drivers. None came.

"Wait, you're serious?" I asked.

"It's got a good vibe. You feel it, right?"

"Yeah, of course!" I humored him.

When his band broke up, the life force had drained from Chris's body. The idea of moving to Oak Hill restored it. One of the things that made me fall in love with my husband was how passionate he could be when he latched on to a new idea. It was like he lit up and shined brighter than he usually did. I'd forgotten how much I'd missed it.

But our home was in the city, where we could get falafel or a pedicure at two in the morning, where a short walk or subway ride was all that separated us from live music and theater. We weren't even thirty, we were still figuring it out. We didn't belong in this area filled with toddlers, found cats, and Stepford dogs.

"We could get a dog!" Chris exclaimed, as if reading my mind.

He beamed, happy, purposeful. How could I not at least look around? I'd "ooh" and "aah" over giant bedrooms and walk-in closets, and then let him come to the obvious conclusion that we weren't suburb material—at least not yet.

"Sure, what the heck? I said, taking his hand and pulling him toward our car. "Let's explore!"

We wound our way through tree-lined streets, following open house signs. Nineteen Woods End, a large Colonial filled with natural light, hardwood floors, and high ceilings, was our final stop. We arrived ten minutes before the open house ended, forcing us to rush from room to room. As we entered each one, I could feel Chris's body hum with excitement beside me, the way it did when he was writing a song.

When we got to the finished basement, he spun around.

"My music studio!" he exclaimed, raising his arms over his head. Even at six foot two, inches remained between Chris's fingertips and the ceiling.

Before leaving, we took a last look at the living room. Built-in bookshelves framed a window seat that overlooked the side yard where a row of mature arborvitaes provided privacy. I would've bought the home on this room alone, but it was what Chris said there that sold me.

"That's where I'll put the piano, start giving lessons." The sparkle I hadn't seen in months returned to his eyes.

"It's lovely." I scanned the information sheet. "But we don't need all this space. It's got five bedrooms!"

"Don't worry." He raised his eyebrows and slid his arm around my waist, pulling me into him. "We'll fill 'em up."

His words lit a fuse. Something electric crackled to life in me—desire, yearning for the next big step in our lives. Chris's parents had died before we met, and my relationship with my sister, Jen—my only sibling—had been fraying for years. It would be nice to start our own family, make new memories, grow instead of shrink.

Chris looked out the French doors that led to a large, flagstone patio, the setting sun a brilliant orange ball that shone a spotlight on him. He looked healthier than he had in months. Was he picturing himself playing catch with the children he imagined filling up all those bedrooms?

We'd been married for a year. I'd started acting at ten years old and had worked ever since. But were we ready to start a family? Of course, we'd talked about it, the word "someday" always in the mix.

As we walked out to the car, Chris turned around to give the house a long, appreciative look.

"Think about it, Al. We could be happy here." He took my hand, brought it to his lips, and smiled.

"We would be happy anywhere," I said, and squeezed his hand, so naive I believed everything would always go our way because, up until that point, it had.

"Our lease is up in December," he said on the drive home.

Our friends were fleeing the city, which grew more expensive by the minute. I was tired of moving the car for street cleaning and garbage day, sick of paying two dollars for an apple, sixteen for a glass of wine, and lugging groceries up three flights of stairs.

"Okay. I'll think about it," I said, because—really—what was stopping us?

I should have known Chris had already made up his mind. Once he set his sights on something, he'd stop at nothing to get it. I was proof of that.

We were in before Christmas. The transition to the suburbs was more isolating than I could've imagined. Gone were the sounds of life I'd been accustomed to—blaring horns, groups of people walking to and from restaurants, cars with the bass thumping beneath our window—replaced by stillness and the scrape of an occasional snowplow.

While this change left me feeling lonely, it energized Chris. He spent most days setting up his basement studio, busy with soundproofing and arranging equipment and instruments he finally had room to acquire.

Because we moved in during the long, cold winter, we didn't meet many of our neighbors. A few came by as we shoveled snow, a novelty that quickly lost its rustic, L.L. Bean-catalog appeal.

We were a bit of a curiosity, the singer and the actress. But much like high school, Oak Hill had its cliques. Most weren't accepting new members. Everyone had a toddler or two, and another on the way. Families met at preschools or music classes. If we wanted to join in, having a baby seemed like the next logical step, moving "someday" up to "now" in our timeline.

One afternoon the following November, nearly a year after we'd moved in, I was slicing an avocado to toss in a salad when Chris came up from the basement. He wrapped his arms around me. I pulled away as the weight of his limbs made my breasts ache. I'd been feeling off for a few days, headachy, sluggish, but we'd only just started trying.

I did a quick calculation and turned around to face him, scared to say the words aloud. "I think I might be pregnant."

I'd barely finished the sentence when Chris was out the door driving to the store to buy a test kit—multiple test kits, actually.

We sat together on our bed, holding hands for the longest three minutes of our lives, waiting for his phone's timer to beep.

Two thin blue lines greeted us.

"Well, that was easy," he said, kissing me long and slow, his hand rubbing my stomach.

Later that afternoon, eager to share the good news, I called my sister, Jen. I didn't know what to say, so I blurted, "Emma and Ethan are going to have a cousin! I'm pregnant!"

"Wow," she said, her voice flat. "When did all this happen?"

"We just found out," I said. "We did one of those pee-on-the-stick tests."

"You're not supposed to tell anyone this soon, Al," Jen said, lowering her voice before yelling to my nephew, "Ethan! I said no snacks. We're having dinner soon. Go find your iPad."

"I know, but I'm just excited." I continued, "I didn't really think it would happen this soon, and you're not 'anyone.' You're my sister. If something goes wrong, I'd tell you then, so why not now, when I'm happy?"

"Well, it's just that there's a lot that can go wrong," she said. "Ethan, put those chips back. What did I just say?"

I wanted her to be excited for me. We were two years apart. When we were little, we'd shared a bedroom. As we'd tuck our dolls into their tiny wooden cradles, we swore our children would be close. But in Jen's voice, I heard the familiar strain that began the spring I was ten and she was twelve.

Most people can't pinpoint the moment that things change in a relationship. It usually isn't a single event that causes a shift to take place. But I knew when and where it started. I could recall everything—right down to the smell of the hot-dog-on-a-stick Jen was eating and the taste of my Auntie Anne's cinnamon pretzel—the day our sisterly bond became a rivalry.

We'd been sitting at the food court at the mall celebrating that our mother had finally relented and let Jen get her ears pierced, which meant I could, too, in just two years. With every sugary bite of my pretzel, I admired the way the sun filtering through the skylights in the food court's atrium made the gold balls in Jen's earlobes glimmer.

We were finishing our snack when a woman approached our table.

"I couldn't help noticing your daughter," she said, pressing a business card into Mom's hand. "She's perfect for a commercial I'm casting. She's not allergic to nuts, is she?"

"I'm not!" Jen proclaimed. Corn dog coating crumbs sprayed out of her mouth. My sister had just starred as Miss Hannigan in our elementary school's production of *Annie*. She was the standout in an otherwise lackluster show, which made her sure this stranger's question was directed toward her.

"Sorry, honey, not you. Your sister." She spoke the words that would forever divide us with a smile, her head tilted in my direction.

I don't know why I thought Jen's bitterness was confined to my career. I'd imagined my pregnancy news would take us back to the days when we promised to give our daughters rhyming names: Carly and Marly, Cara and Tara.

I waited for her to say something else, something positive or hopeful. All I heard was running water in the background filling the awkward pauses.

"Well, I'm happy for you, of course," she said, distracted. "Ethan, I swear, if you don't drop those fruit snacks right now, you're getting a time-out!"

"Could you give him a banana or an apple if he's hungry?" I asked, craving her full attention.

"Oh, you've been pregnant what, two hours, and suddenly you're a parenting expert?" she snickered.

I'd forgotten how quickly she could turn on me. For the rest of the afternoon, the negativity in her voice hovered like a hex I couldn't shake.

When I called my parents to tell them, Mom answered. I asked her to have Dad pick up the extension.

"I have something to tell you both," I said, nearly breathless with excitement, knowing how they doted on Emma and Ethan.

"Oh no, honey, what is it?" Mom asked, always fearing the worst.

"No, Mom, it's good news! I'm pregnant."

Neither of them spoke. Were they each waiting for the other to say something? Were they exchanging glances across their outdated kitchen?

"Hello?" I thought maybe the call had dropped.

"That's terrific, honey," was all Dad said before he hung up.

"And Chris's drinking is under control?" my mother asked, her voice a judgmental murmur.

I sighed. Chris was in the basement recording the first songs he'd written in months. I felt relieved I hadn't put my parents on speakerphone and asked him to come listen to what I thought would be the positive reaction from our child's only set of living grandparents.

It wasn't easy, but I tried to forget about my family and focus on the new one Chris and I were forming. The first few doctor's appointments went well. At eight weeks, Chris and I heard the heartbeat, a thrilling *thwacka, thwacka, thwacka,* like hoofbeats racing toward us.

"Everything looks great," said Dr. Bradford.

I'd chosen him because he got rave reviews, and his office—
a former schoolhouse—was within walking distance of our
home. It was a bonus that he was bald, something I found oddly
reassuring. When we were little, Jen came up with a theory that
bald men must be brilliant because their brains worked so hard
their hair burned right off.

At my first visit, Joyce, the nurse, recognized me from a skin
cream commercial.

"You sold me!" she'd said. "I'm old enough to be your
mother, but I keep applying it, hoping I'll look like you. Not
yet! Hey, do you know Tom Hanks? I love that guy."

During my next appointment, Joyce stood in the corner
scribbling in my chart as Chris and I gazed at the monitor,
already in love with the tiny being we'd created. After spending
a few minutes pointing out our baby's arms, legs, and heart,
Dr. Bradford removed the ultrasound wand and the screen went
dark. I had to stop myself from asking him to go back and start
all over again. Like the best movie I'd ever seen, I wanted to
watch all afternoon.

"Getting past the twelve-week mark is a big deal, kiddo," he
said. "Your baby's got a nice, strong heartbeat. Go home. Relax."

He gave my knee a playful shake, and I exhaled. It seemed
too easy. I'd read so many heartbreaking stories about infertility. I had friends on their third round of in vitro, sinking deeper
into debt, wondering why they'd spent all those years worrying
about birth control.

"I'll see you in four weeks," the doctor said as he left the
room. "Keep up the good work."

Joyce stepped forward to offer me tissues so I could wipe the
gel off my stomach. "By the time we see you again, you'll probably have felt your baby move," she said with a smile. "It's the
most wonderful feeling in the world. It's a little bit like popcorn
kernels at first, just teeny pokes here and there. Then, later it's
all jabs and left hooks."

The three of us laughed, and I wished I could time travel to
the end of forty weeks to hold the baby I couldn't wait to meet.

Each day I expected to feel my little kernel pop as Joyce
predicted, but nothing happened. When Chris wasn't looking,

I stole sips of his coffee, hoping the caffeine jolt would work some magic. I stepped on the scale. For once, I wanted to see the digits increase, but my weight stayed the same. Then, I lost a pound.

"You've been nauseous," Chris reminded me. "What did you have for dinner last week? Rice cakes and almond butter? Don't worry, Al. Everything's good."

I thought about my sister's words, "There's a lot that can go wrong," and tried to ignore them by shifting my focus. After the twelve-week visit, we started keeping a list of potential names. Our baby's due date was July 4.

"How about Independence? Or, what about Liberty Langley?" I suggested.

"I was thinking Roman, as in Roman Candle." Chris laughed. "Or, hey, no one messes with a kid named Firework at recess."

I took the vitamins, drank plenty of water, and pictured our baby, the size of a plum, floating safe and warm inside me.

When I went for the sixteen-week appointment, Chris wasn't with me. He'd been offered a last-minute audition for a narration gig, and I encouraged him to go, insisting there'd be at least a dozen more visits.

I sat in the waiting room, fidgety, flipping through a magazine without looking at the pages. I didn't know if there would be another ultrasound, but I wanted to hear my baby's heartbeat again.

In the exam room, I stepped on the scale and watched Joyce's face as she noted the number, less than my last visit, in my chart.

"Holding pretty steady! Good for you," she said. "After today's appointment, we're going to send you for some blood work, all routine stuff. The doctor will be right in."

I nodded and sat on the table, the white paper crunching beneath me.

When Dr. Bradford came in, we chatted about the weather, how the air smelled like snow, and then he said, "Let's listen to your baby."

I reclined as he placed the Doppler probe on my stomach.

"Well, I hear Mama's heartbeat, but . . ." he paused. "Let's try something else."

He switched off the overhead light and reached for the ultrasound wand, moving it around in circles, then back and forth, as if he were performing some sacred ritual, a spell that would rouse my baby.

Joyce came in the room to grab a chart and glanced at the screen—same black border with a cloud of white in the middle, only this time there was no flicker. She stepped closer and placed a hand on my ankle. The warmth of it through my wool sock made me feel claustrophobic and sick. I wanted to jump up and run from the room before they could tell me the brutal truth that was slowly forming in my mind.

"I'm sorry, Allison, there's no heartbeat." Dr. Bradford stared at me, but I refused to turn away from the monitor. He took measurements, clicking away methodically while my world imploded. "It looks like your baby stopped growing a couple of weeks ago. I wish I could say this is uncommon. It isn't. Unfortunately, approximately ten to fifteen percent of women miscarry before the twenty-week mark . . ."

Miscarry. My face burned. I felt dizzy, like I was floating, watching my useless body from above. I only caught random words and phrases as the doctor continued speaking.

"No reason to believe this would happen again . . ."

"You're young, healthy . . ."

"Schedule a D&C . . . test tissue . . ."

"I'll be in touch."

As tears slid down my cheeks, Joyce handed me a ball of tissues and, when I was ready, helped me off the table. I walked through the waiting room in such a deep fog, I nearly left without my coat.

"Come back, dear," Joyce said, handing me the plaid peacoat that was no match for the weather, her eyes wide with pity. "Get some rest."

Snowflakes swirled around me as I stood outside the office in a state of shock. The future I'd envisioned ripped away in moments. In the parking lot, I looked for the car, forgetting that I'd walked there despite the biting January wind, believing fresh air and exercise would be good for the baby. I wandered home, an emptiness growing inside me. How did this happen? How would I tell Chris?

By the time I reached the house, I felt numb. Sinking into the couch, I pulled my ice-cold cell phone from my pocket and called Chris. He answered right away.

"Hey! How was the appointment? How's Firecracker Langley doing?"

There was no easy way to say it.

"The baby's gone, Chris. There was no heartbeat." I burst into tears.

"Where are you now? I'll come get you. Stay where you are."

"I'm home," I choked out. "On the couch."

"I'll be right there."

I don't know how much time passed before he appeared, beside me, stroking my hair, whispering, "We'll try again. It'll happen, Al. I promise."

A few days later, I called Jen to tell her. "Aw," she said, "I guess it just wasn't meant to be. Look, you'll try again. It'll all work out. Everything always does for you."

She told our mother, who called and said, "You know I had a miscarriage between you and your sister. If everything had gone well with that pregnancy, you wouldn't be here! It's all about the timing."

I had the D&C, the procedure that removed the cells and tissue that remained inside me after the essence of our child had disappeared. I wished I could've stayed anesthetized, safe in those blissful moments of dreamless sleep, the only ones where I wasn't haunted by loss. When the tests came back, we learned the baby had been a boy.

"The results showed a common chromosomal abnormality," Dr. Bradford told me over the phone. "Nothing unusual, so the good news is you're free to try again. But we'll probably want to do the blood work earlier next time. Make an appointment after you get a positive test result, and we'll take it from there."

I thanked him out of habit, knowing I couldn't bear to ever see him or Joyce again.

Two weeks later, I still refused to get off the couch or out of sweatpants. I turned down jobs—a print ad for eyeglasses, another for a designer handbag—and immersed myself in reality show marathons and dramas with complicated subplots that temporarily distracted me.

Chris handled everything while I wallowed, angry with my body for failing me—us—confused at how I could feel such grief and longing for a baby I'd never even held.

It was January. My new year, the one I'd expected to be the best yet, had gotten off to a devastating start. Soon it would be March, then April. Our neighbors would stroll past our home, laughing and pulling their children in red wagons. I couldn't imagine ever wanting to go outside again. I spent most days dozing on the couch until one afternoon I awoke to something licking my face. I opened my eyes to see a puppy, fluffy and golden, his tongue as pink as bubble gum.

Chris knelt down beside the couch to be eye level with me and the pet that would bring me back to life. "His name is Murphy, but he's just a couple months old, so we can always change it."

Oversized paws rested on my shoulders. As tears slipped down my cheeks, he nuzzled my neck with his charcoal nose, tail rhythmically slapping the couch and coffee table like a metronome.

"No," I said, burying my face in his soft downy fur. "Murphy is perfect."

We were done choosing names.

* * *

Later that spring, I saw Rachel Barnes watering her hanging ferns, her belly round as a basketball. Only then did I remember seeing her in the waiting room that awful day as I left the doctor's office. She'd leaned over the front desk, and snapped at the receptionist, demanding to know what was taking so long. I must've blocked it out.

I didn't want to keep jogging by her home. But it was on our regular route. I thought if I said anything to Chris, it would upset him to know how often my mind lingered on our loss. By May, he was ready to try again. I wasn't. We compromised, making a pact to discuss it after we were on the other side of the baby's due date.

As weeks passed, hope began to swell inside me. I'd read a million articles that echoed what Dr. Bradford had said about miscarriage being common. I spent the afternoons Chris gave lessons lurking in pregnancy chat rooms, Murph gently snoring beside me as I skimmed real-life stories of moms who'd lost their babies and went on to have healthy children. Rainbow babies, they called them. I convinced myself there wasn't any reason to believe it would happen again. We'd start over. I'd find a new doctor. Everything would work out.

By mid-July, I was in a better place. I thought I'd overcome the jealousy I felt toward Rachel Barnes. Until I saw it—a giant wooden stork on her front lawn. Standing six feet tall, it was dressed in a blue top hat and bow tie, a white bundle hung from its bright yellow beak announcing the arrival of William Edward Barnes, eight pounds, two ounces.

Chris, Murph, and I had just turned the corner when I spotted it. Unable to catch my breath, I doubled over. Pretending to tie my shoe, I knelt down, my hands trembling. Chris helped me up and kissed my forehead, holding me as I sobbed, my shoulders shaking. When I finally stopped, he said, "C'mon, Murph. U-turn."

We avoided that block for months. But in such a small town, it was inevitable that our paths would cross. Each time I saw Rachel with Billy pressed to her chest in one of those carriers— at the farmers market, the library, walking through the neighborhood—I felt like I'd been sucker punched, or, worse, robbed.

Billy was a reminder from the universe: *This is what your child would be doing now.* I watched him grow, pedaling around the block on a tricycle, then moving on to training wheels. He and our son would've been classmates, possibly even friends. Maybe they'd trick-or-treat together or go sledding. I pictured them, heads together over our kitchen table, building a volcano. I'd eavesdrop on their conversations about school, sports, and video games while serving them hot cocoa.

As much as it made my heart ache whenever I spotted Billy, I felt connected to him. He was a link to the son I'd lost.

In time, I stopped dreading seeing him and looked forward to it. If it's possible to be nostalgic for moments you never experienced, that's what I felt when I saw Billy.

That's why I can't stop thinking about him now.

I return to my inbox to write back to the real estate agent about the apartments I wanted to see when a new email pops

up. Viv knows me too well. I've already set up a Google alert for
Billy.

The headline, *Person of Interest Questioned in Case of Missing
Oak Hill Boy*, makes my pulse pound. I call out to Viv. I want
her beside me if it's awful news, but the shower's running, and
I hear her singing her way through Liz Phair's "Exile in
Guyville."

I read aloud, forcing myself to not skim and miss any details.

*The Oak Hill Police Department confirmed a crossing guard
was questioned Monday night in connection with the disappearance of five-year-old Billy Barnes, who was last seen Thursday
afternoon.*

*This potential break in the case comes after high school student
Sloan Maxwell contacted police to report that the crossing guard—
identified only as a sixty-four-year-old woman from the community—
invited her into her home years earlier as she was leaving school.*

*According to a source, Maxwell, currently a senior at Oak Hill
High, reportedly told police that six years prior, the crossing guard
admired her crocheted handbag. The older woman then allegedly
asked Maxwell if she would be interested in coming home with her
so she could "teach her how to knit."*

*The source said the now-teen didn't tell anyone at the time but
decided to come forward in light of Barnes's disappearance. Maxwell denies that the $50,000 reward offered by the Barnes family
spurred her involvement.*

*After being questioned, the crossing guard, who further raised
suspicions by calling in sick both Friday and Monday, was said to
be visibly shaken, but agreed to allow police to search her home.*

*At press time, police would not confirm nor deny the crossing
guard's role in the missing kindergartner's case.*

Check back for updates as this investigation unfolds.

Veronica Baker. It had to be. I could picture Ronnie, as
most parents called her, on the corner, handing out lollipops,
her reddish curly hair peeking out from under a baseball cap.

Chris would stop to talk with her when he took Murph for
his afternoon walk.

"You were gone forever," I said one day last winter when
Chris returned with just seconds to spare before his first student
arrived.

"I know," he said, unfastening Murph's leash. "Ronnie's going through a rough time. Last Saturday was her birthday. Her daughter didn't call. She lives in L.A. Usually, she lets Ronnie's granddaughter FaceTime. But nothing. Ronnie's pretty down. Lonely, I guess."

"She told you all this at the corner?" I asked.

He hesitated, ruffling his hair, a gesture he made when he was unsure of something. "I shouldn't say this, but she goes to meetings."

"Meetings" was Chris's code for Alcoholics Anonymous. He'd gotten serious about quitting drinking a few months before his band fell apart, a last-ditch effort that was a classic case of too little, too late.

"Ronnie's shared some stuff," he continued, shaking his head. "She hasn't had an easy time these last few years."

I wished Chris hadn't told me any of that. It made me sad to think of Ronnie, all by herself in her small home on Cherry Lane, the only house that hadn't been gutted and built out to look like a starter home on steroids. It also made me anxious. What if she showed up to her corner drunk? That was a busy intersection. I didn't want to be the person who had the woman fired, but was this the right job for her? I couldn't mention any of that to Chris knowing he'd be offended by me questioning anyone's sobriety.

My eyes skim the article: "... *the crossing guard, who further raised suspicions by calling in sick both Friday and Monday* ..."

I don't know Ronnie well, certainly not like Chris did, but she seemed kind, grandmotherly. How could anyone believe that the woman who doles out candy canes before Christmas break would abduct a child? It doesn't make sense. Yes, she may be lonely and a misfit among Oak Hill's well-preserved senior population, but there's no way Ronnie has Billy.

I'm certain of it.

7

Tuesday, June 18
Lindsay

"**D**ID YOU SEE the police cars?" Betsy asks through clenched teeth as she sweeps through the garden gate.

She air-kisses me though we just saw each other a few hours ago at kindergarten pick-up. No one's letting a child walk home unchaperoned in Oak Hill now.

"Three squad cars were pulling up when we came back from tae kwon do." I keep my voice low as Oliver and Betsy's son, Parker, race past me toward the pool. "It's insane. Oliver keeps asking me if they're going to arrest Mrs. Baker. How do I answer that? I mean, can you imagine? The kids adore her."

"The whole thing is just too much." Betsy removes her sunglasses and weaves them through her auburn hair. "I feel like I have to be on high alert at all times now. Each car that passes the house—if I don't recognize it, I stare at the driver, wondering, 'Are you a predator?' I'm snapping at Doug and the kids. I wanted to bring you those raspberry-almond-chia bars you like, but I burned the whole batch. I can't concentrate. And now this? Ronnie Baker, a suspect?"

"Scott won't even let the boys skateboard or ride their bikes!" I shake my head. "The good news is the bar is open. Follow me."

"Oh thank God!" Betsy says as we walk across the bluestone path toward the deck. "Your yard looks gorgeous, by the way." She takes a moment to rustle my lavender, its sweet fragrance momentarily perfuming the air.

"The gardener was here today. I can't take credit."

"You may want to tell him to add coffee grounds to your gardenia. They love acid," she says.

"Thanks for the tip!" I roll my eyes as I head to the bar cart.

Betsy sinks into the outdoor sofa and sighs as if she walked a dozen miles to get here rather than half a block.

"Now, remember, I'm still experimenting," I warn her, adding ice to the cocktail shaker.

We're co-chairing the fall football fundraiser—again. Sampling drinks that could become the event's signature cocktail makes the rest of the planning bearable.

"This is an apple bourbon smash." I hand Betsy a stemless wine glass complete with cinnamon stick garnish. "I know it's hard with this heat, but try to think autumn! Tackles! Touchdowns!"

"Thank you, thank you, thank you!" She sets her phone faceup on the low table where I've put out a lemon-dill dip, carrots, and pita chips. "I didn't want to stand there gawking at Ronnie, so I asked Polly to text me updates. She just wrote, 'Police are inside the house' and added a sad face emoji."

"I know, I can't bear to watch! Plus, Scott would be horrified."

We make our annual toast—*Clear eyes, stiff drinks, can't lose!*—and clink glasses.

I take a sip. It's definitely out of season, but the lemon makes it refreshing, and it's strong, which seems like the most important thing.

"So, about Ronnie . . ." Betsy raises her eyebrows and tucks her chin.

"What?" I mouth.

"I heard she stumbled off the curb last week. Twisted her ankle. Maybe that's why she called out sick?"

I grimace. Of course, we've all heard the rumors about Ronnie—her problems with alcohol. But, in Oak Hill, drinking is practically a competitive sport. I didn't take the gossip seriously. She was in charge of helping schoolchildren cross the street, for God's sake. If Ronnie really had an issue, wouldn't someone have stepped in by now?

"I don't think Ronnie had anything to do with Billy's disappearance." I shake my head and take a long swallow, debating whether to share my theory with Betsy.

"Watch this, Mom!" Oliver shouts. Betsy and I make a big show of applauding, as if we've never seen anyone cannonball into a pool before.

Betsy shudders.

"Too heavy on the bourbon, right?" I ask.

"Any other day, maybe. Today, it's perfect." She takes another sip before placing the glass on the table. "No, I was thinking about the new pool cleaner I hired. Rachel recommended him."

"What about him?"

"I don't know, I have a bad feeling. He's creepy." She frowns. "He drives down the street really slowly, looking right and left," she swans her neck, "like he's trying to see into everyone's backyard."

"Wait, you're following him? Now, who's creepy?" I laugh, pull out my phone, and take a few pics of our cocktails to post to Instagram later. "Maybe he's trying to see who else has a pool—you know, get more business."

Sergeant Pepper circles the table, hoping we'll drop a chip. Scott and the boys let him swim in Oak Hill Pond, and now he smells like feet. I make a mental note to text the mobile groomer.

"I wasn't following my pool guy!" Betsy snaps. "I just happened to be behind him while I was driving Parker to his reading tutor. This guy—I'm not exaggerating—is doing under five miles per hour."

"Maybe he's trying not to hit a child, Bets, c'mon. Plus, his van is hardly an Indy car! How fast can those things go?"

"It makes me very uncomfortable. I'm serious. Something's not right about him." She sips her drink and clucks her tongue. "You're right, a little less bourbon next time—not that I mind."

"So, what are you saying? You think the pool guy abducted Billy? He finished vacuuming and tossing in chlorine and nabbed a kid on his way out of town? Because he has long hair and a tattoo of a jack of hearts on his arm?"

"So, you have noticed him!"

"He said hi to me one afternoon when I was walking the dog past your house. It's not like I'm making a documentary about him."

Betsy takes a deep, dramatic breath. "I didn't want to bring this up because it's mortifying, but last week I'm standing in my driveway about to hop in the Lexus to take Miles to honors orchestra practice, and he struts right up to me—so close, I could smell him!" She wrinkles her nose. "Honest to God, he reeked of crabgrass and chemicals. He says, 'When am I gonna see *you* in a swimsuit?' Then he winked and walked away." Betsy does a full-body squirm. "It was so off-putting, I must've turned the color of that beet hummus I make for the Valentine's Day teachers luncheon."

Maybe it's the bourbon, but I start laughing and can't stop.

"Watch your drink!" Betsy hands me a cocktail napkin as the amber liquid puddles on the sofa cushions.

"Don't worry. It's Sunbrella." I giggle again.

"It's not funny! His behavior is completely inappropriate— and with Miles in the car!"

I pull myself together. "Listen, Bets, at our age, a compliment's a compliment. Your Peloton's paying off. People are noticing— appreciating." I wink at her, but she won't come around.

"I got that thing for Doug. I worry about his heart." She pops a chip into her mouth. "He's up twelve pounds since New Year's. But he's using it as a tie rack! I told him, 'Put on those special shoes and start pedaling or it's going back! Our husbands—it's like having another child!"

I picture Doug, bald and neckless as a newborn. She's not wrong. On the other side of our French doors, I see Scott in the kitchen, punching buttons on the microwave as if he's dialing a phone number he can't remember, and expect him to ask me to come help him any second.

"Speaking of being overwhelmed by children, Sarah Davies seems to be really struggling since having Brent," Betsy continues.

"What do you mean?" I try to sound clueless even as I remember Sarah serving us wine in plastic cups along with Fritos snack bags the night the police dragged Oak Hill Pond.

"Well, I asked her if she wanted to join us and help out with the fall fundraiser—Tucker is registered to play this year—and she said she didn't think she could manage it." Betsy, queen of multitasking, frowns. "I mean, you know how she is, so eager to fit in, I thought she'd jump at the chance. She hasn't signed up for the Meal Train for Rachel and Ted either."

"Going from two kids to three is a big leap. You're totally outnumbered!" I don't know why, but I feel compelled to defend Sarah. Maybe it's because she seems genuinely kinder than the rest of us, like the way she refused to pile on when we pointed out that Ted wasn't at the pond that night.

"Anyway, what do I do about the pool guy?" Betsy's voice pulls me back to the deck. "Go to the police? What if this creep does have something to do with Billy's disappearance?"

"He doesn't, Bets. Trust me."

She narrows her eyes. "What makes you so sure?"

I glance over each shoulder as if Rachel Barnes might burst out from behind our row of lilac bushes. Then, I look back into the kitchen. Raised with three older sisters, Scott hates gossip. Still, I can't keep my suspicions to myself any longer.

"Well, I have a theory. It's awful, but if I'm right, our kids aren't in any danger."

Betsy sits up straighter, sets her glass down on the table. "This fundraiser meeting just got a lot more interesting. Spill it!"

"Mom!" Oliver shrieks. "Watch me!"

"Oh Jesus Christ," I mutter and fish out the mason jar of silver dollars I keep beneath the couch. I fling a fistful toward the water for the boys to dive down and find. "That'll keep them busy."

Betsy nods expectantly. "So?"

I lean toward her and whisper, "I think Ted has something to do with Billy's disappearance."

Betsy squints her hazel eyes. "No!" she gasps, pressing an open palm to her chest.

"I don't want it to be true, but hear me out, Bets." I peek around again to make sure Scott and the boys aren't within earshot. "A few weeks ago, Scott was at the ball field—raking it, dragging it, whatever they call it—after a T-ball game. He and

Oliver were in the dugout packing up, and all of a sudden, Scott hears this booming voice yelling, 'How'd you like it if I left *you* here?' Scott steps out, and it's Ted, screaming at Billy. I guess Billy had brought Evan's catcher's mitt to show the team and left it at the field. Scott said Ted just kept ripping into Billy. So Scott said something like, 'Hey man, he's just a kid. My boys lose stuff all the time.' So Ted says, 'Then maybe you ought to do a better job raising them!' Can you believe it? I'm kind of shocked Scott didn't deck him."

"That's awful." Betsy flicks chip crumbs off her fingers. "Scott and Ted used to be pretty friendly, right?"

"When we first moved in, they'd golf together!"

Betsy shakes her head. "Ted was a totally different person when Jane was alive."

"Well, Jane was so warm and loving. Oliver still sleeps with the quilt she made when he was born."

"I think years of guilt have eaten away at Ted." Betsy finishes her drink and presses the cold glass against her forehead. "Jane would still be alive if he'd just let her use that delivery service. I was the one who told her about it, but she said Ted was very particular about his collars, so he insisted she keep going to that dry cleaner in Pine Ridge."

I close my eyes, remembering Jane, how she volunteered to lead story hour at the library long after Evan was in elementary school.

"I still can't believe she's gone," Betsy says.

"I think things are pretty rocky with Rachel," I add, the bourbon making me share more than I probably should. "Oliver and I were dropping off the flyer about T-ball team photos, and I could hear Ted yelling from inside the house, shouting, 'I'm not stupid, Rachel. I promise this won't end well for you!' Oliver was about to ring the bell, but I scooted him down the steps and into the car. I can't stop hearing Ted's voice. It's keeping me up at night. Seriously, I'm using twice as much concealer to cover the bags under my eyes!"

"Stop!" Betsy sinks a carrot into the dip and snaps it between her teeth. "When was this?"

"About a week before Billy went missing." Even as the late-day sun beats down, a chill creeps up my neck.

"Why not just leave?" Betsy stiffens. "Get a divorce? Ted hurt his own son? I mean, that's crazy. This isn't a Lifetime movie!"

"I know, believe me, I hear how sick it sounds. But what's that expression? 'The best way to punish a woman is to hurt her child.' I hope I'm wrong, but I just have this bad feeling. I was right about the Langleys, wasn't I?"

Betsy sighs. "Ted's got his hands full with Evan too, from what I hear."

"I know." I nod. "He's the one supplying Robin Cooke with weed and Adderall."

"Ted wasn't there the night they dragged the pond." Betsy narrows her eyes again. "Have you told anyone else this theory?"

"Just Scott—who thinks I'm insane."

I glance toward the house. Scott waves at us before disappearing into the family room. I feel a twinge of guilt gossiping about the Barnes family.

"But, I mean, Rachel has to suspect something, right?" I finish my drink. "What a nightmare."

Betsy moves to the bar cart to refill our glasses. "I keep thinking about how she fired her au pair." She shudders as she drops ice cubes into the metal shaker. "That was ugly."

I nod and look at Oliver and Parker laughing and wrestling over an inflatable dolphin raft as the sun slowly dips behind the thick row of evergreens.

It's a horrible thought, but it seems like whatever happened to Billy, it's got more to do with his family's problems than a random predator. And that tracks with what I've believed all along: my family isn't in real danger. If we were, I'd sense it. A mother knows.

8

Tuesday, June 18
Rachel

THE MAXWELL GIRL has come forward about Veronica
Baker. It sounds ridiculous—an elderly woman luring
Billy and trapping him in her home? And yet, anything is possible, and, in many ways, it's preferable to other, more terrifying
options.

Ronnie lives two blocks from us. There's no sugarcoating it;
her property is an eyesore where overgrown hedges aren't tall
enough to hide peeling paint and crooked shutters.

Routinely, I sent her postcards that listed recent home sales
in our area. Of course, her outdated Cape Cod, an obvious tear-
down, would never fetch those prices. Still, I wanted to let her
know she had options. Derek had put the idea in my head.

"The lot is perfect. Work your magic, Ray." He'd winked,
as we drove past it in his truck one afternoon. This was before
we knew the home on Maple Crest Drive we'd invested in
would turn out to be a money pit.

Did I offend her? Perhaps. But it's impossible to imagine
someone would abduct a child because you implied they weren't
maintaining their home properly.

I don't know much about Ronnie other than what I've heard
from neighbors: she's a widow who lost a son to leukemia at a

young age. Her daughter lives in California. Loneliness seems like a given.

Because Billy walked to and from school with Oliver, I've only seen her a handful of times. She was there on the corner in May when I brought Billy to school and stayed for his spring concert. When we returned from the zoo field trip in June, she growled like a bear and roared like a lion to the kindergartners' delight.

Ronnie knew my son by name, calling, "Hey, Bill! Yankees take on the Blue Jays tonight."

"Go Yanks!" he cheered over his shoulder. "See ya, Mrs. Baker!"

"It's possible," I whisper, my pulse quickening. I need to know if Veronica Baker has my son. I've been resting on his bed, holding the stuffed panda he got at the zoo's gift shop, but I can't sit still any longer.

At the bottom of the staircase, I shove my feet into running shoes.

"Taking a walk?" Darcy asks, drying her hands on a dish towel. "I'll join you."

"I'm going to confront Ronnie," I say, tightening my ponytail.

"That's not a good idea, Rachel." Ted appears, licking his lips. "Let the police handle it."

"I'm going," I repeat through gritted teeth.

"Ray, I think Ted's right. They're looking into it. We'll know something soon." Darcy reaches for my arm, but I jerk away and bolt out the door.

At the edge of my driveway, my eyes fix on the flashing police lights, their spinning reds and blues jarring against the silvery evening sky.

"Rachel!" Ted barks.

"Ray! Come back inside!" Darcy calls.

Ignoring them, I stagger down the sidewalk in my new uniform—yoga pants and an old sweatshirt, unwashed hair already spilling out of my ponytail. I don't need to look to know my neighbors gape from behind their plantation shutters and custom window treatments. Out of the corner of my eye, I sense movement—reporters, camera crews hopping out of vans. I force myself forward, heart lodged in my throat.

As I get closer, I see Ronnie standing amid a patch of dandelions. She looks like an overgrown toddler in yellow culottes, a matching floral shirt, and a pair of mint-colored Crocs.

Police officers carry out a hulking PC and a bag of things I can't make out as dusk settles. I feel like I'm walking through a dream. Everything seems close-up yet distant at the same time. Sounds are muffled as my pulse throbs in my ears.

I didn't mean to get as near to her as I do. And I didn't expect her to wheel around on me, face red as a rooster's, dark eyes unblinking, the way she does now.

"I'd never take a child!" she exclaims, her voice a mix of sorrow and righteous disgust. "I agreed to this"—she thrusts her arm toward her house, loose skin swaying above her elbow—"because I've got nothing to hide!"

I stop abruptly, frozen to the sidewalk, so close I can see saliva foaming in the corners of her mouth.

"Just because I'm not as fancy as the rest of you people, that doesn't make me a predator! And you will not drive me out of my home!" Her arm remains extended like a club, her hand clenched in a fist.

As I slowly back away, I know she doesn't have Billy. Staring into her haunted eyes, I see a woman whose world has been rocked by something she never saw coming.

It's like looking in a mirror.

CHAPTER

9

Thursday, June 20
Cassidy

EVEN WITH THE AC jacked, my hair is a giant frizz ball. Normally, I'd care—especially because tonight is graduation—but I don't.

Mom knocks on my bedroom door, tiptoes into the room grinning, and pulls a present from behind her back.

"Now, don't get your hopes up," she says, handing over a small box wrapped in green paper and tied with gold ribbon—Oak Hill High's colors. "It's not the keys to a Jeep or a Mini Cooper or anything like that."

That's the trouble with living in Oak Hill. It's impossible not to compare yourself to everyone else. Mom's spent her whole life in this town—she can't help it. The summer after she graduated high school, she backpacked through Europe and came home two weeks before she was due to start at Vassar with a few surprises: head lice, a broken heart, and an unplanned pregnancy. She's been here ever since.

"Stop, Mom, I'm sure I'll love it. Whatever it is."

"Go on!" She smiles, first at me, then the gift. "Open it!"

I tear the paper slowly. Mom deserves a big reaction no matter what the box holds. After completing the financial aid application for college together, I learned how little money she earns and saw just how small her savings account balance is. We thought that between her finances and my grades, schools would throw oodles of money our way. They didn't.

"It's going to be fine, Cassidy," Mom said when the disappointing aid packages came back. "I'll pick up more shifts at the hospital. It'll all work out. If not, I could always sell the house."

I was sitting at the kitchen table making a playlist, preparing to go for a head-clearing run, only half-listening. But that last sentence got my attention.

"Mom, no! You can't! You love this house."

"Yes, but do I love the cost of maintaining it? Nope. Not one bit." She shook her head. "I don't suppose you've noticed that water stain the shape of Texas on the bathroom ceiling? And I found a few of the roof shingles in the driveway this morning."

Mom kept a list of necessary repairs on a legal pad on the kitchen counter. It grew longer each season.

"It doesn't matter, Cassidy, I'll do whatever it takes. This is your chance . . ."

. . . *a chance I didn't get because I was pregnant with you.* I finished her sentence in my head. Mom would never say that, but she's been so excited for me that I can't help but wonder if that's why it's so important to her.

She's worked her butt off to come up with the money for my first semester. When I ask her about the second one, or the years after that, all she'll say is, "Let *me* worry about that."

So whatever she's spent on this gift, it's too much. I hold the box in my hands, afraid to open it because I doubt I'll be able to fake the kind of excitement she deserves.

Luckily, I don't have to. A dazzling silver necklace with two rows of teardrop-shaped amethyst stones rests beneath layers of tissue paper.

"Mom! It's gorgeous!" My voice catches. The tears that swim in my eyes almost constantly now threaten to spill over.

"It was your grandmother's."

"I know." I nod. "I remember her wearing it." I hold it up and watch the stones sparkle as they catch the light from the lamp on my dresser.

"I only needed to have it shined up and the clasp repaired. Here, turn around, I'll help you."

Mom brings the necklace over my head as I sweep my frizzy hair up into a bun. Our eyes meet in the mirror.

"Gran would be so proud of you, Cass. She loved you like crazy, and even though she and I didn't always get along, she was always there for me. I hope you know that I'm always here for you. That you can come to me and tell me anything no matter what, right?"

My heart plunges to the floor. She knows. She knows about Chris and me. How did I ever think I could hide it from her? Since Gran died three years ago, it's been just the two of us. We can practically read each other's minds. I look down, breaking eye contact, and wipe my tears.

"No, I know," I mumble, wondering if I should tell her everything. Rip off the Band-Aid. She'll be upset, but she'll help me figure it all out. She's always reminding me, "I was young once too, Cassidy!"

Mom had a wild past while my teen years have been pretty tame. I've never even gotten detention. But this isn't something simple like drinking beer in the woods with boys or forgetting to turn in a scholarship essay. This is being so crazy about someone, a guy everyone would say is too old, too complicated, but one I find so fucking perfect I want to spend every second with him. And when I do, it's amazing and so unlike anything I've ever felt that I lose all track of time, to the point that it made me late, and a child went missing. When asked why I wasn't there, waiting for the sweet boy who gave me eighteen sunflowers on my birthday, I lied. First to Kyle. Then to Mrs. B. Later to the police. And, finally, to my own mother.

Those actions, *my* actions—I picture them lined up like dominos, one falling into the next and then the next until everything's destroyed. Thinking about it makes my head pound and my stomach twist. I have to tell Mom the truth, and there's never going to be a right time.

"I—" I swallow as Mom says, "You are—" both of us talking at the same moment.

She laughs. "What were you about to say?"

And just like that, I lose my nerve. "Nothing. You go." I nod.

"Well, I was just going to tell you that you are absolutely beautiful—inside and out." Mom steps back as if she's admiring a work of art instead of her daughter, who's made one bad decision after another.

I look at my reflection. The necklace is perfect with my lilac wrap dress. I touch the delicate stones, thinking I'm the last person on the planet who should be given anything nice.

"Thanks," I say, "but I don't feel beautiful."

Mom rubs my bare arms, which are suddenly coated with goosebumps. "Try to put everything else out of your head for the next few hours. You've worked so hard for so long, Cass. You deserve to enjoy this. Take a night off from punishing yourself. You didn't do anything wrong."

This is my window to say something. I open my mouth.

Mom takes a deep breath. "I'm going to go get ready. Try not to wrinkle your dress. Linen is a beast to iron."

She flashes her regular Mom smile. She doesn't know where I was or who I was with when I should've been at the Barneses' house. A rush of relief at not having to tell her everything right now hits me, and I collapse on my bed, ignoring her wrinkle warning. But it also means I'm still on my own with the secret that's eating me up inside.

I bite my thumbnail and stare at the ceiling. I don't even want to go to the graduation ceremony. It got moved to the gym because the football field is a swamp thanks to today's thunderstorms. But Mom would be crushed if I told her I'd rather skip it. That's the thing about being the only child of a single parent: everything you do matters.

I look at the clock on my nightstand. 5:30 PM. The hours blur into one another. I should get up, dig through my hair products, plug in my straightening iron, put on some mascara and lipstick. Get moving. But the bed sucks me right in, and it's impossible to pretend like things are normal after what's been hands down the worst week of my life.

When I texted Chris as I was leaving Oak Hill Pond Saturday night to ask if I could come over, he wrote back, "Probably not the best time."

Oh my God, now I'm losing him too, was all I could think.

Just Chris and Lexi know the real reason I was late on Thursday, and that makes them the only ones who understand the guilt I'm carrying.

"Why not?" I texted back, hoping I didn't come off as needy or hostile.

"I don't think it's a great idea for us to hang out right now. The streets are crawling with cops and neighbors. Wouldn't look good for either of us."

I stared at his words, devastated, until his next sentence appeared, "As much as I'd love to see you."

I was glad we weren't FaceTiming so he couldn't see the ridiculous grin that crossed my face as I walked away from the pond and toward home.

"I'm eighteen, it's not like hanging out with me is a crime," I texted back, immediately regretting my word choice and feeling grateful to Lexi for telling me to get the burner phone.

Thursday night as we hung flyers on telephone poles all over town, she said, "If you're going to keep seeing him—and I seriously don't know how or why you would now—you do not want any record of your conversations. Trust me."

"Why?" I froze up. "Stop! You're freaking me out even more."

"You lied to the police! I've watched a ton of true crime TV, and when you're dealing with a case where there's a missing kid and a bumbling police force, they'll latch on to anything. Even if you've done nothing wrong, weird stuff like that catches up to you."

"I don't know, Lex, that seems like a crazy overreaction."

"I'm sorry, but holy shit, love really has made you clueless. Think about it: You're seeing a guy nearly twice your age, who, technically, is still married. It doesn't matter how hot he is, this is a small fucking town. And if you don't care about your own reputation, think about his. How does it look for the local music teacher to be bangin' his student? And you know what people are going to say about you?"

I shook my head. "What?"

"Daddy issues."

When Lexi laid it out like that, it did sound creepy and gross. But Chris isn't a predator. I'm the one who initiated it. Though, technically, I blamed Lexi too. She started taking guitar lessons with Chris freshman year, and she wouldn't shut up about his "tropical" blue eyes and the way he smelled faintly of vanilla.

"I could butter my toast with his jawline," she said during one of her lengthy rants about how he was the perfect male specimen.

"What does that even mean?" I asked.

"It's chiseled and fine as hell."

We listened to all of Regrets Only's albums, starting with their first, *Put It on My Tab*, and worked our way toward their sloppy but rollicking finale, *Last Exit Before Rehab*. My favorite was "A Series of Unrelated Symptoms." At the end, Chris's voice moved from a growl to a throaty whisper that left Lexi and me swooning.

Gran had taught me how to play the piano, but I gave it up after she died. Then, one day this spring, Lexi and I ran into Chris at the grocery store, and I felt it. That thing she was talking about—that perfect specimen thing. I was starstruck and giddy, trying not to stare too long at his hypnotizing blue eyes or the Pavement tee beneath his flannel shirt, while Lexi was all cool confidence. He was taller and broader than he appeared in the concert clips we watched on YouTube.

"Hey! I was going to text you." Lexi bounced on her toes. "This week, I totally want to work on 'Valerie,' that Amy Winehouse song. You know it?"

"Sure, but—little known fact—it was actually written by an indie rock band called The Zutons."

Lexi tilted her head and exaggerated a sigh, as if the guy she'd been crushing on nonstop for three years was boring the hell out of her.

"Sorry," he said. "I geek out over this stuff, and it wrecks my soul when the original artists don't get the credit. Anyway, they're from Liverpool. Home of . . ."

"The Beatles, duh." Lexi punched him in the shoulder. "Gimme a hard one next time."

"Ouch. Will do." He smiled at us, his eyes locking onto mine. A warmth spread over me, setting off a chemical reaction that messed with my brain. All I could think about was him, hearing his voice again up close.

When I told Mom I wanted to start playing again, she said, "Aw, honey, I love that idea. I just don't really have the cash right now. I bet you could teach yourself some stuff by looking online, though."

So I used my babysitting money, and every day I counted down the hours until six on Thursdays—the best forty-five minutes of my week.

I only saw Chris's wife twice. Of course, Lexi already told me how perfect she was, which I sort of assumed because I grew up watching her in one of my favorite shows, *I'll Be the Judge of That*.

For three seasons, she played Alex Judge, the sexy but smart RA who settled standard sitcom battles between kids in her dorm. Lexi said she was prettier in person, and nice too. She was right.

"She makes an excellent Arnold Palmer, which makes it super hard for me to hate her," Lexi said.

Allison answered the door when I went for my first couple of lessons. Then she was gone. No one knew why they split. If Phil hadn't watched her leave—and Mrs. Foster hadn't told the whole neighborhood what her son saw—it would've seemed as if she'd vanished.

Sometimes, when Chris was talking about flats and sharps, I'd gaze into his blue eyes and wonder, *What could ever make someone not want to wake up to that face?*

Then, the first Thursday in May, we were in his living room. I sat on the piano bench. Chris stood behind me, so close my body came alive, humming in a whole new key. When he reached out to turn the page of the sheet music, I moved forward and touched my lips to his bare forearm. I don't know what made me do it. It was a crazy impulse, like stealing a lick of someone else's ice-cream cone.

Time froze as I waited to see his reaction. I held my breath, the ticking of the metronome the only thing I heard above the sound of my heart pounding in my ears.

"Cassidy, I—"

I looked into his eyes and felt it again—whatever had made me tingle when Lexi and I saw him in the grocery store. Something passing between us, like a secret or a joke only we understood. Chemistry I'd heard about but never felt.

Mine was the last lesson of the day. No one would be coming to the door, ringing the bell, interrupting us. I didn't wait for him to finish his sentence. I stood, leaned toward him, and brushed my lips against his. Every part of me trembled in the best possible way as we kissed, his hands cupping my face, his fingers rough and calloused from playing guitar. It felt like a movie, right down to the gentle tinkling of music as I touched the piano keys to steady myself. Complete perfection.

He took my hand and led me upstairs. For a second before we walked into the guest room, I wondered what he'd been going to tell me before I stopped him. "Cassidy, I'm still in love with my wife." "Cassidy, I'm your teacher." "Cassidy, I've been thinking about you too."

He didn't say anything as he lowered me onto the down comforter. His mouth, hungry and everywhere, his body, long and knotty with muscles, warm against mine, his strong hands tangled in my hair—every part working together to create a symphony of sensation that made my head swim like it did on the nights Lexi and I mixed strong, terrible cocktails in her basement.

She and I would toast to celebrate our college acceptances or commiserate about the pressure of being the only children of single moms. Then, we'd lay in opposite ends of her hammock, staring up at the stars, talking about how fabulous our lives would be once we got out of Oak Hill. We'd stumble back inside, filled with hope for our futures, before her mom returned from another online dating disaster.

Being with Chris, I saw my better future finally coming into view.

I'd had sex before, but this was completely different. Chris was deliberate, considerate, like he wanted me to enjoy every second. Clay Bennett—a guy in my grade—had been my first. We'd gone to homecoming together last fall and hung out at his house a bunch of times, which mainly consisted of me scrolling through my phone while he played Grand Theft Auto. One Friday night we were fooling around and he said, "If we're gonna do this, now's a good time 'cause my dad's working late and my mom's at a yoga retreat."

I thought about saying no, but I was curious. Clay was cute—ginger hair, hazel eyes, and a dimple in his chin. Plenty of our classmates left campus during lunch to do it while their parents were at work. Not that it was a good reason, but I wanted to see what the fuss was about. After watching her mom date one loser after another, Lexi said she'd probably die a virgin and she was fine with that.

"Maybe I'll donate my body to science," she'd joke, "so some med students can study vaginal atrophy."

Clay's room reeked of an air freshener trying to mask the stink of dirty socks.

I turned my head and stared at a poster of Eli Manning as Clay made a series of fast, jerky movements and attempted to adjust my legs in odd positions that I imagined he'd picked up from Internet porn. This was accompanied by grunting—not good, pleasurable grunting, more like he was straining to push a truck uphill.

After, I went to the bathroom and tried to pee, hovering over the toilet seat, thinking, *That was it? That's what everyone thinks is so great?*

When I walked back into Clay's room, he was wearing boxers and a shirt that read PETA: People Eating Tasty Animals. If regret had a flavor, it would be metallic, and when that steely tang sprang into my mouth, I wished I could travel back in time and leave before he'd tried to unhook my bra with his teeth. Looking up from his phone, Clay smiled and patted a spot on the bed. "Hey, c'mere, I want to show you something."

I hoped it would be a Tiny Desk concert on YouTube or an interesting TED Talk—anything that would make me feel some connection to him and stop me from thinking I'd done something I'd always view as a mistake. But, no, it was just a TikTok of some loser lighting his farts on fire.

"Fucking amazing!" Clay laughed and punched his pillow. "If you want, I can drop you the link."

I went back to Clay's one more time, believing it had to get better. Whole industries were devoted to sex. People blew up their marriages and abandoned their families for it. With Clay, that made no sense. With Chris, I got it immediately.

It wasn't just that I was starstruck, or that his skin felt like velvet. It was more that when he kissed me, slowly, gently, everywhere, I lost myself completely. My mind went deliciously blank. Everything disappeared, and all I could think about was how connected I felt to him.

After he made each cell in my body vibrate with pleasure, we lay there, arms and legs tangled. I was afraid I'd fall asleep, so I forced my eyes open and admired the silver lamp on the nightstand, the orange blossom candle beside it. The whole room looked straight out of one of those five-star hotels Mom and I drooled over on the Travel Channel, complete with a leafy green plant in the corner and a velvet bench at the foot of the bed.

"Stay for dinner?" Chris propped himself up and smiled at me.

I laughed. I'd expected it to be awkward between us. It wasn't. "Wow, is there anything you can't do?"

"Hey, I'm no Bobby Flay, but I can grill some chicken."

"That sounds great, but I should probably go." I bit my lip before I began blabbering about homework or how I needed to get home before Mom so she wouldn't ask why my piano lesson lasted two hours.

Downstairs, I grabbed my jean jacket and backpack from the living room, avoiding looking at the top of the Steinway, where the Langleys' wedding photo stood. Each week I tried not to stare at the image of Chris and Allison, hand-in-hand, beaming at each other through a storm of white rose petals, the picture so perfect it could've come with the frame.

How could she possibly have left him? The thought flitted across my mind as Chris walked me to the door.

"See you next Thursday?"

"Or sooner?" He smiled.

As I stepped out into the rosy dusk, a warm breeze kissed my shoulders. The memory of Chris's mouth on my neck caused me to catch my breath. I couldn't stop grinning. The moon was full, and a chorus of crickets made the air buzz. I hadn't noticed they were back for the season. The world, and everything in it, seemed alive, kind of like when you upgrade your phone and the speed is faster, the colors more brilliant, and you wonder how you ever lived with the old version.

On the sidewalk, I stopped to dig through my backpack, thinking I'd call Lexi on my way home.

"Long lesson?" Phil Foster stood across the street. He wore his army jacket even though the night air was warm. His black hair stood at odd angles, his glasses crooked. Binoculars dangled around his neck. I had no idea how long he'd been watching me.

"Oh hey, Phil. What's up? Say hi to your mom for me!" I tried to sound casual as I walked faster, wondering how I hadn't noticed him, and why I hadn't been smart enough to remember that since Phil got back he acted like it was his job to observe and patrol all of Oak Hill.

I got home about fifteen minutes before Mom returned from another twelve-hour shift.

"How was your day?" she asked. "Anything new or exciting?"

"Good. No, not really." I lied, glad she was sorting through junk mail and not looking at me. "How was your day?"

"It was okay, but I'm beat." She yawned. "I'm going to take a hot bath. You had dinner?"

"Mm-hmm," I lied again. I had a Clif Bar in my backpack. I'd eat that if the manic butterflies in my stomach ever settled down.

As soon as I heard the water running for Mom's bath, I FaceTimed Lexi from inside my bedroom closet, my go-to spot when I wanted to be sure Mom couldn't hear me.

"So these calculus problems are kicking my ass," Lexi said in place of a greeting. "Did you solve number seven?"

"Where are you? Are you alone?"

"Why are you asking me that, weirdo? What's next: What am I wearing?"

I waited.

"Yes, I'm alone," she sighed. "My mom is out with some insurance salesman who—and I quote—'has only one ex-wife.' So he sounds like a real catch. Why? What's up?"

"I hooked up with Chris!"

Lexi's phone had been resting faceup, so all I could see was the ceiling, but my confession made her grab it. Her mouth dropped open, forming an oval. She looked like a scream emoji.

"Shut up!" she shouted. "You did not!"

"Did too!"

"You're kidding me, right?

"Nope."

"What the hell? He hit on you? What a perv!"

"No, it was all me! I told you last week when he was sitting on the bench beside me, our thighs touched, and my whole body went weak? It was like that! I'm still completely light-headed, like when you get off a roller coaster." I waved my arms and rolled my head back to give her the visual.

She stared, like she couldn't process this info. "Okay, so what do you mean by 'hooked up?' Did you make out? More than that?" She started to squeal. "Tell me you did not just have sex with a grown-ass man! But if you did, was it better than with Clay Bennett? Did he at least give you that piano lesson for free?"

Lexi flipped back and forth between curious friend and concerned parent. I imagined it was because she'd watched her mom make so many mistakes with men.

"He's all I can think about, Lex." I grinned. "And you were the one who pointed out how perfect he is at least a billion times!"

She didn't say anything, just shook her head, her eyes closed.

"You're not mad, are you?" I suddenly realized I may have breached some unspoken friend code.

"Look, I know I always talked about being totally into him, but I never would've done anything about it. I've known him since I was thirteen. He's my guitar teacher, and he's seen me in braces for fuck's sake!" She paused and looked off to the side like she was trying to figure out how to say something before turning back to face me. "I'm just—I just think this isn't going to end well for you. Like, what if his wife comes back? She's been gone what? A month? She could just be filming a movie somewhere. Phil Foster was the only one who saw her leave town in the middle of the night without a suitcase." She raised an eyebrow. "Should anyone believe him? Last week, he was convinced a backpack outside the library was filled with explosives."

I'd forgotten about Phil. I hoped it wouldn't get back to Mom that he saw me leave my six o'clock piano lesson at nearly eight.

"I'm sorry, but who knows what he really saw with Mrs. Langley?" Lexi continued. "She could be back tomorrow."

The thought of not being with Chris again seemed impossible. Still, I couldn't help but laugh. "I'm not delusional. I'm not trying to become the next Mrs. Langley or anything like that. It's just—our time is almost up in Oak Hill, right? We leave for college in a couple of months, and it just feels like up until three hours ago, my life has been super dull."

"Um, speaking as your best friend, thanks a lot."

"No, you know what I mean. What do we do? Study, play lacrosse, babysit, get fro-yo. Maybe we stop by a party and watch drunk people make asses of themselves. Then we do it all again the next week." I huffed in frustration. "I can't go off to school and have that be all I've ever done."

"So you decided to *do* former rock star Christopher Langley? Like, as what? An experiment?" Lexi asked. "A graduation gift to yourself?"

"I don't know."

Actually, I knew exactly why I'd done it. But I was too embarrassed to tell even my best friend that each night before I went to bed, I pictured myself kissing Chris beside the piano. I rewound the image over and over in my mind. It helped me block out all the shit that'd kept me up for months, stuff like, can I really leave Mom all alone in this falling-down house? How am I going to pay for school? Would my life be completely different if my dad, whoever he is, were in it?

"Well, if you're happy, I'll try to be happy for you, I guess. Just be careful." Lexi frowned and wagged an index finger at me before smiling and switching back to friend mode. "Now kiss and tell, bitch! I want all the details!"

* * *

That was five weeks ago. How did my life go from a dream come true to a fucking nightmare in such a short time?

"I'm almost ready," Mom calls from down the hall, jolting me back to the present. "Just give me five minutes to put my face on."

That had been Gran's way of saying she was going to pencil in her eyebrows, apply her signature red lipstick, and dust her high cheekbones with pink powder. When I was little, I never missed the chance to leap onto her enormous bed and spread out like a starfish across her rose-patterned quilt to watch Gran transform into a more glamorous version of herself.

I think of Gran, touch her necklace, and remember I need to put my own face on. My game face. The thought of seeing my classmates and their parents packed into the gym makes me so sweaty, I should probably glue sticks of deodorant directly to my armpits. I can picture faceless masses nodding in my direction, whispering, "That's Cassidy! *The babysitter!* You know, the one who was on the news. The babysitter who should've been there for Billy Barnes! Yes, that one!" My stomach pitches and I want to crawl beneath my blankets and refuse to come out.

I look back at the clock on my nightstand. 5:50 PM. I haven't heard from Chris since yesterday. Lexi was right. I am in over my head. She's been awesome this week, staying beside me, acting like my bodyguard any time someone asks any questions. Even a simple, "How are you holding up, Cass?" in the senior parking lot elicits a harsh "Back off!" from my best friend.

When Xander McCall, editor of the school paper, which no one reads anyway, shouted, "Why were you late, Cassidy?" across the crowded hallway on our way to AP French on Monday, I thought Lexi was going to body-slam him into a locker.

I'm going to be late again if I don't get up. It takes all my strength to stand. As I reach for a hairbrush, my phone buzzes against my dresser. It's a Snapchat notification. Lexi. I haven't heard from her since we left graduation practice just before noon, which is weird, considering she's been checking in with me almost continuously since last Thursday.

I open it. "Meet me in the East Wing ladies' room at 6:15!" the Snapchat disappears.

"Sure, what's up?"

She starts to reply. I wait.

"Just be there!" flashes on the screen.

"Why so mysterious?"

She doesn't answer.

"??" I send back.

Nothing. It's unlike Lexi to not respond. She's probably stressed. Her dad flew in from L.A. yesterday with his new wife, and her mom's obsessed with the insurance salesman.

"It's been like a month, and already she thinks he's 'the one.' If I ever act that desperate, I want you to run me over with a car," Lexi said at graduation practice.

"I'll probably never own a car thanks to my student loans."

"Well, then hit me with your bicycle." She shook her head. "This is the one day it's supposed to be about me, and my parents will make it about them."

Maybe Lexi filled a flask and that's why she wants to meet in the bathroom. Whatever it is, not wanting to disappoint her is the only thing that finally motivates me to get moving.

*   *   *

I groan as we round the corner, and Oak Hill High comes into view. The packed parking lot looks like a high-end car lot, Audi here, Ranger Rover there. Meanwhile our car's muffler announces our arrival from a mile away. The entrance is a sea of Burberry umbrellas. Principal Saunders sent an email this morning that there'd be security in the lobby to check purses and backpacks for weapons. Since Billy disappeared, Oak Hill is suddenly on high alert.

We wait in a long line of cars, watching people leap over puddles and rush through the rain.

"It feels like it was just yesterday and a million years ago that I was the one in the cap and gown." Mom's staring at the brick building, ivy snaking up its sides.

Sometimes I wonder if she wishes she could get a do-over. I don't ask. I'm afraid of the answer.

When she finally pulls up to the school's entrance, I grip the seat, not wanting to get out.

"Why don't you park, and I'll walk with you?" I offer.

"Don't be silly. You'll get soaked. Plus, it's six twenty. You'd better hurry."

I take a deep breath and reach for the door handle. Mom touches my arm.

"Cassidy," she says, wincing as the wipers scrape the wind-shield. She needs new ones but keeps putting it off, and I wonder if it's her crazy work schedule or not wanting to spend the money.

I expect her to say, "It isn't your fault," for the millionth time. She can repeat it every minute for the rest of my life, and I still won't believe it, not as long as she doesn't know why I was late.

"You're braver than you believe and stronger than you seem—"

"You're actually quoting Christopher Robin to me?"

"If the Pooh fits . . ." She smiles and nudges me toward the door.

I stop to look at her, really look, and notice the red veins around her blue eyes. Purple half moons hang beneath them. I've been so worried about myself and Billy that I haven't stopped to think about Mom. People are probably talking about her too. The babysitter's mother. *How could a nurse raise such a careless girl? See what happens when you're a single mom?* If I keep looking at her, I'll break down sobbing.

"I love you," she calls as I shut the car door, and all I can think is, "How?"

*   *   *

I'm barely through the entrance marked "Graduates only!" when my phone pulses in my hand. Squeezing my way through the jammed lobby, I struggle to raise my arm to read Lexi's "Where are you??" message.

I keep my eyes down and rush toward the ladies' room. It's a full house, with seniors crowding at the mirrors to fix their hair and makeup, moms congratulating each other and reminiscing before dashing off to find seats in the gym. Standing on tiptoes to scan over grandmothers' hairsprayed heads, I spot Lexi at the far end leaning against the wall.

"Excuse me, excuse me!" I mumble as I make my way toward her, trying to avoid getting poked in the eye by a mortarboard.

"Hey!" I say when I finally reach her.

"I said six fifteen. What took you so long?" She doesn't smile. Her protective bodyguard persona is gone. She looks pissed. My heart beats faster.

"I'm sorry. My mom drives like a tortoise in the rain. Her wipers suck. I—"

She holds up a palm for me to stop talking and then waves her hand under the automatic dryer. It roars to life as she leans in close and whispers in my ear, "The police were just at my house."

With her face so close to mine, I can't read her expression. I pull back. "What? Why? What did they want?"

She rolls her eyes like I'm the dumbest person alive and leans in again, keeping her hand beneath the dryer. "To ask me about you! You told them you were here. At the picnic. Last Thursday. As your best friend, they wanted me to vouch for you."

My stomach flips. I want to go back to when I thought she asked me to meet her here to chug whiskey from a sports bottle she'd snuck in under her gown. I could use a shot right now.

"Why? What did you say? What did you tell them?" I whisper back, scared to look up in case everyone is staring at us, guilt making me more paranoid than ever.

"Hey, can you take your hand away?" barks a girl who's standing at the sink applying concealer. "It's already hot as balls in here."

Lexi ignores her. The dryer continues its gale-force blast at a deafening volume. She looks around and over her shoulder. "I said you were there. Here. I lied. To the police. For you."

Sweat beads on my forehead, and all I can think about is how stupid I've been and how fast it will catch up with me. My face is on fire from the heat in the bathroom and the fact that Lexi, who earned the Girl Scout Gold Award, has just been forced to cover for me.

"Lex, you didn't have to—"

"My mom and dad were standing right there the entire time. What choice did I have? Tell the truth? That you ditched because you have a mad crush that's caused you to—I don't know—lose your fucking mind? Then, they asked me if I had any idea why you'd have gotten stuck in that detour when Cherry Lane isn't anywhere near the train station."

My heart pounds. I want to ask Lexi what she said, but my throat is a desert, my voice nonexistent.

"You've put me in a really shitty position," Lexi hisses.

"Take your hand out from under the fucking dryer!" the same girl yells.

Lexi gives her the finger, then glares at me. My lip quivers, tears springing to my eyes. I need to say something here. Tell her I'll fix it, get her out of this, but I don't know how. My head feels as if it's floating, empty as a balloon. I have no words other than the stupid clichés that tumble out of my mouth. "I'm so sorry. I never meant for any of this to happen."

It's true, I hadn't planned to lie to anyone. My mind flashes to waking up at Chris's. After hunting around for my backpack and keys, I'd raced from his house to the high school to pick up my car. Getting it made me even later, but I had no choice—my phone was inside. If Mom, Mrs. B., or Billy needed me, they'd call or text. Plus, I couldn't leave the rust-spotted Camry in the empty lot, sticking out like a pimple on an otherwise clear face. Sometimes Mom drove past the high school on her way home from work. I'd have no way to explain why I'd left it there. Plus, I never expected *this* to happen. I thought I'd apologize to Billy, make it up to him with an extra snack or by letting him quiz and correct me on baseball trivia. I hadn't meant to lie about the detour. I'd been caught off guard, sitting on the Barneses' porch steps that awful afternoon as I waited for Billy. Once Kyle told his brother, Officer Kinsley, that I was late because of the detour, I had no choice but to stick with that story.

The memory of it leaves me weak. Like Mom said earlier, some things seem like they happened yesterday and a million years ago. I feel like I've lived an entire, awful lifetime since Billy disappeared.

"Ladies!" Mrs. Howell, the vice principal, calls from the doorway. "We're going to start lining up in five minutes. Wrap it up in here!"

Lexi sees I'm trembling and puts her hand on my arm.

"What am I going to do? What the hell am I going to do?" My voice cracks, rising to a panic.

"Shh!" Lexi hisses. "Look, here's what I think: The cops have no leads and no idea what happened to Billy. The story's all over the news. Every day that goes by without a break in the case, they're under more pressure, and they're grasping at straws."

"I don't know, Lex." I can't seem to get my brain to focus, to think clearly.

"I'm not just saying that to make you feel better. Believe me—I'm pissed at you—but, seriously, that whole shitshow with Mrs. Baker makes them look so much worse."

On cue, Sloan Maxwell glides into the bathroom, tosses her iced coffee cup in the trash, and pulls a lipstick out of her bra.

"Speak of the devil!" Lexi pushes past me and marches up to Sloan, who's at the full-length mirror, puckering and winking at herself.

"What the hell were you thinking?"

Sloan doesn't turn, just keeps admiring herself as if she's wearing vintage Versace and not a polyester gown like the rest of us. Lexi takes her arm and spins her around.

A couple of underclassmen who were heading for the door, stop and wait, expecting a showdown.

"Hey, Sloan! I'm talking to you! What made you do it?"

"I don't know what you're talking about."

"The hell you don't!" Between the stress of her parents, the police, and graduation in general, Lexi's ready to explode. "The thing I don't get is why you did it. Just to be a bitch?"

Sloan caps her lipstick and turns back to her reflection as if Lexi's not worthy of her time. We've never liked Sloan. She moved into town at the end of fifth grade and invited the whole class to her house for her birthday party. She had a pool, and it sounded fun—until we got there, and she chose who received Chipwichs and chocolate eclairs and who got freezer-burned lemon or lime popsicles. She wouldn't let certain kids use her slide or diving board. Then she opened her presents in front of everyone and said things like, "I already have this," and "Is this all you got me?"

Sloan's always been obnoxious, but what she did to Mrs. Baker was vile.

"You completely ruined a woman's reputation. For what, a little attention?" Lexi steps between Sloan and the mirror. "'Cause you sure as shit don't need the money."

"Well, what if she did have Billy?" Sloan shrugs. "Then I'd have been a hero, and you'd be thanking me instead of being huddled in a bathroom consoling the world's worst babysitter."

I can't even speak to defend myself. I just keep picturing Sloan's Instagram post. It was a selfie, with her in a tankini and a poster that read "Bring Billy Home!" in big bubble letters. In her caption, she described how Mrs. Baker noticed the turquoise crocheted purse she'd gotten as a birthday gift years ago.

All I said was, "Thanks!" and next thing she's inviting me to go home with her! And she says she'll, get this, "teach me how to knit." WTF, guys!? I mean, that's so creepy, right? Kind of like a luring? It totally freaked me out. I never told anyone until right now. Should I tell my mom? Go to the police? LMK.

And, of course, all Sloan's followers who wanted to be invited to the Friday night drunk fests she hosts, while her parents are upstairs not giving a shit, backed her one hundred percent. Within minutes, they wrote dozens of nasty comments about Mrs. Baker, like:

> She always gave out those cheap Dum Dum lollipops. Now it all makes sense! And, I'm sorry, but nobody wants that shit! At least get Blow Pops or Tootsie Pops!
> She smells like peas.
> I always thought she was gross! Those long purple fingernails?! Total predator!!
> Sloan, you're so, so brave to come forward! Thank you for caring so much about Billy!

Of course, Sloan had "liked" every single comment.

"You will never be a hero!" Lexi sneers at her. "How could you ever even think that about Mrs. Baker? She's like Oak Hill's unofficial grandmother."

"No fucking way!" Sloan says. "She's a weird old woman. Who knows what she does in that dump she lives in? Plus, look at all these teachers you see on the news—male and female—who creep on kids?" Sloan cranes her neck to see her reflection above Lexi's head. "Just so you know, I've been having nightmares about her. That's why I look like shit today."

"And she's having nightmares about you, probably." My voice is back, but it's a whimper compared to Lexi's roar or Sloan's defiant bluster. "My mom saw her at the ER Tuesday night. She had chest pains. She couldn't breathe. She thought she was having a heart attack."

Sloan stares me down. "If you'd done your job, I suppose none of this would have happened."

My shoulders twitch as tears swim in the corner of my eyes.

"Okay, ladies, let's go!" Mrs. Howell shouts into the bathroom. "Your hair and makeup are flawless. Now move it out into the hall!"

"Aw, Cassidy, don't cry," Sloan smirks, striding toward the door. "I'm guessing you can't afford waterproof mascara."

Lexi puts her arm around my shoulder. We both know my problems are way bigger than cosmetics.

10

Thursday, June 20
Rachel

SITTING ON BILLY's bed, I press his pillow to my face. He's been gone a week. The scent of him—coconut shampoo and bubble bath mixed with the raw earthiness of a little boy who'd live outdoors if I let him—fades a bit more each day. I turn the pillow over in my hands and scream into the side that smells only of cotton.

Against my leg, my cell phone pulses, making my stomach lurch. I'm terrified to look at the number. Will this be it—the call that ruins my life? My hands tremble as I turn it over. It's Betsy. I don't want to answer. I haven't spoken to anyone since the disaster with Ronnie two nights ago when I staggered home, my neighbors' eyes burning into my back. Darcy begged me to take a sleeping pill. I refused. I can't.

Betsy's probably calling to cancel our Meal Train or recommend a grief counselor. I'd like to ignore her, but every conversation could offer information I need.

"Rachel?" Her voice is nearly drowned out by the sound of rain. "How are you?"

"I'm—" There are no words for my condition.

"I'm in the car," she says, "waiting for T-ball practice to end. Do you believe Scott went ahead with it in this weather?

Anyway, I don't know if this means anything, but I was just talking to Kelli—"

Talking about Billy and me. She doesn't have to say it.

"—and she said your au pair was in Oak Hill on the afternoon Billy disappeared."

My grip tightens around the phone. With my other hand, I reach for Billy's headboard to steady myself. "Rose?" My ears burn. "Rose was here? What time? Who saw her? Where?" I can't make my mouth form the words fast enough.

"She was visiting Audrey, Kelli's au pair, asking if she knew of any families looking for help this summer. Kelli said Audrey just told her this afternoon. She's worried, said Rose's boyfriend is—and I quote—'kind of an asshole.' According to Audrey, he's upset with Rose for not making any money, and he threatened to kick her out. Kelli wanted to call you, but I told her I'd do it because I wanted to ask—"

"Thank you," I whisper and hang up.

It takes me three tries to find Detective Dubin's number, as my brain leaps from one awful scenario to the next.

When he answers, I babble, speaking in fragments. "I wasn't feeling well. I came home early. Billy was alone for an hour at least. Rose walked in. Her boyfriend, this creep with a vine tattoo snaking around his neck, came in behind her. The two of them were laughing. I lost it."

Silence. Is he judging me, thinking, "So, let me get this straight, Mrs. Barnes, you went from a negligent au pair to an irresponsible babysitter? Have you considered that your willingness to leave your child with just anyone is the real issue here?"

"What do you mean you 'lost it'?" Detective Dubin asks in his even tone.

"I started yelling, fired her, told her to get out. She apologized and asked me to give her another chance. I said no. Her boyfriend got in my face. He told me I'd be sorry."

"What's his name—the boyfriend?"

"Trevor."

"Trevor what?"

His last name—did I ever know it? My thoughts race, trying to reach into the void of memory.

"I don't know. I— I told him—" I pause, hearing how awful

this sounds before I even say the words. "I told him not to come near my family again or I'd have Rose sent back to Ireland."

"Have you tried contacting Rose directly, Mrs. Barnes?"

"No, I—I deleted her contact information after . . ."

More silence.

"Why am I only hearing about this now?" he asks.

"I assumed she'd gone back home. Her visa—"

"Which agency did you use? Forward me the number and I'll—"

I take a deep breath. I didn't go through an agency. Rose had been recommended by a fellow real estate agent in my office, Heather, whose husband had accepted a promotion in London. Rose could've gone with them, but she didn't want to leave her boyfriend. I should've done my own background check, but Heather was meticulous about her business and her family. If she trusted Rose with her children, that had been enough for me. I remember Heather telling me, "She's a nice girl. Plain." She'd arched her eyebrows in a way that said, "You don't have to worry about catching her in the laundry room with your husband," not that Ted was the type.

I hired Rose a week later.

Until the afternoon in April when I fired her, things had been okay. If I'm honest, there were red flags I'd ignored. During the hours Billy was in school, Rose was supposed to be doing our laundry, grocery shopping, and general housekeeping. Over the winter, I found out she was watching other children in the mornings—helping Sarah Davies with her newborn and toddler, watching the Petersons' twins so Polly could teach spin classes. There were probably others, more families I didn't know about. It wasn't the worst thing. Still, it felt dishonest, sneaky. In a small town you can get away with something for just so long, and then it catches up with you. I asked her to stop and that was that.

"She came highly recommended by a colleague," I say.

"Let me see what I can find out." Detective Dubin clears his throat. "I have to caution you, Mrs. Barnes, people want to be helpful, but often they get their facts mixed up."

"What are you saying?" I'm suddenly so tired, I can barely hold my head up.

"I'm saying this other au pair may have her dates wrong. Or, Rose might have been in Oak Hill, but that doesn't mean she even saw your son." He pauses and his words land like a grenade on my chest. "I'm saying that in these situations it's best to manage your expectations." His voice has a slight edge to it now, as if he's annoyed by my constant calling, my need to cling to the smallest shred of hope.

I stifle a cry, knowing he may be right. This is probably nothing. If Rose took Billy because she needed money, she'd have come forward to collect the reward by now. Is it not enough? There's equity in the house. We could double, triple the amount.

"Where is your husband, Mrs. Barnes?"

Billy's room has grown dark. The only light comes from the clock glowing on his nightstand. 8:45 PM. Where is Ted?

"I think he's still at work."

I have no idea where my husband is, where he goes when he isn't here eating or sleeping. But I can't say that because it will sidetrack this investigation. Precious time will be wasted thinking our son's disappearance is somehow connected to problems in our marriage.

"Have him call me when he gets in. I'd like to speak with him."

And just like that, I'm wide awake, questioning everything and everyone I thought I knew.

CHAPTER

11

Friday, June 21
Allison

PEOPLE HATE SPECIFIC sounds—car alarms, microphone feedback, canned laughter in a sitcom. One of the noises I dread most is the ringing before my mother picks up the phone. It isn't the trilling that gets to me necessarily. It's more the unknown as I wait for her to answer and wonder what she'll come out with this week.

After I left Oak Hill, I called my parents on the disposable phone I bought with cash at a bodega, and told them I had a lot of shoots coming up. I suggested we make a standing phone date—every Friday morning at eleven—just to check in. I didn't want to risk her calling the house. Would Chris even answer? If he did, what would he say? I'm sure his pride would stop him from telling her I left.

Some weeks I call from a hotel lobby, so when my mother asks where I am, I can say I'm traveling between jobs and, technically, I'm not lying. I told her I'd lost my regular cell phone. When I've spoken with my parents from Viv's apartment, she's said, "You should probably call them less. You frown the entire time. Or, at least, bill them for your Botox."

Viv's still in Sedona, so I stretch out on the couch and remind myself to keep my face neutral, even as the ringing makes me wince.

"Hello?"

"Hey, Mom! It's me."

"Allison! Your dad and I were just talking about you."

My muscles tense. I stand and walk to the window. "Really? Why?"

"We were wondering if you're going to leave Oak Hill?"

What has she heard? Did my sister stop by and catch Chris in a weak moment? No, he'd never confide in Jen.

"What makes you ask?"

"Don't you watch the news? That poor boy. Billy Bates."

"Barnes," I correct her. "Yes, I saw." I peel back the curtain and glance down across the narrow street below. The man I'm sure followed me isn't there. Still, I can't shake the feeling I'm being watched.

"Your father thought you might know him, but I said, 'How would Allison know him? She doesn't have a child.'"

Can she hear my heart shatter through my cheap Tracfone?

"Maybe Oak Hill isn't the best place to raise a family," she continues. "I know Chris loves that town, but—"

"We both chose it," I interrupt, feeling oddly protective of my estranged husband.

"Well, now they're trying to find the family's au pair. They think she might be involved. Did you see that? I'm telling you, Allison, they're going to turn this into a movie. Maybe you can play yourself? Imagine!"

"Mom, that's totally inappro—"

"Poor kid. Have you or Chris helped with any of the searches? I read that the community has really rallied together. Maybe Oak Hill isn't so bad?" she chuckles, clueless. "Speaking of children, my friend Celine—from my book club? Her son and his partner are adopting. They're so excited. The club's putting together 'baby's first library' as a gift. I'm sure everyone will pick the old standbys—*Goodnight Moon* and *Velveteen Rabbit*—so I asked your sister to give me a few recommendations."

"That's sweet," I say, idly wiping dust off the windowsill.

"Have you and Chris ever talked about adopting?" Her voice creeps higher the way it does when she talks to Emily and Ethan.

I should have anticipated her awkward segue. In the uncomfortable silence, I twist my hair around my fingers, attempting to get into character: "Daughter Who Refuses to Be Rattled During Weekly Call With Mother."

After the last miscarriage, I'd begged Chris to consider adoption.

"How could you even ask me that?" He'd jerked his head back in shock.

Chris had told me about his childhood a few weeks into our relationship. After one of his shows, we'd gone to a bar. I'd been a little bit starstruck. Struggling to make conversation, I'd asked if musical talent ran in his family. He stayed silent for so long I thought maybe he hadn't heard me. When he finally spoke, he told me that Bill and Charlotte Langley awoke one day in their late forties and realized that while they'd succeeded in their careers, amassed wealth beyond their wildest expectations, and traveled the world, they'd forgotten to have a child. So they adopted.

"I was an item on a to-do list," he'd said, polishing off a fresh pint in a single swallow. "They meant well, but they were like people who get a puppy for Christmas and haven't really thought about the day in, day out care that goes into it."

Soon after they brought Chris home, the Langleys resumed traveling. They always returned laden with gifts—exotic toys placed on a high shelf, books no one read to him.

"Don't get me wrong, they were good people," he'd said. "They did a ton of charity work. But I was raised by a rotating cast of housekeepers, who also meant well." His smile faded, and he signaled to the bartender to bring another round though I'd barely touched my pint. "But it was lonely." His leg bounced against the lowest rung of the barstool. "What am I saying? It sucked, actually. It felt like I'd been abandoned twice. Once by my birth parents, and again by the Langleys."

Remembering the darkness in his usually bright eyes, I'd tried to avoid the subject of adoption until it seemed like our only hope.

"It wouldn't be like that with us," I'd argued. "You know our child would be loved."

"Yes, but you don't know what it's like to go through life not knowing your personal history," he'd insisted. "You've got your mom's smile, your dad's thick hair. I spent years studying strangers. Did I have their eyes? Their chin? I wasted decades wondering about the people who chose not to keep me. Was someone out there looking for me too?"

When he'd asked Charlotte about his birth parents, she'd never say more than "They loved you enough to want a better life for you than they could provide. And now you have it!"

I'd suggested we'd get one of those ancestry kits—search for his biological parents together. He'd refused.

"If I find them, and they're absolute losers, then I spend the rest of my life knowing *these* are my people. *This* is what I come from. One of them must battle addiction—that's a given. On the flip side, what if they're amazing? What if they went on to raise the perfect family, filled with beach vacations, homemade birthday cakes, inside jokes? And I missed all of it. Then what? Then I know exactly how much I've lost." He'd thrown his hands up in defeat as if he were unable to conjure the images that would finally convince me. "It still haunts me. I don't want to see my kid have to deal with that."

"Things are different now," I told him. "There's open adoption. The mom or dad—or both—could be a part of our child's life. I've heard stories; it can be great. For everyone."

"With Chris's past, adoption could be a challenge," my mother says now.

I wonder how many times she's rehearsed this conversation. Chris had already raised this red flag. I can see him arguing with me, clear as if I'm back in Oak Hill standing in our bedroom.

"No one's giving me a baby, Al." He'd shaken his head. "Not when there's a background check involved. Not when there's footage of me high out of my mind taking a shit in a bank lobby while Roddy uses an ATM." He'd laughed then and rolled his eyes at me, as if I were the one who'd done those things. "I've been arrested for trying to sneak drugs through an airport. I know you'll say that was years ago, people make mistakes, blah, blah, blah. I only got off because I'm rich and moderately famous."

"Maybe not a baby," my mother muses, as if she can read my thoughts. "Perhaps an older child? Oh, honey, wouldn't that be wonderful?"

I'd said the same to Chris. He'd fought me there too.

"Don't you get it, Al? I want to stare into my son's or daughter's eyes and know that we're connected. By blood. DNA. That's not what you want to hear, and maybe it makes me a selfish asshole, but I want a family of our own," he'd said.

"I am your family," I'd pleaded. "Two people can be a family."

"Two people can be a family," I tell my mother and fake cough to hide my voice cracking.

"No, of course, dear," she says. "Oh, Jen asked me to remind you to RSVP to Ethan's birthday party. She said she sent you an invitation and texts with links to some gift ideas."

I picture my cell phone on the windowsill back in Oak Hill, screen flooded with my sister's demanding messages.

"I still can't find my phone," I lie. "I might miss the party—traveling for work. But I'll send Ethan something expensive—that's all Jen cares about anyway." I return to a part I'm too old to play: "Passive-Aggressive Younger Sister Who Lacks Internal Filter."

"Don't say that, Allison. It's just that you and Chris have so much, you can afford to be generous!"

I scrunch my eyes shut and feel my entire face contort. Fuck the wrinkles, I can't help it. Just as I'm about to turn away from the window, I look out and spot a tall figure across the street, head tucked, shoulders hunched, plume of smoke spiraling up from his hand. My pulse accelerates as I press my forehead to the glass, trying to see if it's the same guy as before, but he turns the corner and I lose sight of him. Or, am I losing my grip on reality?

"Well, I hope you'll be there. I just said to your father, I see you more on television than I do in real life!" my mother cackles.

"Ha!" I exaggerate my laugh, switching to "Daughter Who May Get Day-Drunk After This Call."

"I know your work is important to you, honey." Her tone turns serious. "But family comes first. Just remember that, okay?"

As if I could ever forget.

12

Friday, June 21
Cassidy

I DROP WAFFLES INTO the toaster as the phone rings. "Oak Hill Police Dept." flashes up in the caller ID. I think I might throw up even though I've been expecting this call.

I spent the entire graduation ceremony freaking out about the police after Lexi told me they'd been to her house. I was half-prepared for them to handcuff me right there in the sweltering gym. Could you be arrested for lateness or even telling a small lie like I had? I didn't know, but it's hard not to panic when cops are going around asking questions about you.

The phone rings again. I can't ignore it. They'll just call back. I take a deep breath, hands and voice shaking. "Hello?"

"Cassidy? This is Officer Kinsley."

He doesn't need to introduce himself. His voice is tattooed in my brain.

"Um, yes, hi," I stammer.

"We need you to answer a few questions. Can you to come down to the station?"

Like I have a choice? "Um, okay, when?" I croak. Getting even these few words out feels impossible. How can I sit across from a cop—even if it's only Kyle's brother—and think straight?

"Sooner the better," he says.

"Sure, be right there."

I run up to my room, pull the burner phone from my dresser drawer, and call Chris. It rings a half dozen times before going to voicemail. I hang up without leaving a message. I want to call back, but he's been in his soundproof music studio a lot lately, working on songs for a television series. When I'd asked him to play a few for me, he said they weren't ready yet. I don't want to distract him or be that needy, whiny girlfriend you see in movies.

Because Lexi always watches Investigation Discovery and listens to all the true crime podcasts, I call her.

"Whatever you do, don't act nervous," she advises. "Be confident. Try not to sweat. Stuff an ice pack in your bra if you have to. And remember, you're not guilty of anything other than really bad judgment—oh, and serious lust. But those aren't crimes!"

"Should I be honest and tell them I was with Chris? You know I'm a terrible liar."

"Are you kidding?" Lexi shouts. "Seriously? That won't help anyone. All it's going to do is get you labeled a slut and Chris a pedophile. Just be cool." She paused. "Hey, I never asked, but why were you late? I mean, I know what you were doing— duh—but didn't you check the time or anything?"

I know she doesn't mean it as judgy as it sounds. Lexi fancies herself an amateur detective. I don't get into what Chris and I had done that left me panting, exhausted, wishing I never had to go. I tell her the truth.

"I fell asleep in the bed in the guest room, and when I woke up, Chris was gone," I say, getting that tingly feeling in my legs thinking about that afternoon. "He'd left me a note saying he'd taken his dog for a walk. After I got dressed, I couldn't find my backpack. Without it, I didn't have the keys to my car or the Barneses' house."

"Where was it?" Lexi asks.

"Chris stuck my bag in his hall closet 'cause he found Murphy trying to get into my stash of Clif Bars." I almost laugh at how dumb it sounds. "Chris thought he'd be back before I needed to leave. But he wasn't, and I wasted like ten minutes hunting for my stuff. Then I had to run to get my car 'cause I left my phone in it. Plus, I didn't want my mom to drive past and see it parked at the high school and freak out thinking it had broken down again."

"That's it? A dog sniffing for energy bars made you late?" Lexi snorts. "This is the type of shit that makes me a cat person."

* * *

When I get to the police station, Officer Kinsley is waiting for me. He shows me into a small windowless room and motions for me to sit down in a hard wooden chair.

"Be right back," he says.

I glance around. My eyes stop on the camera in the corner suspended from the ceiling. I hear Lexi's voice in my head. *Just be cool.*

When Officer Kinsley returns, he offers me a cup of water.

"No, thanks," I say. I'm sitting on my hands to stop them from shaking. I don't dare move.

"You holding up all right?" he asks.

"I'm okay, thanks," I lie. Aside from the day Billy disappeared, this is the furthest I've ever been from okay.

Detective Dubin walks in and sits on the edge of the table. He's wearing navy pants and a white shirt with coffee stains dotting a cuff. He looks harmless—like an uncle. Still, I wonder if I need an attorney, but that seems like admitting I've done something wrong. Mom's at work, and I didn't call to tell her I was coming here. And, it's not like we have the extra money.

"You do not need to lawyer up," Lexi insisted on the phone. "Do what I'm telling you. Trust me."

"Miss McLean, we're following up on every piece of information we have regarding the afternoon Billy Barnes disappeared." Detective Dubin rubs his wrinkled forehead as if he's tired of searching for information and coming up empty. "Help us out with something. You told us you left school and headed to the Barneses' house but arrived there late because you"—he skims through his notes—"got caught in the detour?"

"I needed to go to the pharmacy." I wait, hoping that would be enough. It isn't. In the silence, all I can think of is Lexi's advice.

"Mention anything to do with menstruation and men can't deal," she told me.

Even though it's majorly embarrassing, I follow it. "I got my period. At the picnic. I needed to buy tampons."

"Do you have a receipt?" Kyle's brother asks, unable to meet my eyes. If this weren't so serious, I'd laugh, because who saves a receipt from buying feminine hygiene products? I imagine Lexi saying, "Yeah, I stuck it in my period scrapbook. It's glued beside an empty box of Midol. Geez, Cass, get out of there. These cops are hopeless. Poor Billy."

"I never made it to the store because of the detour." I shrug. "I turned around and went to the Barneses' house. But the whole thing made me late." I pause. "Do you have any new information about Billy?"

Lexi told me not to ask because it might piss them off. The general feeling around Oak Hill is that they've done jack shit to find him. But I need to know.

"We're working every lead." Detective Dubin frowns. "Let me ask you, Ms. McLean, you've spent a lot of time in the Barneses' home. Is there anything that struck you as unusual? Within the family?"

I picture them. Mr. and Mrs. B. are rarely together. When Mr. Barnes is home, he looks annoyed, like he'd rather be anywhere else. But maybe that's what dads look like. Mine's God-knows-where, and Lexi's father chose to leave and not come back.

The times I've seen Evan, he's pretty unfriendly, treating the house as if it's his own personal Costco, leaving with bottled water, toilet paper, and as many snacks as he can carry. I remember an afternoon a few weeks ago when Mrs. B. was on a call, screaming at her house-flipping partner. But revealing these small, weird domestic observations would make me feel like a tattletale. Plus, I want to get out of here, so I shrug again and say, "I don't know. They seem like a regular family to me."

"Do you know Rose Finnerty?" Detective Dubin asks.

"Who?"

"The Barneses' au pair. Did your paths ever cross?"

"No. I mean, Mrs. Barnes said something about letting her go, and that it was a bad situation, but she didn't get into the details."

"Well, if you think of anything, you know where to find us." The detective stands and steps to the side so I can leave. "Thank you for your time, Ms. McLean."

As I walk out of the room, legs wobbly, I hear Kyle's brother. "She's a good kid. She went to the prom with my brother, and he's, you know, different. Shame she's mixed up in this."

I don't stick around for Detective Dubin's response.

* * *

Instead of going home, I go to Chris's. My heart races as I rush to his side door, hoping Phil isn't watching.

I knock and wait. If Chris is in the basement, he might not hear because of the soundproofing, so I pound again.

Seconds later, he appears. I'm right. He was in the basement. "Hey!" His blue eyes widen in surprise.

"Hey!" Even though I've just been semi-grilled by two cops, being near Chris makes me forget everything. And even if it only lasts a split second, it's enough. "Can I come in? I—"

"Sorry, now's not a good time. I'm about to hop on a call with my producer."

The air rushes out of my body like I've been punched in the stomach.

"Hey." He takes a longer look at me. "You're shaking, and it's what? Ninety degrees? Everything okay?"

"I had to go to the police station." I try to play it off like it's no big deal. "They had some questions about why I was late." I shift from foot to foot, fighting the urge to bite my nails.

"Shit, really?" He frowns. "They asked you about that? That's crazy. What did you tell them?"

"I said I had to run to the pharmacy and got stuck in that detour. They took some notes and let me go."

"Cool." He nods. "One sec." He pulls his phone from his pocket. "Hey, man, let me call you right back," he says, before focusing on me again. "Are you okay? That must've been majorly stressful."

"It was, but I'm better now." I smile.

"Cool." Chris nods. "Listen, sorry, I've got to get back to this guy." He holds up his phone.

"Maybe I can come back later?"

"Probably not a great idea." He pokes his head out and nods toward the Fosters' house. "Phil's been on his porch most of the morning. He's back with his binoculars again."

"I'll bring my sheet music. He'll think I have a lesson," I offer.

"He's probably figured out that I take summers off by now." He raises his eyebrows. "And what if I wanted you to stay longer than forty-five minutes?" The smile in Chris's voice makes my knees melt.

"So, what are you suggesting?" I ask, unable to stop grinning.

"Well—" he pauses. Just looking at him gives me goose bumps—the good kind. "There's this place, the Riverview Inn in Wallingford, about thirty minutes from here. Meet me there around three?"

"Okay," I nearly squeal. Maybe Lexi's right. Am I in too deep? Too into him? If someone had told me months ago that I'd be rushing off to meet a man in a hotel room, I'd have rolled my eyes like, "Yeah, right." But when it comes to Chris, I'm a different person. One without common sense, Lexi'd argue.

As if he can read my mind, Chris says, "I know it's weird, and I'm sorry. I wish we didn't have to sneak around. But Phil's kind of a wild card. If he says something to the wrong person, it would be bad for both of us."

"No. Right. Of course."

"You'll dig this place. I'll check in and wait for you at the bar."

"Sounds perfect," I say, grateful I won't spend the afternoon in an empty house wondering what the police will ask me next.

*　*　*

At home, I change into my most attractive underwear, grab the keys, switch off my phone in case Mom checks my location, and pray the Camry makes it there and back.

On the drive, I miss turns, ignoring the old GPS I've plugged into the cigarette lighter, wondering how often Chris goes to this inn. Did he take his wife? Another woman? Is that why Allison left? Is he seeing anyone else now? What does Chris see in *me*? I'm crazy about him, and he knows it. Is it an ego thing?

Questions spin inside my brain as I make multiple U-turns. But then I picture his eyes—the way he looks at me like he really sees me—and block out all my doubts.

He's waiting at the bar for me and lets out a low moan as I get closer. His scruffy face tickles my chin as we kiss. He tastes warm and wonderful, like whatever brown liquid was in the glass beside him.

In the room, I tell him all about the police interview, and then we do things that make me forget every detail.

The sun sets, turning the sky a cotton candy pink. The afternoon has gone too fast. I wish we could stay here forever. As Chris swings his legs over the side of the bed and grabs his jeans, I reach for his arm to tug him back down.

"Let's spend the night. Explore." I flick my eyes toward the bathroom, where a giant soaking tub waits. "I'll text my mom and tell her I'm staying at Lexi's. She'd never—"

"Sorry, I can't."

"Why not?" I pout.

"Murphy," Chris answers. "I'm sure he's drooling over his empty bowl right now—or trying to convince a neighbor to help him order takeout." He winks as he leans in and kisses me. "And I've got to get back to work. Songs for a series about a rowdy gang of leprechauns don't just write themselves." He zips his jeans. "And, hey, it's Friday night, don't you have any baby-sitting gigs?"

"No one will hire me because of Billy."

"Shit, I feel terrible. You were late because of me." Chris sits and sweeps the hair off my bare shoulder. "But, hey, I bet you'll be back in business in no time. People have short memories."

I usually think Chris is right about everything, but this time he's wrong. No one's forgetting about Billy or how I wasn't there for him. No amount of time is going to change that.

It's a scar I'll carry with me forever—until he's found.

13

Thursday, June 27
Rachel

I START MY DAYS the same way I end them, praying my son will come back to me and then calling Detective Dubin.

"We're working on it, Mrs. Barnes," he says. "Doing everything we can."

I bite my tongue not to scream, not to call him every vile name I can think of to unleash my fury and see if he's capable of anything other than his usual monotone. But as useless as he seems, and as much as I hate to admit it, I need his help.

"We'll be in touch as soon as we have something," is how he ends every call.

Something? They have nothing. No trace of Billy. No leads on Rose.

"In a situation like this, these nannies from other countries, they meet a guy, they overstay their visas, they find jobs off the books, then they disappear. On purpose. It can be years before it catches up with them."

These officers are out of their depth. They have no experience with a missing child case. How many times have I boasted to clients that Oak Hill is such a safe town, "The worst crimes range from jaywalking teens to kids shoplifting candy!" I'd insisted with a lighthearted chuckle.

This morning, desperate for answers, I asked Darcy for a favor.

"Can you find the medium from your Halloween party?" I couldn't meet her eyes. That party was seven years ago. I waited for a fleeting look of pity to cross my sister's face as she watched her only sibling devolve into a madwoman grasping at straws. Would Darcy even remember who I was talking about? More importantly, could she track down the mysterious woman who'd possessed the ability to peer into my future?

"I'm on it," Darcy said, pulling her phone from her back pocket, never wavering in her role as my protector and hero.

I'd gone to that Halloween party after a full day of showing homes to an indecisive couple. A high school language arts teacher, Darcy had a half dozen costumes on hand. Insisting that "real estate agent" was far too dull, she'd forced me into overalls and a straw hat. Looking like a drunk scarecrow, I spilled zombie punch into a coffee mug that read "I'm Silently Correcting Your Grammar" because I'd misplaced my glass. As I stood at the makeshift bar, a woman in black leather pants, a red headscarf, a ruffly white shirt, and dangling silver earrings appeared beside me. Was she a stylish pirate or funky fortune-teller?

As I handed her the ladle, a crisp, electric shock crackled between us, though the air was balmy for late October.

"Ouch!" I snatched my hand back and dropped the ladle in the bowl, causing the pale pink punch to splash up at us. "Yikes! Sorry."

Her gray-green eyes never left my face. I braced for her to say something bitchy but justified like, "Look what you did to my blouse!" but she just continued staring.

"Come," she said finally. "Sit with me."

I followed her past the fireplace where a pentagram of votive candles flickered. As we sat across from each other at a card table in the corner, the woman stretched out her arms. She had rings on nearly every finger. They made a gentle knock as she placed her palms up, a receiving gesture, they called it at the yoga studio where I'd started taking classes. I glanced at her hands. She nodded. I hesitated. I was about to tell her that while I respected my sister's life choices and adored her partner, Janet,

I liked men. Though I didn't know why; all they did was disappoint me. Hypnotized by her gaze, I didn't utter a syllable.

"Give me your hands," she commanded.

I obeyed and watched as she stared, then traced the barely visible lines on my palm.

"I see marriage in your future."

I laughed and shifted in my chair. "Did Darcy tell you to say that?" I'd just gotten out of a two-year relationship with a man I'd finally admitted would never love me as much as his job. Or his car. Or his gym membership. It had been three months since we'd broken up. I still wasn't over it.

"I mean, it's just starting to seem like I'm going to be alone forever," I continued. "Like, maybe I should get a parrot? Or a couple of cats?"

She didn't laugh, just studied my hands again.

"You will marry." She nodded, deep lines forming an eleven between her eyes. Then she looked up at me and her face relaxed to neutral. It was like someone had drawn the curtains closed behind her eyes.

"And then what?" I pleaded, the boozy punch making me bolder than usual. "You can't stop there! So I get married, and then what? Do I have children? What happens next?"

I'd become obsessed with the idea of the lifestyle I attempted to sell seven days a week. The perfect home with an open layout. A gourmet kitchen connecting to a stylish family room. A spacious, formal dining room for holidays. A mudroom where children's boots could dry on snowy afternoons. I wanted all of it.

I waited.

She sighed. "Let's just say, things are far from perfect."

I pulled my hands away. "You're not supposed to tell me that! It's Saturday night! This is a party!"

She shrugged. "I see what I see. What can I tell you?"

"Look again!" I begged, readjusting my palms atop hers. "Do I have a second marriage? A do-over? A better one, maybe?"

"Hey!" Darcy put her hand on my shoulder. "Help me pass out the Jell-O shots? They look like eyeballs. They probably taste like shit, but they're absolutely terrifying!"

"Okay," I agreed before turning back to the psychic. "Don't leave without telling me the rest!"

Of course, I didn't see her again.

The next day, through a blinding hangover, I'd asked Darcy, "So, who was the fortune-teller? Let me guess—a drama teacher from your school? She really had me going there for a bit."

"Madame Sonya? No, she's legit. Wasn't she amazing? Hiring her was Janet's idea. She read about her in the paper this summer. Apparently, she helped find an elderly man who'd walked out of his nursing home and disappeared. His family contacted Madame Sonya, and when she put on one of his hats, she said she could hear seagulls and screams that sounded like people on a roller coaster. His daughter knew where he was right away— Coney Island! How crazy is that?"

For months after that night, and with each new man I dated, I thought of Madame Sonya's words and how, when she held my hands over that rickety card table, a fake smoking cauldron bubbling behind her, she saw my future far more clearly than I did.

* * *

With the police coming up empty at every turn, I can't stop thinking about Madame Sonya—how right she'd been. Here I am, in the far-from-perfect marriage she predicted. She'd tracked down a man simply by wearing his hat. What if she could find Billy too?

She's agreed to come this afternoon. Ted would say I'm crazy for turning to the occult to find our child, but I have to do something. And he won't know. He's meeting Evan, who lost his latest bartending gig on the Upper West Side weeks ago, to look at less-expensive apartments. That gives me the window I need to sit with Sonya and hope she conjures a vision that will lead me to Billy.

She pulls up in a powder-blue Prius, wearing flip-flops, capri pants, and a Royal Caribbean T-shirt. Without her headscarf and earrings, she looks perfectly ordinary, like any random woman I'd pass in an aisle at Target. My heart sinks. I need her to be mystical, otherworldly. I pray that Darcy's punch all those years ago and my current desperation haven't caused me to overestimate her abilities.

She steps inside and squeezes my hand. "Take me to his room," she whispers.

I lead the way, Jeter, the cat, twisting between my ankles. Darcy follows behind us, staying close for emotional support and to help me remember everything later.

"May I?" Sonya asks.

"Please," I say and watch as she opens his closet and then his dresser drawers.

Her hands look naked without rings as they land on the Aaron Judge jersey Darcy gave Billy for his fifth birthday. Sonya turns the white garment around and upside down, the number 99 on the back transforming into 66. She stands very still, closes her eyes, and moves her hands up and down the shirt slowly as if she's soothing a wounded animal. I wait, mustering all my willpower not to disrupt her by demanding to know what, if anything, she senses.

Just when I can't stand it another second, her eyes fly open. "He's close," she says.

"Where?" I shout. "Where? Do you mean in Oak Hill? In New Jersey? Is he—Is he okay? Is he . . . alive?"

She nods, closing her eyes again. I want to crawl inside her skull, dive behind her pupils, see what she sees. I press my lips tight to not disrupt her concentration.

"He's scared." She pauses to scratch her arms. "The itch—it bothers him."

"Billy has eczema!" My voice shakes; my hands claw through my hair. "It flares up when he's anxious. Please!" I speak so quickly that spit flies out of my mouth. "Where is he? You have to help me. You're our only hope. Please!"

Darcy, who'd been standing in the doorway, crosses the room and sits on the bed, easing me down beside her. I want to bury my face in her shoulder and weep, the way I did when we were kids and our father would hurl his shaving kit into his suitcase, screaming, "This time it's for good, Doreen." But I can't take my eyes off Sonya. I hold Darcy's hand as we wait, the room silent except for the sound of the air conditioning sighing through the floor vents.

"Please, please," I whisper.

Sonya clutches the shirt again, eyes closed, head tilting from side to side, lips moving silently.

"Is he alone? Is he hurt? Does someone have him? Can you see where he is?" I ask quietly, afraid to break the spell.

"I'm sorry," she says, eyelids slowly opening. "It's not clear."
She inhales. "There's plenty of air, but it's damp, and there isn't
much light." She pauses. "Is there a cave in the area?"

"What? A cave?" I demand, willing her to see something
different—an address, coordinates, a direct route to my son. *A
cave?* "I don't think so. I don't know. I—I can find out," I ramble. "Is someone with him? Billy would never just wander off.
Can you see anyone else? Is there a man with a scar on his
cheek? A tattoo of a vine on his neck? A girl named Rose?
Please!"

"I'm sorry." Sonya shakes her head. "That's all."

"Any other details? Anything?" I double over, clutching my
stomach. This can't be it. There has to be more. "Please?" I beg.
"There must be something else." My hands clench into fists,
nails digging into my palms. I want to shake Sonya, knock
something loose in her mind, force her to envision a clue or
marker that leads to my son.

"That's all," she repeats, folding the jersey. "But I feel him.
He's close."

My hopes deflate like a bouncy castle after someone pulls
the plug.

How can she see certain things but not what we need? I
fight the urge to tell Darcy to block the door, to trap Sonya
until she gives us an exact location. My anger quickly settles
into sorrow. I let out a small cry, my chest puffing up and down
as Darcy rubs my shoulders, whispering, "Breathe."

"I'm sorry," Sonya repeats. "I wish I could give you more."

I walk her to her car, my heart and brain ricocheting
between hope and fear. Billy is close. But what difference does
it make if we still don't know where he is? He's scared, in danger. What if I never find him? And what if Sonya is just saying
what I want to hear? But she knows about Billy's "itchy patches,"
his name for the red, blistery bumps that sprout in the crooks of
his elbows.

Opening her car door, Sonya's gray-green eyes fix on my
hands as I tear at a hangnail. "If anything else comes to me, of
course, I'll be in touch."

"Thank you," I whisper. "Wait, what do I owe you?" I realize we never discussed her fee.

"Your sister took care of it." She looks me up and down, her gaze landing on my stomach. "Now you take care of yourself."

A shiver rockets up my spine. Sonya knows things; I'm sure of it. Her final words are all the proof I need.

*   *   *

After Sonya leaves, Darcy heads back home for the weekend to celebrate Janet's birthday. The house is exponentially emptier without her.

Through the window, I spot boys on bicycles, scooters, and skateboards—a summer evening in full swing. From the back, their height and brown hair make me believe for a second that one of them is my son. Beams from cell phone flashlights illuminate the growing darkness as parents or nannies trail behind, reminding me that no one feels safe in Oak Hill now.

I don't go outside during the day anymore, not even to sit on the porch and escape the stale, frigid air inside the house. News vans line the street. Reporters lurk, waiting for me, ready to shout their awful questions: "What do you think happened to your son, Mrs. Barnes?" "Rachel! Do you blame the babysitter?" "What would you say to Billy if he could hear you now?"

At first, I answered them all, hoping it would make a difference. Maybe Billy would hear my voice and know that I'd never stop searching for him. He'd sense my anguish and find a way to break free, to get home. I issued desperate pleas to the public to help find my boy. It did nothing.

These journalists aren't here to be useful. They're here for ratings, to pander to Internet trolls. In the middle of the night, I read their comments:

"I suspect the parents."
"That mother doesn't seem upset enough to me."
"It's not the babysitter's fault. If you don't want to raise your own kids, don't have any!"

It only got worse after everything with Ronnie. The headline, *Crazed Mom of Missing Boy Confronts Beloved Crossing Guard in Sidewalk Showdown,* burned into my brain. I no longer read the news or turn on the television. I simply try to breathe without breaking.

The days are impossibly long. The nights are worse.

While Ted sleeps, I walk miles around Oak Hill, sick to my stomach, looking for anything that might lead me to Billy.

Tonight, I wander in search of the cave Madame Sonya mentioned, though I don't know of any in all of Oak Hill. Maybe it's part of a street name? Could it be something kids built out of fallen branches? I don't know where to begin but I have to try.

I end up at Oak Hill Elementary School's playground. The last place he was. I slump into one of the belt swings, its cool, hard plastic sending a chill through me. Moths beat their wings against a streetlight as my mind drifts back to the day last August when we'd visited the school for orientation.

Billy had been nervous and excited about starting kinder-garten. After we met his teacher and learned about book reports and field trips, we walked out hand-in-hand, greeted by giggles and whoops from kids chasing one another around the jungle gym. Billy began pulling me in that direction.

"Can I go to the playground? Please? Can I?"

"Not today. You know I have things to do this afternoon." I had an appointment for a blowout and makeup ahead of my meeting with the photographer who'd take my new headshot for my marketing materials. "You'll be back here in a couple of weeks."

"I know, but please! Just five minutes! Please, Mommy?"

Why hadn't I just said, "Okay, sure, sweetheart. Go! Meet your new classmates. Have fun!"

If I'd agreed that day nearly a year ago, would it have helped him make friends? And if it had, would he have been on his way to a playdate instead of walking home alone that Thursday afternoon two weeks ago?

Ted always says I spoil Billy, but the images that flood my mind show me all the ways I've disappointed him. I sit until the narrow swing makes my hips ache and the vacant jungle gym causes his sweet, "Please, Mommy?" to echo inside my head.

My phone pings. A text appears beneath the time: 12:28 AM.

"How about now?" Derek. Again.

"I'm not ready to have this conversation." I type.

"Call me. Please."

It isn't fair of me to continue ignoring him, but I can't deal with our situation. Not on top of everything else.

I turn off my phone and head home. Billy's absence is more acute as I walk the path he'd traveled each day. A rustling in the underbrush of hydrangea stops me. A raccoon and I lock eyes before it scurries off. As I freeze there on the corner, catching my breath, I look up at a smallish house that recently sold for well above list price. It's an ideal starter home with impeccable landscaping. The moonlight hits something shiny under the eave near the garage—a camera. Detective Dubin told me they've spoken with all the homeowners in the neighborhood who had any kind of surveillance system.

One resident came forward with footage that showed herds of kids walking home the sunny afternoon Billy disappeared. I'd gone to the station and watched a half dozen groups pass before my child came into view. Seeing him there, animated, swinging his keychain, backpack strapped to his shoulders, alone, vulnerable, oblivious to whatever came next, gutted me.

"So now we know that your son made it as far as the three hundred block of Cherry Lane, but what happened after that?" Officer Kinsley had asked, as if *I* should be providing *him* with answers. "Did he get as far as the corner where Cherry Lane intersects with Woods End or Forest Trail? We're not sure."

Standing at the corner of Forest Trail and Cherry Lane, I don't remember the police offering any information about this house with the camera. I don't care that it's after one in the morning—I turn my phone back on, call Detective Dubin, and leave a rambling message.

I want to ring the doorbell to ask the homeowner if I can come in and see any footage the camera might have captured.

As I move toward the door, a lamppost flicks on at the edge of the lawn across the street. The whispers probably already circulating about Rachel Barnes slipping toward insanity will only grow louder if I don't leave now.

I step back onto the sidewalk. I haven't found a cave, but this, this camera, is more than I had before. The thought that it might reveal something is what I cling to as I turn and head home.

*   *   *

Detective Dubin returns my call twelve hours later.

"We've had trouble contacting that homeowner," he admits. "I've put Officer Kinsley on it. But, Mrs. Barnes, with all due respect, we think it's best if you leave the investigating to us. We know you're anxious, of course, but let us do our jobs."

His tone makes every nerve in my body vibrate with rage.

"With all due respect, if you did your job, maybe I wouldn't have to!" I hang up, wishing I had a rotary phone so I could experience the pathetic thrill of slamming down the receiver.

Now I wait. Helpless. Useless. Carrying my cell phone and the house phone with me from room to room. I answer every call, terrified of what I might be told, and now, of what I might say as my sorrow transforms into fury.

My cell phone pings in my hand.

Another text from Derek. "I'm around, Ray. Let's talk. You can't avoid me forever."

He's right. We need to have a conversation. But I don't know what to say—or what I want to hear. I'd like to believe that neither of us intended for our relationship to evolve the way it did, but that would be a lie.

Derek renovated our kitchen three years ago. When I went back to work last fall, I asked him if he'd help a few of my clients with repairs and improvements before I listed their homes. We'd worked so well together that we decided to invest in a fixer-upper, hoping to flip it quickly for a nice profit. I'd planned to use my share as a springboard to leave Ted. Billy and I could make a fresh start.

As we picked out finishes, hardware, and paint colors, Derek, single and childless, made me laugh with his dating horror stories. Over time, I began to wonder what it would be like to go home to him instead of Ted.

In February, when Derek asked if I wanted to join him in Colorado at a home improvement and remodeling expo, I knew he was inviting me as more than an investment partner and the agent who threw business his way. As I packed, I swapped practical flannel pajamas for silk lingerie I hadn't worn in years, imagining him undressing me in a hotel room far from Oak Hill.

I didn't expect to come home with a souvenir. Inside the house on Maple Crest Drive, amid the chipped pink-and-black tiled bathroom we hadn't gutted yet, I took the test. When I showed Derek the stick, the word "pregnant" staring back, bold as a billboard, he looked older, tired, more concerned than when we discovered mold behind a kitchen wall.

"You know how I feel about you, Ray," he'd said.

Aside from Darcy, Derek was the only person who called me "Ray," and it made me believe that he'd protect me as my sister always had.

"But if I'd wanted a family, I'd have had one by now," he'd continued. "I'm planning to retire in the next ten years, not coach Little League."

Perched on the thin lip of an old clawfoot tub I was determined to salvage, I'd groaned, "I know, I know," through my hands, hoping to hide my disappointment.

Billy was so gentle and kind with toddlers and preschoolers in the neighborhood. I'd always wanted him to have a younger brother or sister, believing it would boost his confidence. But Ted had taken care of that.

Shortly after Billy turned three, he began having night terrors. He'd awaken, inconsolable at 1 or 2 AM. Ted and I barely slept for months. One crisp, fall Saturday during that stretch, we decided to go pumpkin picking. Heading west on our way to the patch, the sun was a brilliant ball of orange. I'd reached for the spare pair of sunglasses I kept in Ted's car's glove box and found a sheet of paper with the credit card receipt stapled to its corner. Ted glanced over and saw me pull out the brochure that was tucked beneath the paper.

"That's just—I wanted to talk to you about—"

My brain had struggled to process the words: "Answers to Common Questions Following Your . . ."

"You got a vasectomy? Three weeks ago?" My voice rose sharply with each word.

"Shh!" Ted hissed.

"What's a vascatomommy?" Billy asked from the back seat.

"You do not get to 'shh!' me!" I'd turned sideways in my seat so I could face Ted, the seatbelt cutting into my neck. "You did this without even talking to me?"

He laughed, a nasty cackle that filled the car. "You're in no position to talk." His dark eyes shifted to the rearview mirror and settled on Billy. "I don't remember you consulting me four years ago."

His words hit me like a punch in the stomach. "I'm forty, Ted! What if I wanted . . ." I didn't finish the sentence. It was clear that what I wanted was irrelevant.

For months after that, we lived like roommates, the seeds of leaving him taking root in my mind.

*   *   *

When I found out that I was pregnant two months ago, after the shock wore off, there was a sweetness there, like opening a window to an entirely different view.

Still, as much as I'd wished for Billy to be a big brother, I'd never meant for it to happen like this. Continuing with this pregnancy meant ending my marriage. Would Billy and I stay in Oak Hill? I could count the single moms I knew in town on one hand. Most were treated as defective, as if their personal shortcomings had driven their spouses to seek better options.

And how many times had Darcy joked, "Some people say their parents screwed them up by getting divorced. I'd say ours messed us up by staying together."

Would Billy be better off growing up in a home with both his parents or in one free of hostility?

Ending this pregnancy meant Billy would never be a big brother. He deserved a sibling closer to his age, nicer to him than Evan was. How would I have survived without my sister?

Darcy. I'd planned to tell her about the pregnancy before Billy disappeared. Now seven weeks have passed since I took the test, and I'm no closer to knowing what to do.

I've seen Derek once since Billy vanished. He came by one night last week.

Each time the doorbell rings, my heart careens between hope and fear, never knowing if the person on the other side has come to tell us Billy is safe or to deliver news that will destroy me completely. Darcy typically answers while I brace, hiding in the kitchen, gripping the marble island until my fingers cramp.

That night, Darcy said, "I'll get it," and squeezed my shoulder for support before heading to the door.

"Hi." Hearing Derek's deep voice filled me with longing and sadness. "I need to speak with Rachel."

"And you are?" Darcy asked.

"Derek, her . . ." I waited to hear how he'd describe himself, "contractor. We're working on a project together."

Darcy's tone softened. "Ah. Want to come in?"

"No, thanks, I'll wait here."

Darcy walked into the kitchen and raised her eyebrows. "*Derek* wants to talk to you."

With broad shoulders and strong hands, Derek was ruggedly handsome. Did Darcy suspect that we might be more than business partners? He had a man-who-can-fix-anything charm. But he couldn't fix this.

As I passed the entryway mirror, I saw my reflection. When was the last time I'd showered, put on makeup, run a brush through my hair? I looked feral compared to my former self, with my stylish clothes and standing Friday afternoon manicure appointment.

I stepped onto the porch and pulled the door closed behind me. He sucked in his breath when he saw me.

"Ray, I'm so sorry." He shook his head and looked off to the side like an actor embarrassed at forgetting his next line. "I don't know what to say except that whatever you decide, with . . . you know, everything, you have my full support."

"Thanks." I nodded, wondering what he meant by that vague offer. As shame spread over me, I couldn't meet his eyes. Was he wondering the same thing I was? *How could I be the mother to a second child when I couldn't even protect my first?*

* * *

I stare at Derek's text now, which reads, "You can't avoid me forever." I'll respond and ask him to meet for coffee a few towns away— far from my neighbors' prying eyes.

I begin typing when the phone pulses. An Oak Hill number I don't recognize flashes up. Probably a credit card scammer or a dentist's office confirming an appointment I've forgotten. Still, the possibility that it might be about Billy makes me answer.

"Rachel?" The woman's voice is tentative.

"Yes?"

"It's Frances. Frances Lewis."

I know the name but can't recall how.

When I say nothing, she continues, "You helped us buy our home. The updated ranch on Hickory Knoll Drive?"

"Oh, yes, of course." Her face, filled with concern as I ran out of the attorney's office after Cassidy's call, pops into my mind. I wait for her to say something about Billy—how sorry she is to hear the news, to ask how she can help.

But instead, she says, "Jack wanted me to call you. You know how we had all that rain last week? Well, there's some water in our basement. And Jack asked—and I agree—isn't that something the home inspector should've caught? I'm calling because you recommended him, and, well, I guess we're wondering what you can do about it?"

"What *I* can do about it?" I'm standing in the kitchen, pressing my head against the fridge, hoping the cold stainless steel will slow the onset of a migraine.

"Right, I mean, it just seems like maybe he should've checked the sump pump or recommended that the former owner install French drains. Something?" She sighs as if annoyed by the effort of explaining the situation to me.

I should hang up, pretend the call dropped. It's terrible timing, of course, made worse by her entitlement. But it's also years of demanding clients who expect me to corral unruly dogs before an open house, or explain why my list price doesn't match their Zestimate. All of it launches me into the wall I've been speeding toward for months.

"Have you seen the flyers around town about the missing child?" I ask through gritted teeth.

"Yes, I did! What an awful shock."

"That's my son." I listen, waiting to hear the swift gulp of air that confirms I'm living a nightmare.

"Oh Rachel, I'm so sorry I had no id—"

I should end the call here, with her feeling deep remorse for bothering me at the worst moment of my life, but I can't stop myself. A demon spawned from fifteen days of fear rises up inside me and refuses to stay silent.

"My son is missing," I growl. "So when you call to tell me that your shithole of an unfinished basement is damp and you want to know what I intend to do about it, my first thought is fuck you, Frances! Fuck you!"

I hurl the phone at the couch. It bounces off a throw pillow, the embroidered words *Thankful. Grateful. Blessed* mocking me.

Real estate careers are built on referrals. Now my business will crash and burn just like every other aspect of my life. I don't care. None of it matters except my son.

*   *   *

I'm resting on Billy's bed, idly stroking Jeter's soft black fur when the doorbell rings. Darcy isn't here to answer it. Adrenaline rushes through me. Peering out the window that faces the street, I see a police car parked beside the curb. An anxious buzz hums in my ears as I wobble down the stairs, knees weak.

I open the door. Detective Dubin and Officer Kinsley step inside. I hold my breath.

"So, bad news." Officer Kinsley shifts from foot to foot. I clutch my stomach, certain I'm going to be sick. "Oh, not bad news like that." He waves his hand like he's swatting at a fly. "The camera you saw? You were right. It could've picked something up, but the new owners didn't have Wi-Fi yet. They only moved in June twelfth. So, basically, we don't know any more than we did before. But the good news is it's all set now. The Wi-Fi, I mean."

Detective Dubin, wearing his out of style and out of season tweed blazer, shakes his head, acknowledging that this "good news" is irrelevant. My shoulders slump. We've hit yet another dead end. I look at my feet, bare, filthy, calloused, and aching from walking miles in search of my son. I nod and wait for these men to give me their usual speech about investigating every lead, but they don't move.

"Mrs. Barnes," the detective says, "there's something I'd like you to look at with me. Is your computer nearby?"

"Of course." I walk toward the kitchen where my laptop rests on the island.

"Can you open Instagram?" he asks. "And go to your posts?"

I scroll past photos of lunches I've ordered at local restaurants, flowers blooming in backyards of the homes I've sold, a few aspirational breakfast nooks, and birthday cakes, when he says, "Stop! That's the one."

His thick finger lands on a shot of Billy, his back to the camera, wearing a yellow rain slicker, holding a Yankees umbrella.

"Can you read the caption aloud, Mrs. Barnes?" Officer Kinsley asks.

I clear my throat. "This is 5! Look at my big boy! Walking to kindergarten @OakHillElementary all by himself! Yay, Billy!" I look up at them. "And?"

I wait. Has someone left a comment I'd missed? A bunch of moms use the app to share recipes, vacation photos, first day of school and holiday pics. For months last summer, it seemed like everyone we knew got a puppy. Billy loved to scroll through, leaving hearts and thumbs-up emojis on posts and videos.

"Your account isn't private, Mrs. Barnes, did you know that? Anyone can see that your young son walked to school—and precisely which school—alone." Detective Dubin's tone isn't shaming yet my face burns as if I've been slapped. He pauses, allowing the words to sink in, gnaw their way through my skin. I didn't think I could feel any worse, but implying I've given predators a road map to Billy leaves me reeling. I bury my face in my hands, shame and all the ways I've failed my son leaving me nauseous and light-headed.

"Mrs. Barnes, we want you to look through your followers," Officer Kinsley says. "Is there anyone here you don't know? Anyone new who followed you within the last few weeks or months? Again, can you think of anyone who has a reason to want to hurt you or your family?"

"I told you about Rose, but—"

"We're still looking into that," Officer Kinsley interrupts. "The boyfriend and his roommates said they haven't seen her in weeks. Cops who interviewed them found some drug paraphernalia, but no sign a child was there. I talked to her family and they're not concerned. She checks in with them every few weeks. They said they'll reach out when they hear from her next."

These cops don't believe she's involved, not really. Audrey, Kelli's au pair, confirmed Rose was in town the afternoon Billy disappeared, but said she left before three in the afternoon. That doesn't mean she left Oak Hill, I pointed out—not that it mattered.

With each day that passes, I feel their eyes turning to me, blaming me for Billy's disappearance. That's why they're here now—to show me how my social media use put my son in danger.

Detective Dubin nods as I click "followers." I scan the list—moms from playgroups, neighbors, interior designers, landscape architects. Officer Kinsley's breath on my neck as he peers over my shoulder makes my skin crawl.

"Amazing how much people are willing to share these days," Detective Dubin scoffs.

I tune him out as my eyes lock onto one face in the "suggested for you" section. Baseball cap backward, a shot glass in one hand, middle finger of the other raised high to the camera.

Evan Barnes.

I stop scrolling and stare as a memory forms in my mind. Back in May, I'd been sitting at the island reviewing a home inspection report when Billy walked into the kitchen, holding a clear plastic bag. At first glance, the assortment of bright colors made me think he'd found some LEGO pieces.

"Is this candy?" Billy asked, his pupils expanding. "Can I have some? I ate all my kale."

"Let me see that, sweetheart." I held out my hand, heart rate quickening.

Inside were a dozen small sandwich baggies half-filled with pills. My face started to tingle. "Where did you find these?" I don't know why I bothered to ask. I knew the answer.

"Evan's closet." Cheeks flushed, Billy avoided my eyes. "I wanted to try on his catcher's mitt, and then I found those." He looked up, hopeful again. "So, can I have some? Do they taste like jelly beans? Or Skittles?"

The seal appeared to be intact. Still, I had to ask. "You didn't take any, did you?" I kept my voice calm, knowing that if I seemed frantic, Billy might be tempted to lie.

"No, I didn't. I promise!"

My relief was fleeting, replaced by rage. "Well, these aren't candy. They're medicine, and they're not for kids, okay?" I explained, causing his shoulders to droop. "But you can have a fruit pop if you'd like," I added to stop him from asking any questions.

I watched him skip toward the freezer, praying he'd told me the truth, thanking my lucky stars that I had a child who asked permission before gobbling down anything he got his hands on. What if he'd swallowed a fistful? The thought made me murderous.

"Ted!" I yelled, turning the bag over in my hands, watching the pinks, blues, whites, and reds swirl together like crystals inside a kaleidoscope. "Ted!"

"What? What is it?" He appeared in the kitchen doorway, clearly irritated that I'd interrupted the post-dinner nap he took nightly in front of the television. With Rose gone and no replacement, Ted was supposed to be playing with Billy until bedtime. If he'd been interacting with our child—building LEGO sets, working on a puzzle—Billy wouldn't have been in Evan's room. But that wasn't even the point. Evan had put my son in danger. It was one more confirmation that I needed to leave, get Billy out of this environment as soon as I could.

I rose from the stool, legs locked as I stood my ground, and thrust the drugs at Ted.

"Billy found these in Evan's closet!" My voice cracked, thinking about how narrowly we'd avoided a tragedy.

"Rachel, Rachel, calm down—"

"Do not tell me to calm down!" I hissed. "Either you talk to Evan and tell him to get his shit together, or I'm calling the police!"

"Rachel—"

"I mean it, Ted. You can't ignore his problems any longer. Deal with this!"

Ted summoned Evan from the city. He arrived an hour later, grudgingly, as if we'd asked him to reshingle the roof.

"What's up?" Evan sauntered into the kitchen, opening the pantry, then the fridge, before grabbing an apple from the fruit bowl and studying it for imperfections.

Ted had hidden the stash in a high cabinet behind the pasta maker we'd been given as a wedding gift but never used. He tossed the bag on the island, pills shining beneath the pendant lights.

"What the fuck, Rachel?" Evan spat, his bloodshot eyes narrowed and fixed on me.

"You do not speak to me like that in my home," I said, trying not to show how irritated I was, how anxious I felt every time we were forced together.

"Your home? Yeah right," he laughed. "How about you stay out of my fucking room?"

"Rachel didn't go in your room," Ted said.

I waited, holding my breath, hoping he'd stop and not say the thing that would only make this worse. But he continued, "Billy found them. He thought they were candy."

I watched, expecting to see something human in Evan's face—surprise, shame, remorse. All I saw was hate.

"How do you know she didn't plant them?" Evan pointed at me, shifting from foot to foot. "You've always hated me, Rachel, admit it!"

"That's not—" I started.

"Don't be ridiculous," Ted interrupted.

Evan reached for the bag, but Ted was faster, snatching it first.

"They're mine," Evan growled. "I want them back."

"I bought you a car; I pay your rent," Ted's voice rose so sharply, I worried that he'd wake Billy. "Your amateur drug-dealing days are over. And if I catch you with this shit again, that's it, you're cut off."

Evan let out a self-righteous snort. Ted leaned forward, and, for a moment, I thought he might slap the arrogant smirk off his son's face. Instead, my husband walked out of the room, leaving me alone with the monster he created.

"Whatever," Evan shrugged. He took a bite of the apple. The crunch sounded like a bone snapping in the silent kitchen. Then, he smiled again, a grin that kept me awake for weeks. "You mess with what's mine, Rachel, I'll mess with what's yours. Remember that."

*   *   *

I've tried not to think about that night, but lately, when I find myself staring at the clock on the kitchen wall at 3 AM, haunted by thoughts of one horrific scenario after another, Evan has crossed my mind.

In these visions, my stepson never blinks when he says, "I'll mess with what's yours," his teeth sharpened to points, licking his lips, smug as a wolf after a kill.

"That's Billy's brother, right?" Officer Kinsley asks, pointing at the profile pic.

"Half brother," I correct him.

"Hmm," Detective Dubin muses.

"What?"

"It's interesting you make that distinction," he says. "They don't get along?"

"Billy adores Evan, but, unfortunately, Evan has never reciprocated. Since Billy's been gone, Evan hasn't even come home. Not to help hang flyers, or join in the search, or just to be here with us. That's odd, right?"

I choose my words and tone carefully, calculating the events they may set in motion. I picture Ted's face when he said, "Rachel, calm down," and Evan's sinister smirk as his father left the room. Just like with Frances Lewis, my reaction is primal. "Fuck you, Ted. Fuck you, Evan."

"Officer Kinsley interviewed your stepson by phone. He said he was working, bartending, the afternoon Billy disappeared. You confirmed that, right, Dan?"

"Actually, I'm still waiting to hear back. I got in touch with a waiter who said the manager who handles the time sheets is on his honeymoon, but he'll call when he's back from Turks and Cacao. Or, is it Caicos? Wait, what's cacao again?"

Detective Dubin presses his lips together until they form a thin flat line as I reach for the edge of the marble island to steady myself.

"Evan lost that job a month ago," I say, mind reeling. "He lied to you."

"We'll follow up this afternoon, Mrs. Barnes," the detective says. "C'mon, Dan. We'll show ourselves out."

I sink onto a stool as the picture in my head shifts. This time it's Evan who does the talking, staring right through me, mouth twisted in that menacing grin, whispering, "Fuck you, Rachel. Fuck. You!"

14

Sunday, June 30
Allison

VIV RETURNS FROM Sedona tonight. She's been stuck there longer than expected. The elderly actor playing her husband had a heart attack, and they had trouble finding a replacement on short notice. She's been complaining about spa food, so I'm making her a homemade "welcome back" risotto.

Walking into the tiny market around the corner from her apartment reminds me of one thing I miss about Oak Hill—wide grocery store aisles. Here, shoppers have to turn sideways to shimmy past one another and practically lift their baskets overhead to get by.

I circle the produce area, hunting for leeks and mushrooms, when I spot a small boy in a stroller wiggling his way out of the straps that restrain him.

"Don't even think about it!" his mother commands, slipping her hands under his armpits and settling him into place. She rolls her eyes at me as if to say, "Motherhood's a lot, isn't it?"

I fake a smile as she goes back to inspecting green beans with one hand, ruffling the child's soft curls with the other. The gesture makes my heart hurt. I turn away and almost knock over a gourmet olive display, sending my thoughts sliding back to one of my weakest moments in Oak Hill.

I'd just returned from shooting a pilot for a series that never got picked up. Chris and I had been apart for weeks—another month we could have been trying for a baby wasted. We were going to make dinner together, but the fridge was empty. I went to the market and wandered the aisles, still unfamiliar with the layout. I roamed in search of balsamic vinegar, passing a couple of women complaining about the snowy forecast. Then I saw her—a baby girl in a pink fleece snowsuit, little ears on the hood. Her car seat rested inside the cart. I stood in awe, admiring her big, dark eyes and full cheeks as she babbled and sucked her small fists. Before I knew what I was doing, my fingers were curled around the cart's handle and I was pushing it forward, my basket banging against my hip. A muzak version of Avril Lavigne's "Complicated" played loudly overhead, but I barely heard it over the thumping of my pulse in my ears. In slow motion, I wheeled this child, who smelled like peaches, past jarred artichokes and canned chickpeas. The Exit sign loomed, its red "X" growing fuzzy. I was light-headed, sweating inside my winter coat. The baby smiled at me, her feet kicking like tiny pinball flippers as a hand clamped my shoulder and spun me around.

"What do you think—"

My face burned every shade of fuchsia as I panicked: *My God, what was I doing? How would I explain this? What could I say?*

"Oh, it's you!" The woman's eyes widened as she pulled her hand away. She recognized me, and I felt the power shift. "I'm sorry, was she—the cart—in your way?"

"It's fine, really." I nodded and reached for a jar of olives I'd never use.

"I shouldn't have left her there clogging the aisle, but it's so quiet here today, and I bumped into my neighbor."

"No worries." I smiled, heart fluttering. "She's beautiful." I nodded toward the little girl.

The woman leaned closer, ignoring her daughter. "I just loved you in that show about those college kids. I read there might be a reunion special. Is it true?"

"Fingers crossed!" I gave her arm a squeeze and moved toward the checkout area, legs weak.

I arrived home shaking, without half the ingredients I was supposed to buy.

"What happened?" Chris had asked as soon as he saw my face.

I told him I'd nearly taken someone else's child. He held me as I wept into his shoulder.

When I'd finally stopped sobbing, Chris's expression changed from sympathetic to serious. "This isn't Chapsticks and training bras, Al."

I'd nodded. When we'd first gotten together, Chris had told me about his arrests and I'd confessed to going through a shoplifting phase during high school. I viewed it as a common deviance, almost a rite of passage in those rebellious teen years. I'd gotten caught a few times and had to flirt with pervy mall cops so they wouldn't call the police.

But Chris was right. This was nothing like that.

"I don't know what happened." I'd started crying again. "I slipped into some crazy autopilot." I shook my head. "I wanted that baby to be mine."

"We'll have our own someday, Al." Chris's palms cupped my face. "Give it time."

I'd given it time. Where had it gotten me? Back where I started, wandering a grocery store admiring children who don't belong to me, looking for things I never seem to find.

15

Thursday, July 4
Cassidy

M Y PHONE VIBRATES against the nightstand. I roll over, hit the snooze button, and squint as the sun peeks in from behind the blinds. For the first time in three weeks, my eyes aren't burning. I slept through the night. The whole night. A long, dreamless, drool-on-my-pillow, sand-in-the-corners-of-my-eyes sleep.

It takes me a few seconds to figure out what day it is and why I set the alarm. July 4. 7:50 AM. I'm supposed to meet Lexi at the gazebo at 8:30 to run the Firecracker 5K. We signed up months ago, part of a tradition we started the summer before our freshman year because Lexi had a crush on a boy on Oak Hill High's cross-country track team. Nothing ever came of it, but we liked the T-shirts we got for entering.

When everything happened with Billy, I told Lexi I was out. No way was I putting myself in the middle of town, where hundreds of people could whisper about me, their side-eye anything but subtle, just so we could get some stupid T-shirts.

But things have changed. I'm no longer Oak Hill's pariah. Even though Billy's still missing, the focus has shifted away from me and toward Evan Barnes. I got a Snapchat from Lexi two nights ago.

"Up?" was all she wrote.

"Of course." It was one in the morning, and, like most nights, I couldn't sleep. "What's up?"

My phone pinged. A text. A video.

"??" I sent back as FaceTime flashed. "Hey!" I whispered, rushing into my closet so I wouldn't wake Mom, even though I doubted she could hear anything over the droning of our hulking, old window air conditioners. "I just got your text. What is it?"

"Evan Barnes. Check it out. Now! Then call me back." She hung up before I could say anything.

I pressed play. Evan's angry face filled the screen.

"Guess where I've been all night? Answering questions at a fucking police station!" He stopped and jerked his thumb toward the red-brick building behind him. He was in Oak Hill. I recognized the cafe's awning as he strutted down Main Street with his usual dickhead swagger.

"Why?" He brought the phone to his face for a close-up. "Because my little brother is missing. And the crazy bitch my father married after my mom died made the cops think I have something to do with it. Me!" He laughed and threw his head back. For a moment, his face was swallowed by the darkness before it reappeared, unsmiling. "Like I'd hurt a kid? My own flesh and blood? That's messed up! You want to know who the real monster is? It's you, Rachel. Yeah, so maybe I lied about where I was. And maybe I spent my rent money on some killer bud and was high as fuck playing bongos in Washington Square Park when Billy went missing. You think I'm a total loser, Rachel. I get it. And maybe you're right. But that doesn't make me a kidnapper. And you're not exactly perfect. Not by a fucking mile—"

The video stopped, interrupted by Lexi's FaceTime call.

"Did you watch? Holy shit, right?"

"Jesus," I whispered. "What the—"

"I'd say the Barnes family is in for one awkward-ass Thanksgiving."

"No kidding." Maybe because it was late and weeks had passed since I'd slept for more than an hour or two at a time, my brain couldn't process it all. "This is so—Why does Mrs. B.

think Evan would take Billy? And why are you watching Evan Barnes's Insta stories?"

"He sent me a follow request after I babysat that time you had a swim meet or something. He stopped by to drop off his laundry and hunt around for cash. It was easier to accept and follow back than ignore him."

"You never told me."

"I didn't really think about it. And what? Am I not allowed to have secrets? That's hilarious coming from you, Miss Sneaks-Off-to-Hotels-With-Her-Piano-Teacher."

She'd groaned when I told her about the afternoon Chris and I spent at the Riverview Inn. I couldn't help it. It had felt so excitingly adult, like I was in a movie.

"You know he's going to break your heart, right?" she'd said. I chalked it up to jealousy.

"Seriously, why would Mrs. B. suspect Evan?" I asked. "He's a dick for sure, but would he abduct his own brother?"

As I waited to hear Lexi's answer, I remembered an after-noon last spring. Billy and I were sitting on the porch when he spotted a rabbit under a lilac bush. Mrs. B. had left rice puffs for Billy's snack, but instead of eating them, he'd lined them up, hoping the bunny would sniff them out and hop over. Billy started on the grass then worked his way toward the porch, leaving a puff every inch. I didn't have the heart to tell him those things were so flavorless, even a starving grizzly bear wouldn't touch them.

Evan pulled up in the Jeep his dad bought him for gradua-tion, music blasting.

"Evan!" Billy had jumped up and down. "I'm making a trail so the rabbit finds me and Cassidy! Like Hansel and Gretel!"

Evan stared at me and smirked as he crunched his way up the walk.

"No! Watch out! Stop!" Billy yelled. "You're messing it up! Stop!"

"Oh, sorry, buddy. I didn't see those there." Evan ground the heel of his Vans into the concrete, and then leaped past us, taking the porch steps two at a time.

Remembering Billy's sad, scrunched-up face broke my heart all over again.

"That dude's so sketchy," Lexi continued. "He's capable of anything."

"That's insane." The closet had gotten so hot I couldn't breathe. I crawled back into bed, dizzy.

I was about to tell Lexi I'd call her in the morning when she said, "But this is good news. For you, I mean."

"How?"

"If Evan has Billy, he probably picked him up on his walk home. It wouldn't have mattered when you got to the house. This was premeditated."

I said nothing, just stared at the ceiling, trying to force her theory to make sense.

Lexi sighed. "Are you even listening? What I'm saying is that you can stop beating yourself up. There's nothing you could've done to stop Evan. Plus, Billy's probably safe. Evan's douchey, and a loser—his words—but that's all."

"But he says he doesn't have Billy."

"Of course he's going to say that! He lied to the cops, remember?"

"That doesn't mean he's guilty. *I* lied to the cops, remember?"

"If you were innocent, would you make that video? He's guilty of something! You can bet on that."

*   *   *

I don't know how many people saw his Insta story, but over the past two days word of Evan Barnes's questioning has spread quick and ugly, like weeds through a garden. He's the new talk of Oak Hill. The mood has lifted as Billy's disappearance has been downgraded to a domestic dispute: "Troubles within the family." Everybody loves this explanation because, while it's terrible, it also means there was never a real predator in Oak Hill. And I'm not a negligent, irresponsible teen. Now I'm "poor Cassidy," just a girl caught in the middle of unexpected local drama. I'm ashamed at the relief I feel.

My alarm buzzes again. If Chris were running the 5K, it would be easier to get out of bed. But I promised Lexi I'd be there.

I throw back the sheet, get dressed, and hurry downstairs. Mom's in the kitchen, sipping coffee and rolling out pie crusts.

"Hey!" she says. "I was just about to check on you!"

As I walk toward the fridge, she blocks my path by holding out the rolling pin, and I stop so she can kiss me on the forehead.

"I don't know what your plans are, but the mayor is honoring Phil tonight before the fireworks start. I thought it would be nice if we were there, you know—front and center—to support him and Mary Alice."

My mind shifts to Chris. Without Phil patrolling the block, maybe we could hang out at his house, watch the fireworks from his backyard, kiss as the sky explodes with color above us.

"Let me check with Lexi and see what she's planned for us," I say, avoiding Mom's eyes, watching her hands as she works the pastry cutter, carving dough into the strips that will create the lattice for her blueberry pie.

"Too cool to hang with your old mother? I get it." Mom laughs.

"I'm not cool, and you're not old." I steal a pinch of pie crust dough and pop it in my mouth. "Let me check with Lexi."

I grab a water bottle, and Mom tosses me a granola bar. I kiss her on the forehead, inhaling the warm scent of melted butter mixed with sugar. It reminds me of Gran. I smile.

"Hey, Cass," she says as I'm almost out the door. I stop and turn to look at her. "It's nice to see you looking a bit more like yourself again. Enjoy the run!"

I give her a big, goofy grin and jump down the back stairs.

* * *

The air's already warm but not humid or gross yet. The sun feels good, golden. Lexi and I meet at the gazebo by Oak Hill Pond every year and then walk to the registration table. The streets are more crowded than they'd usually be at eight fifteen in the morning as runners and spectators make their way to the course. Every few blocks, I slip under caution tape that clears the streets for the race and the Oak Hill Independence Day parade that begins once the last runners cross the finish line.

"Hey, Cassidy!" Mrs. Winslow, a classmate's mom, calls. "Happy Fourth!"

"See you at the finish line, Cassidy!" Mr. Carver, my friend Emma's dad, waves as he jogs past.

Everyone's eager to say hi to me now that Evan's a suspect. I spot Lexi standing near the gazebo stretching, her thick brown hair pulled back in a ponytail. I jog up to her.

"Hey!"

"Hey! Ready to win this thang?" She can't even say it without laughing because neither of us loves running. We'll be lucky to finish in under forty-five minutes.

"I'm just here for the T-shirt, remember?"

As Lexi and I make our way to the registration table and then the starting line, more people smile at us. Me, in particular. Lexi shakes her head.

"That's messed up," she says.

"What?"

"A few days ago, these people would've thrown you into Oak Hill Pond with a boulder around your neck. Now the guilt they feel for judging you makes them extra friendly. What a bunch of phonies."

"Okay, thanks, Holden Caulfield."

"I'm just saying, it's times like these you learn who your true friends are."

I keep my head down as we slip into the pack, do some half-hearted stretches, and wait for the starting gun.

When the race begins, it's amazing, electrifying, the tradition of it—the familiarity of it, being in the middle of it all beside Lexi, like it's just another summer day, and I'm just a regular person under the warm July sun instead of a cloud of suspicion. For the first time in so long, I feel free. Air fills my lungs. The lump in my throat is gone. My muscles work from memory, the ground solid beneath my feet.

Running down Main Street, the energy of the crowd drives me forward. But after the first couple of miles weaving through backstreets, we circle around toward the heart of town. With each landmark we pass—the pond, the elementary school, the block where Billy was last seen, the police station—a sense of dread creeps over me. Evan was questioned, but that doesn't mean anything. It could be just another false alarm, like what happened with Mrs. Baker.

Billy is still missing.

This isn't over.

Suddenly, I'm exhausted. Aching to quit. I want to walk off the course and crawl home—into bed. I look at Lexi. She gives me a thumbs-up.

"Almost there!" she says, barely winded.

Every step feels like its own marathon. On our way to the finish line, we pass the start of the parade route. I see clusters of Cub Scouts, little boys in beige, American flags in hand. Billy should be with them. He'd told me his mom would be riding on her real estate agency's float. So, he could either march with the scouts or sit with her outside a She Shed.

"I don't know who to pick." He'd scratched his head.

"You can't go wrong either way," I assured him, laughing.

For the millionth time, I wonder where he is, and the weight of not knowing nearly buckles my knees as Lexi and I cross the finish line. My face feels like an overinflated balloon that's ready to burst. Stomach cramps double me over. A volunteer hands me a bottle of water, but I can't get the cap off. Lexi, who's hardly broken a sweat, grabs our commemorative T-shirts and steers me away from the crowd, out of the sun. I sink toward the shady steps of the barbershop as she opens the water and hands it to me.

"What's up, bitches?" Bridget Hanley walks over, trailed by a few of her former Oak Hill High basketball teammates. With her auburn hair and freckles, she looks more like Annie, the lovable singing orphan, than the badass she wants to be. "We're going to the diner to eat our body weight in cheese fries. Wanna join?"

The thought is enough to make me almost hurl all over the sidewalk.

"Wait, what about the parade?" Emma Carver asks.

"What are you, twelve? Fuck the parade!" Bridget turns to look at me. "I want to hear how Cassidy is going to go all 'Kill Bill' on Evan Barnes for turning her life to shit for the past three weeks."

"I'm not feeling great," I say, struggling to catch my breath. "Go, Lex. I'm gonna walk home."

"You sure?" she asks.

I nod.

"You guys go ahead," Lexi tells Bridget and Emma. "I'll catch up. Order me a Coke and a banana split."

Last night's chicken burrito swims into my mouth as Lexi sits next to me. "Hey, you okay?" she asks, rubbing my shoulders.

I swallow hard. "Just nauseous and my head . . ."

"You're not pregnant, are you?"

"Oh my God! No! Don't even say that!"

"Calm down! I'm just asking."

"It's the heat, and I didn't drink enough water." And it's Billy, of course. Across the street is the ice-cream shop where I took him for his birthday last July. He told the girl behind the counter he'd just turned five, so she gave him six cherries. "Five and one to grow on!" Mrs. B. would've freaked if she'd seen how fast he ate them, a big, fat smile splashed across his face like he'd just won a lifetime supply of rocky road.

I have to stand up, get away from here, but my legs shake, muscles twitch. I know Lexi won't leave until she thinks I'm okay.

"Go! Eat your . . ." I can't even think about her order. "I'm going to take a shower. Sleep."

"You're sure?"

"Totally. Text you later." I wait for the head rush to pass before walking downhill toward home.

*   *   *

When I open the door, the house is quiet except for the hum of air conditioners. Mom's at the parade. I shower, turning the water to icy cold. The thought of possibly hanging out with Chris later is the only thing that takes my mind off how crappy I feel.

My sheets are cool as I slide between them. My hair, wet from my shower, will dry in a tangled mess, but I don't care. I drift off, dreaming of marching cub scouts, ice cream, blueberry pies, and Chris sitting beside me at the piano.

My ringing phone wakes me. The number looks familiar, but I can't place it.

"Hello?"

"Hey, Cass! It's Sarah Davies! Tucker, Amy-Pat, and Brent's mom!" She always starts off this way, as if her whole identity is tied to being the mother of these kids.

"Oh, hi," I say. I sit up and clear my throat, trying to sound more awake. I look at the clock. It's past noon. I've slept for two hours, but it hasn't helped. My head aches, and my mouth feels as if it's packed with cotton.

"I know it's short notice, but Brian and I were invited to the Moores' barbecue tonight. I was hoping you might be available to babysit? Amy-Pat has been asking about you nonstop!" She sounds so energetic and hopeful. "We'd have called you sooner, but it's been so busy. Amy-Pat's almost fully potty trained, and Brent's cutting teeth. Now that I've said all that, I hope I didn't just scare you out of coming over!" She laughs, and I hear the sound of kid-related mayhem in the background. "What do you think? Maybe six-ish? I'll order pizza for dinner. We won't be home late. I'm still nursing Brent, so I can't get too crazy."

I wish she'd sent a text instead of calling. I hate being put on the spot. Of course, it's my fault for answering. Another sitter must've canceled on her. I know what this is. A show of faith, as if she'd always believed Billy's disappearance wasn't my fault. Lexi would call bullshit on this too because, of course, no one in Oak Hill reached out to ask me to babysit before the whole Evan thing happened.

"Um, I . . ." I don't really have any plans. I haven't called Chris. Lexi and I didn't talk about doing anything specific. I'm sure Sloan Maxwell's having a party, but I'm also positive we're not welcome. It would make Mom happy if I went to the fireworks with her, but that seems like the lamest option.

If Mrs. Davies is willing to hire me and the other Oak Hill moms find out, they will too. With five weeks left before I leave for college, I'm not in a position to refuse any moneymaking opportunities.

". . . I'm available."

"Oh great, Cassidy, thank you!" Mrs. Davies gushes, then lowers her voice. "This is like *the* social event of the year! I'd die if I missed it."

I roll my eyes. Mom always jokes that high school behavior extends well into adulthood in Oak Hill.

"I'll be there at six?"

"Perfect. The kids will be so excited to see you! Thanks again!"

As soon as I hang up, I regret agreeing to it. Even if Evan took Billy, and there's nothing I could've done to stop it, watching someone's children—the responsibility of it—feels like more than I can handle. But if I get there at six and Mr. and Mrs. Davies leave soon after that, it'll be two hours max before the kids go to bed. If they get home by ten—even eleven—I can still hang out with Chris. If he's around.

I try to psych myself up for it by doing the math. I could make close to seventy bucks. Since having Brent almost a year ago, Mrs. Davies increased her hourly rate to seventeen dollars. But I earn every cent.

When I was there in May, I felt more like a zookeeper than a babysitter. But I guess that's what you get when you watch three children under eight years old. Brent crawled and climbed everywhere, as if he were preparing to compete on *American Ninja Warrior*. Amy-Pat had just turned three and wanted to play "fashion show," which meant she ran around naked, changing outfits every ten seconds. And, Tucker, who I've been babysitting since he was three, had become obsessed with electronics and kept asking to use the family's iPad or scroll through my phone. I wish I'd remembered all this before I said I was available.

I call Chris, hoping the sound of his voice will work its usual magic. When I tell him I'm babysitting for the Davieses, he says, "That's great. Sounds like you're back in business."

"Yeah, but I thought maybe we could hang out."

"We've still got a few weeks, right? Before you leave?"

I hesitate, stopping myself from asking what I've been wondering when I can't sleep: *Will you visit me?* I definitely can't add "at school" because that would remind him of our age difference.

"What if I stopped by later tonight—after the Davieses get home? They live sort of around the corner from you. Do you know them?"

"Yeah, actually, Tucker came by for a guitar lesson once, but then I never heard from them again. I should've followed up."

"He'd probably rather play GarageBand. He's obsessed with technology. They're sweet kids, but holy shit, they're a handful." I laugh. "Last time I was there, they'd just gotten this tree house, and I had to keep climbing up and down the ladder delivering snacks and pretending to be a mail carrier. Sorry, I'm rambling. You probably have better things to do. How's the leprechaun soundtrack coming?"

"Needs a wee bit more work," he says, making a sad attempt at an Irish brogue. "See what I did there?"

I love that beneath all his exterior hotness beats the heart of a goofball. "I'll call you when they get home."

"Sounds good. Have fun."

Lexi thinks my obsession is part-lust, part-fangirl, but it's more. Chris listens. When I tell him about some of the kids I watch or how I'm thinking more about becoming a teacher, he asks thoughtful questions. He's paying attention. I love Lexi, but sometimes she'll say things like, "Yeah, yeah cut to the chase!" and "Sorry, Cass, but hearing your babysitting stories might actually be worse than if I had to watch the kids myself."

Knowing I'll see him later will get me through babysitting, but I'm still fighting the anxious feeling I've had since the 5K.

*   *   *

The rest of the afternoon, I sort through my closet, dividing things into piles: take to school, leave at home, donate. Mom pops her head in the doorway to ask about dinner and the fireworks. I tell her my plans. "I think it's a good sign, you know. Like people trust me again."

She smiles. "I'll save some blueberry pie for us to share when you get home."

"It's a date," I say.

*   *   *

As I walk over to the Davieses' house, I pass families hosting barbecues. Some are already heading to the fireworks. Red wagons roll toward town, filled with kids, coolers, blankets, and bug spray. Now that I'm almost there, making sixty-eight dollars seems like nothing. I wish I'd gone with Mom. Lexi made plans to hang out and watch the fireworks with Bridget and her crew in Emma's backyard.

"Come by when you're done. I'm sure we'll still be there," Lexi texted earlier.

They'll only be awake for a couple of hours. Chill, I repeat like a mantra as I approach the front gate. It sticks. I jiggle it, lifting the latch up and out. Laughter spills from the backyard. I walk around to find Tucker and Amy-Pat chasing the bubbles Mr. Davies blows in between sipping a beer.

"Cassidy!" Amy-Pat squeals and throws herself into me, hugging my legs. She's wearing a white dress, navy blue beads she probably got at the parade, and a headband with two glittery, red stars on springs poking out of it.

I bend down so we're eye level. "Hey, I missed you!"

"Do you like my headband?" She shakes her head, sending the stars bouncing back and forth and side to side.

"It's gorgeous!" I say. "Where can I get one?"

"Amazon!" Amy-Pat giggles and pulls her skirt over her head.

Mrs. Davies sighs as she walks toward me with Brent on her hip.

"Another to add to her collection. Picked this one out herself! She slept with it on last night. Got glitter all over her pillowcase!" She air-kisses me, and Brent reaches to pull my hair. "Congratulations! We haven't seen you since you graduated!" She hoists Brent higher on her hip. "We've missed you! Are you so excited for college? Enjoy every single second!"

Brent lets out a wail before I can say anything.

They'll only be awake for a couple of hours. Chill.

"Brian's been trying to wear them out for you." She nods toward the assortment of riding toys, Hula-Hoops, and jump ropes littering the lawn.

"But Amy-Pat took a long nap after the parade, so good luck!" Mr. Davies adds.

"Shh! You're not supposed to tell Cassidy that! She'll make a U-turn!" Mrs. Davies swats him on the shoulder and hands a blubbering Brent to me. "You remember where everything is? Help yourself to anything. I ordered the pizza. Tip money's by the door. Brent goes down at seven, Amy-Pat at seven-thirty, and Tucker at eight." She waves, blowing kisses at Tucker and Amy-Pat, and pinches Brent's rosy cheek. "See you at your 2 AM feeding, mister." She smiles at Brent, then winks at me. "Call or text if you need anything, Cassidy. We'll be right in town."

As we watch them leave, Amy-Pat's lip quivers. Anxiety creeps over me again, but I don't have time to dwell on it. I have to do something before she melts down and there's no return.

This is fine. You're fine.

"Hey! Let's go have a dance party in your playroom," I suggest.

Amy-Pat runs off, shouting, "Alexa, play A.P.'s favorites!"

"Wheels on the Bus" begins. Not my first choice. Tucker marches in after her. "I showed A.P. how to make a playlist," he says proudly.

I follow, Brent heavy on my hip but happier now that he's weaving his sticky fingers through my hair.

Inside, I put him down, and he stands at the coffee table, bouncing up and down to the music. We're mid-way through the song, nailing the horn sounds and wiper motions, when Tucker yells, "This is for babies! I'm going back outside!"

"Wait, Tuck," I say. "The pizza will be here soon."

"I want outside too!" Amy-Pat whines.

I pull out my phone. 6:18 PM. *Time is standing still.* I smell something vaguely foul. My other phone rings. Chris. I pull it from my pocket.

"Why do you have two phones, and I don't have any?" Tucker asks.

"Hey," I say to Chris. I can't hear him with all the noise from the kids and the music. I'm about to duck out of the room when Tucker suddenly chants, "Brent's got di-ar-rhea! Brent's got di-ar-rhea!" He points to his brother's leg, where yellowy-brown liquid trickles down toward the cream shag carpet.

"Ew!!" Amy-Pat screams and jumps onto the couch.

I cringe and move toward Brent slowly as he inches his way around the table on chubby, now-filthy legs. I don't want him to think I'm chasing him because if he falls backward it means shit everywhere—up his back *and* all over the rug.

"Hey," Chris says. "I got a last-minute invitation to Roddy's." Roderick Kelly, Regrets Only's drummer. "I know you said you might stop by when you're done, but these guys tend to go pretty late. I'll probably stay there. I haven't seen them in a while. Might be nice to catch up."

My heart sinks. "Want me to walk your dog for you?" I ask. *Pathetic. Guy's blowing you off, and you're offering to scoop his dog's poop?* I imagine Lexi saying, then following it up with, *Don't you have enough shit to deal with—literally?*

I look at Brent, who's starting to whimper as Tucker continues pointing, and Amy-Pat holds her nose, squealing.

"Nah, I'm bringing Murph with me. But I'll tell him you offered." The warmth in his deep voice, like he's about to tell me a secret, gets me every time. I picture his eyes, his smile, and it almost blocks out Amy-Pat's shrieking and Brent's exploding diaper.

"Well, have fun." I struggle to hide my disappointment.

"What are you up to over there?" Chris asks. "Do I hear 'Head, Shoulders, Knees and Toes'? Sounds like a good time."

"Yeah, just having a dance party. We've got pizza on the way, I have to change the baby. Can I call you back?"

"You don't have to. You've got your hands full. Talk to you soon."

"Okay, bye."

"Why sad?" Amy-Pat asks. She cocks her head, making the glittery red stars on her headband bounce again.

"I'm not sad," I lie. "I'm having so much fun! I'm just going to get your brother cleaned up, and then we'll have dinner, okay?"

"'K," she says, nodding.

"I'm going outside," Tucker yells.

"No!" I can't have them all going in separate directions. I look around. "Find your iPad." I pick up Brent, keeping him at arm's length to avoid getting coated in poop. Tucker and Amy-Pat run from the playroom. I hurry after them, noticing that the basket where Mrs. Davies usually keeps diapers, wipes, and that icky-smelling butt paste is empty. *Shit!*

"Amy-Pat, want to come with me and help me find a new outfit for the baby?" I don't want her getting into trouble while I'm upstairs. Tuck's so focused on the iPad, he'd never notice if she created a mural with Go-Gurt.

"No! Brent stinks!" She jumps up and down, holding her nose again. She's not wrong.

"Fine," I say. "Go back to the playroom. Keep dancing! I'll be right down!"

As I climb the stairs, my legs ache. I think back to the 5K. I can't believe it was this morning. It feels like weeks ago. Brent's room is dark, cool, and quiet. I want to sit in his navy rocker and close my eyes, but I can't because he's crying as poop oozes down his legs.

I place him on his changing table, hold my breath, and get to work. I'm almost done when the doorbell rings. The pizza. *Great timing.* I keep a hand on Brent's belly, so he doesn't roll off the table and yell toward the window, "Be right there!" Of course, it's shut because the Davies family has central air.

Just a few more hours. You need the money!

I pick up a better-smelling Brent and stick him on my hip. As soon as I reach the top step, my heart starts hammering. The front door is wide open. I race toward it, nearly tripping on the toys and shoes on the sides of the steps.

"Tucker!" I call, looking toward the playroom and kitchen. I turn back to the front yard, where the pizza delivery guy wrestles with the gate.

Tucker appears beside me. "I opened the door and got the pizza and gave the man the money Mommy left."

"Tuck, you gave me a heart attack. You shouldn't open the door without a grown-up," I say, then shout toward the deliveryman, "Jiggle it and pull it toward you," causing Brent to fuss.

The gate opens, and the delivery guy waves a "thank you" with his red insulated bag without turning back. Over his shoulder, he barks, "Fix that fuckin' thing!" I flinch as Tuck giggles, his eyes gleaming with mischievous delight.

"He said 'fu—"

"Let's eat!" I cut him off and slam the door.

As we walk into the kitchen, I'm scared to see if Tucker carried the pizza to the table safely, or if melted mozzarella is glued to the top of the box, and if it is, will that cause them to freak out. Lifting the lid, I'm beyond relieved that the pie is still intact.

"Amy-Pat! Pizza's here!" I yell, slipping Brent into his seat, ready to find the pureed mush he'll have for dinner. "Tuck, you handled that like a champ, but next time wait for your mom or dad or me before you open the door for a stranger, okay?" I start to frown but then ruffle his hair. "I know I was busy with Brent, and you just wanted to help, so thank you."

"No problem!" He smiles.

"Hey! You lost a tooth since the last time I was here!"

"I'm losing them, and Brent's getting them!"

We laugh and look at Brent, who's chomping on his fist.

"Hey, where'd your sister go?" Was she dancing in the playroom? I don't remember seeing her on our way into the kitchen, but I can hear "The Ants Go Marching."

"Using the potty? I don't know." Tucker digs into a slice.

"Amy-Pat, let's go! Pizza's here!" As I look around, my eyes land on the back door. It's partially open.

"Shit!" I curse. Tucker giggles again. If she's in that tree house, I'm going to have to climb up and get her. My legs ache in advance.

"Amy-Pat," I yell. "Come on in! Pizza's here."

I wait, hoping to see her face in the window of the tree house or her white dress float into view from around the corner, her sparkly stars bobbing. No luck.

"Tuck, keep an eye on Brent. I'm going to get your sister."

I step into the yard, the grass thick beneath my bare feet. It's warm and damp from the sprinkler. I listen for Amy-Pat but hear only crickets. Every family on the block is probably in the heart of town, waiting for the fireworks to begin. The air is still. There's not even a whisper of a breeze. I see a flicker behind the tree. A firefly flits past.

"Amy-Pat, let's go, come inside. Now!"

I hear rustling near the garage. A squirrel darts out. I look around the yard, at the swing set. The slide is empty, the swings motionless. The riding toys, Hula-Hoops, and jump ropes are exactly where they were thirty minutes ago. I check under a blue tarp where bricks are piled beside the half-built pizza oven. She's not there. I turn toward the tree house. The ladder. I have no other choice but to climb up and get her. I'm pissed and trying hard not to completely lose it. *Where is she?* I should've stayed home. Or gone with Mom. Maybe if I didn't have plans, Chris would've invited me to go to Roddy's with him.

I want to be anywhere but here. I'm going to get a splinter from climbing the wooden rungs without shoes.

"Amy-Pat!" It comes out more like a whimper than a growl because I'm almost at the top and I'm tired.

She's not here. The ceiling is low. I squat for a second and take a deep breath. Something on the lawn below catches my eye. A flash of red near the back gate under the arbor where pink roses bloom.

I feel dizzy, disoriented, limbs shaking as I climb down. My stomach's a field of butterflies as my mind jumps to Billy. This can't be happening.

"Amy-Pat!" I shout her name, bellow it toward the treetops. I don't care if the neighbors hear. I wait for her to pop out from behind the swing set, giggling. She doesn't.

Adrenaline floods my body, making my aching legs strong as I race toward the gate. It's unlatched, open several inches. Tears blur my vision as I fall to my knees just feet away from the thing I spotted from the tree house. I reach out my hand and pluck Amy-Pat's headband from the lush green grass, a lone strand of blond hair still attached.

16

Friday, July 5
Allison

"Hey! You still alive in there?" Viv sits on her coffee table and lifts the sheet I burrowed beneath when a car alarm started blaring at four in the morning.

"Barely," I groan.

"Tell me what or *who* you did last night?" I open one eye and see Viv smirking, an empty wine bottle swinging between her fingertips. "Please say you finally took my advice and hooked up with Jayson."

"Who?"

"The hot chef in Three-C!" She's losing patience. "So I guess that's a no? Don't tell me you stayed home on the Fourth of July and drank alone."

"Okay, I won't tell you." I won't tell her that I went back to Oak Hill yesterday. I had to be there. It would've been our son's sixth birthday, and I needed to see it—the tree I planted on what should've been the day he came into the world. I chose a Japanese maple because they symbolize peace and rest. If I could've taken one thing with me when I left Oak Hill, it would've been that tree. It stood in our front yard growing taller each year.

I know I was crazy to go back. I'd put so much time and thought into leaving, into not being found.

What if Chris recognizes me? I worried as I adjusted the mid-length, white-blond wig I pulled from the back of Viv's closet. In her loose sundress and the nonprescription eyeglasses she wore when she wanted to appear "brainy," I looked nothing like myself.

Goose bumps pricked my skin in the air-conditioned train car. "You're insane," I whispered as it lurched into the station. Stepping off the platform, the air smelled sweet, like funnel cake. The town was empty, the annual parade and 5K long over. I passed the pond and the gazebo. It felt like years since I'd been there and, at the same time, as if I'd never left.

Across the street from the home Chris and I had shared, I stood, attempting to block out every bad thing that happened there, forcing myself to simply admire the tree's crimson leaves, the way they fanned out like fingers reaching toward the blanket of green grass. I wanted to believe that our child lived on in that tree, his soul nourished by its timber, his spirit dancing in its branches. But I was fooling myself. He was gone. They all were.

I shut my eyes and saw my other life, the one in which we hosted a barbecue, balloons swaying in the soft breeze, a two-wheeler, adorned with a big blue bow, waiting in the garage. I could almost hear the laughter, the music, the gentle *whoosh* as birthday candles change from fire to smoke. Sounds of life, of love, of happiness.

For a moment, my heart was tender, and I thought about knocking on the door, telling Chris how sad and sorry I was that we'd ended up like this.

"We almost had everything, but it wasn't meant to be," I wanted to say, but then I heard Mary Alice Foster on the other side of her screen door and I hurried away.

I stayed in Oak Hill longer than I should have, feeling furious, robbed. I got back to Viv's in time to see the last fireworks fade against the black velvet sky above the Hudson River.

* * *

"Seriously, Al," Viv says now, rubbing my arm. "This is getting kind of sad. You're in the most exciting city in the whole world, and you barely leave this apartment. You're gorgeous, but you sit around all day in boxer shorts and a weird shirt."

I glance at the faded blue tee. A stick figure hovers above the words, "Running late is my cardio."

"This is *your* shirt!"

She continues as if I haven't said a word. "You had the whole place to yourself for a few days, and you spent them alone. Hot gal busts up her marriage, chugs rosé—cheap rosé, I might add—by herself on Independence Day. You're a pair of cowboy boots and a pickup truck away from the beginning of a Nicholas Sparks novel. Maybe I can play the sassy BFF who tries to save you from yourself in the film adaptation?"

I adore Viv, but sometimes she's a lot. I want to pull the sheet over my head, but she still holds the corner.

"You're back early," I mumble, surprised she hasn't spent the rest of the holiday weekend in the Hamptons with her cousin and family as she'd planned.

"Honestly, the place they're renting is spectacular, but I couldn't wait to get out of there." Viv walks five feet to the kitchen, where she examines an overripe banana before tossing it in the trash. "They invited too many people, and do you believe they made me sleep in the same room with their insomniac toddler? They gave the nanny the weekend off. That little demon woke me up at five-thirty for the past three days. This morning, I was like, 'Fuck this, I'm outta here.' Plus, it's not the same. Lara used to know about the best parties, the hottest bars. Now it's all ice-cream shops and nap schedules."

"Napping sounds nice." I plump my pillow and nuzzle into it.

She opens and shuts the refrigerator door, sighs, and walks back to me.

"C'mon, get up. I'm taking you to lunch."

"Lunch?"

"It's almost noon." She shakes my arm. "I'm starving, and the only thing in the fridge is ketchup. Oh, and more shitty rosé."

I sit up slowly, my head aching. When Chris stopped drinking, I did too. Initially, I missed it—a lot. On crisp fall evenings, my mouth would water at the thought of pouring a glass of cabernet and sitting on our patio or beside the fireplace. When we went to a restaurant, I'd watch a woman sip a glistening cocktail, almost able to feel the stem of the glass, the elegant weight of it in my hand, imagining the stinging cold of a martini on my tongue. Most of all, I missed the blissful oblivion that overtook me as the alcohol swam through my bloodstream.

As time passed, I got used to not drinking, and I didn't miss how awful it made me feel or look the next day.

In Viv's bathroom mirror, my reflection startles me. Compared to her glowing skin, mine's bloated, blotchy. I don't want to keep her waiting, so instead of showering, I wash my face, brush my teeth, and sweep my hair into a bun. I grab my makeup bag from the shelf above the toilet, where Viv has a framed print that reads, "Better late than ugly." I dab concealer at the bluish-purple pockets beneath my eyes, add a swipe of lipgloss, and hope Viv isn't horrified to be seen with me.

Though it's overcast, I put on sunglasses. When we went out a few weeks ago, a woman recognized me from "I'll Be the Judge of That." It always starts with, "Aren't you that girl . . . ?"

In the past, I never minded, but now I just want to lay low and not end up in the washed-up actress-lets-herself-go section of the tabloids, especially if it reveals my location. So far, Chris has respected the request I made in the note I left—to give me space and not try to find me. Still, I worry that it's only a matter of time before he tracks me down and attempts to convince me that we'll have our fairy-tale ending.

A wall of heat smacks us as we exit the building, but it's good to be out of the apartment. I take a deep breath. Viv's right. I need to start living again. That's why I came here. To heal, to remember who I used to be. I believe that woman is still in there, only hidden. I have to stop looking back, focus on what I have rather than what I've lost.

This afternoon, I'll email the real estate agent again, find my own place. Maybe I'll even humor Viv and agree to meet the hot chef in 3-C for coffee or a drink. I think about something a yoga instructor in Oak Hill used to say, "Inhale possibility; exhale doubt." I turn my face toward the sun, and though it's behind a cloud, I know it's there, only hidden.

It's a short walk to the restaurant Viv picks. Even so, I'm sweating. Twelve-dollar rosé seeps out of my pores by the time we arrive. I'm relieved when I hear her ask for a table indoors, away from the humidity and smells of summer in Manhattan. I want a booth in the back where I can hide, rest my head on a cool wooden table, but because Viv's eye candy, we're seated in the middle of the place. I force myself to sit up rather than slouch and cross my legs instead of letting them splay open like a baseball catcher's.

The city's quiet after the holiday. There's not much traffic. On the sidewalk, slow-moving tourists slog their way through the heat.

Our waiter arrives with two glasses of water. Viv orders a salad, no dressing. Next week, she's auditioning for a main role—sexy lifeguard who gets murdered by a guy she meets online.

"Just when you thought it was safe to go back on Tinder . . ." she's been saying in a menacing voice ever since she got the call from her agent.

I order the first thing my eyes land on— a western omelet with bacon and hash browns. "I'll share," I promise.

"Let me introduce you to my new mantra: 'My body is a temple!'" She closes her eyes, raises her prayer hands, then laughs. "It's also my sole source of income."

If Viv's body is a temple, mine is a dumpster, the source of my bitter disappointments. After being careful for so long— first with modeling, and then trying to get and stay pregnant— the list of foods I've denied myself—sugar, flour, sushi, soft cheeses—could fill a grocery store aisle. I'm not sorry to be done with all that.

Viv takes a sip of water and starts choking. She points toward something behind me.

"Don't look, Al," she splutters. "Seriously." Her eyes widen. "It's only going to freak you out."

I make no effort to turn. My neck is stiff from sleeping on the couch so I wait for Viv to tell me what's caught her eye. Plus, I'm used to her dramatics. She could witness a murder or spot a ladybug and she'd have the same reaction.

"These cops are about as ineffective as natural deodorant." She puts her glass down, coughs, and leans in, though I have no idea what she's talking about. "Did I tell you that I was

cyberbullied by a bride after I did those chemical-free deodorant ads? This bitch had the balls to accuse me of ruining her
wedding day because she 'smelled like a high school wrestler.'
She threatened to sue. As if I'm a fucking chemist! Maybe you've
got a gland problem, lady!"

Her eyes flick back up. My head pounds. I should drink my
water, but all I want is coffee. I swivel around to look for the
waiter, and that's when I see it. The thing that's captured Viv's
attention. The TV above the bar. On the screen are the gazebo,
the clock, Oak Hill Pond. I squint and make out captions,
"Town rocked as second child goes missing in three weeks." I've
been half asleep. Now I'm wide awake with a sick feeling in the
pit of my stomach.

"Amelia-Patricia Davies!" Viv snorts, reading along as the
words at the bottom of the screen change. "Jesus, I thought
L.A. parents were crazy with the names." She lets out a long
sigh. "When I lived with Mark, the twins next door were called
Luna and Lyric. I'd nicknamed them Urethra and Areola. But
this? Amelia-Patricia? That's a mouthful."

Photos of the little girl flash up. In one, she's dressed as a
princess, a sparkly tiara nests in her blond curls. In another,
she's sitting in a stroller on a boardwalk licking an ice-cream
cone. A headband adorned with an orange gerbera daisy sweeps
her ringlets away from her face. Next, the picture of Billy at the
zoo pops up.

"It's likely the disappearances are linked," the caption states.
The news anchor grimaces. "A cell phone was found on the
family's property. It's the lone clue police hope will lead them to
these children," she says before moving on to the next story.

I pat my pocket for my phone. I must've left it in the
apartment.

"They're going to start microchipping these kids. Just
watch," Viv says, shaking her head.

Our waiter sets down Viv's cucumber-lime seltzer and my
coffee. I desperately want to gulp it, but I'm frozen.

"Meals will be up in a sec." He starts to walk off but stops
and stares.

"Great, thanks!" Viv waves him off politely before he works
up the courage to ask why we look familiar. She frowns at me.

"My God, Al, you're whiter than the Pillsbury Doughboy's ass. Promise me you won't go digging around for news about that little girl. It'll only make you feel worse."

"I've met her," I whisper. "And her mom. They were in our house. Her brother came for a guitar lesson."

"That's messed up. These parents have to be completely losing their shit," Viv says before pulling out her phone to scroll idly through Instagram. She looks up to inspect my face. "If you think you're gonna hurl, the bathroom's downstairs."

I picture Sarah Davies. The day she came for the guitar lesson wasn't the first time I'd seen her. We'd met three years earlier. She was pregnant. And I was too. Murph and I were at the park one afternoon in late fall. The days were growing dark earlier. It made me happy, the idea that time was moving forward, each day bringing me closer to the end of forty weeks. Even thirty-seven would be enough to be considered full-term, which meant I was more than halfway there.

At nineteen weeks, our baby was the size of a mango, according to the Pea in Your Pod pregnancy email that waited at the top of my inbox each morning. By that point, it had been two years and three more miscarriages since my first pregnancy loss.

As Murph sniffed his way through the last leaves of the season, a little boy walked over to pet him.

"Ask permission first, Tuck," said the woman strolling behind him.

The boy asked, and I nodded. "This is Murphy. He's super friendly. He may even try to lick you."

"Well, I hope Murphy likes yogurt because snack time got a little wild back there, and this kid's coated in it." The woman held up a bouquet of berry-stained crumpled napkins as proof. When she laughed, her quilted jacket opened, revealing a baby bump. "I'm Sarah, Tucker's mom."

"I'm Allison. When are you due?"

"May eleventh."

"June first!" I blurted, pointing toward my stomach.

I can still see her expression. Surprised. I didn't look nearly as pregnant as she did. I'd read that you showed earlier with each pregnancy. But though it was my fifth, it was also the furthest I'd ever gotten. Maybe that was why her stomach was shaped like a small watermelon, while mine was barely the size of a cantaloupe.

Chris and I hadn't told anyone yet. We'd announced three of the other pregnancies only to have to share the devastating news when they ended. The comments people made in an effort to be sympathetic only made us feel worse. "You're young and healthy. Just try again!" "It wasn't meant to be," and the most disturbing, "It's all part of God's plan!" As if God decided to give us a baby, and then had a change of heart.

Chris and I vowed to keep that pregnancy a secret as long as we could. But acknowledging it aloud, even to a stranger, made me believe it could really happen. Something about Sarah—her calm confidence, her casual ease, her cute red Keds—made her seem like she belonged in the world I desperately wanted to inhabit. A land of playgrounds, story hours, and jogging strollers, where making friends seemed effortless.

"Congratulations!" she gushed, no doubt overcompensating for her initial surprise. "Is this your first?"

I hated that question. No one could've imagined what I'd endured, the heartbreak, the tests, the fruitless search for answers. The grief was always with me, yet I rarely spoke about how my body repeatedly failed me, and when I did, it was only with Chris. So I smiled at Sarah, betraying the souls of the children we'd lost, and nodded.

"Oh, how exciting! Do you know what you're having?"

"A girl." The exhilaration of saying that part, too, gave me a slight headrush. My voice oozed happiness. I sounded nothing like the fraught and fearful woman I was. The one who, every time she used the bathroom, prayed she didn't find red dots freckling white cotton underpants. Spots that turned into a trickle, then a river, and later, a raging flood. The thought that I could lose the pregnancy at any moment left me perpetually anxious, restless. I lay awake in the middle of the night, tracing small hearts on my stomach, whispering, "Please stay, baby," praying I wouldn't wake to find blood forming a scarlet amaryllis across our white sheets.

Chris and I no longer joked about names or picked out paint colors for the nursery. We didn't talk about the future. We took each day as a gift, a small miracle that brought us a step closer to a bigger one.

Sarah was expecting a daughter too. She lived on Forest Trail, just a block away from us.

"Our girls will be in the same class!" she said before Tucker threw himself backward into the leaf pile, demanding a dog. "Yikes! Looks like someone's ready for his nap."

She squatted, scooped up her flailing toddler, and bundled him into his stroller, offering him a sippy cup and a tiny container of crackers. A graceful, maternal dance. Would I ever get the chance to make these simple, loving gestures?

"It was great to meet you, Allison! I'm sure we'll see each other back here in the spring. We can commiserate about how swollen and achy we are." She placed a hand on her lower back and smiled.

I laughed, like, of course, that would happen. I forced myself to embrace that optimism because, after all, didn't this baby deserve a mother who believed she'd live?

"It's a date!" I said.

A warm feeling stayed with me as Murph and I walked home, even as clouds crossed over the sun, and the wind stripped the trees of their final leaves.

Two days later, the baby was gone. A knot in the umbilical cord cut off her oxygen, we were told.

"Such a freak thing, no one could've anticipated it," the doctor added, as if that might provide some comfort.

Chris took a picture of our perfect, birdlike girl as I held her in the palm of my hand, fully formed in miniature, her skin translucent, her eyes tightly closed, the way they'd always be. I spent days, weeks, months staring at that photo, reminding myself that she was real, my grief valid. I lost *her*.

Months later, I saw Sarah at the grocery store. She was holding Tucker's hand. Pink socks, small as rose petals, poked out of the infant carrier that balanced on the front part of the shopping cart. I dropped my basket and left.

When Tucker came for a trial lesson last year, I answered the door without knowing who waited on the other side. Seeing them—a visibly pregnant Sarah flanked by her son and adorable daughter—unnerved me. The easiest thing for me to do was to flip into actress mode and pretend we'd never met.

"I'm Allison," I'd said, my skin on fire with envy and shame. "Nice to meet you. Please come in." I turned my back to them, but not before the light of recognition that flickered in Sarah's eyes moments earlier faded. I hated being part of that bitchy thing women do where they pretend they don't remember each other. She'd probably chalked it up to me being a self-involved, B-level celebrity, which made me feel worse. But what were my other options? Say something like, "Oh, hi, Sarah! I remember you. Congratulations! Your daughter is perfect. Mine is dead." If she'd pointed out that we'd met, wouldn't she have asked, "Where's your little girl?" and how would we navigate that? She didn't know it, but I was doing us both a favor.

After I invited them to have a seat on the benches in our foyer, I went to find Murph, who'd been out back on the patio, snarling at squirrels. I grabbed his leash, and we walked until the sun set, and I'd taken us so far from home, I had to call Chris to pick us up.

When Sarah texted to say Tucker complained that the guitar strings hurt his fingers and they'd have to hold off lessons, Chris had been in the basement. I knew if he read the message, he'd suggest a lighter gauge set of strings and invite Tucker back the following week. I couldn't bear to see them, the happy little family, again, so I wrote, "No problem. Thanks for letting me know." Then I deleted her text and mine.

I tried not to think about them after that. But sometimes when I couldn't sleep, I pictured their home, so close to ours and yet so different. I could practically hear the echo of their laughter, the scampering of small feet racing down the hall, the tiny cry of the healthy baby they welcomed months after that lesson.

Some nights I couldn't help but wonder: What would happen if their luck ran out?

CHAPTER

17

Friday, July 5
Sarah

I STARE OUT THE kitchen window. My eyes flick to the back
gate where the latch dangles, held in place by a single screw.
Useless.

How many times had I asked Brian to fix it? How many
times had he promised he'd get to it?

"I know, I know, the front gate won't open, and the back
won't close. Sounds like a lyric in a country song, doesn't it?"
He'd laughed just last weekend. "It's on my list."

I want to blame him. Hate him. Believe he's the reason our
precious daughter isn't upstairs asleep in her favorite purple
pajamas. But I can't. Because it's my fault. *I* wanted to go to the
party. *I* called Cassidy in a panic after the other sitter backed
out at the last minute.

Why? Why was it so important to me? What made me so
desperate that I'd hire a girl who'd just been part of a missing
child investigation? That question consumes me. But I know
the answer. I'm a pathetic, middle-aged mom plagued with a
teenager's fear of missing out. I've been this way ever since we
moved to Oak Hill.

What was it I was so afraid of missing? Lobster rolls? Gossip? I didn't want to hear stories—who wore what and who

drank too much—secondhand. I needed to be there. In it. I'd been dying for a night away from my children, their mouths constantly moving, dripping with demands, needing something that lately I felt too tired to give, get, or find.

Now, all I want is to see my daughter's face, her bright eyes, the dimple in her chin, hear her proud, squeaky voice. "*I* do it, Mommy!"

My fingers brush my throat, thinking about how she'd burrow into my shoulder, her soft curls, pale as butter, tickling my neck.

For the second time, I've had my heart ripped from my body and been forced to keep on living. Ever since Mama died the summer I turned nine, all I ever wanted was to be a mother. To be there for my children. To make them feel loved, special, cared for, protected.

I've failed.

It's been nineteen hours since I blew my baby girl a kiss and hurried down the driveway without so much as a peek over my shoulder. That's how eager I was to sit without a kid on my lap and sip whatever fancy thing Kelli Moore decided to serve as this year's signature cocktail—even if it meant I had to pump and dump later.

Brian didn't want to go. "I'm tired," he'd said when I reminded him about the party just before leaving for the parade. "I worked yesterday. I've got to work tomorrow. Why can't we permanently move July Fourth to a three-day weekend?"

He was still talking as I walked out of the house to add more water bottles and snacks to the stroller. I knew he wanted to stay home.

As we headed up Main Street, heat already rising off the sidewalk in little waves, he tried to convince me, "I'll go to the store, pick up burgers and dogs. We'll grill, then take the kids to the fireworks. It'll be fun!"

I was distracted, hoping I'd packed sunscreen and wondering why it was always up to me to remember everything.

"No way!" I'd said. "That's hours past their bedtime. It'll be a nightmare."

"Maybe they'll sleep a little later tomorrow."

"You know that never works," I whined. "I love this party! I've been looking forward to it for weeks. Kelli and Kip go all out." I glanced over each shoulder and lowered my voice. "Plus, I heard if you skip it one year, they don't invite you back the next."

"Well, that's nice!" Brian laughed and shook his head. "And these are the people you want as your friends? If we don't get invited again, consider it a blessing. That whole white-gloved caterer thing at a backyard barbecue makes me uncomfortable. And the flowers and candles floating in the pool? It's so over the top."

Brian grew up in a town like Oak Hill. I didn't. After Mama died, my childhood July Fourth celebrations were spent visiting Dad's brother, Uncle Roy, in upstate New York. We'd stand around his condo parking lot, my brother, Tom, and me holding sparklers that fizzled almost as soon as Dad lit them. We sat on the curb, kicking gravel around a pothole, watching Uncle Roy shoot off Roman candles and bottle rockets while Dad drank beer and said, "Jesus, Roy, this may be the year you finally lose a finger."

After neighbors called the cops, Tom and I would shimmy into our sleeping bags on Uncle Roy's living room floor, split a pint of cherry vanilla ice cream, and pretend the carpet didn't smell like dog pee.

The Moores' party was as far from Uncle Roy's as you could get. Their backyard had a pool *and* a koi pond. Round tables waited under an air-conditioned tent. Each had its own lush centerpiece—scarlet and ivory peonies that turned the night air sweet and fragrant. Last year, they'd hired a jazz band. Brian and I danced on the lawn until one in the morning, even though I was six months pregnant with Brent.

It was more than just the fantastic spectacle of it. I wanted to fit in, be part of the "cool mom" crowd. Not just for myself, but for the kids.

Brian can't understand the importance of belonging to the right group. But these moms are like an underground network; they have all the intel. They're how you find out about the best music classes, the gentle dentists, the secret basketball leagues for vertically challenged youth.

Even as I ordered the pizza, Brian tried to talk me out of going to the party. "That's not a very patriotic dinner, is it? There's still time for me to fire up the grill!"

"Give it a rest, Uncle Sam," I'd joked. "Mommy needs a night away from all this." I waved my hands at the books, toys, and stuffed animals that had taken over every corner and countertop. "You're around grown-ups all day. I can't even shower without an audience."

"Fine. If you want, we'll go. But I'm going to cannonball into the pool if that's what it takes to get away from Scott Jordan and his bragging about grooming the next A-Rod. Maybe I'll make a game of it and do a shot every time he says 'slugger' or 'RBI.'"

"Whatever it takes!" I kissed his cheek, knowing I was lucky. My husband was kind. Funny. He made pancakes shaped like animals for the kids on weekend mornings so I could have a few hours to myself. He'd roll over and go to sleep when I told him I was too tired to have sex after a day of wrangling toddlers and changing diapers. He supported my decision to stop teaching kindergarten and stay home full-time after Tucker was born. Basically, he was perfect, just like our children. My life had turned out better than I'd ever dreamed.

Now, I'm living a nightmare. Our daughter is gone. Vanished. As many times as I say or even think those words, it still seems impossible. How? How did this happen? Questions whip like a cyclone inside my head. Did Amy-Pat simply walk out of the backyard through the garden gate? The gate that wouldn't latch? Was she looking for me?

Before we left for the party, she'd been bouncing on our bed while I put on my makeup, chanting, "Don't go, Mommy! Stay! Play ponies with me!"

"We're only going a few blocks away. I'll give you the biggest smooch as soon as we're back! We have all day tomorrow to play ponies."

"No! Stay home!" She pouted, tiny arms crossed, the sparkly red stars on her headband bobbing defiantly.

She'd been so independent, following Tucker everywhere, until Brent was born. I blamed myself for her clinginess, the way she regressed with potty training. She needed more of my attention. Each day I swore we'd spend some special time together, just the two of us. But then Brent would be fussy, cutting teeth, or Tucker needed help with a scouting project. She always sought me out, and I was too busy.

"Can you remove my little blond barnacle while I dump this pasta?" I'd ask Brian, nodding down at our daughter, who'd hug my legs while I attempted to make dinner.

Would she have left the backyard to try to find me? That was my first thought. But no. Never without her headband.

Someone took her. Someone who dropped a cell phone in our shrubs. *Why wasn't Cassidy watching her?* This question repeats in my mind until I expect my head to explode.

When I couldn't stop shaking and screaming after we'd gotten back from the Moores' and the police wrapped our backyard in yellow crime scene tape, Brian pulled me into the half bathroom and pressed a pill into my palm. The anxiety medication I'd taken after Dad died.

"No! No!" I'd yanked my hand away. "I can't be numb. I need to find her."

"You're scaring the children," Brian whispered, holding me tight. "I know it's impossible, but we have to try to be strong for Tuck and Brent. They need us too."

I'd always loved that Brian was calm and reasonable. He'd saved us from buying a termite-infested home I'd adored because of its fancy molding. But hearing him suggest that I pull myself together, even if it was for our sons' sake, made me want to claw at his eyes, eyes I saw struggling to hold back tears.

I swallowed the small white circle, and then another when the first began to wear off, and more after that. They're the only thing stopping me from running through the streets, screaming my sweet girl's name.

Now, I stand by the window, clutching a cold cup of coffee in a state of shock, my body fighting an all-over pins-and-needles tingle that never lets up. The clock tells me it's nearly two in the afternoon. I've lost all sense of time. All I know is the sweet *before* and the devastating *now*. I cannot imagine going one more minute without her. And then I do. I have to. How? How have I gone from a woman whose main concern was choosing the perfect hostess gift for a barbecue to a mother whose beautiful baby girl is missing?

I see the night unfold over and over, bringing us to the same awful ending. We'd been at the party for less than an hour. I'd finished my first drink, a Pinterest-worthy pomegranate Paloma, and craved another. My eyes scanned for Brian, hoping he'd fetch me a fresh cocktail.

I didn't want to give up my seat until I'd gotten the scoop about Oak Hill Elementary's second-grade teachers. We'd received the class list emails and teacher assignments the day before. Tucker had gotten Mr. Franklin. As soon as Betsy Gallagher was done outlining her upcoming kitchen renovation and debating the merits of garbage disposals, I was going to ask if Franklin was the one who gave a ton of homework and was tougher on the boys. And, if so, I needed to know how difficult it was to request a new teacher. Tucker could be sensitive. I already anticipated Amy-Pat having separation anxiety once preschool started. How much could I handle?

Before I could ask, Lindsay Jordan sighed. "It's getting impossible to find a sitter in this town. These kids are so busy. Who's watching your guys tonight, Sarah?"

"Cassidy McLean." Heads whipped in my direction, eyes wide. A hush fell over the table. Even the sounds of the fiddle from the bluegrass band beside the renovated barn fell away.

"Wow." Betsy looked around the table and then directly at me. "That's—you heard about Evan Barnes, right?"

"That they think he may be involved? With Billy . . ." I fumbled, unsure how to phrase it.

Lindsay shook her head as her manicured nails clicked across her phone screen. "No . . . he . . . here. Watch. My niece knows him. She sent me this a couple hours ago."

She held out her phone with a video queued up. Evan Barnes's face filled most of the screen. I wouldn't have known him if I hadn't seen his picture on TV. I leaned in. Lindsay pressed play and turned up the volume.

"Hey, what's up, guys? Happy Fourth!" He strolled through Manhattan, the Washington Square Arch and fountain behind him. "Guess who's celebrating July Fourth and freedom like never before? That's right. It's your boy, Evan! Got cleared by the cops today. Here's a tip: always make sure your dealer has a doorman and a security camera in case you need an alibi. Peace out."

He has an alibi. Evan didn't take Billy.

"What an asshole, right?" Lindsay said. "Anyway, I couldn't find a sitter, and after that, Scott insisted we take the boys to his mom's in Toms River. The traffic was killer."

Someone else has Billy. Someone who may still be out there.

"Poor Rachel," Betsy said. "Has anyone seen her lately? I brought her a meal a few weeks ago." She lowered her voice. "She still hasn't returned my Le Creuset."

My children are with the sitter who was supposed to be watching Billy Barnes.

"I haven't seen Rachel, but Oliver's still a mess." Lindsay frowned. "He and Billy were really tight. I worry about the long-term. Like, what impact this will have on him, you know? If he hadn't had that dentist appointment, he'd have been walking home with Billy that afternoon. I'm afraid he'll have that—what do you call it? Survivor's guilt?"

"You are literally giving me chills right now." Betsy shivered and stabbed at her ice cubes with a skinny straw. "Who else is ready for another drink?"

I'd only had one cocktail but felt unsteady. My brain pinwheeled, replaying how out of it Cassidy sounded that afternoon when I'd called her. I should've hung up and found someone else.

My phone sat tucked beneath the Tory Burch wristlet Brian had the kids give me for Mother's Day. I slipped it out and stared at the screen. Three missed calls. All from Cassidy. In an instant, I felt my heartbeat vibrate throughout my entire body.

"Be right back," I said, though no one was listening. They'd already moved on to the subject of dog breeders. As I walked toward an empty corner by the pool, the phone buzzed in my hand. Cassidy. Again. I swiped frantically at the screen, fingers greasy from caramelized onion and gruyère tartlets.

"Cassidy, what's—"

I heard her crying, gasping, trying to form words I could barely make out over the banjos' twang.

I pressed the phone to my skull and cupped my hand over my other ear, straining to hear.

"She's gone. Amy-Pat. I can't find Amy-Pat! She's gone!"

My knees buckled. I collapsed into a thicket of hydrangeas, phone clattering against flagstones.

"That's it, lady, you're cut off!" Kelli Moore giggled, extending a hand. "How many have you had? Didn't you just get here?"

"Oh my God! Sarah just fell into the bushes! It's like 'Real Housewives of Oak Hill!'" Betsy shrieked.

Lindsay hurried over and knelt beside me, frowning and calling, "Brian! Brian! Sarah needs you!"

"She probably hasn't eaten . . . doing that intermittent fasting thing . . . so hard to lose the baby weight . . . after three kids!" Betsy's murmur faded in and out.

The music stopped. Brian's face swam in front of mine. He'd been smiling until he looked into my eyes.

"Sarah, what happ—"

"We—we have to go." I took his hands and struggled to my feet, the wedge of my shoe caught between pavers wrenching my ankle. "We need to leave! Now!"

"Are you going to be sick? What's wrong?"

"It's Amy-Pat! Cassidy can't find her!" I spun in a circle, disoriented, and watched Lindsay's jaw drop. "We have to go. Where's the car?"

"We walked here." Brian took my elbow and steered me away from the crowd closing in around us. A chorus of whispers clashed with the ocean-like roaring in my head.

"I'll drive you," Lindsay offered, taking my other arm.

I don't remember climbing into her enormous SUV, only feeling small and terrified in the back seat, Brian squeezing my hand.

"She's probably up in the tree house or hiding in your closet," he said. "Remember when she stuffed herself inside your suitcase and asked us to ship her to Disney World?"

Lindsay let out a nervous laugh. "Aw! So sweet!"

I wanted to believe Brian was right, but somewhere deep inside, I knew she was gone. I felt it—the void of her. The invisible thread that connected us had snapped.

As Lindsay turned the corner, I saw the squad cars. Before she could park, I spilled out of the SUV and lunged toward the house. *That fucking gate.* I threw myself at it. It finally yielded, groaning against my weight.

Inside, Brent howled in his high chair as a police officer stood beside him offering Cheerios. Tucker ran from room to room looking under couches, behind chairs, opening closet doors, yelling, "A.P.! I know you're in here! Come out!"

Cassidy's face, splotchy and wet, crumpled when she saw us. I rushed at her. It took everything I had not to grab her shoulders, shake her, and demand, "How did you let this happen? How did you lose my child?"

"She was right here. With Tuck." Her voice cracked as she struggled to be heard above Brent's wailing.

I pulled my baby from his high chair, my arms heavy, weak.

"I took Brent up to change his diaper, and when I came down, the back door was . . ." She wiped her nose with the back of her arm and pointed toward the patio and beyond it to the backyard, bright as midday from police searchlights.

I waited for her to say the words, the part that came next. It couldn't be real. This couldn't be happening. "The back door was what?" I screamed.

"Open," she mumbled between cries, unable to meet our eyes.

Police officers escorted her to the backyard to walk them through it all again.

The rest of the night skidded into a terrible jumble of sobbing and disbelief, Brian's arm around my shoulder holding me up, police officers tearing apart our home, asking endless questions. I needed to talk to Cassidy again, but she'd been taken to the station before I had a chance.

At some point, the police found the phone. It looked so cheap and fake, I thought it was a toy Amy-Pat left in the tree house. Officers located it in the bushes, near the gate. The thought of someone watching our home, our children, waiting for an opportunity, made me feel faint. I sunk into a lawn chair.

"Most often, these prepaid phones are purchased by individuals who wish to remain anonymous," a young policeman, Officer Kinsley, explained, as if he were talking about a philanthropist rather than a criminal.

"But you'll be able to find out who owns it? And that will lead us to Amy-Pat?" I gasped, foolishly believing my daughter would be returned to us within minutes.

"You don't need ID to buy one." Brian hung his head. "They're the kind drug dealers use."

An older officer told us that they'd check it for fingerprints and get a warrant to unlock and search it. We'd hear from them as soon as they had news.

* * *

Now we wait, that phone a lifeline.

After the AMBER alert went out around midnight, Phil Foster called the police. He told them he'd seen a child's silver sandal on the sidewalk on his way to the fireworks.

"We sent officers to the scene; there was nothing." Mike Pruitt, the FBI agent they'd brought in to assist Oak Hill's police department, sighed after he shared that this morning when Brian and I called, pleading with him for any other leads. "I know it's disappointing, but what you have to understand about Mr. Foster is that he has a history of making false claims. He inserts himself in and creates—or perhaps 'imagines' is a better word—situations. It's not uncommon among former members of the military. While deployed, Mr. Foster lived in a heightened state of awareness. Once you've had that experience over a prolonged period, it's difficult to readjust to an uneventful life in a small town."

"But what if he did see something? My daughter has a pair of silver sandals!" Amy-Pat had worn them everywhere, believing they looked like Cinderella's glass slippers.

"It's a cry for attention, ma'am," he'd said. "Officers spoke with Mr. Foster and checked the street, the sidewalks, even the sewers. I'm sorry."

* * *

I stare at the tree house and picture my daughter, her tiny legs climbing the ladder in those cheap slip-ons that reminded me of jellyfish, pink purse swinging from her wrist. Did someone go up and pull her out? Did she scream? How did Tucker and Cassidy—even the neighbors—not hear her? Did she go willingly? And, if so, does that mean our little girl was taken by someone we know?

18

Friday, July 5
Allison

"HERE YOU GO!" Our waiter places our meals in front of us. "Enjoy, ladies!"

Viv stops scrolling through Instagram. "Fucking finally," she mutters when he's out of earshot.

I've lost my appetite. I want to grab her phone and search for information about Amy-Pat's disappearance. I missed most of that news segment because I'd been too lazy to turn around. Days ago I'd read that the FBI had gotten involved once Evan Barnes became a suspect—something about drugs and crossing state lines.

"Let's do some touristy shit after this," Viv says, arugula stems poking out of her mouth.

While Billy and Amy-Pat are all I can think about, they're the furthest things from Viv's mind.

"Sounds good." I nod, not meaning it. I want to go back to the apartment and use her laptop to look for news, but I know she'll call me out for becoming a hermit or an amateur detective.

I watch, stomach churning, as Viv stuffs her "temple" with my untouched hash browns and bacon. When she's done, she balls up her napkin and tosses it into a puddle of ketchup.

"We've gotta walk this off! I know this director, and she'll never hire a lifeguard shaped like a manatee."

Viv and I wander along the High Line toward the Vessel, the metal-and-glass centerpiece of Hudson Yards. Families determined to make the most of the long weekend surround us. Perspiring parents with babies in carriers cuddled against their chests pass us, some push pink-cheeked toddlers napping in strollers. The familiar longing returns. I watch as Viv winks at a puppy.

"Is it weird that my ovaries ache for a French bulldog?" she jokes. "Seriously, why would anyone want a baby when you could have a sweet, cuddly pooch who won't leave you with stretch marks or completely destroy your vagina?"

I look at her, but before I can speak, she says, "Oh shit, Al. I'm so sorry. That was totally insensitive."

Her words make me catch my breath. I stop, breaking our slow, meandering stride. How does she know? Has she heard me crying at three in the morning after another nightmare filled with lost children jolts me from sleep? Did Chris find her and ask if she's heard from me? And if so, what does that mean?

Just as I'm about to speak, she continues. "You must miss your guy like crazy. What's his name? Sully? I remember his photos from Facebook. Such a cutie!"

"Murphy." My body melts with relief. I can't talk about anything as serious as what I thought she meant, especially with this hangover.

She touches my arm. "I'm really sorry. I get this insensitive asshole gene from my dad."

"It's fine," I say, meaning it.

Viv shares nearly every thought she has with me—for better or worse—while I'm hiding an enormous chunk of my life from her. But what I love about our friendship is the fact that she's completely herself. Uncensored. Talking with someone who doesn't weigh every word is a refreshing change.

It's been a long time since I've had that. After Chris and I left Brooklyn and our friends scattered to various leafy suburbs, we'd meet for drinks in the city, or someone would host a barbecue to show off their new house. We were eager to flaunt the things we couldn't have during our city-living days, the upgrades we'd made—kitchen renovations, home theaters. For Chris, it was his man-cave music studio.

After lamenting the endless work homeownership entailed, the conversation would turn to babies—everything from cracked nipples to sleep training. The guys patted each other's stomachs and joked about their "dad bods." Across a newly installed deck, Chris and I would look at each other. We no longer fit in. Often, we drove home in silence. Without a baby snuggled in a car seat, the back seat loomed, menacing as a hitchhiker.

Our get-togethers rarely ended without the question we dreaded: "When are you two gonna have kids?" Someone would fill the awkward silence with "It would be nice to see the perfect couple as miserable as the rest of us!" followed by forced laughter.

At first, we said my work schedule was crazy—too much traveling. Then we'd joked that we were adjusting to life as puppy parents—we couldn't imagine caring for a tiny human.

When I'd stopped drinking, they'd whisper until one friend, nursing her perfect infant, would sidle up to me grinning to ask, "So, you and Chris have any good news to share?"

Sometimes I felt their pity, all those big, life-defining moments we were missing. Other times I sensed their resentment that we could sleep in or catch a movie or a concert on a whim.

During our Brooklyn days, I'd listened as several friends struggled through IVF. But they'd gotten their happy endings. The embryos they fretted over—from their cost to their viability—were beautiful, thriving toddlers. Would these couples even remember what it was like to long for the babies who now woke them at dawn, left them unshowered, with messy rooms, devoid of any free time?

When I finally told my friends about the miscarriages, they were sympathetic, showering me with advice: "Try acupuncture! Maybe yoga?" They referred me to doctors we'd already seen. In the months that followed, they peppered me with texts filled with links to articles on infertility and grief, recommendations for herbs and supplements, and the always-hard-to-answer, "How are you holding up?" followed by hearts and sad face emojis. It only made me feel worse.

We stopped inviting them to our place and found excuses not to go to theirs. I skipped baby showers and gender reveal parties. It was less painful, but it also meant losing touch with those friends.

At the same time, my relationship with my sister offered little comfort. When I suffered another loss days before Thanksgiving, I insisted on hosting the holiday, needing a distraction, determined to focus on something other than myself and our latest heartbreak.

"This has to be really hard for you," Jen had said as we watched Chris and her husband, Pete, kick a soccer ball with Emily and Ethan.

"It is." Tears, always on standby, swam into the corners of my eyes. I swallowed the sadness, stuffed it down, and took a deep breath. The air smelled smoky, a fire burning somewhere in the distance.

"I mean, you and Chris always get what you want—the cool jobs, the big house in this fancy neighborhood." She waved her arms, as if we were on the grounds of Versailles instead of a suburban backyard. Wine spilled over the rim of her glass and onto her jeans. She didn't notice. She'd uncorked a second bottle from the half case she brought, knowing we no longer kept any in the house. "Shit, I've even seen people stop to admire your dog. It seems like this is the first time things aren't going your way. Disappointment sucks, right?"

I refused to give her the satisfaction of knowing how much her words hurt me.

"I'm sure it'll all work out soon. I'm seeing a new doctor."

"Yeah, Al, but what if the doctor's not the problem? I'm just saying, Chris's past . . ." She shivered as the wind kicked up and the sky darkened. "And you've always been so skeletal. Do you even still get your period?"

I wanted to leave, abandon my home and the holiday I was hosting, because as much as I hated to admit it, Jen was right. The doctors weren't the problem. Chris and I had submitted to every test imaginable. I'd been poked, stuck, scanned, and shot full of dye. The results always came back the same: no definitive answer.

"Hmmm . . ." Specialists invariably paused while scrolling through reports, then turned to me. "We don't know why this is happening. We should try sending you for . . ." They'd name another obscure condition that warranted more tests, simultaneously giving me false hope and the impression they were grasping at straws.

Often, as these experts stumbled toward the part where they admitted they were stumped, there'd be a moment when they felt inclined to share personal anecdotes.

"You seem to be having a run of bad luck. Same thing happened to my cousin. Today, she has three healthy sons. Just between us, I think she wouldn't mind having one less!"

As we sat in cold rooms where photos of "miracle babies" lined the walls, I'd watch Chris, handsome even as he scowled and pressed his lips together, stopping himself from saying the words I knew were forming in his mind: "There's got to be some mistake. Look at us! We're perfect. We've been on magazine covers. People want to be us. Look again!"

I wanted them to find something, to beg them, "You don't know my husband. He'll never accept this. Please help me."

* * *

While I'd been changing in and out of disposable paper gowns in doctors' offices and hospitals, Viv had been donning evening gowns, strutting down runways in fashion shows in Paris and London. Even when she moved to L.A. and we were in touch more frequently, I didn't share my problems with her. It seemed too hard, too personal to explain via email or text. And anytime I tried to talk about it, I couldn't do it without dissolving into tears.

Now I'm glad I never told Viv because she doesn't see me as "poor, defective Allison," the way so many others do. She thinks my sadness stems from problems in my marriage. It's better this way. More common, less intimate.

Since going back to Oak Hill yesterday, seeing the tree, thinking about all we lost, I've been wondering how Chris is coping. People don't think infertility affects a man, but it does. I sat there, helpless, witnessing how each loss crushed him, compounding my sense of failure. In his eyes, I saw the disappointment each time we walked Murph and spotted families out for a bike ride or watched parents pushing kids on swings in the park. The life we'd never have was constantly reflected back at us.

When Chris gave lessons, he was funny, patient, encouraging. *"That was amazing! Now tell me what you think if we tried it a bit like this . . ."* His students adored him. He'd be a wonderful father. If there were any other way to make it happen, I'd have stayed. But the last miscarriage broke me.

Without telling Chris, I'd filled the prescription for sleeping pills, storing them in a Tampax box in the bathroom. After we got home from the D&C, I'd taken two, longing to sleep without a single nightmare. When I woke up the next morning, the ache—that gnawing hollowness that I knew too well—was there, waiting to ruin another day.

I smelled coffee and pancakes. Chris always worked overtime to make me feel better and stronger afterward. I drifted downstairs, that familiar trickle of blood between my legs a reminder of my body's ongoing betrayal.

"Hey, there's my girl," Chris said, kissing me lightly on the forehead before sprinkling chocolate chips over the bubbling pancakes. "Have a seat." He gestured toward the kitchen table, where a package waited at my place—a square white box with a baby blue ribbon.

"Chris," I started, "I don't want a—"

"Good, because, technically, it's not for you." He smiled. "Open it."

Following each loss, he'd bought me things—necklaces, bracelets, cashmere wraps. I donated them to auctions for charities that supported animals, children, or survivors of domestic abuse.

I hesitated as I untied the ribbon, eased the lid off, and removed a cloud of tissue paper.

"Take it out!" Chris insisted.

I reached in and removed a mobile. A tiny guitar, baby grand piano, mini drum set, harmonica, and a French horn dangled from golden, harp-like strings.

"It's got a built-in MP3 player." Chris smiled again. "I can create and record my own lullabies. Check it out."

He pressed a button. His tinny rendition of "You Are My Sunshine" pierced the silence.

"How? Why?" I dropped the mobile on the table, delicate strings tangling, music stopping.

"I found it online and ordered it before—" He looked down. "We'll keep it for next time."

"I told you at the hospital," my voice cracked, strength seeping out of me, "I'm done. There isn't a 'next time.' I can't do this anymore."

He pulled me close, smoothed my hair matted from sleep, and whispered, "You say that now, Al, but you'll change your mind." His fingers stroked the back of my neck. I recoiled. "Give it time. You'll come around. You always do."

"No!" I wrestled out of his arms. "No. I mean it, Chris. I'm done."

I left him there, shaking his head as if I were a confused or disobedient child, smoke rising from the griddle.

Upstairs, I swallowed two more pills and waited for everything to fade back to nothingness.

As tension built a wall between us, I started seeing someone. A therapist. I needed support if I was going to move forward, pack all my sorrow into a box, shelve it, and continue trying to have a baby. I wanted someone to show me where to find hope. Without it, how could I have my heart broken over and over and still tell myself it might turn out differently?

"Let's put aside what Chris wants. What do *you* want, Allison?" the therapist asked one February afternoon as I sat in her office, empty, hypnotized by the sound of sleet clinking against the window behind her head.

"I want to be done." A thrilling clarity washed over me. It was like slipping on a dress that fit perfectly.

I'd known the terrible statistics—after three previous miscarriages, the risk of another is forty-three percent. It got worse from there. What made me think I could beat those odds?

At some point, it stopped being about having a child. It morphed into achieving a goal that was always out of reach. It was about pleasing Chris, even as he became blind to the toll it took on me. It turned into trying to show my sister that I could have everything and proving to myself that I could be a mother, just like the women surrounding me in Oak Hill.

But none of that happened, and I hated who I'd become—someone who averted her eyes each time she saw a happy family, someone who pretended not to know her neighbor because that woman's child had lived.

That sleety February afternoon, the numbness began to melt, and the idea of leaving started forming in my mind. When Viv got in touch later that week to tell me she was moving to New York, it felt like a sign.

I decided I'd be gone by early spring before the dogwoods bloomed and dozens of mothers flocked to the park, their perfect, round bellies preceding them, toddlers waddling like ducklings in their wake.

"Start again with someone else," I told Chris in the note I left. "Create the life I can't give you. Be happy."

* * *

Am *I* happier now? It's hard to say. I just want to be whole again, complete, without needing or wanting anyone else. Days I've spent sipping cocktails with Viv overlooking the Hudson or wandering alone through a museum, lingering as long as I like, in those rare moments, I've felt I could get back to who I was, and that sustains me.

As Viv and I walk back to her building, I sneak a look across the street. No strange man waiting there. I breathe a sigh of relief as Viv's phone beeps. She reads the text, smiles, and taps her reply.

"Date tonight," she says. "I started talking to this guy, Dex, on the train back this morning." She grins. "A little, old conductor sneezed and farted at the same time, and I started laughing—I totally get that that makes me a weirdo—but I looked across the aisle, and this guy was cracking up too."

I shake my head, the heat zapping me of the strength to point out that's hardly a meet-cute anyone would repeat.

"What? You know a twisted sense of humor is important to me. Well, that and a thick dick," she says as we pass an elderly woman walking a corgi.

"Jesus, Viv!"

"He seems cool. But now I barely remember what he looks like. He must've been hot if I was willing to talk to him at eight in the morning, right?"

"Based on how fast you wrote back, I'd say you liked something about him."

"He probably has a wife, three kids, and a farmhouse in Connecticut. You can't trust anyone these days."

We climb the stairs, panting and groaning until a welcome blast of air conditioning greets us inside her apartment.

"I'm beat!" Viv drops her keys in a bowl beside the door. "I'm gonna lie down for a bit."

I flop onto the couch, kick off my sandals, and wait for her to leave the room so I can be alone with her computer, my mind returning, as it always does, to lost children.

Once I hear her bedroom door close, I grab the laptop, pop in earbuds, and type "Amelia-Patricia Davies Oak Hill." Three weeks ago, I did the same with Billy Barnes.

Stories fill the page. It's now national news. Cassidy McLean is the headline.

Nanny Dearest: Is Babysitter to Blame for Jersey Girl's Disappearance?
Suburban Babysitter Back in Spotlight as Second Child Vanishes on Her Watch
Who's Watching the Sitter? 2 Oak Hill, NJ, Children Go Missing in 3 Weeks

I only met Cassidy a couple of times. She'd taken lessons, wanting to learn Joni Mitchell's "River" for her mom's birthday. There's no way she could have anything to do with missing children. Instead of clicking on the article from The Acorn, Oak Hill's online news, I choose a trashy, tabloid-style site because it will have more details.

Double Trouble: Two Kids Snatched From Snooty Suburb Watched By Same Sitter

Fireworks weren't the only thing that shook residents in the sleepy suburb of Oak Hill, NJ, last night. Three-year-old Amelia-Patricia Davies went missing before 7 PM. Her disappearance comes just three weeks after five-year-old Billy Barnes vanished from the affluent community without a trace.

In addition to sharing a zip code, the children have something else in common: their babysitter, Cassidy McLean. An eighteen-year-old Oak Hill High graduate, McLean has maintained that she arrived late to the Barneses' home on June 13, the day the boy went missing, due to a detour. McLean was on duty again last evening, minding Davies and her siblings. The sitter called police when she was unable to locate the little girl.

Photos show volunteers posting flyers and tying ribbons on trees at Oak Hill playground. My eyes reflexively scan the dog park for Chris and Murph.

Residents who asked not to be identified said they believe parents may have let their guard down after Evan Barnes, Billy's twenty-two-year-old half brother, was brought in for questioning in connection with his disappearance.

"I think maybe we all got a little lax, thinking that what happened to Billy was just a bad family situation," said an Oak Hill mother of two speaking on the condition of anonymity.

Some Oak Hill residents are reluctant to point a finger at McLean but admit it's an "eerie coincidence."

Police aren't sharing many details as both investigations remain ongoing, but confirmed another odd link. The Barnes family's former au pair, whom police have been unable to locate, also minded the Davieses' children occasionally. A spokesperson for Oak Hill's police department refused to comment on efforts to find the Irish-born caregiver.

Both families now wait, hoping that a cell phone found in the Davieses' backyard will lead to the safe return of their children.

I glance around the apartment, wondering where I've left my phone. It's usually on the coffee table, but it's not there. I dig around beneath the sofa cushions and come up empty-handed. It's so small and cheap, if I can't find it, I'll just get another at the bodega.

In the meantime, parents in Oak Hill are keeping their doors locked and their children close.

Even though I'm sick to my stomach, I can't help it. I scroll to the comments section and brace for the worst. At the height of my acting career, I received plenty of hate from assholes with too much time on their hands. "That's part of life in the spotlight," my agent would remind me.

Chris understood. For him, it cut even deeper—it was his art. His essence. Yet, he'd shrug it off. "As long as you're still a fan, that's what counts," he'd say with a wink, pulling me toward our bedroom.

The memory fills me with a warm feeling I've nearly forgotten, and for a second I think about shutting the laptop. Why upset myself? But now, just like then, I can't help it.

"RIP Billy and Amy-Pat! Too bad your parents didn't care enough to watch you themselves."

"Sitter's hot. Just sayin'"

"I don't know what happened to this little girl, but I still say five was way too young to let that boy walk home alone!"

"There's no greater heartache in life than losing a child."

A bunch offer "thoughts and prayers," while others speculate on the children's terrible fates. The more I read, the sicker I feel.

"You know some pedo has them chained to his furnace."

"My condolences to the families, but these two are in pieces somewhere at the bottom of a landfill. Or, worse, sold to traffickers. They're never coming back and anyone who thinks differently is living in la la land."

I shut the laptop and close my eyes, not that it does any good. Billy and Amy-Pat's faces remain, seared into my brain.

CHAPTER

19

Friday, July 5
Lindsay

I DOUBLE-CHECK TO MAKE sure the front door is locked, and the garage doors are closed. Then I set the alarm before walking to Betsy's. She texted earlier about organizing a candlelight vigil for Sunday night at Oak Hill Pond if Billy and Amy-Pat aren't found by then.

I'm halfway down the driveway when I realize I forgot my phone. I turn around and go back into the house. My hands fumble reentering the security system's code. Since last night when I drove Sarah and Brian home, I'm having trouble focusing, my head aches, and I can't stop trembling. I'd been so sure Ted or Evan was responsible, I'd dismissed all possibility of a real threat until I heard Sarah wail, "It's Amy-Pat! Cassidy can't find her!" Sarah's face, white with fear, told me how wrong I'd been.

I shouldn't have driven. I'd only had one drink, but it was strong and I hadn't eaten in hours. The air in the car was hot and stale. I wanted to say something reassuring, but my mind went blank.

Sarah opened the door and leaped toward her house before I'd barely turned the corner. I didn't know what to do. Should I park and stay to help look for Amy-Pat? Or would I be an intruder, a voyeur, stepping in to observe my neighbors at their darkest moment?

I remembered when Oliver was three and had wandered off at the supermarket. Those seconds before I found him in the seafood department talking to lobsters were easily the most frightening of my life.

After Brian jumped out, I gripped the steering wheel until I couldn't feel my fingers and circled the empty streets. Everyone who wasn't invited to the Moores' was at the fireworks. Scott called my cell to tell me the party had broken up and he'd meet me at home.

I wasn't ready to see him, to hear him give me a hard time for not taking this seriously. I drove slowly as dusk settled, squinting at porches, side yards, backyard trampolines, praying for a glimpse of Amy-Pat. I would find her and bring her home. I coasted from stop sign to stop sign, hoping to spot her wandering down a sidewalk, lost, barefoot. *Why barefoot?* I wondered. Then my mind flashed to something I'd passed a few streets back—a gray thing my brain registered as a squirrel on the side of the road. Was it a child's shoe? A little silver sandal? Did it belong to Amy-Pat? Why hadn't I stopped? Which street was it? I couldn't remember.

I looped back to the Davieses', saw their backyard bathed in unnatural light, and tried to re-create the route I'd taken. Whatever I'd seen was no longer there. Who knows? Maybe I imagined it. That's when my headache started.

*   *   *

I ring Betsy's doorbell.

"Coming!" she calls.

No one's leaving any doors unlocked now.

"Hi," she says, brushing her fingers against her floral apron. "Come in."

No air kiss. She must be distracted by thoughts of the vigil. I follow her into the gorgeous kitchen she's planning to gut in a few weeks, her heels tapping on the stone floor.

"Sorry about the mess." She gestures toward the double sink where a pot and pan soak. "I just took a baked ziti over to Sarah's."

"How is she?" I flinch, afraid of the answer.

"Brian said she was resting. He looked awful. He's wearing the same clothes he had on at the party last night." Betsy shudders.

"Where is everyone?" I check my phone for the time. 7:10 PM. "You invited Polly and Robin?"

"I told them seven thirty. I asked you to come a little early so we could talk first. Wine?"

"Just a splash, I have a killer headache." I settle onto a barstool and look around. On the island rests a clipboard with a checklist of the tasks Betsy plans to assign tonight. As she opens a Riesling, I read through it: "Candles. Music. Posters of Billy and Amy-Pat. Contact local and national media!! Find minister??"

Betsy sets out two glasses, fills them well beyond a splash, and takes a long swallow.

"Where are Doug and the boys?" I ask, noticing the house is quiet except for the dripping of the copper faucet and the almost-imperceptible purr of her Bosch dishwasher.

"Mini golfing. I told Doug, 'Do not let them out of your sight for a second!'"

"I know." I sip the wine, so sweet that my headache instantly worsens. "Scott has the boys at the park fielding grounders, and I said the same to him."

"Honestly, Lindsay." Betsy shakes her head. "I can't believe you convinced me we had nothing to worry about."

"I—"

"That Ted Barnes would hurt his own child?" She looks up at the vaulted ceiling before narrowing her eyes at me. "What if something happened to my boys because I believed you?"

Her tone shames me into silence.

"And, what's your 'feeling' about Sarah?" She sneers. "Let me guess. Is she jealous of Rachel getting all the attention, so she faked her daughter's kidnapping?"

"Betsy, stop!" I smack my glass down so hard on the island, I expect the stem to snap. "Please! Where is this coming from? I'd never say anything like that."

"Wouldn't you?" She drains her wine, and puts her hand on her hip.

"Obviously, I-I was wrong," I stammer. "It's just, in a town like Oak Hill, you don't think—"

"No, you don't think," Betsy continues, pointing a long, manicured finger in my face. "You just blithely spread rumors about Ted. I saw him this morning at the market. The man is distraught."

"I wasn't spreading rumors! You're the only one I told!" My face burns, first with embarrassment, then anger. "And you're no better. Everyone knows you deliver your pity meals so you can get a front-row seat to their misery. Then, you complain if you're not immediately thanked and complimented!" Betsy rears back as if I've slapped her. "The petition, this vigil— they're not about the children. They're about you!" My voice comes out high, squeaky, undermining me. Betsy's face is a mask as she stares at me, shoulders squared, regaining her strength. "And that au pair?" I can't stop. "You're the one who told the whole town she left Billy home alone! You made sure she'd never work in Oak Hill again. What if she's getting her revenge now?"

We glare at each other as the doorbell chimes.

"Get out," Betsy says, lips curling in toward her teeth.

"I'm already leaving." My legs tremble as I slide off the stool and follow her to the front door.

Robin and Polly step back, confused as I rush past them, tears stinging my eyes.

"Lindsay isn't feeling well," Betsy explains.

Over my shoulder, I see her air kiss our neighbors and whisk them inside. She scowls at me as she shuts the door. From the sidewalk, I hear the deadbolt jam into place.

As I hurry home, a squirrel zigzags across the street. I close my eyes, trying to picture whatever it was I saw in the road last night.

Do I go to the police? Or have I already said too much?

20

Friday, July 5
Rachel

T HE NIGHT SKY is a deep, dark blue, the color of an ink
stain. I look through the window, waiting for the slideshow to load so I can torture myself, watching my son grow
from a pink newborn to a toddler in overalls, crawling through
lush green grass, and then into the beautiful boy whose laughter
I'd give my life to hear once more.

His face fills the screen, so close and real I want to reach in
and pull him through the desktop computer into the home
office Ted and I shared during better days. Billy loved to sit
here, swiveling in circles in the brown leather chair, his legs
dangling inches above the floor, marveling, "I was so small!
Now I'm so big!" as the photos changed.

The brightness of the images sears my already-burning eyes,
but I can't look away. Each day feels like a century since I've
seen my son's face. I need to memorize the way his dimples
crease and his nose crinkles when he smiles.

I pause to study a photo taken in an orchard. Ted's hand
rests dutifully on my right shoulder. Billy is perched on the
crook of my left arm. He reaches for an apple as branches bend
toward us, dripping with fruit. I'd asked one of the farmhands
to take this shot.

"Beautiful family," he'd said as he handed back my phone.

We had the potential to be, once. Everything I ever wanted is there in that image. Now it's gone. A sob catches in my throat as I press play and watch us dissolve. Billy, sitting in a bubble bath, comes into focus. He was two, maybe three at the time.

My mind shifts to Amy-Pat, to her family, reeling from the shock and anguish that I wear like a second skin now. When I heard she was missing, the baby inside me leaped—this other child that somehow grows while everything else within me dies. I'm ashamed to admit that when Betsy called to tell me Amy-Pat disappeared, I felt a small, bitter thrill that made my heart race—an evil *Ah-ha!* aimed at police who act like I'm a nuisance, who are no closer to finding my son than on the day he disappeared three weeks ago.

The hairs on my neck prick with white-hot rage when I picture Detective Dubin standing on my walkway the afternoon Billy went missing. He'd wiped sweat off his brow as if he'd been hard at work instead of what I imagined he'd done all day: sit in his air-conditioned office, waiting to collect his pension.

I ball my fists and dig them into the armrests, my brain calling up all the times he's offered me his empty, "We'll be in touch." They've been unable to track Rose. They've written off Evan as your average lost millennial with a run-of-the-mill drug habit, even though he lied to them. And how is Cassidy involved? This is more than a coincidence. Are they investigating her? Or has she been acquitted because, being young and beautiful, she doesn't fit the profile?

But the police can't dismiss me any longer. Things are different now, thanks to Amy-Pat. A glaring spotlight shines on sleepy Oak Hill. This is no longer just my family's misfortune. The whole town is on edge. I think about Madame Sonya. *He's close.* Something has to happen—soon.

On the screen, the photo from the day at the zoo flashes up. It's the one I gave police, the one that stares back at me from every poster stuck to every telephone pole, hanging in every storefront.

I wasn't supposed to go on that field trip. Chaperones' names were picked from a hat. I threw mine in, never expecting it to be chosen. I was selected as an alternate. At five thirty on the morning of the outing, I got the call. Billy's classmate Cecelia Ryan had been up all night with a stomach bug. She and her mother, one of the original chaperones, would be staying home.

"Shit!" I'd cursed loudly enough to wake Ted, who'd managed to sleep through the phone ringing and my fake-cheery, "Sure, no problem. Happy to do it!" side of the conversation.

"What?" he'd grumbled. His breath, similar to the stench of a full Diaper Genie, traveled across the king-size bed, causing me to recoil.

"I have to chaperone this stupid field trip." I'd spat, pawing at the nightstand for my glasses and struggling to remember my original plans for the day. A home inspection, a showing, a closing? I'd groaned as I scrolled through my calendar and began sending cancellation texts along with my apologies.

Of course, now I wish I could go back and savor every moment. I wish I'd given Billy a thoughtful answer when he asked, "How much hay do horses eat in a day?" rather than tossing out my careless response: "A lot."

If I'd known what was coming, I'd have put my phone in my purse and paid attention when he turned to me, pointed, and said, "Look, Mommy! A lion cub!"

But I was preoccupied—responding to emails, sending texts, my focus divided among all the wrong things. I'd missed what was right in front of me.

Even as I sat beside him on the bus, I ignored him, choosing the company of my fellow chaperones over his—the sweet boy who believed in the tooth fairy, who timed himself reciting the alphabet backward, who rejoiced each summer at the return of lightning bugs.

I look out the window again. Can he see them from wherever he is now? I rest my face in my hands, tears wet my palms. I startle as Jeter leaps into my lap, nudging my arm. *Did I give him dinner?* Time has lost all meaning.

As I close the slideshow, my eyes land on a folder on the desktop, one I haven't seen before. I click and photos of a dozen houses pop up. I don't recognize any of them. Smallish, nothing fancy, these aren't my listings. My brutal call with Frances Lewis has been the only work-related contact I've had in weeks.

Did Derek send them as possible investment properties? Some overlook water, tiny whitecaps lap clay-colored rocks in the foreground. These don't look like any homes in Oak Hill. *Where is this? Why is this here?* I feel disoriented.

I open the search history. "Homes for sale in Maine."

Maine? I read the words again, my brain struggling to connect invisible dots. My heart beats faster.

I move the mouse back to the search history, scan the list:

"Good school districts in Maine."

"Public schools in Portland, ME."

"Best private schools in Maine."

"Jobs in Maine."

I close my eyes to stop the dizziness.

Ted's moving to Maine? Does he know about Derek and me? We'd had a fight about the amount of time and money I was spending with Derek weeks before Billy disappeared. I remember him threatening me, "I promise this won't end well for you!" I thought he'd been talking about the home flip. Was he planning to leave and take Billy with him? To punish me? My limbs turn to jelly. I force my hand to move the mouse to the menu bar. These searches are from a week ago. *A week ago.*

I picture Ted—that smug prick, sleeping and eating while I tear my fucking hair out with worry. Has he had Billy this whole time? All the nights he's told me he's with Evan, has he been with his other son? *My son!* Where is Ted now? Where is Billy? I scoop up Jeter and place him on the carpet. I have to call Ted. With trembling fingers, I press my phone. It's dead. I need the charger. I fumble through the drawers. It's not there.

I stand too quickly and sway, blinded by a headrush. It feels like all the air has been sucked out of the room. I can't catch my breath, overcome with relief that Billy might be safe, murderous that my husband could be capable of something so twisted and sinister. *Did he think he'd get away with this? That I wouldn't find out? Could this nightmare almost be over?*

The hallway is dark as I lurch toward the stairs. I miss a step, sending me tumbling. My head hits the floor just as a new thought strikes me: If Ted has Billy, who took Amy-Pat?

21

Saturday, July 6
Sarah

I T'S BEEN DECADES since I've said a prayer. Even when my water broke at the farmers market last October, and I thought Brent might drop right out of me beside a gourd display, I refused to call upon the same God who let my mother die when I was a child. But now I close my eyes and whisper desperate bargains. *Please! If my daughter comes home, I'll never lose my patience, never take my family for granted, never be so selfish that I choose a party over my children again.*

My pleas are interrupted by a sound. At first, I think I've imagined it, then it comes again—the doorbell. It's six in the morning. Only bad news arrives before breakfast. Brian's in Brent's room, giving him a bottle. I turn toward the door, tightening the belt on my robe, my body suddenly chilled by cold sweat.

In the entryway, I see Brian at the top of the staircase, Brent squirming in his arms. We exchange a look, knowing a devastating new reality may wait on the other side of the door. I don't want to open it. At least in the unbearable not-knowing, there is hope. I'm not ready for that to be ripped away from us too.

I take a deep breath. Brian nods but doesn't speak, not wanting to wake Tucker, who was up most of the night again, asking, "When's A.P. coming home? Where do you think she is? Who took her? Why? What do you think she's doing right now?"

I unlock the door and turn the knob.

*   *   *

"Morning, Mrs. Davies." Agent Pruitt removes his sunglasses.

His gaze is steady. I can't read it. My heart jackhammers, body preparing mind and soul for the worst. There's a ringing in my ears—the kind I get before I faint. I grip the doorknob like it is the only thing tethering me to this earth.

"I know it's early, but I figured you'd be up," he says. "We haven't located your daughter, ma'am, but we do have some new information I'd like to share. May I—?"

I step back, tightening my robe, and bump into Brian. I never heard him come down the stairs.

"What? What is it?" he asks. He's still in the same clothes he wore to the Moores' party. His unwashed hair points in all directions. My husband, who's been holding us together, is coming undone.

"Let's talk in here." Agent Pruitt nods toward the kitchen as if this is his home and we're his guests.

Brian and I follow him to the table where dishes from last night's dinner—a ziti Betsy delivered—sit, mozzarella hardened like Elmer's glue. I stack the plates and shove them to the side while Brian wiggles Brent into his high chair, reattaching the tray, crusty with bits of pasta and pureed peas. I should be embarrassed, but I don't care.

"We were able to unlock the phone," Agent Pruitt says, his eyes shift from Brian to me and back again. "We don't know who owns the device yet. There's nothing stored on it in terms of personal information, but I can tell you that both outgoing and incoming calls were made to only one number."

We wait, barely breathing, staring at him, willing him to say more.

"The calls were going to and coming from a number registered to Allison Langley."

He lets the name land, gauging our reaction. Brian and I look at each other, confused.

"Do you know Ms. Langley?" Agent Pruitt continues, hands on hips.

Do I know Allison Langley? Does anyone?

I shake my head. "I know who she is," I say.

"That's the actress, right?" Brian asks.

"I met her in the park, years ago, I'm sure I told you," I remind Brian before looking back at Agent Pruitt, "and then again when our son Tucker went for that guitar lesson with her husband."

Agent Pruitt shifts his weight from one side to the other like he's waiting for me to say something that will help him piece this together. Nothing comes to me.

"She was sort of reclusive," I babble, "not really friends with anyone in the neighborhood that I know of."

Allison Langley? I fight through the fog in my mind, trying to force this new information to make sense.

"She left town in April," I add. "Everyone talked about it, but no one knew why. What happened, I mean."

My thoughts crawl back to that day in the park. She'd told me she was pregnant. I didn't see her again until Tuck's lesson. On our walk to the Langleys' house, I'd wondered if she'd remember me, if Amy-Pat and her little girl would become friends. I imagined introducing her to my mom circle, scoring cool points with Lindsay, Betsy, and the others. "Oh! We didn't know you were friends with *her*!" they'd say. I pictured her spilling secrets about the costars she'd kissed and the skin products that made her glow like she'd just returned from vacation.

But that never happened.

Allison had answered the door and looked right through me. It was as if we'd never met. Her home was stunning, but like a showroom or a fancy hotel. Sterile, cold. Not lived-in. There were no toys or stuffed animals, no evidence of the daughter she'd said she was expecting. Had she been playing a part, prepping for an audition? Did she lose the baby?

She turned her head so I couldn't make eye contact. "Follow me," was all she said as she led us to a bench where we waited for Chris. Where was the friendly, forthcoming woman from the park? This Allison was cold, joyless. But what could I say? "Hey! Remember me? We had that nice chat ages ago?" No.

Instead, I'd just sat there, checking my watch, wishing time would speed up. Chris had been great with Tuck. Funny, kind, encouraging. I'd expected some big rock-star ego, especially when I saw how much cuter he was in person. I heard Tuck laugh when Chris high-fived him and said, "Dude, you nailed that ending. You sure this is your first lesson?"

Still, those few moments with Allison made me so uncomfortable I didn't want to go back there again—certainly not weekly.

On the walk home, Tuck showed me his hands. Little lines creased his fingertips where the guitar strings had dug in. I seized on it as an excuse to not return to their house.

I wasn't surprised when I heard Allison had left Oak Hill. She seemed miserable here.

"We're going to contact Ms. Langley," Agent Pruitt says, his deep voice pulling me back into the kitchen. "See what we can find out. In the meantime, there's something else I want to ask: "You hired the Barneses' former au pair, Rose Finnerty, occasionally, is that correct?"

I nod. "Rose helped me a bit after I had Brent. She'd play with Amy-Pat, read to her, things like that, while I caught up on laundry or showered. But then she told me Rachel didn't want her working outside their home—even though Billy was in school."

"Did Rose seem angry with Mrs. Barnes?"

"No, not really." I shake my head, trying to remember. Nothing sticks out. "She seemed kind of disappointed that she couldn't make more money—that's how I took it." I pause, a memory swims to the surface. "A few months after that, I'd heard that Rose left Billy home alone and Rachel let her go."

He nodded, as if this confirmed something he already knew.

"I—I didn't know if it was true?" I add.

In Oak Hill, gossip is like oxygen—it's everywhere, sustaining us. I gobbled it up like everyone else. But because I wasn't part of the true inner circle, I never knew how much to believe. When I'd heard that story about Rose, I'd had my doubts. I'd wondered if Rachel Barnes had made it up as a way to stop neighbors from speculating about why the au pair was spotted leaving their home in such a hurry.

A few evenings ago, I saw Rachel circling the streets. Shrunken and stoop-shouldered in black leggings and an enormous sweatshirt despite the oppressive heat, she looked ravaged—nothing like the crisp professional I'd seen at Oak Hill Elementary functions, tapping her Apple watch with her gel manicure, passing out business cards to pregnant moms, hoping they were ready to upgrade from their starter homes. I'd been pulling Amy-Pat in her red wagon. We were headed to the library to return the "Llama Llama" books she'd picked when I spotted Rachel turning the corner. I'd crossed the street to avoid her, as if her misfortune was contagious. I should've gone up to her, told her how sorry I was, asked her what I desperately want to know now: "How have you gotten through the haunted minutes of every hour?"

After Mama died, Dad always introduced himself as a widower. When he passed last year, my brother, Tom, and I cleaned out his closet. "We're orphans now, kiddo," Tom had said. Is there a word for a woman who's lost a child? Other than *broken*?

"When was the last time you saw Rose?" Agent Pruitt asks.

"It has to be months ago," I rub my forehead as if that will help me call up a date.

Brent fusses in his chair, tossing the Cheerios Brian piled on his tray toward the floor.

I cross my arms in front of my chest as my milk comes in.

Agent Pruitt's phone rings. He pulls it from his pocket and answers in one movement. He listens, staring down at his burgundy loafers. Brian and I stiffen, waiting.

"On my way," he says, and returns the phone to his pocket, eyes on us. "Thank you for your time. We'll find Ms. Langley. Then we'll be in touch."

"When? How will you find her?" I blurt. I don't want him to leave. He is taller than Brian, and older than both of us. In his clean, pressed khakis, white shirt, and dark blazer, he has an almost fatherly presence. I need him to stay, to tell us how we will get through whatever happens next. "Is there anything we can do? What should we be doing?" I swallow a scream. "Shouldn't we do something?"

"Sit tight. We're doing everything we can, Mrs. Davies." He places his business card on the table. "We hope to know more soon."

Soon. Fucking soon. Thursday night, when I asked the young officer who found the phone when they'd know whose it was, he'd said, "Hopefully soon."

"How soon is 'soon'?" Brian had asked.

"Here's the thing, people watch these CSI shows, and then they think we can solve a crime in an hour—forty-five minutes if you skip the commercials. It doesn't work like that."

It took everything I had not to slap his boyish face.

*   *   *

As Brian walks Agent Pruitt to the door, I scoop Brent out of the high chair and press him to me. I bury my face in his neck to stifle a wail so Brian doesn't hand me another pill. I can't nurse if I keep taking them, and all I want is to feel the weight of Brent's small body connected to mine.

I sink into a chair, my brain attempting to arrange what I know—facts, not gossip. A childless woman flees Oak Hill in the middle of the night. Two months later, a boy vanishes. Three weeks later, my daughter disappears. A phone found in our backyard links Allison to the person who stole my child. How are these connected? Am I delirious? Crazy from worry and no sleep?

I look at Agent Pruitt's card. Should I call and tell him what Allison said to me about expecting a child? A child who never existed. He'll think I've lost my mind. The Oak Hill Police Department will treat me like I'm the next Phil Foster.

It's a risk I have to take because, while my theory could be nothing, it might be everything.

22

Saturday, July 6
Cassidy

L EXI SLIPS THROUGH the gap in the beat-up back fence to
avoid the news vans parked in front of my house. Reporters
and camera crews film in the street, waiting for the police to
pounce on me. Until that happens, they stop our neighbors to
ask what they know about "the babysitter."

I've circled the kitchen, waiting for Lexi ever since Mom left
for work hours ago. Even though it's Saturday and she's been at
the hospital all week, Mom picked up an extra shift. I should be
grateful because she's doing it for me, but instead, I just want
her home, telling me things will be okay, though neither of us
believes that.

As Lexi gets closer, a lump swells in my throat, and I blink
back tears. She'd planned to spend the day at the beach with
Bridget and Emma but bailed to be with me.

"Hey." She steps inside and hugs me. "Sorry it took me so
long. The deli was packed." She heads to the table, opens a bag,
and tosses out a couple of sandwiches. I'm not surprised she got
me one even though I told her my stomach hurt and I didn't
want anything.

"You have to eat," she'd texted back. "You need to stay
strong. Now more than ever."

I wonder if it's the same thing she tells her mom after her relationships fall apart. Lexi sets out two bottles of iced tea—beads of moisture drip down their sides. I'm sweating too. The heat wave shows no sign of letting up, and the air conditioner in the kitchen window barely works. Constant fear of what may happen next makes me feel like my whole body is on fire.

"Did you decide what you're gonna do?" Lexi tears into a BLT, bits of bacon and a blob of mayo fall onto the foil wrapper. Her eyes widen as she waits for my answer.

I shake my head. "I've looked fucking everywhere and I can't find it. It has to be my phone. It must've fallen out of my pocket when I ran across the backyard." My stomach twists each time I think about it. "I never should've listened to you and gotten that stupid thing."

"I said if you weren't going to stop seeing Chris, at least don't use your own phone. I never told you to lose it!"

I didn't even know I'd lost the burner phone until Lexi called me Thursday night as I waited in a small room at the police station to answer more questions. Or, really, the same questions asked a million different ways, just like when Billy disappeared.

"I can barely hear you," Lexi had screamed after I whimpered hello. "Are you coming to Emma's? There's a taco truck here. It's epic!" she shouted.

"I'm at the police station. Amy-Pat is gone. She's missing. Just like Billy." Even as I said the words, it didn't seem real.

"No fucking way!" Lexi was drunk. "Are you serious? Are you okay? Want me to come and meet you?"

I heard fireworks, music, and laughter in the background. *Why hadn't I gone with her?* She said something I couldn't understand. I saw the profile of a police officer in the doorway, so I hung up. I hoped it would be Kyle's brother, but he'd stayed at the Davieses' house. An officer I didn't recognize peeked in, but then turned and continued down the hall. Even though my head ached and I thought I might throw up, I couldn't sit still. I was dying to call Chris. But he was at Roddy's. Still, if I told him what had happened, he'd listen. He'd find a quiet spot and calm me down. Just hearing his voice would be a tiny bit of comfort. I reached into my pocket, and that's when I knew. The burner phone was gone.

My heart hasn't stopped racing since. The police found one on the Davieses' property, and it's got to be mine. I keep praying maybe it belongs to whoever took Amy-Pat, but that seems like too much to hope for.

Pacing around the table, I stop at the window and peek through the blinds. The number of news vans has doubled since yesterday afternoon when the story attracted national attention. I turn back toward Lexi, my mind a mess of paranoid thoughts.

"Could someone be framing me?" I ask. "I hear how crazy that sounds, but this is more than me having bad luck or being negligent. Someone's setting me up, right? Is that possible? But why? What have I done? I swear, Lex, it has to be personal. Am I insane? I feel like I'm literally going insane."

Lexi's mouth is full of toast and lettuce. She can't answer, so I continue. "What about Sloan? She hated me for winning homecoming queen last fall." I rake my hands through my hair. Loose strands twist between my fingers. Adrenaline takes over. I circle the table faster, feeling like I could run a marathon.

Lexi flicks crumbs onto a napkin. "Sloan just won prom queen, and she had a huge party on July Fourth. Her alibi's rock solid."

"What about Clay Bennett? I sort of ghosted him over winter break."

"No way." A *pop* punctuates Lexi's words as she opens her iced tea. "He's been seeing some junior since March. Plus— sorry—but he's not smart enough to abduct two kids without leaving his DNA everywhere."

"Allison Langley? What if she knows about Chris and me?"

Lexi shakes her head. "That's the guilt talking. You think she'd leave her husband and then go on a kidnapping spree? Not likely."

"Then, what, Lex? Who? Who took them? Where are they? How is this happening?" I go over it and over it. Why didn't I insist that Amy-Pat come upstairs with me while I changed Brent? Why didn't the Davieses have extra diapers and wipes in the playroom so I could keep an eye on all three kids at once? Why did I agree to watch them in the first place?

Lexi shrugs her shoulders. My stomach cramps. I'm not used to seeing her stumped and speechless.

"Any chance you changed your trip?" I ask.

Lexi leaves tomorrow to visit her dad in California for two weeks. I wish I could hide in her suitcase and leave my entire life behind.

"You know I would, but my dad will say it's my mom's idea, and they'll get into another huge fight. I can't deal. Plus, the insurance salesman just dumped her. He's getting back together with his wife. My mom's heartbroken. Again." Lexi sighs and chugs the rest of her iced tea. "Which sort of makes me want to get out of here. Sorry," she adds. "You can call, text, FaceTime me, and I'll be there. I'll be glad to get away from my new stepmother, believe me."

It's completely irrational, but I'm jealous that these are her only problems. I want to beg her to cancel, to stay with me. "I need you! My life is over!" I scream in my head, but even in my frantic state, I hear how selfish that sounds, especially knowing how her parents use her to get back at each other. So I say nothing.

The doorbell rings. Is it another soulless reporter asking if I'm ready to tell my side of the story in an attempt to clear my name? Is it the police? It rings again, but I can't move. I'm stuck to the floor, heart knocking against my ribs, fear pumping through my bloodstream.

"Sit. I got it." Lexi hops up and slowly walks toward the front hall.

I drop into a chair, legs unable to support me another second, and rest my head on the kitchen table. The cool wood surface smells like lemons. I think about Mom, how she cleans when she's anxious.

When we got home from the police station Thursday night, we sat together on the couch. I put my head on Mom's shoulder, and she smoothed my hair while I tried to stop shaking.

"Everything I do is a mistake," I'd said. In that moment, I asked her what I've always wondered but never dared to say aloud. "Do you regret having me?"

"Oh, honey!" She sat up, placed her hands on my shoulders, and brought me so close our noses nearly touched. "Did you come into my life sooner than expected? Yes. Did I ever wish things had turned out differently? Not for a single second."

Then she pulled me toward her, kissed the top of my head, and whispered. "We'll get through this, Cass, I promise."

She said everything right, but I heard her crying in the bathroom last night after she called Mr. Carver, Emma's dad. They'd gone to high school together, and he moved back to Oak Hill to start his practice after law school. Criminal law isn't his specialty, but he offered to recommend a good defense attorney if I needed one.

"I've gotta warn you, Katie, even if I can wrangle you a discount, his retainer's a hefty chunk. Just want you to be prepared."

After that, Mom took it off speakerphone.

The doorbell rings again. I close my eyes and wish I could disappear.

"It's only Kyle," Lexi calls.

"Thank you for that less-than-enthusiastic introduction, Lexi." Kyle strides into the kitchen and sweeps imaginary crumbs from a chair before sitting. "Cassidy, I have good news for you."

I jolt upright, praying he's about to say Billy and Amy-Pat have been found alive and unharmed. "What? What is it?"

"I overheard my brother Dan—he's a police officer—"

"I know he's a police officer! He's questioned me at least twice! What's the news?" I shout, causing Kyle to jerk back and cover his ears.

"It's okay, Kyle." Lexi nods, shooting me a look that says *Keep it together.* "Go ahead."

"I heard Dan talking to my parents. The cell phone found in the Davieses' bushes was used to call a number belonging to Allison Langley."

Chris's phone must be registered in his wife's name. My eyes dart to Lexi. She's frowning, no doubt calculating what this means for me.

"Shit!" I hiss.

"No, Cassidy. This is a good thing," Kyle says. "Dan said they're going to find Mrs. Langley, figure out who's calling her, and that will lead them to Amy-Pat—and, hopefully, Billy. Then you'll be cleared." He waves his long arms like he's a magician who's just made all my problems vanish.

"It's mine, Kyle. The phone is mine."

"Isn't that your phone? There on the counter? Charging?"

"I have a second phone."

"Why do you need two phones?" Kyle, who isn't big on eye contact, stares directly at me. "And why would you call Mrs. Langley?"

I ignore his questions. Too many of my own cartwheel through my head. "Did Dan say anything else?" I spin away from Kyle to face Lexi. "They're going to know the phone's mine. My fingerprints are all over it. Should I go to the police station now? I should, right? But I need to tell Chris first."

"Who's Chris?" Kyle demands. "Why do you have two phones?"

"Yes, you have to tell the police!" Lexi raises her voice. "If you don't, they're going to waste time investigating the wrong people—time they should be searching for Amy-Pat and Billy," she warns. "You could end up getting charged with hindering an investigation. Or obstructing it. I forget what it's called, but it's not good. Obviously."

"Who's Chris?" Kyle shouts.

Lexi and I look at him, then each other. It's all going to come out now anyway. Still, I don't want to be the one to say it.

"Cass has been hooking up with Mr.— Chris Langley. She got a burner phone so her mom wouldn't find out," Lexi tells half the truth. Again, she's lying for me. I wonder how many more times that'll happen before she's had enough.

"Mr. Langley? The washed-up rock star who gives music lessons to children?" Kyle asks. "What do you mean by 'hooking up'? Are you referring to sex? He's old. That's—what's the word? Gross." Kyle makes a face like he just licked the inside of a urinal.

"Well, it doesn't matter now because I doubt he'll want to keep seeing me. I've got a shitload of baggage." I hold up my hands and tick off all my mistakes. "Let's see, two children I was supposed to be watching are now missing. Mom talked to Mr. Carver last night. I could be charged with negligence—or worse." My voice starts to shake. "If that happens, I'll lose my scholarships. If my college acceptance isn't rescinded, that'll be a miracle. The only thing that matters is finding Amy-Pat and

Billy, but—no offense, Kyle—it doesn't seem like Oak Hill's finest is up to the job. I could end up going to prison. So, basically, my life is over. I'm completely fucked."

When I stop to catch my breath, the only sounds come from the mechanical whirring of ancient appliances. I know things are bad when Lexi doesn't offer any reassurances and Kyle doesn't tell me to stop cursing.

"I need to see Chris, tell him that I lost the phone before the police show up at his house and he's blindsided." I'm pacing again, babbling, trying to convince myself that I can control one part of this giant nightmare. "Then, I'll go to the police station, explain that the phone is mine. If they know that the phone number is Chris's, I'll make up a story about asking him to send me sheet music or something. Our relationship is no one else's business. If I can deal with this—keep Chris out of it—maybe we can still be together? Maybe it'll bring us closer?"

"Slow down," Lexi says. "You're spiraling. I know you don't want to hear this, but your *relationship*"—she makes air quotes. It shouldn't bother me considering everything else, but it does— "was going to end anyway. This isn't the time to think about Chris. Think about yourself. Your future."

I do think about my future—a lot. I thought I'd like to be a teacher. Now I wonder if I'll ever be more than "the Oak Hill babysitter."

"I know you think it's wrong or weird, but what Chris and I have—it's important to me." My tone is defensive, pleading. I hear how pathetic I sound.

"When's the last time you talked to him?" Lexi asks.

"I wanted to go over to his house last night, but I couldn't leave with these reporters parked outside, and then I thought about Phil Foster sitting on his front porch watching everything. So I stayed home. I haven't talked to Chris since Thursday night. He called before he left for Roddy's party in Brooklyn."

Lexi pushes away from the table. Her chair makes an awful squeak as it scrapes the linoleum.

I know what she's thinking: *you're dealing with some major shit and your boyfriend's basically bailed on you.* I look from her to Kyle. Neither speaks. Shame and self-doubt wriggle under my skin. Is he seeing someone else? The afternoon we met at the

Riverview Inn flashes through my mind. How many other women has he been with this whole time I've thought he was mine? Maybe he went to find Allison? Why did I ever believe what we had was real? I haven't seen him in days; he's been so busy working on that soundtrack. But he'd called Tuesday night. He said he missed me. Then, he made me a playlist. The songs he picked, "Northern Sky" by Nick Drake, Shawn Colvin's cover of "You're Gonna Make Me Lonesome When You Go," they meant something.

"Thank you, I love it. Every single song." I'd told him, lying on the floor of my hot closet talking on my now-missing phone. "I'd never even heard of half these songs."

"Then it's a good thing we met," he'd said.

"It's the best thing," I'd whispered. Just listening to him breathe made me ache to be near him.

I know Lexi will think I'm a fool, but I don't care. "I'm going over there. Before the police do. I don't want him to get caught up in this because of me."

Lexi rolls her eyes like I'm delusional, and I get it. I sound totally desperate. But my relationship with Chris is the last good thing I have. I don't want to lose that too.

Horns honk out front. Our neighbors are pissed about the news vans clogging the street. It doesn't matter who's out there. I have to go. I need to see Chris.

On my way to the side door, I grab a baseball hat and sunglasses from the counter and pray no one sees me. On most Saturdays in July, Oak Hill residents are either at their beach houses or the country club. Still, I can't take any chances.

"Want me to go with you?" Lexi offers.

I shake my head. "I'll call you later."

"Cassidy!" Kyle shouts as I'm almost out the door. "Your secret about Mr. Langley is safe with me."

The lump returns to my throat. I swallow it before I start sobbing.

23

Saturday, July 6
Rachel

"I'M SO SORRY, Ray." Darcy reaches over and squeezes my hand as I slide into the passenger seat.

I shake my head. "It's not your—"

"Still, I should've told you. I feel awful."

Last night, after I fell down the stairs, I hobbled to the kitchen to find the phone, clutching my stomach, momentarily relieved when I felt a small, flutter kick inside me. I called Ted a dozen times, leaving violent, threatening messages. When I couldn't reach him, I called my sister.

"Ted's moving!" I shouted. "To Maine! I found a folder of house photos on the computer. He's been searching for schools, Dar. *Schools!* I think he has Billy. He's not answering his phone. Do I call the police? Will they think I'm out of my mind? Should I put a tracking device on his car and follow him? What, Dar? What do I do?"

She said nothing. "Darcy? Are you there?" I stared at the phone to make sure the call hadn't dropped. Then I heard movement, traffic, like she'd stepped outside.

"Ray." Her voice got that low, I-have-bad-news tone I recognized from when she'd called to tell me our father died or our mother was having an off day. "It's not Ted." She sighed. "I created that folder. I'm so sorry. I didn't want to tell you like this."

My thoughts spun. *Darcy? Maine?* I collapsed into the sofa. Ted didn't have Billy. Tears slid into my mouth. I felt my heart shatter all over again. "What? Why?"

"I was searching for schools—for a job." She lowered her voice. "Janet wants— She's retiring in September, and this has always been her dream—to live by the water, have a boat. She sends me listings. She thinks a change would be good for us. I didn't know how to tell you—with everything else. Ray, I'm so sorry."

Endless seconds passed before I could form words. "Maine? Darcy? You're leaving me?"

"No, of course not," she said. "Not now. Not right away. In time. We're just looking ahead. Keeping our options open. I was thinking maybe you could come join us. In time," she repeated. "Not to live, but to visit maybe. It could be good for you too, you know, if . . ."

She didn't need to finish the sentence. I knew exactly what she meant.

*   *   *

For that brief window when I thought Ted had Billy, I had hope. Now I'm back to nothing. I haven't lost anything additional, yet I feel like another gaping wound has opened.

I meant it when I told Darcy it wasn't her fault, but it's hard for me to see her, to think that she's considering moving and didn't share it with me—not that I haven't been keeping my own secrets from her.

"You really don't have to do this," Darcy says now, arching a dubious eyebrow as she backs out of my driveway.

"I know. I want to," I assure her. She frowns. "You know what I mean," I add, buckling my seat belt. Though it's light, the weight presses down on my tender breasts, reminding me of the conversation I keep avoiding. "I haven't been there in almost two months. Not that she'll remember."

Birthday balloons knock against the headrests and windows as Darcy blasts the air conditioning. Seventy-eight years old today, our mother is frail, "forgetful," we say because we can't bear the "A" word.

Mother's Day was the last time I saw her. I'd brought Billy with me. On the drive home, I let him have his phone—a desperate attempt to make him forget how depressing the visit had been. He looked up from whatever game he'd been playing, meeting my eyes in the rearview mirror. "Is Nana one hundred years old?" he'd asked. "Why can't she remember us?"

Billy's birthday is Wednesday. His pediatrician's office sent a reminder notice about scheduling his physical. After I opened it, grief, strong as quicksand, sucked me into the couch, where I sat for hours. Billy loved those appointments—hearing how much weight he'd gained, how many inches he'd grown, reporting it all back to Ted at dinner. How tall is he now, wherever he is?

When I think the ache of losing him can't possibly hurt more, it deepens, divides, and spreads until it leaches beyond the soft tissue into every cell.

"Let's just hope it's one of her good days," Darcy says. "You don't need any more stress."

I glance over, but she's staring straight ahead. I can't read her expression. Does she know I'm pregnant? I've never been able to hide anything from my sister for long. Still, I've gained less than five pounds. I have no appetite. Just the thought of anything other than crackers makes me nauseous. When I was expecting Billy, I craved cheeseburgers and strawberry milkshakes night and day.

I want to tell Darcy everything. I have to. Today. Once I find the words.

As we roll down Cherry Lane toward the stop sign, I spot the pool company's van, an indigo wave on its side, parked in front of Betsy's house. The cleaning guy salutes me with a skimmer on a long pole, and I jerk my head in the opposite direction.

"What?" Darcy asks.

"I don't know." I put on sunglasses. "This new pool guy— Ted hired him and I recommended him to Betsy. But he's odd. Last week, I didn't know he was there. I went into the backyard to get some air and he came right up to me, put his hand on my arm, and said, 'Sorry to hear about your boy.' He recognized Billy from the flyers. Then he said, 'Cute kid. Little shy at first, but get him talking about baseball, and he won't shut up.' I just stood there, Dar, almost relieved, you know, to hear someone speak about Billy in the present tense—to talk to someone who wasn't afraid to say my son's name. Then he did this weird thing where he pulled his arms toward his chest and flapped his hands, and said, 'I was really into dinosaurs too at that age.' Later, I realized he was imitating the Tyrannosaurus rex on Billy's backpack." The image makes me shudder.

"If you think something's off, Ray, you should tell the police," Darcy says. "Don't wait."

Of course, she's right. Still.

"I don't know." I shake my head. "After everything last night, and then before, with Evan, I . . ."

I look out the window. As we weave our way out of Oak Hill, I lift my handbag from the car floor and rifle through it, looking for nothing in particular. I can't bear to see the trees. Pink ribbons for Amy-Pat are tied above blue ones for Billy. Will there be more? More children taken from us?

I think about Amy-Pat. Is she with Billy? It can't be a coincidence.

"Any word from Ted?" Darcy asks.

"Nothing. I left another message, explaining the others. Things were bad before last night. After I accused Evan . . ."

"You did nothing wrong, Ray." She checks her mirrors and merges onto the highway. I wish we could just drive forever like we did the summer Darcy got her license, when we'd roll down the windows and speed as far away as we could from our parents and their endless screaming matches. We'd listen to Tracy Chapman's "Fast Car," twisting down backroads and looping over highways until we nearly ran out of gas.

"You listened to your gut," Darcy says now, turning down the air conditioning, silencing the radio. "Evan lied to the police. What kind of a person does that?"

I'm the kind of person who does that. I think back to the afternoon Billy disappeared, to the moment when Detective Dubin asked, "Any problems in your marriage?"

"No, nope. Everything's fine," I'd lied.

"Ted's never going to see reality when it comes to that kid," Darcy shakes her head, "and it's not doing either of them any favors."

The first time my sister met Evan and Ted was Christmas Eve when I was expecting Billy. It was early in the pregnancy, and only Ted and I knew. I'd invited Darcy, Janet, Evan, Ted, and his mother to my tiny condo for dinner. I wanted everyone to get along, to create good, new holiday memories that would replace the unpleasant ones Darcy and I had from childhood. I imagined it might help Ted and Evan see a future in which the three of us, and the child I was carrying, would be a happy family.

But it hadn't gone that way. When he thought no one was looking, Evan stuffed shrimp tails under my couch cushions. Later, he locked the door to my only bathroom after he'd exited. Ted had to pick it with a coat hanger, while Evan sat in the living room making fun of Jimmy Stewart in *It's a Wonderful Life*.

"That kid's trouble," Darcy had whispered to me in the kitchen. "Trust me, I'm a high school teacher. I know."

"He's a teenager!" I'd said, defending him. "And he lost his mom around this time last year. Give him a chance."

"He's probably in your bedroom right now peeing in your artificial ficus," Janet had joked, "and then he'll blame you for not having a second bathroom."

"Sorry, Ray, he's a dealbreaker," Darcy said. "Janet works with this really nice guy. She'd be happy to intro—"

"I'm pregnant!" I blurted, so jittery I accidentally basted my thumb with hot turkey drippings. "Ted and I are getting married. In the new year. Probably at the courthouse. I'll let you know when."

Darcy forced her open mouth into a smile before rushing to hug me. "Well, congratulations then! Me? An aunt! Oh, Ray, I'm going to spoil this kid like crazy."

The relief I'd felt at having my sister's support was fleeting. On my way back to the living room, I heard Ted's mother whisper, "I still don't understand what we're doing at the home of your real estate agent on Christmas Eve!"

"We're seeing each other, Mom," he'd said. "I told you. Let's not make a big deal out of it."

Later, after Darcy and Janet had gone home, Adele Barnes, with her silver helmet of perfectly coiffed hair and Talbots sweater set, flounced into the kitchen. Under the guise of helping me clean up, she'd said, "I don't think my son is in the market to start over, and you—" she wrinkled her long nose, appraising me as if I were a carton of milk on the verge of expiring, "—you probably don't have much time to waste, do you, dear?"

*   *   *

"If I'm honest, things were bad even before Billy disappeared," I say now, wanting to lay the groundwork to tell her about Derek, this pregnancy, but I'm lost, exhausted. I stare out the window. Wilting wildflowers on the hillside blur as little waves of heat rise off the asphalt. "My marriage is over, Dar."

She takes a hand off the steering wheel and squeezes my arm, probably expecting me to burst into tears, but I have none to spare for Ted. Ted, who—when he is around—devours the food that arrives from the Meal Train Betsy organized, offering everyone an up-close look at our misery in exchange for a casserole. I tried to stop it. I sent her a text telling her we appreciated the thought and everyone's efforts, but we were just two people. We couldn't consume the lasagnas and chickens that were delivered to the hulking cooler Betsy placed on our porch. The thought of returning cookware and sending thank-you notes seemed impossible.

"Nonsense! People like to help!" Betsy insisted yesterday afternoon when she called to tell me she was coming by to pick up her Le Creuset. "I want to make a decent meal for Christopher Langley," she'd continued. "I saw him at the market with a basket of frozen dinners and boxes of mac and cheese. It was the organic kind, but still. He's gotten so thin. And I think he's growing a beard." She fake-gagged. "I heard he's working on a new album. Let's hope it's better than that last one."

I'd seen Chris earlier this week, walking his dog after midnight. I turned the corner, and we nearly collided. The smell of beer on his breath turned my stomach as we exchanged an awkward, "Oh! Sorry, hi."

When I'd seen him in the past, I usually found myself tongue-tied. This time, the sight of him caught me off guard for a different reason. He barely resembled the famous musician who'd graced the cover of *Rolling Stone*. Now, he looked like someone you'd find busking in a subway station. Beneath the amber glow of the streetlight, I noticed dark rings circling his eyes. A dingy concert T-shirt hung from his stooped shoulders. It struck me that he'd recently lost someone too. His wife— under entirely different circumstances, of course—but still. He was obviously devastated.

As Betsy had prattled on, I thought about Chris, about how money, good looks, and even fame weren't enough to save you from heartbreak.

"I want to do *something*, you know," Betsy continued. "Without Chris, Miles never would've gotten into honors orchestra at Oak Hill Middle School."

"I'll leave your dish on the porch. I'm getting another call," I'd lied and hung up, worn out by the effort of listening.

*   *   *

The Langleys. It's been almost three months since Allison left and the spotlight still shines on them. This morning, Sarah Davies called to ask about Allison. I've seen Sarah at school functions, but we don't know each other well. Billy is older than Amy-Pat, but younger than her son Tucker. We were acquaintances, but now we're forever bound by a shared horror, a limitless grief.

In a voice barely above a whisper, Sarah asked me how well I knew Allison. I'd just gotten the call from Agent Pruitt about the phone and its connection to Allison. When he told me, I felt nothing. How many times had I gotten my hopes up only to have them obliterated?

I told Sarah the same thing I told Agent Pruitt—that I'd seen Allison around the neighborhood, but we weren't in the same circles.

"I didn't really know her either," Sarah said. "But tell me if you think this means anything."

She shared a strange story about Allison possibly pretending to be pregnant and, later, acting as if they'd never met.

"Am I crazy?" Sarah had asked me. "Could she have taken Amy-Pat and Billy? Tell me I'm losing my mind. That phone connects her to my backyard. Brian says the police will call when they know more, and I should try to rest so

I'm ready. Ready for what? How can I rest when my daughter is missing, and these awful thoughts keep racing through my head?"

I know this madness. I've lived inside it for three weeks and two days. In this desperate state, a person will believe anything. How else would I have thought a crossing guard, my stepson, or even Ted could have taken Billy? But Allison Langley?

I thought back to the first time I'd spotted her in Oak Hill. There'd been a buzz in town: "Have you seen her? What about him?" We waited, like fans at a Broadway stage door, clamoring for a peek. I'd been at the ob-gyn's office, standing at the front desk, seething because I'd been waiting for thirty minutes. Allison rushed from an exam room into the reception area, shoulders shaking, cheeks flushed, attempting to hide behind her mane of chestnut hair. The nurse chased after her with her coat. Even if I hadn't seen her sitcom or shampoo commercials, I'd have noticed her. She had a presence—an aura—the thing that makes someone a star.

Could she be pregnant? I'd wondered, and if so, was she upset that it might sideline her career? I'd hoped to see her again at the doctor's office. I never did. But that didn't stop me from indulging in fantasies in which we became friends, and she sent celebrity clients my way, as if all of Hollywood was dying to move to Oak Hill.

I'd envied her. She had a job where people threw gobs of money her way, while in mine, clients constantly asked me to cut my commission. My new husband mourned his late wife, while her husband had flown to another continent to woo her. I'd read an article about them—how they met. He'd seen her in a magazine, an advertisement for gin or vodka, and told his bandmates, "I'm going to marry that girl." He made some calls, found out she'd be walking in a fashion show in Milan, and boarded a plane twenty-four hours later.

"I knew she was it for me," he'd said. "The one."

"I didn't know who he was at first, but I noticed him. Of course, I did," Allison had gushed. "He was waiting for me after the show with a huge bouquet of lavender roses."

"They symbolize love at first sight," Chris had told the interviewer. "I wanted her to know I was all in."

Allison's life had unfolded like a rom-com. Could it have taken such a radically dark turn that she'd go from leading lady to villain? It seemed ridiculous.

I didn't know what to tell Sarah other than to trust her maternal instincts. If I'd listened to mine, Billy would never have been walking to and from kindergarten without an adult.

* * *

Darcy exits the highway, and a few turns later, the assisted living center comes into view. With its sprawling veranda and cheerful mix of annuals and perennials, it looks more like a bed and breakfast than what it is: a storage locker for loved ones who no longer recognize you and can't care for themselves.

As we walk inside, I'm hit with overpowering smells: egg salad, a steamed broccoli and cauliflower medley. I gag, reminded once again of how pregnancy intensifies every aroma.

"I know, right?" Darcy bumps my elbow. "For what this place costs, they ought to serve T-bone steaks and lobster tails."

We're directed toward the day room, where a teen volunteer calls a Bingo game. Our mother's small, golden head droops toward her chest, like a sunflower at dusk, making me think she's asleep.

"Look, Doreen! N33! You have that! Cover it with this chip," an aide instructs.

Mom brings the blue plastic disc toward her mouth as the aide gently redirects her.

"Hey, Mom," I whisper, bending to kiss her cheek, soft with peach fuzz. Her hair has thinned, her curls fall flat. I should be here more. The guilt that consumes me presses down, causing an instant migraine. She is smaller each time I visit, shriveling like the Shrinky Dinks Darcy and I made on snow days.

"Happy birthday, Mom!" Darcy's voice booms, full of forced cheer.

Mom glances from my sister to me with a wary smile.

"Let's take your mother to her room," the aide suggests. "You'll all be more comfortable there."

Mom hoists herself up and stands behind her walker. We wait for her to lead the way, but she inches left, then right before stopping. "This looks completely different in the daylight," she muses.

I look at Darcy and bite my lip, hoping to stop the tears that spring to my eyes. The aide takes her by the elbow and guides her down the hall, nodding for us to follow.

When Mom's settled in her chair near the window, my sister pulls a bakery box from a bag. Three carrot cupcakes rest on a white doily, grease dotting its lacy edges. Darcy pokes a candle into the middle one. "Is this illegal?" she asks before mumbling, "Fuck it," and striking a match.

Darcy and I sing off-key. Our mother looks at us, her watery hazel eyes searching our faces. Despite my best efforts, tears slip down my cheeks. My mother is becoming a child, and my child is gone. I sink onto the bed, weighed down by my inability to protect them.

"I'm sorry," Mom says as wax from the birthday candle pools atop cream cheese frosting. "If I'd known you were coming, I'd have made some tea." She gestures toward an imagined kitchen. There's only a closet and a tiny bathroom with grab bars every few feet. "Are you here about the insurance? Because I already have some. But thank you."

"We're your daughters, Mom," Darcy reminds her. "I'm Darcy." She nods to me. "This is Rachel." Darcy smiles. "It's your birthday! We want to celebrate with you. Blow out your candle. Make a wish."

"Okay." She nods, eyes closed. Her breath wheezes like a faint whistle.

Darcy sits on the edge of the bed, cuts Mom's cupcake into quarters, and pulls a small photo album from her bag.

"I thought we'd look at some pictures together for fun," she offers. "If you want to?"

"Sure, why not?" Mom shrugs.

Darcy raises her eyebrows at me. I know what she's thinking: *Who's this gentle lady? And what has she done with the miserable woman who'd ground us for not looking happy enough to see her when we returned from school?*

As Darcy narrates, putting a rosy spin on our childhood vacations and family holidays, I stare out the window and watch a woman on a bench brush the shoulders of a white-haired gentleman. Nearby, a boy and girl chase a pair of butterflies. I check my phone, never out of reach.

In the past, the device brought me tiny doses of happiness each time I received a referral or someone shared my tips on home staging. Research says every "like" delivers a hit of dopamine. I believe it. Sometimes Billy would text me selfies with Jeter, and I'd post those, eagerly awaiting comments about my handsome boy.

Now I'm afraid of my phone. It's a time bomb threatening to detonate in my handbag, one call with the power to destroy my life. Still, I check it compulsively, never knowing if I should feel relief or sadness when there's no news.

"Ray-Ray! Are you still afraid of horses?" Darcy asks, pointing to a photo of me at age three or four, sobbing while riding a pony at the zoo.

I glance at the picture and laugh. It seems like such a stupid fear now. When I look up, Mom is staring at me, frowning. "Didn't you used to come here with a little boy? Bobby, was it?"

Darcy stops flipping the album's pages, her face a mix of alarm that our mother's words will upset me, and hope that she still knows who we are.

Before I can answer, our mother continues, "I had children once. It wasn't easy. I made a lot of mistakes." She rubs her chin, her fingers thick, shapeless as the gummy worms Billy always asked for at the checkout line. My stomach clenches thinking about how I never bought them, telling him they'd rot his teeth and give him a bellyache.

"When is this next one due?" She points at my midsection.

Darcy winces.

"December," I say.

My sister's jaw drops. Her mouth forms an "O." I try to send her a message telepathically, a game we used to play when we were little. I think, *I'm sorry, I did not want to tell you this way*, and beam it toward her, but she packs up the photo album and avoids my gaze.

All of our secrets are out in the open now.

"I thought something was different about you . . ." Mom says. "I'm sorry, dear, tell me your name again?"

* * *

We walk to the car in silence. Darcy unlocks the doors. Through the windshield, I watch the sky darken. In the distance, it's bruised, the color of eggplant. A storm is coming. We wait for the air conditioning to turn from hot to cool. The cauliflower smell lingering in my nostrils, coupled with the conversation Darcy and I need to have, makes me want to vomit.

Hot leather squeaks beneath Darcy as she shifts in her seat to face me. "That contractor?" she asks quietly. "The one who came by a few weeks ago?"

"Derek." I nod. I'd told her about Ted's vasectomy as soon as we'd gotten home from the pumpkin patch the afternoon I'd discovered the brochure in his glove box.

"What an asshole," Darcy had hissed at the time.

Now I'm the asshole. The fact that I've been unfaithful—this is the part I've dreaded. Before she met Janet, Darcy had a girlfriend who cheated on her and moved out, leaving her stuck in an apartment she couldn't afford on her own. She'd put on a brave face, attempting to joke, saying, "I don't know which is worse: finding out my partner lied to me or moving back in with Mom at age thirty because teachers get paid shit."

"Why didn't you tell me?" she asks now.

"I'm not sure I can do it again, Dar. Not alone." Hot tears sting my eyes. "This wasn't how I wanted to tell you. It's all too much—Mom's fading. Billy is gone. How can I have this baby? What if Billy comes home—even if it's years from now—and thinks I replaced him?"

Darcy frowns. Does she think I'm delusional? Does she believe Billy will never be found?

"You aren't alone, Ray. You know that. Whatever you need. I'm here."

"But you're . . ."

"I'm not going anywhere, Ray. Not now."

"Thank you," are the only words I get out before I'm sobbing. She reaches across to hold me, water bottles and a phone charger wedged between us. I rest my heavy head on her shoulder as rain begins knocking on the car's roof.

When we separate, she dries her eyes and shifts the car into reverse. "Let's get you home."

"Thanks, Dar," I say, but what I think is, *I don't have a home. Not without Billy.*

*   *   *

We're back on the highway when my phone rings. I brace for Ted's wrath, for him to tell me he's saved my frantic, accusatory messages from last night, that I'm unhinged, that I need help, that if Billy returns, he will fight me for custody because I'm an unfit mother. But the call comes from a phone number I don't recognize. I answer anyway.

"Mrs. Barnes? Agent Pruitt."

I grunt, words trapped in my throat.

"I'm outside your house," he continues. "I'd like to come in . . . speak with you."

My knees go weak. I slump in the seat, head bumping against the window. This is it—the moment that will confirm my worst fears.

"I'm, I'm on my way home now," I finally manage. "What? What is it?"

In my peripheral vision, Darcy slowly turns her head toward me. Time stops.

"We've found your former au pair, Mrs. Barnes."

24

Saturday, July 6
Sarah

BRENT'S MILK-DRUNK, HEAVY in my arms. He's been asleep for an hour, but I refuse to put him down, even as our skin sticks together from the heat.

It's three in the afternoon. Amy-Pat's been gone almost forty-five hours. I hear every precious second tick by on the fire engine clock in Brent's nursery.

The week after Billy disappeared, Betsy hosted a gathering to discuss neighborhood safety and update us on the status of her petition that would prevent elementary and middle school children from walking home alone.

"Any excuse to show off her latest home improvement," Lindsay had whispered, rolling her eyes as Betsy led us to her multilevel terrace.

After we admired her outdoor sofas and smokeless fire pit, Betsy handed out fact sheets with information and frightening statistics she'd pulled from government and crime-stopper sites.

The first 72 hours in a missing persons investigation are the most critical, according to experts. But in the case of a missing child, that window shrinks to the first 48 hours!

I remember my heart breaking for the Barnes family when I read that.

The next stat, *Forty-nine percent of kidnappings involve a relative of the victim,* came rushing back to me once rumors about Evan Barnes started swirling. In my mind, it cleared Cassidy of any involvement, making me comfortable enough to hire her.

How long will it be before Brian turns on me and blames me for leaving our children with a teen I knew may have been responsible for another child's disappearance?

I choke back tears, careful not to wake Brent. Last night, I found Brian kneeling, head in his hands, sobbing on the floor in front of Amy-Pat's closet. I knew what he was doing there—searching for her silver sandals. I'd already looked. I sunk to the floor. We clung to each other, a tangle of elbows and shoulders, grief making us awkward, unfamiliar.

Betsy didn't include the data on marriages that end in divorce after the loss of a child, but I'm sure it's staggering. I picture Rachel walking in circles alone at night. Everyone's whispered about it. *Poor Rachel Barnes. She's totally gone off the rails!* Where is her husband?

We barely know each other, but I called her this morning to share my suspicions about Allison Langley. I'm certain she's involved somehow. Rachel told me to listen to my intuition. But accusing a semi-celebrity who left town months ago, seems so bizarre, I keep talking myself out of it. Still, the thought nags at me. I want to call Agent Pruitt. I've been waiting for a quiet moment. I stand and transfer Brent to his crib. My arms feel like lead. Tuck is on his iPad in our bed while Brian dozes beside him. It's the first time he's closed his eyes since Thursday.

In the kitchen, I find Agent Pruitt's card on the table and dial before I lose my nerve. When he answers, I babble about the day I met Allison in the park.

"And then when we got to her house for Tucker's lesson, she pretended not to know me. It was like we'd never met," I ramble.

He says "uh-huh" a few times, and I hear how petty and paranoid I sound.

"I'm sorry, it might be nothing," I backtrack, embarrassed and confused. "I don't know. I-I haven't slept much."

"Any and all information is helpful," he says, and clears his throat. "I was just about to call you and Mr. Davies."

I hold my breath. Should I wake Brian?

"Mrs. Davies, we've found the Barneses' au pair, Rose Finnerty." He pauses. "She's dead. Boyfriend too."

"What?" The room feels as if it's tilting. My mouth goes dry. "How?"

"Drugs," he says. "Happened yesterday."

"I don't understand. Rose didn't seem like the type who'd . . ." She'd been here fewer than a dozen times, but I can't wrap my head around this.

"We just got the call. Unfortunately, it seems Ms. Finnerty got involved with some bad people. We have detectives at their apartment, going through their things. But at this time, there's no evidence that suggests she had anything to do with your daughter's disappearance."

I picture Rose—her black curls and green eyes, the way she'd tickle Amy-Pat, making my daughter giggle and squeal, "Again! Again!"

Her family owned a small flower shop in Carlingford. She'd grimaced when I'd said that sounded lovely.

"I'll do anything so long as I don't have to return to a life of standing around making centerpieces for grumpy old church ladies!" she'd snorted.

At the time, I'd laughed too. Now, tears spill down my cheeks. Another family has lost a daughter—a daughter whose chance to return home safely is gone.

25

Saturday, July 6
Cassidy

S LIPPING THROUGH THE gap in the fence, the grass blurs beneath my feet. I wish I'd eaten something. The sky's turned cloudy, and a light rain starts to fall. Still, I'm burning up. My tongue feels thick as I struggle to practice what I'll say when I see Chris—if he's even home.

It's less than a ten-minute walk, but for the first time, I wish it were longer. With each step that brings me closer, my heart somersaults. I feel dizzy, but not in the usual good way I do before I'm with him.

Will Phil be wandering the streets or sitting on his porch? I block it out, force my eyes down, determined to keep moving forward. I want to go around the back way, cut through the row of evergreens that separates Chris's house from the one behind it, but now isn't the time for me to sneak through anyone's backyard.

I'm drenched in sweat as I hurry down Woods End. Rushing up to his side door, I don't look around for Phil or anyone else. I still have no clue what I'm about to say.

As I lift my hand to knock, the door opens a crack, like he's been expecting me. For a second, butterflies fill my stomach the way they always do when I'm near him. But looking into his hypnotizing blue eyes, I'm not sure he's happy to see me.

My heart races. I want to kiss his perfect mouth, step inside, and ease my way into explaining that the police found my phone, but I'll straighten it out. His frown and the way he stands, arms crossed, blocking the doorway—it all throws me off. He's silent. Not even offering his usual "Hey, Cassidy," that never fails to make my insides shimmer. The warm light in his eyes that made me feel that instant connection is missing.

"I lost my phone," I blurt. "I'm so, so sorry. The police have it. I'm going to the station now to tell them it's mine, and that I was calling to ask you some questions about songs—about piano. I never meant to involve—"

"They were here." His voice is low, more monotone than mean. "Two officers. You just missed them. Not exactly how I wanted to spend my Saturday afternoon." His nostrils flare as he takes a deep breath, like he's trying to control his temper. "My phone is registered to Allison—my wife. They had plenty of questions about where she is, why she left. So that's not a good look."

He'd never referred to his wife before whenever he talked to me, never said her name. He's a different person. A stranger. I rock back and forth, heel to toe, unable to speak.

"How, Cassidy? How did you let this happen?" He shakes his head. "You lose everything, don't you? First those kids, now this phone? Did you stop to think about what *I* could lose if—"

"I'm going to talk to the police! I'll fix it! I swear. No one has to know about us." The butterflies that filled my stomach are gone, replaced by waves of nausea.

In the distance, a child giggles, a lawn mower drones. Behind Chris, Murphy whines and scratches at the basement door.

"I think he wants—"

"I know what he wants. He left a bone down there. I'll get it later." He turns to the whimpering retriever and hisses, "Quiet!"

His simmering anger makes it impossible for me to think straight.

"I'm so sorry," I say again. "The phone must've fallen out of my pocket when I was looking for Amy-Pat. I've been searching for it nonstop."

My apologies mean nothing. His glare sucks the oxygen out of my lungs. Gulping for air, my voice comes out small as a child's as I force myself to ask, "What— What did you tell them? The police?"

"I told them the phone's yours." His eyes narrow, thin lines crease the edges. He looks older, tired. "I said you're a piano student who has a crush on me, and I didn't want to hurt you. I told them you've been spiraling ever since that Barnes kid went missing. I said I was worried. You've seemed off lately, so I tried to be there for you, listen to your problems. But after this latest—whatever happened with that little girl—I want to distance myself from you."

"What?" I step back. His words destroy me. I don't want to cry in front of him, but the lump in my throat is back, larger than a fist. "How could you—"

"I don't have time for this shit, Cassidy. I might as well tell you now, I'm moving."

"Moving? When? Where?"

"Doesn't matter. We're done. Goodbye, Cassidy."

I stand there, mute, as he closes the door and turns the lock, swift and forceful.

We're done.

I lurch toward the sidewalk in a daze. A black Jeep slows and then speeds up. *Evan Barnes?*

Across the street, Phil Foster holds a shovel. I watch as he carries it into his house. I lift my hand to wave, but it's too late. Another door closes in my face.

CHAPTER

26

Saturday, July 6
Allison

I'M DRINKING ALONE. Again. But this time I'm celebrating. Two good things happened today. First, I found an apartment. It may be small and basic—or as the realtor spun it, "cozy with universal charm!"—but it will be all mine as of September 1.

Before Chris, I'd bounced around apartments where models who were in town for short stays could pay by the week, sometimes by the night. For far less than I'd spend at a hotel, I'd claim a spot among beautiful women and bunk beds, rice cakes, and roaches.

The thought of a place that's truly my own has sent me down a delightful rabbit hole. For the past hour, I've sipped champagne and scrolled through site after site, adding furniture to virtual shopping carts, picking out paint colors, learning how to create whimsical wall galleries. I nearly jumped up and down at the thought of purchasing a bed. Viv's couch has been a life raft, but my stiff neck and achy hip tell me it's definitely time to move on.

My mind fast forwards to winter. I picture myself sitting by a window in an overstuffed chair, reading, listening to the sounds of life in the city—horns, music, the chatter of people on their way to somewhere interesting. So different from Oak Hill's white noise soundtrack of sprinklers, leaf blowers, and snowplows.

The second good thing: As I approached Viv's building, he was there. The guy who'd followed me. Waiting.

"Fuck this," I huffed through clenched teeth.

If I was really about to start over, I refused to live in constant fear. Darting across the street on rubbery legs, a horn blared, brakes screeched. I focused solely on this man, this stranger who stood between my old life and my new one.

"Who are you? What do you want?" I shouted before I'd even reached the sidewalk, face tingling with adrenaline, terrified of who he was, and enraged at the thought that I might never really be free.

"Allison?"

At the sound of my name, I stepped back, nearly stumbling off the curb, my mind reeling. He was here to take me back. Chris had sent him. I was certain of it.

He stood straighter. "It *is* you! I thought—"

My heart beat so loudly in my ears, I barely heard my own voice. "Who are you?" I demanded, tightening my grip around the neck of the champagne bottle, a makeshift weapon.

"It's me, Dave. Dave Hollander." His dark eyes searched my face, waiting to see a flicker of recognition.

His name meant nothing to me. It had been a short sprint across the street, but I was panting, panic and the unrelenting heat making me light-headed.

"We were in *The Crucible* together. In high school." He waved his hand over his shoulder as if gesturing toward the past. "You were a freshman. I was a senior. You were Abigail Williams. I played Reverend Samuel Parris."

I stood, silent, trying to slow the furious pumping of my heart, my mind calling up images of poorly constructed sets and cheap costumes made by tired mothers.

"I thought it was you!" he continued. "But I'd read that you'd moved to a fancy suburb with a musician or something, so I didn't think it could be. Then I checked your social media, and you said—"

"What?" I roared, palms sweating. "What do you want? Why are you following me or waiting for me or whatever the hell you're doing?"

He shrunk back as if hurt by my impatience, like I'd scared him instead of it being the other way around—*him* hunting *me* for the past month.

When you have even the smallest amount of fame because someone bought a ticket to your movie, or watched your show every Tuesday night at eight, they think you owe them something—your time, your attention. I was done trying to please other people.

"What?" I repeated, the edge in my voice sharpening.

"I-I— I've been trying to make a go of the acting thing. I did a little off-Broadway."

I waited, trying to not scream the sentence circling through my head: *Did my husband send you?*

"Off-off-Broadway, actually. In Brooklyn. Jersey. Anyway, I'm staring down forty in a couple years, definitely feeling like my dream is dying, and when I saw you, I just thought maybe, I don't know, you might know someone. Maybe put me in touch with your agent? Anything you can do would be—"

The breath I'd been holding rushed out, and I nearly doubled over. I'd been scared to leave the apartment and this—my help—was all he wanted.

"Give me your phone." I reached out my hand, exhausted.

"You're not going to throw it in front of a taxi, are you? I'm down to my last few dollars, and I—"

"Give it to me!"

He placed the device in my hand. It had been months since I'd used a smartphone. I opened his contacts, typed my agent's name, phone number, and email address, then handed it back. "Tell her I sent you, but do not tell anyone where I am."

"Thanks, you wouldn't happen to know if she's looking for comedic actors? I joined this improv troupe—"

I reached into my bag and gave him a wad of cash and one of my prepaid gift cards.

"Good luck, Dave. Don't come back here, okay? I'm leaving."

"Right, I won't," he said, counting the bills. "Thank you, Al—Abigail Williams!" he called out, but I was already safely back across the street.

* * *

I sit back, raise my champagne flute, wondering where I can put a wine fridge in my new apartment, and smile. I wish Viv could see me now.

Before she went out last night, she noticed I'd been crying. I tried to tell her it was allergies, but she didn't buy it. She sat beside me on the couch, smelling like high-end hair products. Her black dress showed off her tanned and toned shoulders. Dangling jade earrings highlighted her blue-green eyes. She looked gorgeous. I felt a stab of jealousy. I used to look like that—before everything fell apart.

"It's the missing kids, isn't it?" She took my hand in hers.

I nodded. There it was—my chance to tell her everything. I hesitated. Where would I begin?

"Have you thought about seeing a therapist, maybe? I'm no mental health expert, but sitting inside on perfect summer days by yourself being super sad? It isn't a good look for you, Al, and I'm out of tricks."

Her gentle smile, the warmth of it, reminded me of my sister, the way she was when we were kids. For months, I'd feared monsters lurked beneath my bed. To help me fall back to sleep, Jen would slip out of her twin bed, crawl to mine, pat my back, and whisper, "It's okay. I'm here. Nothing will hurt you."

Though it felt like a million years ago, the memory brought tears to my eyes, prompting Viv to continue.

"You didn't want to go to the Hamptons with me. I've been trying to set you up with the hot chef in Three-C, and you refuse. You stay up all night watching infomercials, and you don't even buy anything." She gave my knee a playful pat, an attempt to make her next words sound less serious. "When you first got here, I thought it would just take a little time for you to snap out of whatever you were going through. But it's been almost three months. I'm legit worried, Al. I don't know how to help."

"Thanks, Viv." I wiped my eyes with one hand and squeezed her arm with the other. "Don't worry. Please. You've been so generous already. I'm going to pull it together. Soon. I promise."

"I get that those kids were your neighbors, and it's horrible—obviously. But you can't save them."

I nodded. "No. I know. You're totally right."

And she was. I'd come to Manhattan to move on, but, instead, I was clinging to the past. Ghosts of my lost children hovered all around me. I'd grown so accustomed to their company, to ignore them now seemed like a betrayal. And yet the weight of it all anchored me to a place I no longer wanted to be.

After Viv left, I felt a bit better but drained. I stretched out, closed my eyes, and drifted off. A hazy, early morning glow filtered through Viv's curtains when I woke up this morning. When I couldn't fall back to sleep, I went for a run, showered, and headed off to find an apartment. After hours of climbing stairs, inspecting kitchens and closets, and hearing agents try to present fire escapes as balconies, I found the perfect two-bedroom on Perry Street. I floated home, euphoric, dying to tell Viv all about it. But by the time I got back, she'd gone out, leaving me a note on the coffee table.

Sorry about last night. Hope I didn't violate "girl code" and you're okay today. Going out with Dex again tonight. Too much too soon? Fuck it—life's short! XO

I read it a second time, unsure what she meant by "girl code." Did she think she'd overstepped by suggesting I see a therapist? Some people might've been offended, but I thought her concern was touching. Viv's softer side was a sweet departure from her usual swearing and sarcasm.

If she doesn't spend the night at Dex's, I'll pour her some champagne as soon as she comes in, and we'll toast to my apartment and to her being there for me. *Really there*. Like family.

I refill my flute, giddy, watching the bubbles rise and pop. Drunk on the endless possibilities of a new future.

The rental application needs only my signature and the date. Since I've been at Viv's, days and weeks slip by in an odd blur. I look at the calendar icon at the bottom of the laptop—July 6. A strange nostalgia sneaks up on me. Our eighth wedding anniversary is in three days. Does it count if you're no longer together?

For the millionth time since April, I stare at my bare hands.
I left my rings in Oak Hill. At first, each time I felt the naked-
ness of my fingers, I'd panic, thinking I'd lost the emerald-cut
diamond and sparkling platinum band. But now I don't miss
them. What does that mean? What do I do next? Find a lawyer?
File for divorce? If I'm going to move forward, I should figure
that out.

Maybe it's the champagne or the date, but I think of Chris—
of how we were in the beginning. Madly in love. Convinced
we'd found our happily-ever-after. He'd given me a glimpse of
the perfect life. As long as we were together, we'd believed we
had everything. When had that stopped being enough? How is
he? Where is he? I've resisted checking my old email account.
My resolve weakens as curiosity outweighs my willpower. Has
Chris written? If he has, am I ready to read his words, to hear
his voice in my head? I've promised myself I'll move forward.
Would this set me back? I won't know until I look.

Outside Viv's window, leaves rustle on a lone tree. Skinny
branches sway in a fevered dance, an offering to the darkening
sky. There's a restlessness in the atmosphere. After the heat of
the last few days, a storm is coming.

With two clicks, I log out of my new email. "Sign in as a
new user," the screen commands. A voice in my head begs me
to stop. *Don't!* it whispers. *This is why you didn't take your cell
phone!* A louder one pops in, *What are you going to do? Hide
forever? Open it!*

I type my old username and password, holding my breath.
Six hundred and forty-two new messages appear. My eyes scan
the list. Sprinkled among clothing sales, newsletters from fertil-
ity specialists, and a reminder about Ethan's birthday party,
there it is—Christopher Langley.

My wrists go limp against the laptop. Just seeing his name—
the familiarity of it—fills me with a dizzying combination of
comfort and dread.

Maybe he'll apologize, admit he couldn't see the toll everything took on me. He'll suggest a time for me to stop by and
collect my things. We'll agree to go our separate ways. Maybe
we'll keep in touch on birthdays, holidays—part as friends who
ultimately want different things.

That's the champagne talking. He's probably furious. No one likes being left behind—especially not Christopher Langley. It took him nearly a year to get over Roddy and Edward ditching him, breaking up the band. Even when I'd thought he'd moved on, he continued brooding. We'd be at the beach, and he'd see a tattoo that reminded him of Roddy's, and he'd start up again about their "desertion, betrayal, and ingratitude!" We'd hear one of their hits on the car stereo or at Whole Foods, and Chris would launch into a tirade about how they'd abandoned him.

I'd begged him to record a solo album, channel his anger into a new project. I played the role of supportive wife, but I wanted to tell him that he should've seen it coming. His drinking was out of control. His live shows ranged from sloppy to disastrous, with him mangling the lyrics or falling off a stage.

It was the same with our marriage. Like Roddy and Edward, I'd issued clear warnings: "Things need to change." If Chris was surprised I left, it was because he wasn't paying attention.

I filter my inbox so only his messages appear. I scan the dates. He'd sent one, sometimes two, emails per day. The subject line of each shows nothing more than an asterisk.

"Creates a little suspense, a bit of mystery," he'd told me with a smirk when I'd asked him why he didn't fill in the subject like everyone else. "It gets people to open your message faster."

At the time, I'd thought it was clever. Now, I realize it's manipulative. With a few keystrokes, I could delete his emails, continue on the path to healing, avoid looking back.

Fingers trembling above the keyboard, my stomach aches as emptiness grows like a dark weed inside me. I know what I should do. But I can't. Not knowing what he's written will torment me more than reading his words.

I scroll to the oldest message, sent in April on the morning I left. I expect to feel something big, powerful—longing for the man I adored for nearly a decade, rage that he still doesn't get it. Instead, I'm numb. I drain my glass, refill it, and open the message.

Come home, Al. I read your note and found your phone. The house is all echoes and shadows. There's no life in it when you're not here. Funny how this was once our dream home. Now it's just a big, dull box. I can't sleep without you. I haven't felt this alone in a long time. Murph's sitting by the door, waiting for you. Not saying that to make you feel guilty. Just to let you know we miss you like crazy. Come back. Soon.

I want to read the messages in order like someone with more patience would. I'm not that person. I click one from the end of April.

I don't know if you're checking these. If you are, let me know you're okay. Please. You asked me not to find you, and I'm trying to respect that, but I want to know you're all right. We've weathered some terrible things, Al, but we always got through them. Together. Come home. Now.

Are those last lines a plea or an order? Fear runs through me. Outside, the bluish-purple sky has turned black. Rain beats against the windows. My champagne buzz morphs into a throbbing headache. I never should've logged into this email.

About a month ago, Viv asked if I'd heard from Chris. I'd shrugged. She knew I'd left my phone in Oak Hill.

"He could be sending emails, but I haven't checked the account," I'd told her.

"I totally get it. Pandora's inbox. Your willpower is badass. Keep it up!" She'd high-fived me.

Whenever I've felt weak, I've thought of her words. Now I've gone too far to turn back. Tears slip down my cheeks. I want to believe that Chris is capable of changing, but I don't trust him. He'll say all the right things and then, after a few months, he'll find another specialist, a different test or treatment, and convince me to try again. He'll never let this go, and it will ruin me.

I scroll to mid-May.

I've made some mistakes, Ally.

Ally. A low-level hum clogs my ears. A sour taste springs into my mouth. He only calls me that when he's drinking. Six years of sobriety. Gone. I'm scared to read on. I can't look away.

You kinda left me no choice. I'm not blaming you. I know you're on your own "journey" or whatever bullshit that therapist fed you. But journey's over, Ally, time to get back to real life.

I click the up arrow and the next message loads.

I'm drinking again, Ally, not gonna lie. Right now, actually. On the patio. Looking up at the stars, thinking about you and the life we built together. We were happy once. We can be again. I just need you to believe in us. Is that so fucking hard?

I skip to the next one and the next, then slam the laptop shut and rub my temples. My mouth is so dry, I can barely swallow. I pull a water bottle from the fridge, gulp it, pacing in the small space between the kitchen and couch. How did I not think he'd go off the rails? Maybe deep down I knew but didn't care. The voice of the therapist I saw back in Oak Hill rings in my ears, *What do you want, Allison?*

I'll read his most recent message, respond, and beg him to get help. I'll tell him we'll talk again after he does, when he's thinking clearly. Then I'll delete the account. Any future emails will bounce back. He'll know I'm not going to engage in this.

I perch on the couch, insides quaking, and reopen the computer to find his latest message, sent minutes ago at 9:47 PM.

Guess who called me last night? Viv.

My stomach plunges. I reread the sentence. Twice. Three times. *Viv. Viv. Viv.* My Viv? No. Sweat slicks my palms, soaks my armpits. The room tilts, and the floor beneath my feet gives way as her note, her words, "violate girl code," float through my mind. Still, it can't be. Viv? No. He's bluffing. She would never betray me like this. I force my eyes back to the screen.

Maybe she told you. Maybe she didn't. I wonder if she's there with you right now. Awkward! She's worried about you, Ally. She didn't know who else to call. She thinks you miss me, our life, Oak Hill. I hope she's right. She gave me her address.

I'm on my way, Ally. Our new life together starts now.

27

Saturday, July 6
Cassidy

"I'M SCARED TO ask, but how did it go?" Lexi cringes.

We're FaceTiming. I sit on the floor of my hot closet, sweaty and dying inside. This is the first chance I've had to talk to her since I left this afternoon for Chris's and the police station. Once Mom got home from work, she hovered nonstop.

"With Chris? Terrible," I say, picturing the man I've fucking worshipped for the last two months basically slamming the door in my face.

I tell Lexi everything—how the police beat me to Chris's house, how he told them the phone was mine, and that I've been calling because I'm obsessed with him.

"He was super pissed, Lex. I'd never seen him like that. He told me—and I quote—'we're done.' Oh, and he's moving."

She's been rushing around her bedroom, tossing shorts, shirts, and bathing suits into a giant travel backpack, getting ready for her trip to visit her dad, but now she stops to stare straight into the phone.

"Holy shit!" She raises her eyebrows. "What a dick! Not gonna lie, I'm glad it's over." She sighs. "I know you don't feel that way and—sorry—you probably don't want to hear this, but it's for the best. It was going to end in a couple weeks anyway. Now that you know he's a complete asshole, you won't miss him. You're free!"

I wish I could be that rational. But I can't. Not with it ending like this. I've had this awful, empty ache in my stomach since the second I walked away from his house. I want to tell Lexi it's not that simple. She's never been in love, never even moved beyond a crush. But I don't say anything. If I talk about Chris any longer, I'll start bawling.

"What about the police?" she asks. "How'd that go?"

"Better than expected. I talked to Kyle's brother. Since it's Saturday, none of the higher-ranking cops were there. They know the phone is mine because Chris told them. Officer Kinsley said I should've come forward sooner—that I wasted their time and resources. He said Agent Pruitt's following up on a new lead, and will be in touch soon."

"All right, well, that definitely could've been worse, I guess, right?"

In the background, her mom calls for her to come downstairs.

"Shit, I have to go," Lexi whispers in annoyance. "My mom's driving me to the airport, and it's about to start pouring. Nothing like a cross-country red-eye in a storm."

I groan. "I hate that you're leaving. Call me tomorrow?"

Thunder rumbles overhead. I hear it through the phone, above Lexi's house too.

"Maybe my plane will be struck by lightning, and I won't have to go back-to-school shopping with my new stepmom."

"Don't even joke, Lex. Seriously, you're all I've got."

She stops mid-packing, makeup bag in hand. "I'm sorry. I wish I could stay. Believe me." Her mom shouts again. "Coming!" Lexi yells. "I gotta go, just stay strong. Focus on you, okay?"

"Right, thanks, Lex." I nod.

When we hang up, the emptiness inside me spreads, trickling to every part of my body. I sit in the closet listening to the pitter-patter of rain hitting the roof, soft at first but building. I get up and flop onto my bed. I glance at the clock. It's after 10 PM. I should be exhausted, but I'm wired like I've had a double espresso and chased it with a can of Red Bull. I'm freaking out about Billy and Amy-Pat, about what Agent Pruitt will say or ask me, and, now, how I've ruined everything with Chris.

When I got back from the police station, I tried calling him to apologize again and tell him that I never meant to involve him. It rang once before it went to voicemail. Then Mom came home. She made my favorite—penne with vodka sauce—for dinner, and we tried to pretend like it was just another Saturday night.

"We need something light, with a happy ending," Mom said as she scrolled through Netflix. "How about *Sleepless in Seattle*?"

The whole time, I panicked, checking my phone every thirty seconds, terrified of a call from Agent Pruitt, praying for one from Chris.

Before Mom went up to bed, she said, "I'm off tomorrow. I was going to clean the basement, but why don't we do something together? Get out of Oak Hill for the day. Maybe go to Longwood Lake? Rent kayaks?"

"Sounds good." I almost added, *Let's go early before Agent Pruitt shows up.*

* * *

I haven't told her about the phone, about everything with Chris. I've disappointed her enough. Every moment she doesn't know what I've done feels like a small gift I'm giving her. Or a disease I'm not spreading.

I stare up at my bedroom ceiling. Leaving Oak Hill never sounded better. I remember spending Sundays at the lake with Gran. We'd pack a picnic lunch, and I'd waste hours trying to catch minnows or tadpoles. I want to focus on these good, pure memories, but instead, my mind spins back to Chris. The disgust in his eyes. I cannot let it end like this. After everything, I do not want his angry face, saying *We're done*, to be the way I remember him. I need to fix it. I need to see him.

Returning to the closet, I grab my running shoes, then fish out a pair of socks from my dresser drawer.

In the hall, I peek at the bottom of Mom's door to make sure her light is off before tiptoeing past her room. The steps creak in the middle, so I stick close to the wall, carrying my socks and sneakers. If Mom wakes up, I'll tell her I'm going for a run to clear my head.

At the kitchen table, I lace up my sneakers. Rain pelts the windows. I'm wearing shorts, but I'm not going to risk going back upstairs to put on leggings or jeans. On the counter, the vodka bottle, still out from when Mom made the sauce, gleams beside the kitchen night-light. I get up, unscrew it, and choke down two terrible gulps. The bitter liquid burns the back of my throat, but it's a small price to pay if it quiets the hornet's nest of nerves buzzing inside my chest.

By the side door, I grab a slicker from the hook and flip up the hood. Before I head out, I check for news vans. They're gone. Maybe parking under the canopy of oak trees in a storm scared them off. Whatever the reason, I'm glad the street's deserted. I step out and pull the door closed gently, careful not to wake Mom, though there's little chance she'd hear it over the thunder.

Outside, the air is cooler, thick with the scent of simmering pavement. The rain falls so hard and fast, the earth can't absorb it. There's no way to avoid the puddles that swell into rivers rushing toward the sewer. By the time I'm halfway down the block, my feet are soaked, my socks drinking in water like sponges. Trees bend and bow in the wind, silvery sheets of rain blow sideways, stinging my face.

Every few seconds, lightning streaks the sky, and I think back to my first piano lesson with Chris. I stood on his doorstep and raised my hand to knock, but suddenly, he was there. He looked at me. His eyes, blue as the sea, opened wider. He remembered me from that day at the store with Lexi. The spark that flickered inside me then reignited. He felt it too, I was sure of it. The girl who'd had the lesson ahead of mine stepped out, carrying a songbook. She looked about twelve, maybe thirteen.

"See you next week," he said as she walked toward a waiting minivan.

"Don't forget! I want to learn, 'Love Yourself,'" the girl called over her shoulder.

"You got it," he hollered back, rubbing his chin, a smirk forming on his lips. "C'mon in," he said to me, "but please tell me you're not here to learn Justin Bieber's greatest hits."

"I got my name from a Grateful Dead song, so no. I'm here to learn Joni Mitchell's 'River' for my mom's birthday.

I was lying. I was there for *him*.

* * *

Now I wish I could travel back in time and undo everything—never take those lessons, never kiss Chris and fall under his spell. I should've gotten a job at Starbucks instead of babysitting. But it's too late. I can't undo the past, but if I can see him again, I can try to make it right. He has to let me in. He can't leave me standing outside, apologizing in the rain.

Turning the corner onto Woods End, the vodka loosens me up. Running seems effortless even though I'm panting. The rain's steady drumbeat against the leaves isn't loud enough to drown out my heartbeat pounding in my ears. Still, I'm thankful that this downpour means there are few cars on the streets, and I probably won't bump into Phil or Mrs. B.

In the distance, Chris's house is dark. Not a single light glows in any of the windows. I quicken my pace. With every step, my anxiety spikes. What am I doing? How do I begin? *Can you forgive me? Can we still hang out? I love you, and I can't bear to let it end like this.*

28

Saturday, July 6
Allison

I PACE FROM THE kitchen to the living room, down the short hall, and back again. Furious with Viv. Mad at myself. I'd only planned to stay a few nights. But she was gone so often, it was easy. Comfortable. It became a matter of inertia. I was an object at rest who would remain at rest until acted on by an external force—like Viv calling Chris.

I should have been smarter. Not let her see inside me, my pain. How many people are as happy as they pretend to be? I could've faked it—put on makeup, gone on a few dates with the hot chef Viv kept promoting. But I'd left Oak Hill to stop trying to be someone else's desired version of me.

Now, who will I become? A woman continually on the run from her husband? Or, one who confronts him and tells him she's never going back?

Gulping black coffee, I consider fleeing. I could toss the few things I brought with me into a bag and disappear before Chris arrives. But I can't hide from him forever. Once he sets his mind on something, he's relentless. I know that better than anyone.

Chris's need to get his way wasn't only what tore us apart; it was the thing that brought us together. He loved sharing his version of how we met.

"I saw her in a magazine; it was love at first sight," he'd say, charming his listeners, adding how he flew across the world to see if I felt the same way.

Friends, family, interviewers swooned. It sounded so romantic, like a fairy tale. How long had I believed it too?

At our wedding rehearsal dinner, Roddy, the best man, had wrapped his arm around me.

"It was supposed to be me," he'd laughed, giving my shoulder a squeeze. "You know that, right?" He'd been drinking gin and tonics in a pint glass.

How many has he had? I'd wondered, wanting to return to my soon-to-be-husband and our guests.

"I was the one who saw you in that magazine." He tightened his grip and whistled. "I said, 'Damn, I'd like to meet that girl!' And Chris, that cocky motherfucker, goes, 'I could get her if I wanted to. Bet me! Bet me ten grand!' Me and Ed were like, 'Yeah, right!' Next thing, he's halfway to Milan."

My stomach twisted, but I played it off like I'd known all along.

"I bet you still owe him ten grand!" I joked. "Will that be cash or check?"

Roddy laughed. "Your man's crazy, Al. Just know what you're getting yourself into. He wants something? He doesn't go after it; he fuckin' takes it. But, hey, if I had his balls, maybe you'd be marrying me tomorrow."

When I wrenched myself free from Roddy, I found Chris and asked him to explain. He took my hands in his and shook his head. "What difference does it make, Ally? We're here now, aren't we?"

Guests were getting ready to leave, aunts slinking off with floral centerpieces and leftovers tucked inside foil swans. I kept my voice low. "Yeah, but it's . . . I don't know. That story? That you saw my picture, and you felt something—that you just knew?" I paused. "I believed it. It meant something to me."

Chris gazed into my eyes, hypnotizing me. What was I going to do? Stop the wedding?

"I love you, Al," he said. "I'd do anything for you. That's all you need to know."

* * *

I flinch at the memory, at all the red flags I ignored while cling-ing to the idea of the perfect life, even as my real one crumbled. The champagne, coffee, and anxiety boil inside me, burning a hole in my stomach. It's almost eleven at night. Even with traf-fic, Chris should be here any second.

I hold my breath, listening for footsteps in the hallway. Nothing. Rain lashes the window, but inside the building, it's quiet as a morgue. Like Viv, everyone is out making the most of a midsummer Saturday night.

I tiptoe toward the door and peer into the hallway. It's empty, flat, wide. The convex lens of the peephole is like a funhouse mirror distorting my view. As I turn away, a flash catches my eye. Then, there it is—thunderous knocking that shatters the silence and shakes the vase on the coffee table. Urgent. Primal. Life and death.

"Ally." His sharp hiss slices through the stillness like a knife in my ears.

We're inches apart with only the door between us. I force myself not to move before I'm ready.

I will never be ready. It's been almost three months since I've seen him. With the sound of his voice, time erases itself.

"Ally." It comes again. Rough, haunting. "I know you're there."

I lean in, see his red-rimmed eyes, wide open, wild, his hair slick with rain. I step back, shivering, knowing this moment would arrive, yet completely unprepared for it. I take a deep breath, shut my eyes, and picture the apartment on Perry Street, my new life. If I can get through this, I can emerge on the other side. Free.

"Ally!" His low growl verges on a whimper.

This doesn't need to be complicated. It can be as simple as portraying a character: "Strong Woman Who Stands Her Ground" rather than "Submissive Wife Who Allows Her Hus-band to Drag Her Home Caveman-Style to Breed."

I open the door. He rushes at me, burying his wet face in my hair. His arms lock around me.

"Why would you do this?" he slurs, clawing at my back, my neck. "You shouldn't have left, Ally."

My heart pounds hard against my ribs. Can he feel it? He pulls back. With hands clenching my shoulders, he holds me at a distance, appraising me like an instrument he might buy.

"You hurt me, but you didn't break me." He jerks me back into him and laughs a deep, drunken howl before pressing his lips to my forehead. Sweat, whiskey, and desperation ooze out of his pores. "I forgive you," he whispers.

Rage and fear churn in my gut. *Why did I think he'd ever let me go?* My eyes flick to the half-open door. *Why didn't I leave after I read his email?*

Chris turns, follows my gaze. He smiles. "Ready? Let's go home." He tugs my arm.

I've been weak for so long. I need to be strong now. A soft buzz hums in my ears. A hive of doubt and darkness descends. I think I might pass out as dots float before my eyes. I blink them away, pull my arm out of his grasp.

"No. I'm not going back." I sidestep my way toward the kitchen, barely feeling the floor beneath my feet. "It's over. I'm done."

"You're not leaving me, Ally." He shakes his head. "No one is leaving me again!" His roar terrifies me. I sink to the floor, shaking.

"I'm sorry, I'm sorry." He frowns and squats beside me, rubbing his glassy eyes. His pupils are dime-size black holes boring into me. I wonder what mix of booze and pills he's taken. "Lemme start again." He clears his throat, reaches out, brushes my cheek. Blood rushes to my face as my pulse beats a steady drumroll. He grins and tilts my chin up.

I start to cry. Frustration, exhaustion, and the thought that I may never be free swallow me.

He clasps my trembling hands in his and presses them to his lips. "Let's go home."

I'm never going with you! My mind screams, but I have no voice. Could I push him out of the way, throw him off balance, and bolt through the door, down two flights, and out of the building? When we ran together, he was always faster, always ahead of me, slowing his pace to match mine. I stifle a cry. *I will never outrun him.*

He pulls me to my feet. I'm powerless. My body, betraying me once again, goes along with whatever he tells me.

"I got you something," he smiles, "for our anniversary. I can't wait to show you."

29

Saturday, July 6
Cassidy

I'M ALMOST THERE, just across the street, when I spot something on Chris's front lawn. Movement. Is it a shadow? A
trick played by the darkness and the wind?

I'm on his sidewalk when lightning brightens the yard. The
grass shines, slick with rain. Something's there. Squatting now.
Larger than a dog or even a deer. Raindrops catch in my eye-
lashes, blurring my vision. I blink hard, take a few more steps,
and stumble over a large rock that's been rolled away from its
usual spot in a line of landscaping stones. I startle at a sound, a
shovel tearing into roots.

"Chris?" I inch closer and lean toward the noise.

A flashlight blinds me.

"Cassidy?"

I know this voice. I step backward, my mind swimming in
a cocktail of confusion, alarm, and alcohol. "Phil?"

"Help me, Cassidy!"

"What are you doing?" I ask, though I can see exactly what
he's up to because he's leaned the flashlight against the house. It
casts a halo around the basement window. He's removed one
shrub that blocked it. Now he's digging out another. I can't
process why.

The clammy skin on my neck and arms sticks to the insides of my slicker, making me hot, claustrophobic. I want to peel it off, run back home, but my legs won't work.

Phil says something, but it's lost between cracks of thunder and the dog barking inside the house.

I spot the rope curled by his boot. A knife beside it. My mouth goes dry. "Holy shit, Phil! What are you doing?"

"I saw the lights, Cassidy! The signal! I have to do this. Now!"

He's not making sense. I spin around as if someone will be there to offer guidance. Should I get his mother? What will Mary Alice do? Call the police? An ambulance?

"Phil! Stop!"

He ignores me, yanking out the second bush, tossing it to the side.

"Where's Chris?" I shout, suddenly shivering, staring up at the house. Is Chris inside? If he was pissed this afternoon, he's going to be enraged now that I'm back and Phil is destroying his property. I have to stop Phil, but I'm paralyzed. I try to stay calm despite my heart thumping a billion beats per minute.

"Phil? Phil, stop! Please. What are you doing here? Why are you—"

He doesn't speak, just points to the window with one hand and reaches for me with the other. I don't want to get any closer. Phil and I have known each other forever, but with his face dripping and eyes wild, I'm afraid of him. I remember he's seen—and maybe done—horrible things in the line of duty. I need to get out of here. Go home. Now. My teeth rattle as thunder rocks the ground. I look up at the sky, a reflex. Phil grabs me by the wrist and pulls me down to the ground beside him. My knees sink into the mud. The smell of damp earth floods my nostrils.

"Let go! Please!" I plead, attempting to twist my arm free from his grasp.

"C'mere! Get closer!" He yells to be heard above the torrential rain and Murphy's howling.

With his hand pressing on my back, he forces me toward the window.

"Look!" he commands, handing me his flashlight.

If I do what he says, maybe he'll let me go. I aim the beam into Chris's basement, searching for the thing that has brought Phil here at night in the middle of a storm.

The light hits Chris's guitars, cymbals, a keyboard. I adjust it and scan the soundproofed walls and his recording equipment.

I turn to Phil, confused, praying he'll snap out of this, and we can leave before Chris finds us.

"Look again!" he shouts, wrenching the flashlight from my hand, pointing it down toward the basement floor.

My knees sink deeper into the ground, sticks and mulch stab at my bare skin.

He drops the beam lower. I squint, waiting for my eyes to adjust. In the ring of light, I see two heads. Pale cheeks. Small hands. A headband adorned with tiny, pink rosebuds.

I look at Phil, my breath coming in short gasps. "Phil? Oh my God, Phil! What the hell—"

"I saw the flashes, Cassidy—the signal." His eyes widen like he's possessed. He points the beam toward Billy's hand. I lean in again. Looking down, I spot a small flashlight in Billy's fist. Next to it, plastic bottles, the kind that hold liquid medicine, lie on their sides, lids off.

"Are they—are they alive?" I press my head against the house. Dizzy. Sick. *This can't be happening. This cannot be happening. Billy and Amy-Pat? In Chris's basement? This whole time?*

Phil yanks me back. He's holding a hammer.

"I'm going to break the window!" He's shouting in my face though we're inches apart. "Climb down. Pass them up to me before Langley comes back."

My head's spinning. I don't understand any of this. *Chris? Chris took Billy and Amy-Pat? And then watched me lose my mind for the past three weeks and two days?*

"Shouldn't we call the police? Wait for them?"

Phil shoves me toward the window as a car passes, head-lights sweeping over us.

"Fuck the police!" Phil hisses in my ear. "Help me get these kids out of there. Dead or alive, I'll carry them home."

"Phil, I—" I'm shivering. His words "dead or alive" scream in my ears like a siren, a warning that comes too late. *How did I not know?* My legs shake. "I—"

"Now, Cassidy!" Phil roars before the sounds of glass shattering and his knife slicing through the window screen become all I can hear.

30

Sunday, July 7
Allison

H ORNS BLARE BEHIND us as we speed out of the tunnel. Chris weaves from lane to lane without signaling. The windshield wipers can't keep up with the driving rain that sounds like machine gun fire as it pelts the roof. The air conditioning is turned all the way up; I can't stop shivering.

Chris barely watches the road as he stares at my profile, veering toward the median on the left, then the shoulder on the right, one hand on the wheel, the other squeezing mine until I think he's going to crush the bones in my fingers.

"You're a sight for sore eyes, Ally," he says.

Something in me breaks, and I start to cry.

"Hey, hey, hey." He releases my hand and strokes the back of my neck. I remember a time when his touch would've made my whole body tingle. Now I flinch. "Don't be like that." He turns down the AC. "Listen, I'm sorry. I pushed you too hard. I see it now. I drove you away. I never meant to. All I've ever wanted is to make you happy. You've got to believe me. Do you believe me?"

He cups my chin, forcing me to face him. I nod, and he wipes away a tear with his finger. Lightning tasers the sky, and for a second, the inside of the car brightens and we stare at each other.

Journalists always mentioned his eyes, usually with some over-wrought metaphor, calling them "more intoxicating than a bottle of Bombay Sapphire gin" or as "stunning as Santorini's rooftops."

But it wasn't the color that got me. It was the way he looked at me—like I was the only thing that mattered, like he truly saw me—past the surface to the real me, deep down. And he loved me anyway.

When we met, we each felt like some part of us was missing. Together, we formed a whole. Now we are more fractured and broken than when we began.

As if he can read my mind he says, "I don't like who I am without you, Ally. I've done some things I'm not proud of. Hurt some people who didn't deserve it."

My heart races as he clears his throat. *What has he done? Who has he hurt?*

"But this is our fresh start." Out of the corner of my eye, I see he's grinning. My whole body tenses, afraid of whatever he might say next. "I wanted to surprise you, but I'll just tell you now. We're moving. I found a place. In Canada—near a lake. We'll be different there. Better."

We rocket off the exit ramp, heading toward Oak Hill's downtown. The streets are dark, deserted.

"Let's be honest, you and I never really fit in here." He laughs, a throaty cackle that fills the car.

He takes the corner onto Woods End too fast and the car fishtails, skidding toward a telephone pole. I shut my eyes and brace for impact. He pulls the wheel hard, and when I look, we narrowly miss hitting the Fosters' mailbox.

"Remember, Ally, we're not like other people," he says as he floors it into our driveway. "We don't play by the rules; we make the rules."

The high beams graze a lump on the lawn. It's moving, rocking like a wounded animal.

"Is that Murph?" It's the first time I've spoken since we left Viv's apartment and my voice sounds hoarse, scratchy.

Chris doesn't answer. He throws the gear shift into park and jumps out, leaving the engine running.

The figure stands. It's a woman. The rain has let up, but her hair is soaked. Her bare legs are mud-streaked.

"How— How could you do this?" she screams.

I watch through the windshield as Chris puts his arms out toward her. To calm her? I can't tell. Is this my chance to run while he's distracted? How far could I make it on foot in a storm without money or a phone?

"Get away from me!" the woman shrieks as Chris closes in on her.

I open the car door, not sure of my next move.

"What the fuck are you doing here, Cassidy?" he growls.

Cassidy? His piano student? The babysitter!

"You're a . . . you're a fucking monster!" Her face twists and contorts. "I know what you did! I saw them! I saw them . . ." She's crying, hysterical, running her hands through her hair, then hiding her face like she can't bear to look at him.

I picture the afternoon of her first lesson, the way she smiled at Chris, awe in her eyes, already under his spell.

He darts toward the house where a bush has been uprooted. "Where are they? Cassidy!"

"I loved you, and you used me! You took them! You took them . . . and you . . . and you . . ." She's trembling so hard she can't finish.

I loved you . . . You took them! Her words whip through my mind. My stomach drops. I think I might throw up.

"Billy Barnes, Amy-Pat Davies," I whisper their names like a prayer. *No! No! No!* I try to scream, but nothing comes out. My heart is lodged in my throat. My anniversary gift. The children we could never have.

"Where are they?" he roars, shaking her by the shoulders until her head bobs like a doll's.

As I leap out of the car, Cassidy's cries are swallowed by sirens.

* * *

I feel as if I'm floating, watching it all from above. Neighbors spill from their homes onto the street as the blue and red lights spin and flash, bouncing off every tree, window, and garage. Mary Alice Foster paces at the edge of the sidewalk, wringing her hands and repeating, "Have you seen Phil? Has anyone seen my son?"

"Search the house. There could be others still in there," one police officer tells another.

"Take him down to the station; we'll question her here," a man with a badge in a tweed blazer commands.

"Mrs. Langley. Mrs. Langley."

How many times do they say my name before I tear my eyes away from my husband as he's eased into the back of a police car, his lips forming the words that will haunt me forever: "I did this for you."

A police officer removes the keys from the ignition and tells me to unlock the house. Every light is too bright, every sound too loud. Murph runs at me and I want to kneel and bury my face in his soft, golden fur.

Billy and Amy-Pat? Here? In my home. This whole time.

"Where are the children?" I ask. No one answers.

Another officer takes me by the elbow, guiding me through my former home, opening doors Chris and I firmly shut.

I stare in horror and disbelief at the rooms as they ransack closets and overturn drawers. *How did it come to this? How did we lose our minds in this perfect place?*

These spaces feel like they're from a movie set for a part I never got to play. I remember painting the sleepy blue walls of the first nursery, the one with the sailing motif, where the navy anchor we picked up at that shop in Newport rests on the dresser.

Inside the second one sits a half-filled bookcase. Everything is silver, sage, and pink. Hooks shaped like dragonflies stand ready to hold bonnets and tiny sweaters. A white crib waits, always empty.

The third is vacant except for the musical instrument mobile peeking out from its box in the middle of the plush cream carpet.

In each nursery, framed sonograms hang on the wall. Our almost-family, suspended in time.

Police remove a long, strawberry-blond strand of hair from a pillow in the guest room with tweezers and place it in a see-through bag. *Cassidy and Chris?* I picture them together and shut my eyes to block the image, but a new one surfaces—Chris before he got into the squad car mouthing, "I did this for you."

A young police officer finds fake birth certificates for Billy and Amy-Pat tucked inside a shoebox at the bottom of our bedroom closet.

"Where are the children?" I ask again, not sure if I can bear the answer.

"Mrs. Langley, we're going to need you to come down to the basement."

CHAPTER

31

Sunday, July 7
Rachel

THUNDER ROCKS ME from a deep sleep. I bolt upright, pulse racing. I drifted off on the living room couch. The only light comes from the faint glow of the microwave's clock, and lightning as it flashes behind the blinds.

I grab a tissue and wipe a patch of drool from my cheek before tapping my phone. The battery is low from my obsessive checking. 12:11 AM. It's Sunday. Another new day. Each one spools out dark and endless, as unrelenting as the ocean. Yesterday exhausted me more than most—starting with the call from Sarah, asking me what I knew about Allison Langley. I could smell her fear through the phone, her desperation to connect any possible dots if they'll lead to our children. Then the visit with my mother. Confusion has stolen her face to the point that I barely recognize her. She is here and yet gone. Darcy knows about the baby. It feels real now. I don't know if that's good or bad. My life consists of waiting by the phone for a call that never comes.

I'm halfway to the kitchen for a glass of water when I hear it. A thud. On the porch. I creep closer, holding my breath. For a moment, I picture Betsy coming back to collect her cooler to deliver it to someone more appreciative—the Davies family or

Christopher Langley. I almost laugh at the absurdity of the image, but there it is again. Now at the door. Someone's trying the knob. Attempting to get in. A key drops. The gentle clank of metal hitting the porch floor. Evan? It has to be. No doubt he's high or drunk or both. I back away. *Am I in danger?* I'm not ready for a midnight showdown with my stepson, but what choice do I have? I refuse to flick on the porch light or open the door. Let him struggle. I will not make things easier for him the way Ted does.

The phone buzzes in my hand. Sarah. I swipe to answer as the screen goes black. Dead. I need to find the charger. I turn toward the kitchen when I hear the key thrust into the lock.

I stand there in the dark, waiting, crossing and uncrossing my arms, panic rising in my chest, palms perspiring.

Finally, the door opens. A small silhouette steps inside. My knees give way, certain I'm hallucinating—until I hear it. The voice that calls for me in my nightmares, saying the words that make me whole again, "Mommy, I'm home."

Six Months Later
Sarah

A MY-PAT WOULD'VE STARTED preschool this fall, but I've kept
her home. When Brent naps, we read, finger paint, or play
with her ponies. I try not to let her catch me watching her, checking to see how deep the cracks are, how permanent the scars.

Sometimes we'll be making cookies, our hands nested on a
mixing spoon, and I have to stop and catch my breath as the
thought of how close we came to losing her washes over me as
if for the first time.

She looks different now with her pixie cut.

"No more headbands, Mommy," she announced the day
after she came home as she carried her collection into the hallway and dumped them on the floor, a pile of plaids and floral
prints.

Brian and I considered selling the house, moving out of
Oak Hill. But Amy-Pat's attachment to Billy is more important
than my desire to start over. We see him and Rachel a few times
a week. When they're coming to our house, Amy-Pat waits by
the door. She and Billy hug the way people do when they've
survived the unthinkable. Rachel and I look on, knowing that
we may never fully understand what they experienced and what
they mean to each other.

The first few weeks after Amy-Pat came home, Brian and I found Tucker asleep on the floor beside her toddler bed, his arm stretching upward, reaching for her, making sure she's still there.

On Wednesday afternoons, we see a family therapist who's been helping all of us try to move forward. I see someone separately too.

Almost losing Amy-Pat brought up so much unresolved trauma from my mother's death. I struggle to get through each day without panicking that tragedy will come calling again when I least expect it. I try to just be in each moment and not think about the *what ifs*, or the possible disasters that could tear my life apart once more. I take a deep breath and focus on all the good surrounding me—my children's laughter, Brian's patience, and my friendship with Rachel.

I want to believe in time I will feel better, more normal, whatever that means. Still, there are nights when I wake up in a cold sweat, heart pounding, and race from room to room, making sure my children are safe.

Cassidy wasn't directly responsible for what happened, but I don't know if I will ever forgive myself for hiring her, for being careless with the people who matter most.

If Brian and I go out together, my brother, Tom, stays with the kids. We are never gone for long.

When I make dinner now and Amy-Pat clings to my leg, I stop what I'm doing, scoop her up, and hold her like I'll never let her go.

Rachel

THE TOWNHOUSE ISN'T luxurious. There's no marble island or saltwater pool. But it's big enough for the three of us, and it's in town, so Billy can continue to attend Oak Hill Elementary.

I'm there waiting on the sidewalk at the end of every school day, baby nuzzled to my chest.

With her brown hair and wide chocolate eyes, she looks like Billy. We named her Phylicia. Phil, for short.

"Philly and Billy!" Billy exclaimed when I introduced her to him at the hospital.

I didn't tell him I don't love that. Instead, I laughed and repeated, "Philly and Billy, it is."

Born just before Christmas, she is the gift I didn't know how much I wanted until I held her. When she's hungry, she shakes her tiny fists, and I laugh, knowing she will be fierce like Darcy.

Derek and I sold the flip house for a modest profit, enough to allow me to cut back my hours. He spends time with us when Billy is at school or with Ted. I try to minimize the number of changes my son has had to endure these past months.

Mothers from Oak Hill Elementary constantly ask, "How's Billy doing?"

As they wait for my response, their faces crinkle with concern, afraid to hear the answer. My son has been the subject of enough gossip and speculation, so I say, "Amazing. Just amazing. The resilience and strength of the human spirit should never be underestimated."

I read that last bit on a pillow at my therapist's office.

What I don't tell them is that Billy is afraid of dogs now. Or, that he sleeps with the flashlight under his pillow, a pyramid of new batteries stacked on his dresser.

Did I even know that the Cub Scouts taught children Morse Code?

"This is how you spell SOS, Mommy," he tells me, illustrating with his flashlight. "Three short flashes, then three long flashes, then three more short ones, okay, Mommy? Don't forget."

How many nights did I walk past that house and not know he was there? *Dozens.* Did he try to signal me, and in my despair, I'd been too dazed to notice? Focusing on all the wrong things had been my specialty. I don't make that mistake anymore.

Sometimes, just before I kiss him good night, Billy will notice me frowning, or see the worry in my face, as permanent as a tattoo, and he'll say, "He's not a bad man, Mommy. He was lonely. He just wanted a family. He didn't hurt me or Amy-Pat."

Where does it come from? This compassion? How can he be filled with it when I'm seething with rage?

"The main thing is that they're home, alive," Sarah repeats when I tell her that sometimes if I can't open a jar, I tighten my grasp and squeeze, picturing my hands around Christopher Langley's neck. I twist until I hear a loud snap.

"How many families never get that?" she'll continue. "We're the lucky ones, Rachel."

I know she's right.

Cassidy

THE STORY OF Chris and me swept through town faster than a stomach bug. Of course it did. I'd expect nothing less. Mom knew that once I left for school, I wouldn't want to go back to Oak Hill, so she sold the house.

"Say what you want about this town, but the properties hold their value," she'd said when she called to tell me she'd accepted a good offer.

She moved to Boston to be near me. She got a new job at a hospital here and rented a studio apartment. With the money from the house sale, she bought a cottage on Cape Cod. We'll spend next summer there together. It's good to look forward to something.

I still think about Chris. Sometimes. (Okay, all the time.) I'll go to a party or the grocery store, and a Regrets Only song will come on, and I'll need to leave. His voice makes me dizzy, weak. Not in the same way it once did. That feeling of being tricked, used, it stays—a stain you can't remove. I know now that he'd moved my backpack and keys so I would be late the afternoon he took Billy, that I'd slept so deeply because he'd crushed a small piece of one of his wife's sleeping pills into the iced tea he'd given me.

You'd think these facts would make me feel less awful. They don't.

When there's a thunderstorm, or I can't sleep, my mind takes me back to Oak Hill against my will. To that night when I climbed through the window, not knowing if Billy and Amy-Pat were dead or alive. I picture myself rocking them gently, their eyes glassy from whatever he gave them, cheeks white as a January moon, whispering "You're safe," over and over. I see Phil carrying them home.

As I waited for the police, I sat on the wet grass, replaying all the times I'd been with Chris. Like a recording stuck in a loop in my mind, I heard myself telling him about Billy's love for dogs and Amy-Pat's obsession with headbands—details he used as bait.

After Phil brought Amy-Pat and Billy home, he caught a ride to Florida and has been living there ever since. Mom said Mary Alice was horrified that he'd hitchhiked eleven hundred miles, but then Phil asked his mother something I think about a lot: "Who's more dangerous: the stranger who picks you up on a highway or the people in your neighborhood?"

*   *   *

College has been a welcome distraction. I keep my head down, get my work done. It's not like Oak Hill, where everyone knows your business. Students don't pay attention to the news, and when they do, it's not to stay on top of small-town kidnappings.

I've made a couple of friends, but I struggle with letting anyone get too close. Mom said that's natural and to give myself time. We have dinner together every Sunday.

I got a waitressing job so I could save up enough to buy a plane ticket to meet Lexi in California at her dad's. We have the same spring break, which feels like a miracle.

Last Friday, at the end of my American Lit class, the professor said, "It's my husband's birthday, and I was able to score tickets to tonight's Bruins game. Anyone available to babysit?"

My face flushed, and my body went stiff and cold as an icicle. I dropped my eyes and listened for gasps, expecting heads to spin in my direction.

"For extra credit? Anyone? I'd really prefer it to be one of you as opposed to someone from my Vonnegut seminar!" She'd laughed the way she did when she discovered she'd lectured on *A Farewell to Arms* with a soiled burp cloth over her shoulder.

I was in no position to offer advice, but I wanted to tell her not to leave her child with just anyone. Even when you think you've found the most trustworthy person in the world, you never know who's watching your babysitter.

Allison

B ILLY AND AMY-PAT are safe.
      Am I?
   I move from one city to the next. Still, Chris's notes find
me. The first arrived in August. Murph and I were checking out
of a motel in Tennessee. As I handed the key back to the clerk,
she smiled.
   "This came for you." Wiggling her eyebrows, she slid a
square envelope across the worn wooden counter. "Someone's
got an admirer."
   I took it, my stomach twisting. And yet, it was almost a
relief. I'd been expecting it. I knew the words I'd find there
even before I read them.
   You didn't think I'd let you disappear again, did you, Al?
   It wasn't his handwriting, of course. It never is. He'll be
away for a decade at least. He dictates them to someone—different people, I imagine—who place them in my mailbox, slide
them under my door, leave them with a neighbor to deliver.
   They're all a variation on the same theme: *Wait for me, Al.
We'll start over.*
   That feeling of being followed, watched, is always there, a
constant sensation like a breath on the back of my neck, but
when I turn to find its source, I'm alone.

The cream-colored note card in my hand is proof that it doesn't matter how many miles I put between my old life and this one, I'll never outrun it.

I've started to wonder: Despite your desire to become someone new, can you change who you were? Who you are?

I read the note for the dozenth time. I found it tucked beneath a wiper blade on the windshield this morning as Murph and I hopped in the car for our daily trip to the park. It's the longest one yet.

We're not that different, Al, you and I. We want the same things—love, happiness, family. We can still have it. The idea was yours, remember? That baby girl in the grocery store? I only finished what you started.

Murph's beside my feet, gnawing on a stick, turning it around in his front paws, as a boy toddles toward us. Bundled in a navy vest, his cheeks are rosy, round, infinitely pinchable.

We're not that different, Al.

Murph and I used to make it a point to try new parks. San Diego has so many. But lately, we've been coming back to this one. It's nice to see familiar faces, like this little guy, who inches closer, his tiny sneakers flashing with each step. He's been here every day this week. I've watched him looking at Murph from a distance, working up the nerve to pet him. This dog's a magnet, always has been.

My eyes flick to the boy's babysitter. She's sitting on the low bench of a picnic table near the jungle gym. She rocks the boy's sibling in a stroller with one hand. Her phone in the other captures her full attention. Is she playing a game, texting a friend? I can't say, but I do know that the stretches between when she looks up to search for this boy and his older brother get longer.

It's crowded for a Friday. Parents and nannies at tables set out late breakfasts or early lunches, bolting down napkins with piles of juice boxes. The air is warm for January, filled with a deceptive hint of spring.

We want the same things—love, happiness, family.

I glance over my shoulder at the car. We got a good parking spot today. Close. I turn to the boy. He grins shyly, dimples flashing, front tooth missing. I smile back.

We can still have it.

ACKNOWLEDGMENTS

THANK YOU TO my mom, Margaret Brue, my first and favorite storyteller (and enthusiastic typo finder). Thank you for always believing in me.

Thank you to my cousin Kim Breen for being my constant cheerleader and pro bono publicist, who charms friends and strangers into buying my words. You are the best!

Thank you to the amazingly generous Keri Kelly, who always says (and writes) the right thing.

Thanks to the Writers Circle where I workshopped early drafts. Michelle Cameron, Alison Poe, and Joan Halperin, your encouragement kept me going.

Thank you to my dear friends Celeste Romano and Kris Pfeifer, whose keen eyes and unwavering support mean the world to me.

Thank you to Amy Tipton of Feral Girl Books, who went above and beyond to provide editorial expertise and perfectly timed pep talks. You are truly a writer's champion.

Thank you to Kiri Blakeley for listening and commiserating. I'm glad we're in this together!

Thank you to Victoria Di Santo for years of thoughtful notes and fabulous book recommendations.

Thank you to Cari Rosen, whom I've adored since our first email exchange, and the entire team at Legend Press. Thank you to Faith Black Ross for her kindness and enthusiasm. And to the team at Crooked Lane, I'm so grateful for all your help and hard work in bringing this book to readers.

I'd be remiss if I didn't acknowledge Bubbles, my cat, who sits by my side (and sometimes directly on my laptop) as I type, delete, and sigh.

Thank you most of all to Rich, Sam, Ben, and Charlie for putting up with my endless requests for synonyms and character names and for not running in the other direction when I say, "Hey, can I read you something?" I love you more than you'll ever know.